CONTENTS

A Bright Pen Book

Text Copyright © James Roy Pickard 2012

Cover design by © Elizabeth Fitt

British Library Cataloguing Publication Data.
A catalogue record for this book is available from the British Library

ISBN 978-0-7552-1520-1

FT
Pbk

Authors OnLine Ltd
19 The Cinques
Gamlingay, Sandy
Bedfordshire SG19 3NU
England

This book is also available in e-book format, details of which are available at
www.authorsonline.co.uk

1: Ballater–The Pass–Craig Coillich

On Friday morning, 5 June 1914, as mystic Lochnagar soared above the dreaming Coyles of Muick, to the north-east in the Dee Valley below a Great North of Scotland Railway train arrived at the terminus in Ballater. The forty-three mile journey from Aberdeen had taken ninety-five minutes. Curves and gradients restricted speed as the scenery changed gradually from charming pastoral to sublime pine-capped crags and lofty, austere summits. Now the iron steed snorted jets of white steam, as if mocking patches of snow which still lingered in mountain corries. Occasionally snow was evident all the year round. An old legend, implying a colder climate, presaged that when the White Mounth, the high plateau south-west of Lochnagar, was snow free doomsday was drawing near.

Sergeant Andrew Mackay with three comrades of the Gordon Highlanders alighted and passed the royal waiting room, for Balmoral Castle lay further up the valley. They emerged from the white and red building in bright sunshine. Their military bearing revealed the occupation, although they were on leave and bore climbing ropes.

As they crossed Station Square to the south the ginger haired sergeant breathed in deeply, then his eyes sparkled as he commented, 'I have visited many places, but none compares with Ballater's sunny peace and pure mountain air. We will go first to Douglas Gordon, a grocer. He served in the regiment until he was injured in the Second Boer War.'

Entering Bridge Street they soon traversed Church Square where imposing Glenmuick Parish Church faced east towards each dawn and the theme of resurrection. It was set alone on the green, the sides of which were lined with trees. The effect was of God and Nature being at the heart of the burgh, an impression heightened by the wider, lofty setting. The men reached the shop near the top of a continuation of Bridge Street and on their right side. Durable goods were displayed in the windows, including packets of shortbread, oatcakes and tea, with jars of heather honey and confectionery. A leaving housewife held the door open for the sergeant. The soldiers entered, including Private Gavin Fraser. Lithe and slim, he had grey-green eyes set in sharp yet homely features with dark hair. Smiling affably he welcomed the old world serenity of the place, including a picture beyond the counter of Queen Victoria on a Highland pony, as if in spirit she still ruled this favoured part of her Empire.

Then he heard a young woman singing a Gaelic song up a ladder, as she restocked a shelf. He was struck by the voice, because it had more than roundness, richness and feeling. Refined, peaceful chords both chided and charmed the confused bustle below. He glanced up to meet her blue-green eyes and lightning smile, before she turned towards the proprietor who greeted the arrivals.

'Sergeant Mackay, my old friend, and fellow Gordons! Come down, Iona dear, and help serve the soldiers. It may be fine and peaceful today, but with rivalry among European countries over trade, colonies and military and naval power, I fear there may be war before long. The King and the Kaiser are cousins, but the Kaiser is a German first. His spirit is as withered as his left arm.'

Mackay replied, 'Sufficient unto the day is the evil thereof. We are going rock climbing in the nearby pass. Hector and I will return to Aberdeen this evening, but Donald and Gavin will spend a week's holiday in the area. We are all currently based at the Crownhill Hutments, Plymouth.'

As the old friends renewed their acquaintance, a teenage male civilian was being served by another female assistant, and he said with a smile, 'You remind me of Diana, the goddess of hunting and the woodlands. When Actaeon surprised her bathing with her nymphs, he was changed into a stag.'

Morag Brockie replied coldly, 'Very interesting, Alec. Previously I only heard that a stag symbolized a cuckold.'

Incensed by the remark Mr Gordon retorted, 'You would be better to remember that a stag's head appears on the Gordon Highlander's glengarry badge, with the Gordon family's proud motto "Bydand" meaning steadfast.'

The soldiers cheered the words, but she was furious at being corrected, for she was trying to draw their positive attention. She was further enraged by the socially immature youth raising his arms aloft to imitate a stag's antlers.

To divert him she looked at Iona and said, 'Snowdrop knows more about mythology and woodlands than I do.'

Iona remarked, 'When I was younger I associated Diana with the moon and chastity.'

Turning back to Morag Alec Reid said, 'I admire your locks. Do you think that long-haired girls are more spirited and passionate than shorter ones?'

With a coquettish toss of her blonde locks she replied vainly, 'Yes.'

'What do you think, Iona?' he teasingly asked, evoking a dismissive faint smile as she continued to serve Hector.

Morag, however, leaned forward and whispered, 'Don't ask Snowdrop. She's a model of composure. She doesn't know what passion means.'

His right arm rested on the counter, but as he turned to reach forward for groceries he felt a sudden wetness on his hand and exclaimed, 'I'm bleeding!'

Gavin joked, 'You are luckier than Actaeon. When he was turned into a stag, he was torn to pieces by his own hounds.'

Iona gave a cold look at Morag when she saw her quietly giggling. She slipped round and glanced at Alec's hand, which annoyed Morag, because the soldiers' attention was drawn to Iona.

'It's Morag's concoction. She's fond of pranks.'

He was given a paper bag which he furiously tore open to clean his hand, but Iona attentively pointed out, 'There is still a stain on your jacket. Give it to me and I will quickly wash it.'

'Och, don't mind,' he impatiently replied, a brief struggle over the jacket following, before she silently coaxed him to let go and disappeared with it. Her father glowered at Morag, while the soldiers smiled at Alec in his white shirt.

The sergeant, having been supplied by Mr Gordon, boomed at Alec, 'You poor snow bunting, terrified by artificial blood!'

'It was just a brief misunderstanding. Actually a snow bunting is tough.'

'Yes, would you like to come rock climbing with us?'

'No thanks, I'm going fishing.'

'Do you wade into the fast flowing current where the action is?'

'No, I sit on the bank and read. I am particularly interested in St Thomas Aquinas' works and am hoping to study at Aberdeen University.'

'You are a dry, peaceful fisherman! It's as well you are not coming with us. There is a colony of noisy jackdaws.'

He swung his arms like wings and mimicked the bird's 'chack' note a few times, followed by the very raucous alarm note of 'caw.' Alec defensively held his hands before his face, as if the colony was about to attack him.

Seeing Iona return Mackay remarked, 'A very prompt valet service!'

He beamed and his comrades chuckled as she held the jacket while Alec put it back on, before he grudgingly muttered, 'Thanks,' and strode outside.

After she and Gavin had exchanged a quick smile over the incident, he asked for a quarter of a pound of Aberdeen Angus beef, the same amount of cheese and a loaf. He mused on her as he looked down, she being slightly below average height. Her dark brown hair, which was not luxurious but had a golden sheen, was parted at the left and fell towards her shoulders, from which it was set off with little curls. It was managed in a practical way. There were no ornate locks hanging over her forehead, coyly pointing down to her eyes, or locks hiding the corners of the jaw. Her hair was swept behind the ears, so that her full face was visible. She was a slender spire, and apart from the long nose the emphasis was on economy down to small hands. The graceful neck was distinctive, but the eyes transformed her. They had a haunting mystic purity which shone near a window and had a thoughtful penetration when she bent down in a shadow. They showed that her life was vigorous, but a balance between her of gentle placidity and constant application produced a sense of stillness in motion. A combination of graceful simplicity and abundant yet controlled vitality achieved a perfect unity of form and spirit. He had not seen before a woman who was so uniquely the consummation of many generations. Yet she had a strange power which made him reticent. Then her still spirit suddenly woke with an angelic smile, as she saw a little girl enter, nervously clutching her mother's dress, for she was not used to seeing such a group of robust men there.

This informality encouraged Gavin to remark, 'You were singing "Mo Nighean Donn Bhoidheach–My Brown-Hair'd Maiden."'

'Yes,' she replied, looking curiously at his mouth. 'My father likes the song. It helps to keep alive my mother's memory.'

'I see,' he said sympathetically.

Politely she commented, 'You are not originally from the north-east. You have a western accent.'

'Last year my parents and I moved from a hamlet in Lochaber to Aberdeen, so they could work in clothing.'

'Lochaber is a beautiful area with Ben Nevis and many lochs. It has produced fine Gaelic poets.'

'And cattle thieves,' Morag teased.

Ignoring her he asked Iona, 'Have you always lived here?'

'No, my first four years were spent in Coleraine to the north-east of Londonderry.'

Wishing to prolong the conversation briefly he asked, 'Is the Highland toffee popular?' pointing to a tray of bars on the counter.

Before Iona could reply Morag interjected, 'Yes, among the children.'

Glancing aside on hearing his friend Donald Grant snigger, he said, 'No thanks,' but while Iona was at the till Morag took it upon herself to place the purchases quickly in his bag. Then Iona handed him the change with a gentle smile.

As he walked north-west with his comrades up the rising Braemar Road towards the Pass of Ballater, his heart was at one with the swelling hills. He looked forward to the stiff challenge of climbing, but there was lightness in his spirit as he thought of the woman in whom there was a perfect balance of graceful and homely qualities. He loved her instantly he saw her up the ladder. To cynics the song was full of clichés, but for him its sentiments applied well. Her enchanting smile was the rarest, excelling in brightness, purity, kindliness and demureness.

When the party turned right into the pass, the gateway to the Highlands, there was peace in the refreshing breeze, and soon they gazed left at towering crags, before the sergeant pointed and said, 'There's the ancient face of Caledonia, Creag an t-Seabhaig or precipice of the hawk. Let us eat first.'

Gavin laughed as he produced a bar of toffee with other items from his bag.

'What's funny?' asked fair-haired Donald.

'One of the women slipped this extra item in my bag.'

'Deliberately?'

'I'm not sure. I'll return there later.'

'Morag served me. I hope she hasn't put in something else, such as a mousetrap. No!'

As they ate Mackay commented, 'Martial sounds have echoed in the pass. On the snowy 10 February 1654 the longbow was used for the last time in a British battle. A Royalist force was trying to gain support for Charles II, and it held the pass. A Roundhead force under Colonel Morgan got onto the north slopes of Craigendarroch to the south there. The Royalists hampered by bog were defeated.

There is a wonderful legend about John Farquharson, the Black Colonel of Inverey to the west of Braemar. He was presumably called black because of dark skin and hair. Unlike most of the Highland chiefs he had not made his submission after the Battle of Killiecrankie. From either end of this pass a party of mounted redcoats charged with the aim of crushing him between them. Overhanging rocks echoed their triumphant cries. His fine black mare, however, cleared the burn and masses of fallen rocks. The dragoons' horses met with a loud clash. Inverey bounded up, using his dirk as a spur. It seemed repeatedly that they would fall on the spectators' heads. Yet he continued until he was free on the crag's summit. An officer said that if they had been told he could fly as well as run, they might have spared themselves the roughest ride he ever had.'

Hector Macgregor, large, dark haired, dour and taciturn, sat opposite the sergeant, and he showed no reaction to the legend. Yet he gave the impression that in the storm of battle he would be true to his forename's meaning of hold fast, which was similar to his regimental motto.

As Gavin was not in the sergeant's direct line of vision, to Donald's amusement he shook his head in disbelief at the legend. While they ate he was in a philosophical mood. He saw the sunny, reddish granite as a figurative expression of man's body, and through it as a vision of his spirit. A man had to aspire until he found his place in Creation. Gavin sternly observed the defensive wall, which he was to climb until he walked free along the rampart topped with pines. How could he conquer a foe, if he was not the master of himself? He envied Iona's natural, spiritual grace. He had to empty himself to be filled with favour. That day was the gateway to his life and spirit.

After eating he prepared by rubbing his hands together, before turning them inward, interlocking the left and right digits and stretching them down. Then he held his right palm at an angle and passed his left hand over it, interlocking the digits and straining his arms against them. He knew also that the mental approach was just as important as the physical one, and if Iona had only stirred his emotions she would have been a distraction. Instead he found it easier to be calm.

The sergeant and Hector formed one pair, Gavin and Donald the other. They ascended routes of intermediate difficulty, before Mackay decided to hold a contest between the pairs up a more difficult area of 118 feet.

He taunted Gavin and Donald, 'Hector and I will make you two look like clumsy mountain goats. In the unlikely event that you beat us, however, I will buy you both a drink. Otherwise you can buy drinks for us. Is it agreed?' he added with a grin.

'Yes, Sergeant,' they replied impassively.

As they were getting ready Donald asked Gavin, 'How do you like being described as a goat?'

Smiling his companion replied, 'I have been born under Capricorn or the Goat, while Pan, part man, part goat, is the Greek rural god and the spirit of Nature, so we are in excellent company.'

Mackay signalled the start and his pair led initially with an impetuous rush, while the other stayed briefly on the ground as Gavin finished his consideration of a precise route. Then more assured he enjoyed ascending the unyielding granite, which was as steadfast as a friend. He clutched horizontal and vertical crevices and small lumps of rock. He swayed to put his left foot in a crevice, before making a swing of momentum as he raised his right hand to a projection. Then his legs were splayed while he gained a new hold. The breeze became fresher and more invigorating. The dark burn below got smaller and smaller. Approaching a wide ledge, he paused when a loud 'caw' was instantly followed by a startled flock of jackdaws flying away in a black and grey blur. He would have liked to rest for a while on the ledge like a bird and survey the varied landscape, but time pressed him up the ancient crag. He gasped with delight as he mastered a jutting large slab. Gazing aloft he thought how attuned were the pure, beautiful sky and Iona's serene, joyful spirit. He recalled how her hands were lightly and gracefully moulded round items, contrasting with his frown of concentration as he arduously turned the seeming impossible into the possible. Yet the curious combination of military discipline and her gentle inspiration taught him that the harder the task the calmer he had to be. Ironically the last few feet were easy, but he had been so preoccupied with the route and thoughts about her that, when he pulled up the rope and greeted Donald at the top, it was only of secondary importance to him that they had won.

He was gazing quietly at Craigendarroch, when to his alarm Donald raised his arms aloft and gave a triumphant 'Yes!' which was considerably amplified across the narrow pass. Even on leave he should have been careful to show respect for the sergeant.

Soon Mackay's strained, frowning face appeared, but when Hector had joined him at the top he generously raised a thumb of salute and said, 'Well done you two. The Black Colonel would have been proud of you.'

The victors exchanged a quizzical look, but said nothing.

Returning to Ballater the group was in Bridge Street on the way to a meal at the Invercauld Arms Hotel near the River Dee, when Gavin excused himself and slipped into Gordons' shop, quietly followed by Donald.

The proprietor was serving a customer, but Morag came along behind the counter to Gavin with a facile grin and a coquettish toss of her locks, asking, 'Can I help you?'

He leaned over and replied, 'Yes,' and bent further still, as if he was about to impart something confidential. She eagerly shot her head forward, so that there was only about a foot between them.

'Is the colleague you call Snowdrop around?' he enquired with a smile.

Morag raised her eyebrows in disbelief, but Mr Gordon heard the query and explained, 'Iona? She took some groceries to an elderly couple, and as it was nearly closing time she was going for a walk up Craig Coillich,' pointing south-east.

'It means the witch's rocky crag,' Morag whispered maliciously.

As Gavin thanked Mr Gordon and turned to leave, the owner advised him, 'Don't try and find her up there. She takes a wild detour near the top. You should wait down here for her return.'

'Thank you. I think I'll find her.'

Morag whispered round a customer she was about to serve, 'Mike's with her.'

Gavin asked with a dejected look, 'Mike?'

She arched her eyebrows in affected surprise and replied, 'The dog!'

'I'll be wary of him,' he responded with a civil nod and left.

Looking down the street he saw Hector walking ahead, but Mackay had stopped to look at fishing tackle displayed in a shop window, and approaching him he said, 'I would prefer to eat later, Sergeant. As I am staying with Donald and his aunt, I will say goodbye now, in case I do not see you again before you return to Aberdeen.'

'But you could have the free drink I owe you.'

'No thanks. I prefer not to drink on an empty stomach.'

'You are not hungry with a hollow stomach?'

Donald smiled and said, 'What he really means is that he would like to find Iona Gordon, because he has learned that she has taken her dog for a walk up Craig Coillich.'

Mackay's tone softened as he said to Gavin, 'Why didn't you say so? I will tell Hector you have something urgent to do. Just hang back for a few minutes until we are out of sight.'

'Thanks, Sergeant. I will see you later, Donald.'

He walked back to the church and gazed at the spire towering over the little lives of passers-by, and at the hands of time on one of the clock faces. He welcomed the chance to compose his thoughts, but the two minutes passed with leaden slowness, until his heart leaped when the bell chimed at 5.30. Returning resolutely down Bridge Street he sensed Morag give him a puzzled look as she turned to her left outside the shop and went home.

When the road rose towards the bridge the Invercauld Arms Hotel's white walls appeared to the left, but the wider view had far greater charm. He heard the Dee before he saw it, the beckoning loud chant of water flowing over little rocks. On the bridge he looked right and was moved by the reflection of a cloud resting like a spirit of peace on the broad, stately river, its banks adorned with trees.

Crossing the south road he found different tracks near the base of the hill. As Iona was to make a wild detour near the top, he decided to take a steep central path. At first he was enclosed by graceful birches with grass and young ferns below. Then came a steeper firebreak through a massive basically pine plantation. The path twisted and turned, but the cool calmness and soft light refreshed him after his recent exertions, besides instilling a mood of deep tranquillity. He paused and looked back at bright Craigendarroch in the distance. He continued with heather, bright green blaeberry and moss giving an enchanted air.

Not far from the summit the path veered to the right round a rocky outcrop, where a brother and his younger sister, both in their early teens, slowly ascended, and when they parted to let him pass he said, 'Thank you. Has a young woman with a dog passed you coming up the hill?'

'Yes, Iona Gordon, about five minutes ago,' the boy answered.

'Do you know where she was going?'

'She was off to her witch's lair.'

'That is not her description, is it?'

'No, it's ours.'

'Where does it lie?'

The girl replied, 'We saw her there last year by accident. She made us promise not to tell other people where she went.'

'Thank you.'

'She may not be pleased to see you,' the boy cautioned him.

'I will approach warily.'

The girl said with a coy smile, 'She will cast a spell on you.'

'She already has.'

They looked mystified, before the boy warned him, 'If you leave a path and walk through trees, be cautious lest you meet Kaiser Bill, a capercaillie with a vicious beak.'

'Oh yes,' Gavin replied dismissively.

When he proceeded the girl said, 'Be careful, it can be rough at the top if you don't know where you are going.'

Turning Gavin responded proudly, 'A Gordon Highlander is ready for anything.'

His heart rose as the path veered more south-east towards two sunlit trees. At the summit was a cairn to the left overlooking the valley and beyond a flat bed of heather and rock. A short tree-lined path led to a horizontal firebreak. He looked south-west and saw no one. Turning north-east he saw a lesser, curving, grassy path, and he recalled Mr Gordon's remark that Iona would take a wild detour. The way inclined gently down like a carpet, with a steep slope to the right. Again he was surrounded by trees and passed through increasing young ferns. Then he turned south-east into a rising, wilder firebreak, as he remembered the warning that it could be rough at the top.

Climbing over the first of several fallen, mossy trees, he muttered, 'You will not out master me, Iona.'

He strode on, until ahead just to the left was a sublime mound of sunny heather capped by a plantation of waving pines, and he murmured, 'Wild haven, where is your nymph?'

On top of the mound he touched a hoary trunk, a piece of bark crumbling in his fingers. The lower branches of many trees were dead and debris littered the ground, but spaces enabled the sun to nourish heather and rich green vegetation.

He reflected, 'In a dream I have seen such a peaceful vista. May this waking dream end in love's vision.'

To the south he saw more trees with rising moorland beyond, while far below to the north the meandering Dee was held in peace by the heights it served. He wandered on until a gully lay shortly ahead. Just as he thought of returning, he saw the subject of his search glide away to the right among more scattered trees.

He halted by a tree and mused, 'She walks in grace and loving beauty, with the mystery of art sublime. Here her gentle spirit reigns, but with a modesty which seeks neither a halo nor a crown.'

Her gliding ceased beside two pine trunks dividing from a common base, with a backward tilting boulder at the east side. A bird's song on a high branch evoked her smile. She looked cool in the slight shade which blended with the carpet of pine needles. Free of the smock she wore down below, she stood in her full Highland glory, wearing a white blouse and a Gordon dark tartan skirt, coloured black and blue with green, but enlivened with the variant of a yellow line. She raised her hands, the fingers splayed and curved, as if she was about to accompany the bird on a pipe.

He would have admired her longer where he stood, but her collie had spotted him, so he advanced towards them. Instead of the dog turning aggressive, as Morag had implied, he wagged his tail and cantered to him through the trees in a friendly way. Iona glanced at Mike and then she saw Gavin. Her blissful upward smile had suggested that more than the bird had roused her feelings, and her instant recognition of Gavin in a gentle not surprised tone showed that she had been thinking about him. They shared a glance, then a longer look, after he cleared an intervening tree. Their expressions were placid, but he was filled with transport.

He knew that a demure woman would look a man in the eyes at a distance, but become more modest when they were closer. She did not smile at him, averting her gaze to the bird when he approached. He felt greater joy than if he was meeting a woman who smiled broadly from the heart. His was a spiritual love which ruled the heart. Yet he felt a strange wonder which caused an alternating blissful fear and fearful bliss. She remained composed, only a quiver of her hands hinting that he may have come too soon to her alone. He did not feel impetuous, however, for he knew intuitively that they were kindred spirits. Then he saw her more clearly, as she turned her head towards him and her eyes shone through the enveloping shade.

Not wishing to disturb the bird, he whispered, 'The Gordon tartan may help to camouflage a man in war and stalking, but it has the opposite effect on a woman. You are not hunting now.'

'Absolutely not. My father likes me to wear the tartan. It is 120 years since 1794, when it was designed for the new regiment and later adopted by the clan. I was intrigued to learn of the romantic tradition that the very beautiful Jane, Duchess of Gordon, helped initial recruitment to her husband's regiment by travelling to country fairs wearing a Highland bonnet and regimental jacket, and gave a kiss and a coin. Her recruits were proud to have been enlisted by the leading woman in the region. My mother came first to my father, but she called him to love not arms. Unlike Jane I do not have six pipers.'

Nodding he asked, 'Is this your haven?'

'Yes, this fully developed dual tree is much sturdier and far more graceful than close-set ones.'

'Yet there is a wild aspect on every side.'

'Birdsong tames the wild.'

'Yes, and there is a dove here that sheds ineffable peace.'

Modestly ignoring his tribute she pointed above and exclaimed, 'A skylark! You can see the crest on his head.' Turning to him she added, 'The bird! Why look at me? I am not a sylvan sprite. I may just have elemental beauty.'

'I have not seen such beauty before, and when you smile your eyes are poems of Heaven. Yet, as this is the first day we have met, even a few words of love may be too many.'

She replied gently, 'Love is a song without words. The shadows lengthen. In disembodied night silence is love's perfect song, as winged spirits beat at one with the stars.'

Then he stood on a dead piece of branch which noisily snapped. Iona giggled as the startled bird flew a short distance north to another tree which overlooked the valley. The tension of the meeting was eased, and, beginning to follow Mike who was walking south-west, she gained more space and could lead Gavin.

'Mike and I usually visit the plantation down there before returning. You can join us if you like. His name was suggested by a Roman Catholic female friend, as he was born on 29 September, the feast of St Michael.'

They walked through scattered trees with rich humps of heather and blaeberry on the way to the plantation, and at its edge she attached the dog's lead, saying, 'We occasionally see roe deer in here, but, if Mike were to run towards them in a friendly manner, they might not understand and could be disturbed. Not only are they smaller than red deer, but also they tend not to associate in such distinct groups.'

'I had experience of stalking red deer in the West Highlands, before I joined the Gordons.'

'That is interesting.'

The way initially went sharply down. The trees were close with only stumps for lower branches, while the green tops swayed noisily in a stiff breeze, creating the sound of an inland sea. Below was a sequestered, peaceful air, as the trio walked silently on lush green vegetation. Iona glanced about her, until suddenly with an excited smile she crouched down beside a tree and signalled Gavin to do the same. Through binoculars she looked intently to the south-west. She handed the glasses to Gavin, who focused on a grazing hind. Then he saw a young fawn that was beginning to walk, but still had spots as camouflage.

After they returned some distance she commented, 'I hope that the fawn will meet another and enjoy races and leaping over minor obstacles. I discourage children from coming here, because if they were noisily to approach a newly born fawn lying by itself, it might squeal, and, if the mother is in hearing while she eats to maintain a milk supply, she would quickly return in a distressed state. Even worse would be if children were to handle a new fawn, for the human scent could drive the mother away.'

Near the outer area of the plantation, when Mike's lead was removed, he rubbed against Gavin's left leg, as he had become separated from Iona by a short distance, and he laughed, saying, 'He is shepherding me in the right direction.'

'How did you find me among all the trees?'

'Your father told me that you took a wild detour near the summit, and a young girl with her brother warned me to be careful on the top. They linked your wish for privacy round here to sorcery, but with respect, as if you were a white witch who confined herself to beneficial magic.'

When they headed for the mound over which he had walked earlier, he said, 'Inside my bag I later found a bar of toffee which I had not bought.'

'Morag slipped it in. You may not have noticed her admiring gaze. You deserved the gift, because when you entered the shop and smiled it was as if you blessed the place. I remembered the Gaelic Rune of Hospitality in which one gave a stranger food, drink and music, and in the name of the Trinity he blessed those there and the building. The rune continues that in her song the lark says how frequently "Goes the Christ in the stranger's guise."'

Half in jest Gavin replied, 'Yet Morag speaks slightingly of you.'

'She does liken me to a snowdrop and herself to a rose, but I take it as a compliment, because she knows that the snowdrop is my favourite flower. Its dainty, drooping head is like beauty at prayer. In the language of flowers it means hope and purity. According to legend, after being expelled from the Garden of Eden Eve sat weeping, for snow fell ceaselessly. An angel comforted her and, catching a snowflake in his hand, breathed on it, and it fell to earth as the first snowdrop. He called it Hope. In medieval times the white blooms were a symbol of Candlemas, a festival held on 2 February to commemorate the purification of the Virgin Mary, the second Eve, and Jesus' presentation in the Temple. Candles were blessed at the festival. Less seriously Morag and I are friendly rival dancers each year at the Ballater Games.'

They paused in calm amid the trees near the mound's north-west edge, and gazed at the boisterous high branches. They smiled at each other, at the concord between peace and tumult, and at the varied yet united views. Their nascent love was in mystic harmony with the trees, the river flowing through verdant pastures, and the mountains and hills.

'There is a Celtic cross on your necklace.'

'It bestows a blessing on life's journey.'

She looked so composed and serene, he asked, 'How does one earn grace?'

'Grace is not earned. God gives it freely to his humble and grateful children.'

She lightly led the way down the mound, but when they were in a cleft heading to the firebreak her sharp eyes detected a sudden movement beside a larch above to the left, which made her pause and call, 'Callum!'

The boy Gavin met earlier reluctantly rose from a crouching position.

Iona added, 'Where's Helen?' upon which the girl moved from a shadow beside two close pines to the boy's left, which suggested that it had been his idea to lie in wait.

'You shouldn't spy on people,' Iona chided them and continued on her way.

Gavin was amused that she insisted on decorum in the wild, while he waved at them, evoking grins and waves, before he said to Iona, 'They are attractive children.'

'Yes, some years ago they were described as cherubs. They should try to fulfil their early outward promise. I recently told the boy that his Christian name was a form of that of sixth century St Columba, which came from the Latin for dove. He settled on Iona, from which his influence spread through Scotland.'

'You and the boy should become good friends.'

'Hopefully. Their father, Kyle Leslie, is in the 6th Battalion of the Gordon Highlanders. I have seen Sergeant Mackay in Ballater on previous occasions, so I know that you are in the 1st one.'

When they were descending north-west in the nearby firebreak, Gavin looked through trees to the left and said, 'I hear a capercaillie.'

They halted and Iona replied, 'Yes, the word comes from the Gaelic meaning the horse of the wood. Male sounds like the clip-clop of a horse's hoofs have earned the name. It's the female "kock-kock" sound you hear. Last spring Callum and Helen got a fright when they investigated a male's display call in the lek. At school Miss Clark had recently given a vivid description of how between April and May the male started with clip-clop tones which quickened, followed by a sound like the drawing of a cork and ending with one like grinding a knife! During the display the mail's tail was raised and spread like a fan. When the children got close, however, he chased them away. The size of a turkey, mainly blue-black with a dark green breast and brown wings, plus white marks, a heavy pale bill and a red wattle above each eye, he made an impression on them! Generally the males are not aggressive to humans, but they have found an unusual one that lives near. I keep Mike at heel, so he does not disturb any of them.'

Gavin smiled and suggested, 'The female's repetitive note may be an alarm that she has heard us, but we could go a little closer and try to see her with your binoculars.'

They advanced carefully until Iona raised her glasses to see the female camouflaged in ruddy brown and heavily barred black, with her chicks that were in and around the nest, a hollow among fallen needles at the base of a pine. Kaiser Bill kept guard on a branch, but looked obliquely away from the visitors. The sun glistened on the glasses, however, when Gavin raised them, and the male was disturbed. There was an explosive flapping which forced them to flee. With an extended neck the bird rapidly beat his wings just over Gavin's head, and then glided a short way down the firebreak, jealously patrolling the boundary of his territory before returning to keep guard. The children were some distance ahead, but on hearing beating wings they looked back. Callum frowned at his earlier warning having been ignored.

As the children walked on Gavin said, 'It is fitting that they should learn early that life is not a fairy wood.'

Iona corrected him, 'It is better that they should achieve a proper balance between imagination and rational fear.'

Looking about him he remarked, 'The trees here are a welcome change to those in Aberdeen.'

'A more natural, wild setting has its charms, but you are fortunate there. I was in the city last month with a female friend from Glenmuick Parish Church. We attended the sixth North-East of Scotland Music Festival as spectators. Beforehand we enjoyed a walk in the west end, admiring the varied late spring trees which flourished away from the east winds and sea air. Aberdeen is a leader in Scotland for urban trees. The festival has also improved annually, at least for range, and this year there has been a need for specialization. There were eighteen children's choirs competing in the afternoon, including a large number of entrants from country districts. While they have been taught to express the spontaneous beauty and grace of gestures and actions, some children can by themselves express the pure beauty of life in a way we cannot.'

When they stood on a rocky slab to the right of the cairn he passed earlier, she said, 'There is a beautiful view of the valley and Ballater.'

'The river is sublime.'

'Yes, Dee means goddess. In ancient times it was believed that she determined whether or not the river would flood. People were concerned about livestock or anything else they had near the river. It was here when the hills were still evolving. Its source is a spring at the foot of a bank of grass and moss on the summit plateau of Braeriach, the second highest Cairngorm mountain to the north-west. In its eighty-five mile journey to the sea it drops 4,000 feet, the greatest fall of any British river. Look north and see how the sun often graces green Morven or large hill. Immediately overlooking Ballater from the north is Craigendarroch or rocky hill of oaks, which many people prefer to Craig Coillich, but I have to attach Mike's lead at the top there, because of the crags. If you take the binoculars you can get a good view of Glenmuick Parish Church, as well as make out the cairn on Craigendarroch. Before the present burgh there was a hamlet at the east end of the Pass of Ballater called Baladar, meaning settlement at the wooded stream or perhaps stream at the pass.'

After he had finished she added, 'Craig Coillich is a spur of the extensive Pannanich Hill. An interpretation of the name Pannanich is that it comes from Gaelic words meaning the hill beside the river. About two miles down the road below are Pannanich Wells. The water is beneficial for my father's arthritis and it is the key to the growth of modern Ballater. Around the mid eighteenth century an old woman, Elspet Michie, who had been bathing in and drinking water from the wells, was said to have had a miraculous cure from scrofula or tuberculosis of the lymph nodes. The water's dual reputation spread. For visitors buildings were erected around the church, the more impressive current one opening in 1874. In 1847 Queen Victoria and Prince Albert had poor weather in the West Highlands, but their doctor, Sir James Clark, told them that his convalescent son was enjoying better weather at Balmoral Castle. In due course the royal connection helped to bring people for the scenery and the pure, dry, bracing mountain air. Ballater thus became a wider health resort. Some people regard this area as a little Switzerland.'

Admiring the views and the even more charming subject beside him, Gavin replied, 'I am staying here for a week with Donald and his aunt, Mrs Jean Grant, but we have not finalized what we are going to do.'

'After rock climbing you could try the less arduous golf course, while tennis and bowling are also popular. Tourists are advised as well to take the new walk round the shoulder of Craigendarroch and climb to the top. There is an unusual variety of woodland and other scenery, with a very fine view, although the Cairngorms can be seen better from here. In good weather visitors tend first to travel up Glen Muick and climb Lochnagar to appreciate the contrasting two corries and the panorama. Then they journey further up Deeside.'

As he led the way down, so that if he slipped she would not be sent tumbling, Mike moved between them to follow the strong, athletic man, and she said thoughtfully, 'This area is idyllic, but recently we have had a shock. A frost of unprecedented severity occurred between Saturday night and Sunday morning on 23 to 24 May. The oaks on Craigendarroch had a blackened look, as did many potatoes which were through the ground in the district. On beeches spring leaves turned an autumnal russet. There has been some other damage, but hopefully there will be a second set of leaves. The main victim on Deeside, however, has been the very important strawberry crop. Whole fields of the fruit, especially down in the Banchory area, have been ruined. Raspberries have also suffered greatly. Living in the sheltered valley we sometimes forget that in the Cairngorms blizzards can occur in May, although lingering snow on Lochnagar should be a warning. Not being superstitious my father did not speak of a connection between the unseasonal damage and his fears of an international conflict, but he was preoccupied for a time.'

Far too quickly for Gavin they reached the base of the hill, where she put the lead on Mike before crossing the road. When they mounted the bridge Gavin saw Donald in a small safety and viewing recess gazing upriver. Gavin suddenly realized that in his haste to climb the hill he had forgotten to ask where Donald's aunt lived, and so his devoted friend was waiting for him. Donald gazed intently at the broad, peaceful evening river. The air was filled with the paeans of water pouring over little rocks. The rich medley was ceaseless, but it defied the monotony sometimes associated with human chants. He seemed to be lost in reverie, as if taking stock, but then he noticed activity on the north bank. A large dog had arrived with his male owner, and he rushed into the water. In spate the river struck awe and fear, but now it beckoned, and the dog wanted to cool down, so he swam out some distance and surged through the delightful element. While his owner stayed on the bank, now he was the master, revelling in the power and freedom of staging a spectacle.

Donald turned to smile at Iona and Gavin when they approached, and he said to his friend, 'I have asked my aunt to delay our meal.'

On seeing the dog in the water Iona warned, 'Mike would like a quick cooling down, but I will take him a little further up, because otherwise if the larger, temperamental dog sees him he might regard it as a challenge, and on a fight breaking out they could not be quickly separated.'

There was a sizeable area of light brown stones at the edge which had been covered earlier in the year. Mike dashed across them and drank eagerly, before swimming out until only his head was visible. Yet after his exertions on the hill he swam in a relaxed manner for a short time, before emerging he shook himself and returned to Iona.

Gavin said to her, 'You have a striking name.'

Smiling she replied, 'Gordon comes from a place in Berwickshire, apparently meaning spacious fort. My parents visited Iona during their honeymoon. Established by St Columba it became an island of contemplation, pilgrimage and the final resting place of Scottish and Irish kings. I am proud of my parents and try to live up to the name.'

'Could we meet again?'

There was a pause as she gazed wistfully at the river of life, and then she quietly said, 'Tomorrow is Saturday. I will ask my father. Perhaps you could call at the shop just before 12.30.'

They rejoined Donald who was standing discreetly to one side. The two men then led the way up Bridge Street, until Gavin turned and exchanged a smile with Iona, before she disappeared.

Donald's aunt lived in the south-west part of Church Square. Her husband, Ben, and son, Peter, were away at sea, Ben being the master of a merchant ship, while Peter worked on another vessel. She had a trim figure with a bob to her black hair and was a good cook. The conversation at table and afterwards was lively and interesting, but Gavin was puzzled that, when he tried to talk about Iona, she changed the topic.

After a renewed attempt by him she explained, 'Iona has roused interest in two other fellows in the past, but her father has a reputation of being fiercely protective and he has discouraged them. She is regarded as being almost unapproachable on that level, and she is somewhat shy of men, which does not help, although she is very pleasant in herself. I do not want you to build up hopes too high, in case they are dashed.'

He protested, 'She was uncommonly agreeable to me this evening.'

'You must understand her situation. The father exercises such strict control she is like a caged bird in the shop. Many people believe that she goes on long walks with the dog, because of the freedom. I think another factor is that she finds in Nature to some extent what she lacks through the loss of her mother. She is unusually gifted for her age and is deeply conversant with all aspects of the Highlands. Her affable manner to you, however, may have been just gratitude to a kind stranger, rather than a positive response to you on a personal level.'

He recalled that Iona had referred to a stranger when speaking of a Gaelic rune, and he realized now that when she said she would ask her father about meeting him again, it was more than a formality.

The bedroom he shared with Donald overlooked the square, and he opened a window that warm night, so the chimes reverberated around them. In spite of the uncertain prospect the day had yielded such rich memories that his life had never shone more brightly. His was the generous love of the spirit, not the possessive, physical love of the heart, and he fell into a tranquil sleep.

2: Glen Muick–The Ballater Dance

As a soldier Gavin was used to rising early. Woken by the church clock chiming at 5.30, he quietly pulled a curtain back a little, while Donald turned over onto his right side and slept on. He stood by the open window, considering what they could do until he called at the shop just before 12.30. Then he heard light steps below coming from the right suddenly cease, and, after the slight sound of an item being pushed through the letter box, they receded. He looked outside and saw the back of Iona's head. He went downstairs and found an envelope addressed to him just by his forename. He realized with a smile that, when he asked if he could meet her again, he had not given his name. The sergeant, however, had called him Gavin in the shop. He anxiously returned to the bedroom, fearing the worst from this secretive errand. The puzzle deepened when he read a brief note in graceful handwriting which simply asked him to call round at 9 a.m. Was he to be summarily dismissed by her father, like the previous two suitors, or were there to be conditions such as limited access?

Later, turning into Bridge Street, he saw a female customer enter the shop. A delivery van was outside. He could hear the driver and Mr Gordon talking out of sight behind it. Inside was a middle-aged female assistant, apparently deputizing for Iona, while Morag was further along the counter serving Miss Lesley Clark, her old schoolteacher. Small with grey hair, but with a fresh complexion and booming voice, she stated that she was to retire at Christmas.

While Gavin hovered impatiently in the background, she began to digress about age, seeing elements of comparison and contrast between her and Morag, for she remarked, 'In youth we dream of maturity and in maturity we dream of youth.'

Then Graeme Nicolson, a pale, retired teacher with straw coloured hair entered, and, on telling Miss Clark that he was reading Goethe's *Faust*, evoked her reply, 'It would be better if the Kaiser, instead of forever vainly changing from one uniform into another, were to read that work objectively. Faust is reconciled with God after being influenced by Mephistopheles, the spirit of the Devil. Yet, while Germany flourishes, I protest against Lowlanders teaching in our Highland schools, because I am sure that it will lead to a slow death of the Gaelic tongue. Also, I have mixed feelings about English tourists visiting Upper Deeside, because the native language is likely to retreat before the English invasion.'

When Morag had nearly finished dealing with her list, there was a lull in the conversation, and Morag seized the chance to take revenge for the implicit rebuff Gavin had given her the day before by asking for Snowdrop.

'There are two things a girl never forgets–compliments and insults. While some men attach no significance to me and I may not be learned in Gaelic, I am a muse who can inspire poetry in many a man's heart.'

Thinking that she was being flippant, Miss Clark asked, 'Really, you recall what the seat of the Muses is called?'

'No.'

'The Museum! Every woman is an exhibitionist, but the secret is to do it subtly to preserve the mystery.'

'There's nothing mysterious about me.'

When Miss Clark had left Gavin said to Morag, 'She has a fine voice.'

Speaking quietly so that Mr Nicolson could not hear, she replied, 'Yes, like a rocky burn it can be heard far and wide.'

As Mr Gordon and the van driver entered heavy laden, the owner greeted Gavin, but then frowned at Morag and nodded at an item at the back of the shop, indicating that she had been dilatory about it.

She petulantly wheeled forth a man's bicycle and instructed Gavin, 'Hold the door open.' On the pavement she explained, 'This is for you. Iona has gone on ahead to Glen Muick or the glen of the wild boar. She doesn't want the youths over there to see you together, in case they give inquisitive looks. She's always the perfect lady. Pass over the bridge, turn right at the junction and left after the monument to where Gordon Highlanders marched past Queen Vic when she was out driving one day. After four miles the glen narrows sharply. Look out for the beige cottage on a rise to the left, and you will find her by the Linn of Muick further on in the gorge to the right. A path leads down from the road among rowans. I hope you like waterfalls. She has a passion for them and will show you several today. Is it melting tenderness between you?'

'No, I hope it's strong tenderness.'

'Is she the object of your heart already?'

'Yes and the subject of my spirit.'

'Why should a serving girl arouse such devotion?'

'Heaven's concept of a hierarchy contrasts with ours.'

He thanked her, but she gazed after him in confusion when he rode away. As he and Iona had only just met, he assumed that her father was being tactful until they were clearer about their feelings. It was clear, however, that Mr Gordon had considerable trust in him.

Riding over the bridge he heard the proud elemental cry of water pouring over rocks, but, when cycling beside the river on the south road, after a while there was a long stretch in which the main body flowed with silent grace, only ripples lapping the edge being audible. There was a flat bridge over a burn gently pouring between rocks and marked by tall trees.

Shortly he paused before a monument to the left of the glen's entrance. A plaque in white lettering on a black background described it as a cairn, but it was like a dramatic work of art, as if many of the stones had not been added to form a conventional cairn, so that the plaque could be placed at its heart and the vertical central section and angular sides could shelter a memorial bench. The inscription stated that the cairn marked the spot where on 16 September 1899 Queen Victoria, while driving, met the 1st Battalion of the Gordon Highlanders which, 'in camp at Glenmuick,' was to be presented two days later with new colours by the Prince of Wales. The Queen met Lieutenant-Colonel Downman, the Commanding Officer. The battalion at her special request marched past her. Soon afterwards the battalion embarked for South Africa, where Downman and a large number of his officers and men died. The cairn was erected in 1902.

Gavin was reminded that a soldier should live to the full and with honour the years he was given. It was appropriate that the Gordons had marched past the Queen near the bridge under which the River Muick eagerly rushed to embrace the main living waters of the Dee or goddess. He recalled Miss Clark's wistful comment about generations dreaming about the future or the past. In contrast the Queen, after allowing for her grief over Albert's death, and many of her soldiers who had been here on that day were no more, but maturity and youth had done their duty to the present until death.

Turning south-west into the glen he saw the River Muick to the right, and then closer on that side were charming cottages, the gardens having some frostbitten lupins. The road took its own varying course, although burns flowed beneath on their way to the river. There were birches in fields and conifers higher up. Now and then isolated cottages in picturesque settings caught his eye, the cultivated gardens contrasting with Nature's wild yet regulated garden. The glen like many others had a partly tragic past, but today was marked by peace and joy. A breeze blew in upper branches of pines, although it was still below. Small, invisible birds on treetops sweetly chirped and trilled, creating heavenly rills. A wind rose and swept through conifers with the sound of a stream. He was intrigued to the left by an enormous granite mansion with a high tower set in a commanding position amid extensive plantations. Later he was struck by the distinctive charms of the Coyles of Muick on the right. There was Craig of Loinmuie or rocky hill of the enclosed field, while Meall Dubh or black lump, a dark heathery hill, was a little to the west and higher, and the Coyle or the wood was to the south and the highest. A long, straight stretch of road was enlivened by broom and wild rose bushes. At the end was a broad, rocky burn, and then the looming forested Auchnacraig (field of the crag) Hill forced the road to the right. Glancing back he saw smiling green Morven and recalled his father say that some of the best Scottish scenes opened up behind the traveller. Then the view steadily narrowed with increasing trees, first birches and then others, both deciduous and conifers. The Linn of Muick Cottage came into view. As he entered the gorge a welcome cool breeze blowing down from the hills fanned his face.

Crossing to the other side of the road he dismounted, and through banks of tall trees he was enraptured by the beautiful, bounding falls shine like a loving spirit. He perceived that the euphonic thunder came not just from the falls, but also from the rocky bed, the whole amplified by the echoing sides. He rode on and soon found the path set amid rowans leading down to the falls. Iona's bicycle lent against a tree, but then the steep, twisting path claimed his attention. Rounding a bend he saw the upper branches of a fallen pine blocking his way.

Smiling Iona appeared beyond the obstacle and said, 'Hello. The pine fell in a gale last winter.'

'Did you climb over or go round the tree?'

'Neither, I crawled beneath. It was much easier.'

He nodded and replied, 'Crafty,' before pushing his way below. As he did so he grasped an upper branch which to her amusement caused a cloud of hoary dust to shoot up. Descending from a rocky slab they stood beside the head of the falls. There was an eloquent contrast between the endless roar and her beauty's silent song. Yet her white cardigan and green dress blended with the foaming water and summer green. Her gaze was sharp, but the eyes had mysterious depths.

She said, 'Many tourists see the falls at a distance from the east road, but, when they are parallel with the linn the view is somewhat obscured by trees, they are apt to miss the path and go on their way. There's calm in the thunder!'

'Yes, a crescendo of peaceful praise.'

With a smile of light she enthused, 'See the central dark brown mane where the water begins to fall, succeeded by white hurled sheets, bounding drops and rising spume. The word linn comes from a combination of two words, the Gaelic "linne" meaning a pool and the Old English "blynn" meaning a torrent. The water makes two leaps into a pool which according to an old folk tradition is unfathomable.'

'Like yourself! I see the spirit of the Highlands, luminous, intense and sublime.'

Laughing she replied, 'In common parlance the spirit of the Highlands means distilled whisky.'

'Yes, but we Highland spirits don't use common parlance. Nor I dare say is either of us too familiar with drams.'

'No, but as you know the Gaelic form "uisge beatha" means water of life. A long time ago well-to-do people in these parts drank birch wine. Some of them said that it was sweeter than champagne. On a more practical level juice from under birch bark makes a good shampoo.'

'Strangely I have heard that nettles also can be used for making wine and preventing dandruff!'

Thinking that he was teasing her, albeit with a truthful comparison, she playfully pushed a hand against his arm, before signalling for them to sit and rest for a while. As the sun shone on the tall trees stretching up the other side of the gorge, he felt an outer and inner sense of perfect peace.

Then he remarked, 'Morag has said that Glen Muick means the glen of the wild boar.'

'Yes, the name lives on, although the inhabitants have changed. When the glen was very wild there were many boars plus wolves. The last wolf in the whole area was probably killed towards the middle of the eighteenth century. Yet while the glen is one of the most attractive in Scotland, in human terms it has changed. In the 1830's and 1840's many people emigrated to the New World and Australasia, because of poor harvests and the amalgamation of farms. During that century, however, the Linn of Muick Cottage was built and a gamekeeper settled in it. Then many trees were planted around the falls. The graceful larches hopefully will have bright foliage. There are different types of trees, so the varied autumnal hues, including the larches' soft yellow needles and russet beech leaves, are beautiful. In late autumn, when the rowan leaves have fallen, clusters of red berries still cling tenaciously to the branches.'

She sat like a dove at home in the wild. As she turned alternately to him and the fleeting water, her locks more golden in the sun swung charmingly. His attentive gaze made her thoughtful expression dissolve in a blissful smile. Their cup was full to overflowing. She controlled herself by glancing at the top of a pine high up on the other side. More potently than the falls she sang in his heart, as her eyes' pearly lustre reflected love's early wonder. Her inspired vital spirit was a revelation. Happiness for her came through total commitment to life. Suddenly the sun caught her radiant purity, her essence, a perfect fusion of childlike and adult qualities.

He said, 'It must be wonderful to be a child in this area.'

'Yes, but it may sometimes involve a greater shift from fancies to informed imagination. There was a time for me when ferns were fairy trees, there was a magic gleam on river and burn, and golden clouds beyond the Coyles of Muick were the gates of Heaven. When I found that my dreamland broke natural laws, it was here by the falls that I turned from magic to mysticism. I was rejuvenated by the Holy Spirit and began to drink deep of Nature's endless draught. I saw the falls representing the spiritual heights plunging into the depths of the heart in incalculable joy. Equally in the constant falls the wild was tamed with stasis in motion. So much beauty is brief and/or passive, but a waterfall's charm is active and passive, forever changing and yet forever the same. It is part of the cosmic dance of time, uniting masculine power and feminine grace, like the stars which move in orbit and yet seem still. When occasionally I feel subdued in the shop, I think of the falls. Life must be harmonized with the joy of Creation.

My childhood became rooted in reality, but with true enchantment. Once I visited Loch Muick to the south-west and saw a female goosander with a reddish-brown head and grey body, and her ten young resembling a dull female, as they began their passage to the Dee, where she felt safe. The brood must have had great faith in her on the rough, noisy journey. The equally striking drake had a glossy green-black head and mainly white body with a salmon-pink tint when breeding, plus red bill and legs. Yet he had previously left for Norway!'

Gavin remarked, 'If it had not been for the recent severe frost, I would have seen many small flowers near the Dee and up the glen.'

'Yes, some Highland flowers are little, but there may be myriads of them like stars.'

'Why are you and your kind so enamoured of flowers?'

'They are symbols of femininity, with beauty and grace, innocence and peace.'

'I prefer your smiles, the flowers of the spirit. There is the beauty of this world, sublime, elemental harmony and the beauty of another one.'

She gazed at the plunging falls and thoughtfully replied, 'We must try to combine the two. Transcendent beauty is divine purity of which there are many signs in this life. They enable us to surmount pantheism and occasional narcissism, where we vainly fall in love with our reflections, both literal and mental. Joy and contentment are found in seeking spiritual beauty within and without on our journey. We must turn our mortal prose into a greater awareness of divine passion, for on earth only loving souls are eternal. While pure, elemental water lacks colour, taste and scent, it is transformed on a religious level as a symbol of the Holy Spirit, purifying baptism and Jesus' gift of eternal life.'

When they continued the journey together, the wooded gorge and resounding water pouring over rocks continued for a while, before they gave way to open, rising moorland and distant waves of hills. The river meandered and conifers adorned the far right side which was open to the sun.

As he admired the austere prospect, she beamed and said, 'You should be here when the first snow is on the hills. There is a subarctic wilderness of godlike peace. Och, it's grand! The road is still fine, but one has to watch out for occasional icy patches.'

Their spirits rose in the spaciousness and cooling wind, with alternating sunshine and shade. A mystic cloudy veil lay on the summit of Conachcraig to the south-west. They passed a medium-sized burn which gave a joyful, pouring sound, and later they heard a tinkling rill, before they saw young foxgloves around boulders to the right.

She commented, 'Purple and white foxgloves are common in the glen. In the past native remedies included using digitalis from them for heart trouble. There is still design in the apparently random way in which a wind deposits seeds. Arranging flowers in a vase may require some art, but I like the surprise of foxgloves rising between boulders, or a foxglove blooming amid a wild rose bush. I prefer such roses to cultivated ones, especially as the five petals remind me of the wounds of Christ.'

As they reached the last stage of the road, she pointed west and identified part of the dark cliffs of Lochnagar which had haunted artists and poets. Soon they turned and initially descended into the glen's further south-west section. As they passed over a rocky burn, she gave its name as Allt Darrarie or burn of loud rattling noise, but now it had a sleepy, muffled sound on its way to join the River Muick. The pines lying beside part of the track leading to Loch Muick stood out. A stripped cone fell among other cones and scales, as a red squirrel ate seeds on a high branch.

Laughing she said, 'They are easier to spot in winter, because they form a thick chestnut red coat and very bushy tail. Near here used to be the Spittal or hospice of Muick. It was visited by drovers who crossed the southern Capel Mounth or hill of horses leading to Glen Clova. Mountain dew was also taken south by the route.'

'You mean smuggling whisky illicitly distilled in the glen?'

'Yes.'

They halted beside a flattish stone near the Capel Road, really a track, above the end of the loch, as she said, 'The scene is sheltering and benign today. Last century, however, there was reputedly a lad called Menzies who was herding cattle when he perished in a snowstorm, and he was buried here.'

Continuing they saw a group of stags grazing beside the river which meandered from the loch, with one stag standing in the river, and she said, 'They are growing new antlers. When I was a child I once found part of a discarded antler, but my father told me not to bring it home, because the deer nibbled shed antlers for the nutrients, particularly calcium. Originally British deer lived in forests, but as they often disappeared the deer had to live on exposed moorland. In view of the harsh conditions here red deer usually only live between twelve and fourteen years.'

Gavin added, 'Stalking is still necessary, because there are no longer natural predators.'

Some trees once grew by the end of the loch, but only light, skeletal trailing roots remained. Walking beside the loch, they paused while she knelt and scooped up a handful of sand from among pebbles. She showed how it was in different sizes and was a simple example of evolution in progress. Then they stood and watched the broad outlet where the river very gently began, with no hint of the noisy journey to come. The loch's north-east corner was a little deeper, so they drank water gathered in cupped hands from incoming ripples. She had a water bottle for each of them, but it was warm.

A steep path led to the smooth road by the loch's upper side, and they leisurely cycled. The loch was over three miles long. There were birches on the gently meandering bank, with some near the water's edge. Their graceful, swaying branches evoked joy and a few rowans added variety. The loch's other side had fewer bare patches, and a bright green sheen on its bank spilt onto the water. Sunlight pierced gaps in the clouds to cast a varied radiance on the loch, while a breeze spread a pattern of ripples. Through branches they saw a rushing burn on the far side glisten down a green slope. Iona said that it was called the Black Burn, because it ran through peaty ground and so the water tended to be dark, but now it belied its name. The distant sound intensified the calm on their side. They felt held in the serenity of the loch and hillside. Lochnagar to the north-west was hidden beyond the steep rise, but it still made them feel more enclosed.

She commented, 'The loch is so high above sea level, it is like an inner sea imparting peace, joy and freedom. When I have been here alone, surrounded by the heights, I have felt very small. One must be humble to appreciate infinity and find one's place in Creation. Many people seek God through the mystery and wonder of human relationships. I am afraid that Morag has yet to find a partner on that level. She can be hard on a fellow who fancies her, but she does not care for him. You are not afraid of me,' she added lightly.

'No, there is a beauty which protects itself with pain, like a rose with thorns, and there is a beauty which needs no defence, because it is the beauty of grace itself. Yet Donald's aunt has referred to two men who have shown an interest in you before me.'

'My father did not think that I was special to either man, and so he discouraged them. He is not proud, but he and my mother have been unusually close, and he has seen too many false romantic dawns elsewhere. He was thinking of the fellows' interests as well as mine. True enough, they soon transferred their affections elsewhere. When my father heard that you were going to search for me up Craig Coillich, he knew that it was different.'

They saw towards the end of the loch an idyllic pine covered delta which had been formed by the burn running down the hillside. Soon the cyclists stopped outside a house which was inscribed above the front door, 'VICTORIA REGINA. 1868.'

'This is the Glas-allt-Shiel or the shieling of the green burn,' she explained. 'During the steep flow there are large grassy patches as well as heather on the banks. Prince Albert had intended to build here, as it was a royal picnic spot, but it was after his death Queen Victoria had the shieling built. She described the house-warming on 1 October 1868 in her journal, but also referred to "the first Widow's house." The road was made initially. Look at that small pier. The Queen had a boat on the loch. She took a piper and some of the men sang as they rowed. She always came here in October, towards the end of her autumn stay at Balmoral, and spent a night or two in the lodge, preferably when the hills bore the first snow.'

They left their bicycles among trees, soon taking a rising north-west path which led to the Dubh Loch at the end of the glen. He was told that it was a pony track made for Queen Victoria. After a while they were charmed on the right by the cascades of The Stulan or little cataract issuing from the hidden Loch Buidhe or yellow loch. Later to the left they saw a haunting sunny green hue in a gully. Then below they admired the Dubh Loch which was much smaller than Loch Muick. The Allt an Dubh-loch tumbled and then meandered before coursing over rocky shelves and foaming into pools on its descent to Loch Muick.

They stood on the upper side of the main body of water as she commented, 'The name Dubh means black, due to the granite cliff opposite, Creag an Dubh-loch, which keeps out much of the sun. This factor and lingering Scotch mists explain why there is much greenery on its weathered side. The cliff is split by the wide scree on the gully which can be walked up to the plateau. Whereas Loch Muick is popular, relaxing and achieves a fine balance in its appeal to emotional and spiritual feelings, relatively few people come here. The wilder, even more enclosed and isolated scene, where the breeze blows the ripples urgently, has greater vitality and appeals to the spirit alone. The path peters out in soft peat before the end of the loch, a sign that on earth the spirit never reaches the end of its journey, but is still questing into the beyond, represented here to the north-west by the Allt an Dubh-loch cascading down and the rounded Carn an t-Sagairt Mór or big hill of the priest in the distance.

There is a legend about the hill. Long ago Braemar suffered an exceptionally long and severe frost. In May the ground was so hard a famine was feared, and Phadruig or Peter, the priest, led his flock to a well, a little mineral spring joining Loch Callater, and deemed to be of saintly origin. After repeated prayers the well began to thaw and the melting became general. That was the large hill on which the clouds indicating the coming of rain were first seen. According to another version the priest and people stayed on the hill until the thaw set in. The memorable frost which Deeside had last month was not as bad as that one!'

Viewing the immediate dark, brooding scene Gavin asked, 'Are there any tales connected with this place?'

'There was the incident in which the Duke of Edinburgh, Queen Victoria's son, swam to the centre of the loch after a wounded stag and killed it in the cold water. One reason for his perseverance was that the Queen regarded it as a grave offence not to dispatch a deer humanely. At Balmoral in the 1860's a German prince was sent into Abergeldie Forest, but he wounded two stags. He did not see a deer forest there again and was never afterwards invited to Balmoral.

Beyond the cliff there is Coire Uilleim Mhóir or Muckle Willie's Corrie. It is out of sight, but its burn joins the one to the north-west which flows into the loch. When I was at school Miss Clark gave a dreadful account involving the corrie. About the beginning of the eighteenth century a shepherd called William Cameron lived by Loch Callater. Tall and handsome, he excelled in Highland sports. He had won the love of the famed beauty Elasaid Gordon, the only child of Alasdair, an old shepherd who lived at the Glas Allt. Willie was making his last visit to her before the wedding, and he stayed late. Her father, who was regarded as having second sight, urged him not to leave for Loch Callater that night. Confident Willie set out, but as he reached The Stulan a violent storm made him take refuge in a bothy used by whisky smugglers. Ian Farquharson, who had been beaten by him in sport and love, was there with Rob and Donald Macintosh. The smugglers welcomed him and whisky was freely drunk. When the storm eased he went home, but the others, whose passions had been raised against him, overtook him nearly half a mile above the Dubh Loch. They set upon him with dirks, Farquharson offering him his life if he would give up Elasaid. Willie refused and fell by the burn stabbed in the heart, but not before he had fatally wounded Farquharson. The Macintoshes carried Cameron's body into the corrie beyond the cliff there and hid it in moss. Donald Macintosh met a violent end far away in the Highlands several years later, but before he died he confessed to the crime and Cameron's body was recovered. Elasaid did not long survive Willie's disappearance. Miss Clark told us, however, that there was reason to doubt the authenticity of that version of the incident. Yet such a vivid story will survive, although it is tragic when men behave worse than rutting stags. Let us take the descending path back and picnic higher up the Glas Allt.'

When the pine plantation on the delta appeared again, they saw an islet near it on Loch Muick. The water was lower in summer, and through the ripples was visible a sandy stretch linking the bank to the islet. Turning north-west beside the Widow's House, they took at first a barely perceptible path amid coolness cast by soaring trees. She led as the gentle way soon became steeper and twisting, and the pines gave way to birches by the burn.

In the open Gavin, amused by their continued slow progress, said, 'The route is zigzag.'

'It is another pony path.'

Later a steep, sometimes rocky path with occasional drops to the right ran above the tumbling burn, with many boulders on the bed and banks. The walkers were hemmed in by Craig Moseen or rocky hill of the stormy weather to the left and another sharp rise to the right leading to Monelpie Moss. They paused and glanced back at the triangular group of birches and the wider band of pines, with the peaceful loch beyond. As they advanced he was struck by the austere, even rockier stretch of the gorge, which ended in a weathered cliff, although extensive stretches of heather on it gave relief.

She pointed to an indentation in the cliff and exclaimed, 'The Falls of the Glasallt!'

'What a sublime surprise!'

'When Morag and I were here last year the falls reminded her of a wedding dress, with the suggestion of a train further below.'

Nature wrought beauty as the stream made its chaotic, tortuous way. At one point were mini cascades when the flow was divided between yards of heather. He was amused later by the foaming stretch which had given Morag the fancy of part of a bridal train. It was caused by the stream being split first by a boulder and then by a larger rocky mass. The path curved to the right until they took a minor one beside the cliff and carefully advanced until they gazed up at the falls. At the top a short stretch bent to their right, before the water levelled and then leaped down rocky steps on the left, with a separate white ribbon for part of the way on the right. Then the flow broadened on a ledge and fell more widely at a less steep angle. The white tumult and dark rocks accentuated each other, and wet rocks shone with greater power.

She commented, 'Prince Albert was very fond of the scene. Queen Victoria was enthusiastic about all waterfalls. The Linn of Muick is about thirty feet and has a concentrated roar. These falls are about 150 feet and steeper. The sheets of water have a ghostly white sheen and give a liberating cry. I am reminded of the triumphant chords of the Toccata from Charles-Marie Widor's Fifth Symphony. Appropriately the Toccata is built from elemental materials. It is often played by the organist in Glenmuick Parish Church. The main path is used chiefly by walkers making a long descent from Lochnagar. Such a fine Saturday will attract more of them. We will picnic by this side path.'

Sitting on wild grass backed by heather, they ate for a while united by mingled sounds of the falls, before he said, 'This holiday began like an interlude in a drama. Now I hope that the interlude will develop into the real drama of my life.'

She smiled demurely and replied, 'You should be careful. People can imagine strange things in the Highlands, such as kelpies in lochs and ghosts in mountain mists, on crags at twilight and in old, lonely houses.'

'As spirits of the living, not of the dead, we can be closer than bodies. A passion of the heart may be just a passing flame, but a spiritual passion is overwhelming. It inspires one's life.'

'My father fears that there may be war before long. If you serve abroad you will pass through towns and villages, being greeted by many attractive women. Comparison is all. Who knows, you might return with a foreign bride.'

'You are beyond compare.'

'Yet you have other dreams.'

'One vision is worth a thousand dreams.'

After a pause she said quietly, 'My father is so troubled about the future, he would like me to share the rest of your holiday, if you are agree.'

'Och, that is very kind of him. Wonderful!'

'You can spend part of the time roaming with Donald.'

'We met but yesterday. It is too soon to talk of parting. I will not roam except with you, for you surpass what you extol, my song of creation. What mountain has your mystery, what river has your grace, what bird has your melody, what flower has your fragrance? If you banish me for a while, I will follow in your shadow and hide my envy of the sun.'

They were interrupted by the leader of a small group of descending walkers who shouted, 'Good afternoon,' and they responded, before she said, 'My eyes and lips express restraint, because a woman's decision about a man is not hasty. Love comes not in pride and emotional passion, but in the still peace of the spirit which rules the heart.'

'Yes, I speak of my love. Use not that brief and infinite, that simple and wondrous word, until its golden wings uplift you and its mystic paeans inspire immortal joy. There are couples who enjoy love's simple pleasures and leave the mystery to God. If our love is realized, it will be an approach to mystical communion with God.'

They exchanged greetings with another walker and shortly followed him. Remounting their bicycles they saw the sunny, green bank where the Glas Allt joined the loch. Highland weather being changeable, after a while they glanced back at the loch's end cast in shadow, but the rest shone in summer tranquillity. When they left the loch behind, instead of crossing the River Muick and rejoining the east road, to see more of the glen they kept to the west one.

Shortly she pointed a little to the north-west and commented, 'There is Allt-na-giubhsaich Lodge. The first part means burn of the Scots pine. The lodge was often used by Queen Victoria and Prince Albert, and they knew it as "The Hut," but she gave the Gaelic name. She could not bear to stay there after his death, and so used her Widow's House. Albert's love of the Falls of the Glasallt and the lower picnic area on which he had planned to build, plus the more remote location and the sound of the burn's living water flowing down to the peaceful loch, would have made the retreat a great solace to her. It was appropriate that she stayed there towards the end of her autumn visits, when Nature sanctified the season of death in the annual cycle, harmonizing with Albert's deathless spirit.'

They passed over a green iron bridge traversing the Allt na Giubhsaich. To the right the broad River Muick meandered down a gently declining plain. To the left were pines, the grey, weathered lower trunks contrasting with the red upper trunks and protective branches.

She said, 'I like to return by this quieter west side. It is something of a wildlife sanctuary with food and shelter. The way is straighter and I love to see deer and rabbits crossing the road some distance ahead, and the varied plumages of feeding birds. In the freedom of the glen it is wonderful to hear their ecstatic cries in flight.'

Shortly after a young deer cantered across and away to the left in dappled forest shades, they paused and looked through her binoculars at a pair of sprightly lapwings on the ground, before the male flew a little east and circled twice, calling loudly before rejoining his mate. The road bent gradually round to the river which gathered pace. Then they were in the gorge with the echoing chant of foaming rocks. Soon they turned right and stood near the head of the Linn of Muick. As the brown and frothy water began to pass into a narrower channel, on the other side the river's edge was forced back in a contrary flow, which over time had worn a cavity in the rock. They saw where they had been earlier.

Returning to the road they passed a small mound, before taking a path to the side of the linn where she said, 'Now we get a fuller view of the water making two leaps into a deep pool, before darkly flowing on and foaming over smaller rocks. Only a minority of people get this close. Near a waterfall you hear the spirit of a river or burn, and as it is the water of life it is like listening to life itself. When thick snow transforms the area and the rocks are icy, the linn is even more sublime than in summer or autumn. The rushing clamour is always refreshing, yet one learns not to stay long, but to pursue one's life with greater vigour.'

Cycling on they lost sight of the river and felt more enclosed by trees. A rabbit some way in front leisurely hopped from the right, but vanished on the left. Later they laughed on seeing a rabbit lying motionless to the right of the road. Unusually he lay doggo with the ears folded back.

They took the side road by Mill of Sterin, so that they could cross the river and regain the east road. They paused on the bridge and looked up the tree-lined flow sweeping round a bend and pouring over rocks and stones. They crossed to the other side, where a barely submerged rock caused a long line of foam to the right, and branches overhung the river until it meandered out of sight.

She explained, 'The name Sterin means stepping stones. There was a corn mill by the river before the glen's depopulation. Now the machinery is used for a sawmill. Again here are views which few tourists enjoy and they are very peaceful. The flow is lower than in spring, but it is still vibrant. On this side in autumn the sunny, russet beech leaves are picturesque.'

Continuing they soon passed a school on the left, but the rising gradient forced them to walk, as she warned, 'The road becomes very steep and twisted. It is aptly called the Cock's Neck. I pity children who use this stretch when there are snow and ice.'

Shortly after cycling back down the east road they stopped and looked right as she commented, 'The neo-Tudor Glenmuick House blends with the surrounding scenery. It was built between 1868 and 1870. I admire the seventy-five foot tower. In 1890 the owner became Sir James Thompson Mackenzie of Glenmuick, 1st Baronet. Further down the estate is St Nathalan's Episcopal chapel with a religious tower! The saint introduced Christianity into Upper Deeside. Ironically the mansion of the royal estate of Birkhall on the other side of the Muick is much more modest. It was built in the unquiet year of 1715, being later enlarged. Birkhall means birch riverside meadow. Prince Albert greatly improved the estate by extensive planting. Birkhall Woods are now a well known resort of roe deer. There have been sightings in and outside the house of a ghost called the Green Lady. Florence Nightingale was a guest in 1856. On her first visit to Balmoral Castle she had an afternoon talk of over two hours with the Queen and Prince Albert, and she went there repeatedly. The Queen also paid her private visits. One day she appeared alone driving a little pony carriage and took her for a long walk. Lord Clarendon observed that the Queen was enchanted by her. Florence had a successful interview at Birkhall with Lord Panmure about reforms of military hospitals. He was struck by her powerful, clear mind and modest manner.'

'I recently met a lady of that description,' Gavin teasingly replied.

They turned right at the glen's mouth, soon halting on the flat bridge over a gentle burn which he had noticed earlier, and she explained, 'This is the Brackley Burn. As a Gordon Highlander you will be interested in a historical incident. In 1666 John Gordon, the last Baron of Brackley, and others were killed in a skirmish involving John Farquharson of Inverey, the Black Colonel. The matter is covered in the Ballad of Brackley, but there are four versions and two separate events have been combined in one story, so it should be treated with much caution. According to the most popular version Inverey called at the Baron's castle to the south with a challenge. Brackley, realizing that he and his few followers would be greatly outnumbered, was unwilling to accept the challenge, but he was goaded into action by his wife's taunts. After he had been murdered, however, she invited Inverey into the castle. The Gordons, outraged at her conduct, informed the redcoats of Inverey's whereabouts. On her black horse he escaped by climbing up the steep rocks in the Pass of Ballater. When he was outlawed he associated with evil men, but as a Jacobite he was regarded as a hero and the High Court of Justiciary reached no firm conclusion as to guilt about the event in 1666. The castle is no more. The peaceful and pleasing Brackley House, however, was built in 1898. It bears some similarity to Glenmuick House, but lacks a high tower.'

Smiling Gavin replied, 'When I was in the pass Sergeant Mackay said that Inverey escaped there because he had not made his submission after the Battle of Killiekrankie, which was in 1689! When a story is widely told the circumstances are likely to change.'

Iona now revealed that she had another reason for halting over the harmonious flow, as she said softly, 'There is a dance in Ballater's Albert Memorial Hall this evening. I should like you to accompany me. I am sorry about the short notice. We only met yesterday and I wanted to be sure that you were genuinely interested in me. Have you been to dances?'

'A few.'

'Good. You will enjoy the company and you appear to have similar measurements to my father, so you could wear his Sunday suit.'

Returning to Ballater they went upstairs over the shop, and he found that the suit was a reasonable fit. She said that she would come round for him at 7.15. When they met again he was charmed to see her slender figure wearing a dark blue evening frock and a matching light pair of shoes with heels an inch or so high. As they walked to the hall in Station Square she was excited about the event which would crown her day. Also, dances were infrequent and there were few other forms of public entertainment. She spoke animatedly about some of the people who would be there. He was equally happy, not so much about mixing with strangers, but learning about her broader social charms. As they entered he noticed that two young men wore patent leather shoes, but he was proud to wear the suit of a Gordon Highlander who had fought well.

A prominent farmer looking around fifty and his younger wife warmly welcomed arrivals. The father and son wore kilts; the wife and daughter were in dinner frocks. Two pipers also wore kilts. A Highland welcome had long been renowned for its warmth, and in a side room the farmer had generously provided a choice of whisky, wine or spring water. Iona modestly chose water and Gavin thought it wise to follow suit.

Then the bright faces turned to each other in the hall. The ladies behaved in a way they seldom did in public. Most of them smiled openly and a few girls smiled shyly, whereas Iona shone with geniality, hiding her true bliss. Basically the ladies enjoyed the dancing more than the men, for they were the spectacle and their hearts were more attuned to the rhythms. There was little talk, but much shining beauty and grace in motion. Those with long locks let them fly. Even the eyes of men which were normally dour and hard had gentle warmth. The people varied widely in age, but they were all young at heart, for the dance of life sprang from youth's innocent joy which was never lost.

They began with the Scotch Reel, a combination of the Foursome Reel and the Reel of Tulloch, being performed by groups of two couples. Iona told Gavin there was a controversy about the Reel of Tulloch's origin, but many people believed that it related to the kirkyard of Tullich a little to the east, where on a wintry Sunday morning the congregation kept warm by dancing with increasing lack of restraint, as it waited for the minister to come and let it into the kirk. Now two ladies stood at the ends of a line with two men in the centre, and all faced their partners. When the music struck up Gavin conventionally bowed and Iona curtsied with such ineffable grace he was deeply moved and felt that she was a Highland princess. The dancers followed each other round a track in the shape of a figure eight with an extra loop added. The men set to the opposite ladies during the first eight bar setting period, then to their own partners during the second setting period, and so on. The dancers performed the basic sequence of reeling and setting four times to strathspey tunes and four times to reels. At different stages the men raised one or both arms or placed them akimbo, while the ladies had their arms akimbo, but in swinging in the Reel of Tulloch they raised the free arm. Both sexes snapped finger and thumb. The men performed the setting steps with great vigour, although Gavin modestly left the 'heuching' to others. The Reel of Tulloch was performed to the tune of the same name. Initially the dancers stood beside their partners, each lady on her partner's right, facing the opposite couple. The dance consisted of alternate setting and swinging. After the start the dancers formed a line of four, and in setting and swinging each dancer went along the line, one place at a time. On reaching an end position they stood still for sixteen bars, then began to return along the line. The progression continued, forward and back, and forward again, until all had regained their original places. Other reels were danced that evening.

For the Circassian Circle Dance there was a large circle round the hall, with the ladies on the left of their partners. With joined hands they all advanced four steps, before retiring four steps. The inner-outward movements were repeated. Then the ladies advanced to a charming inner circle, clapped their hands and retired. The men advanced, clapped and turned round to face their partners. Like the rest Iona and Gavin criss-crossed their hands on each other's wrists and spun for the count of sixteen. He perceived the irony that such close contact did not occur when they were alone in the wild. Now they were being more private in public. She realized the irony and avoided his eyes, but smiled at his strong hold. Then the men with their partners on the right and hands crossed in front promenaded anticlockwise round the hall. The sequence was repeated eight times, the lively movements making everyone smile.

In a pause before the next dance he asked her, 'Why are people looking at me instead of you? Is it because I look more striking in your company, or is it just the novelty of a stranger?'

'Neither, they have noticed the handsome stranger.'

'It is a while since I have been described as good-looking.'

The very popular Dashing White Sergeant was for groups of six arranged in a circle round the outside of the floor. Each group comprised two sets of three people. Iona was central in a set with Gavin to her right. They all joined hands and circled clockwise and anticlockwise. Miss Clark could be heard pedantically counting the two sets of eight beats. Breaking into a line with a set of three Iona turned to face Gavin. They set to each other, then linked their right arms and circled for the count of four. She turned to another male and repeated the movements. Linking right arms she alternately spun with Gavin, then the other man, and both again. As a line the three held hands side by side and stepped towards the other set, before stamping their feet three times. The sets stepped backwards from each other and clapped hands three times. Iona's line moved forward again to the other set, raising arms, the other passing underneath. The dance was performed three more times with new sets, so it was a great mixer. Morag was in a good mood, treating Gavin like other males.

The Waltz Country Dance was gentler, being a circle dance for two couples. The other man with Gavin was well built with rugged features, and he was an agricultural worker, the class which provided the backbone of Highland regiments. His partner was a similar height to Iona, but rounder. To lilting music they all swayed forward then backwards before the dancers facing them, the men setting to ladies opposite. Then they changed places with those to whom they had set, passing by the right, the ladies doing a full turn. This sequence was repeated until they were back in their original places. Making a circle they moved forward and backwards. The men gave both hands to the opposite lady and brought her across to their right hand. Making a circle they set and brought their own partners back to place. The demureness which Iona had shown to Gavin in previous dances disappeared and she smiled openly at him. The last two circles and following movements were repeated, before the couples changed places with a poussette, dancing round and round with joined hands. The dance was performed four times. Gavin was amused by the other lady's behaviour. The partner had her spellbound. She lowered her gaze, as if he was the sun and she was the bashful moon shining in his reflected light. It seemed that at any moment she might swoon for joy. Her extreme emotional state contrasted with Iona's controlled feelings.

Strip the Willow was a set dance with four ladies facing four men. When any of the members were not dancing they clapped. Iona and Gavin were the first couple. After spinning together she turned alternately with each of the other men, starting with the second, and Gavin, before the couple spun again. He turned alternately with the other ladies, starting with number four, and Iona, before they spun again. She worked down the men, while he worked down the ladies, starting with number two, and alternately with each other. Finally they spun together and other pairs took their turn. He was struck by her light form and steps, but above all by her shining spirit. Some ladies had longer, more cultivated locks and abandoned themselves, yet for grace she was outstanding both for formal and less formal dances.

As they clapped he told her, 'This dance is even better than the Dashing White Sergeant.'

She smiled and asked him, 'Do you see parts of some of the women in me?'

'No, I see you in parts in some of them. You are the belle of the evening.'

'Hush.'

After three repeats the finale was Babbity Bowster (Bob at the Bolster), a kissing dance. Originally a bolster or pillow was used instead of a handkerchief. The use of a pillow may have been an indirect reference to the bridal bed. The dancers sat round the walls and the prominent farmer led the dance. A piper struck up 'The White Cockade,' the other piper standing by to relieve him. The leader pranced to his wife, spread the handkerchief in front of her and knelt on it. He invited her to kneel on it opposite him and kissed her. She was thus the formal belle of the evening. The pair rose and he marched round the room with the lady carrying the handkerchief behind him. She chose a jolly, retired widower, demurely dropping the handkerchief in his lap. He followed and, gently putting the handkerchief round her neck, respectfully kissed her. She joined the leader and arm in arm they went round the room, while the second man came behind waving the handkerchief. He teasingly danced before a lady, before turning away. Then he chose another lady, threw the handkerchief unceremoniously round her neck and kissed her. He joined the procession and the second lady followed with the handkerchief. She selected a third man, threw him the handkerchief and they kissed. She joined the second man to make the second couple. So the process continued, although the dance was briefly held up when a shy girl tried to flee, after being approached by a male she did not wish to partner. She was playfully dragged back and accepted a later male.

When a lady threw the handkerchief at Gavin, he rose and kissed her as a stranger. He went straight to Iona and carefully spread the handkerchief before her. He knelt on it and formally invited her to be kissed on it opposite him. She slipped down and modestly lowered her eyes. He hesitated, wondering whether to kiss her on the brow or on a cheek.

She whispered, 'I would prefer an evening to a dawn kiss.'

He quickly kissed her on the left cheek and they rose. When the selection had finished the piper stopped, but almost at once struck up a final reel.

The farmer's concluding remarks were applauded and the dancers, bright with exercise and geniality, streamed outside. Iona and Gavin wished to calm and cool down in the fresh air, as well as enjoy a little time alone before parting. They walked leisurely south to the bridge. Outwardly they had played that evening, but in the course of performing dances to various tunes and tempos they had learned more about each other. Through physical contact, including a kiss, the spiritual and emotional elements were more harmonized, strengthening each other. In the right recess they stood silent for a while, gazing at the moonlit water and abiding stars, in blissful union with each other and the night.

Then she said, 'The event has resembled the short dance of life, but the dance of time's river goes on and on.'

He added, 'We look back over its flow to gain strength from our origins.'

'Yes, and we have a new beginning, with the growth of God's Kingdom in our lives.'

As they turned back she smiled radiantly at him. He understood that, as her spirit and heart had united in the hall, she had reached a decision about him sooner than expected, and the beginning of their love was the transformation of their lives.

Before they parted in Bridge Street she said, 'I will sing in the church choir tomorrow morning. At this time of year the congregation increases with tourists, but you should have no difficulty in finding a seat. If you call for me at 2 p.m. we could take Mike for a walk, and then have a meal with father.'

3: Glenmuick Parish Church–Seven Bridges Circular Walk, Knock Castle and Craigendarroch–An Evening with the Gordons

Gavin responded promptly next morning when the bell began to call worshippers. The church's grey and red granite stones were attractive. As he mounted the east steps he admired the fitting plant motifs both in the ironwork which was on the two open blue doors and at the top of the seven narrow stone columns beside the doors. Above hung a lamp set in an oval stone. In the vestibule he opened the left entrance door. The interior was spacious with creamy white walls and a gallery. Sunlight shining through south windows enhanced the air of holy peace. At each end were three sets of diamond leaded windows and a tripartite cupola which reminded him of the Trinity. The window sections at the west end each contained a large dove, the Holy Spirit, at the top, with a cross in the centre surrounded by four smaller but pink doves which represented the inspired Evangelists and would catch the evening sun. He remembered referring to Iona as a dove when they met on Craig Coillich. On each side of the church were four pillars and five cupolas. The gallery was partly supported on a central brown pillar. The plant motif at the top of the pillars bore some similarity to that on the stone columns outside. The high, majestic pulpit was backed by the organ.

He sat halfway down in the middle, two pews behind Mr Gordon. Suddenly organ music filled the large church. It was the Toccata from Widor's Fifth Symphony. At first he thought that the volume was too loud, before realizing that the great waves were meant to overwhelm the spirit and heart with the heights and depths, the ecstasy and agony of God's triumphant love. After the final chords the choir filed in, Iona looking fresh in a green frock. She glanced at her father and then further back at Gavin, as if she knew instinctively where he gazed at her. The atmosphere was very different to that of the dance, but her sublime figure made a smooth transition.

In view of her father's deep concern about the German threat, Gavin was struck by the first hymn, 'Lead us, heav'nly Father, lead us / o'er the world's tempestuous sea.' As the second verse began with the word 'Saviour' and the third with 'Spirit,' the singers were strengthened by the invocation of the Trinity.

The regular minister was on holiday and the semi-retired Rev. William Farquharson officiated. He was tall and slender with grey hair, but had a vibrant personality. The text for his sermon was Matthew 6.24, 'No man can serve two masters: for either he will hate the one, and love the other; or else he will hold to the one, and despise the other. Ye cannot serve God and mammon.' The minister reminded the congregation that the verse was from Christ's Sermon on the Mount to his disciples and a large crowd of disciples in a broader sense. Mammon was an Aramaic expression indicating money or wealth. Just as Jesus was self-effacing and focused on people in greatest need, he bid his disciples to do likewise. In Luke 12.33 he told them, 'Sell that ye have, and give alms.' When he taught in the Temple at Jerusalem, spies were sent by the chief priests and scribes to trap him. They asked, 'Is it lawful for us to give tribute unto Caesar, or no?' (Luke 20.22). He asked them to show him a penny and then he enquired, 'Whose image and superscription hath it? They answered and said, Caesar's' (v. 24). By feigning ignorance in asking the question, he implied that God rejected the pagan values of Roman emperors. He replied, 'Render therefore unto Caesar the things which be Caesar's, and unto God the things which be God's' (v. 25). There was a syntactic balance in which Jesus rejected the nationalist interpretation of the Kingdom of God. Basically, however, the statement was an antithesis, abandoning illusory temporal wealth and power for gaining the eternal favour of God's love. Was Jesus not thinking of Roman emperors, when in Matthew 16.26 he asked, 'For what is a man profited, if he shall gain the whole world, and lose his own soul?'

The preacher turned to the remaining verses of Matthew 6 which expanded on verse 24. Against a background of poorer people especially having much of their attention absorbed by material concerns, the disciples were not to worry about what they were to eat, drink or wear. God fed the wild birds and were not his listeners worth much more than them? St Luke gave the birds as ravens, which were unclean and among

42

the least respected of birds. Yet God cared even for them. Gavin thought of the jackdaws in the Pass of Ballater.

Jesus injected humour by emphasizing the futility of anxiety by asking which of them could add a cubit to his height by troubling about it. A cubit was eighteen to twenty-two inches. The words could also be translated to mean extending one's length of days.

As for clothing, 'Consider the lilies of the field, how they grow; they toil not, neither do they spin: And yet I say unto you, That even Solomon in all his glory was not arrayed like one of these' (vv. 28-29). Gavin looked at Iona and recalled the expression 'lilies and roses,' meaning a fair complexion. Yet it was her pure spirit which suffused the clothing of her flesh. The minister commented that in the West they thought of the white madonna lily, which was often seen in representations of the Annunciation as a symbol of the Virgin Mary. It was shaped like a trumpet. From knowledge of the botany of Palestine, however, it was believed that 'lilies of the field' applied to a variety of flowers growing profusely in different brilliant colours. Yet, as a comparison was made with Solomon's regal robes and he was legendary for his wealth, the scarlet anemone was the most obvious one. The anemone was known as the windflower, because its bloom seemed to be blown open by the wind.

Jesus observed that if God clothed the grass—a symbol of transience—which next day was cast into the oven, would he not much more clothe them who were of little faith? Gentiles or pagans concerned themselves much about material things, but his disciples were to seek 'first the kingdom of God, and his righteousness,' and material things would be added (v. 33). They were not to be concerned about the next day. 'Sufficient unto the day is the evil thereof' (v. 34). Gavin had a chilly feeling, for Sergeant Mackay had uttered those words on Friday, when Mr Gordon, who was now again in front, had expressed apprehension about the dangers of international war. The Rev. Farquharson stated that the inference was they were to live each day to the full, as if it was life in little. Instead of troubling about personal needs which reflected a poor faith, they were to serve the needs of others with an absolute faith in the providence of God's love.

The preacher turned to criticize the present worldly world which attached undue significance to the appearance of national power and pride, whereas the emphasis should be on achieving inner maturity and advancing the family of society as a whole. Of course some aspects of national progress were good, such as mechanized transport and the telephone. Yet in various countries the traditional life on the land was being replaced by the power of industrial cities, where riches could go to a few and poverty to multitudes.

To domestic tensions were added international rivalries over trade, colonies and armed power. When Kaiser Wilhelm II came to the throne his first public words were to the Army. He declared that he was the Army. They were born for each other and would inseparably adhere to each other. He promised he would always remember that from Heaven the eyes of his forefathers looked down on him, and that he would one day be accountable to them for the Army's glory and honour. Thus he was ultimately responsible to German ghosts! Laughter rang through the church at this remark. The minister asserted that the Kaiser was in some ways a new Caesar. He worshipped the god of this world, the Devil. Yet he was very proud to have been Queen Victoria's grandson and she had died in his arms.

Fair, civilized, republican France, which had previously lost Alsace and Lorraine, had a basically land economy, and the country would suffer grievously if it was attacked by Germany. In Russia democracy was rejected. In 1905 a revolt had been crushed and in 1906 the Imperial Council reaffirmed the Tsar's supreme autocratic power even more firmly, for it was commanded by God. As a result there had been riots and strikes.

Scotland would not lose its dream of independence, although if it was to be achieved it would be by peaceful means. In Europe there was the danger of a cataclysmic conflict, but in the Scottish Highlands it was easier to see life in perspective. Queen Victoria recorded in her journal that when she first arrived at Balmoral on 8 September 1848 and admired the view from the top of Craig Gowan, 'All seemed to breathe freedom and peace, and to make one forget the world and its sad turmoils.' Yet Nature should be used for inspiration and renewal not escapism. Highlanders knew the reality of harsh elements as well as the romance of landscape. Moreover, despite changing continents they realized that, whatever human progress was made, they must remain God's humble children and give the glory to him without whom they were nothing.

They looked forward to 6 August, when they would celebrate the vision of Christ's Transfiguration on a mountain, traditionally identified as Mount Tabor, when before Peter, James and John he was confirmed in the presence of Moses the lawgiver and Elijah the prophet. It was aimed to strengthen the Apostles' faith in anticipation of his death on Calvary, which would achieve the resurrection of the dead on the last day.

The closing hymn was the stirring 'The Church's one foundation, / is

Jesus Christ, her Lord,' including the assertion that amid the 'tumult of her war, / she waits the consummation / of peace for evermore.'

Filing out Gavin shook hands with the minister, but he had felt closer to him spiritually when he was preaching than when he met him in the flesh. Amid the throng he did not expect to see Iona again until 2 p.m. He was thus delighted to see her green form gliding round the south-east corner of the church. Her earlier reserved glance was replaced by a bright smile.

He remarked, 'It has been a memorable service in a very fine church.'

'Yes, the tall, cast iron Corinthian columns give a greater height and span to the roof.'

'I am fond of the bell.'

'It was actually cast in your Old Aberdeen in 1688. It came from St Machar's Cathedral there, being presented to the earlier Glenmuick Church in 1798, the year of its foundation. In 1873 the present church was founded and the bell was later transferred to the steeple. Part of the Latin inscription on the bell's lip reads in translation, "Sabbaths I proclaim: festivals I announce: funerals I bewail."

We have one of the best church organs on Deeside. Recently it was decided to electrify it. An electric light system is to be introduced in the burgh. It is a famous resort, but complaints have been made about the paraffin lamps. Last July there was a plan to lay a cable along the railway from Aberdeen and bring electricity here, lighting Banchory and Aboyne on the way. The scheme fell through because Banchory would not take part. A number of men in Ballater, however, are determined that we will have our own supply. It is hoped that it will be available by the end of the year and the tourist season will be extended.'

As they passed through shadows cast by a tree, she said, 'There are different kinds of trees in the square, and I hope that rowan over there will bear scarlet berries later. Some superstitious people used to plant a rowan near their homes to keep away witches and evil spirits!'

At 2 p.m. she wore a dark blue frock as they walked with Mike down Bridge Street. Shops joined in the Sabbath calm. The only sign of work was a man holding the base of a ladder on the other side, while another man at the top replaced a slate which had slipped and projected over the street. When the road ascended to the bridge, their hearts lightened as the grey granite became subordinated to the wide blue river. If the birches on Craig Coillich recovered from the recent harsh frost, they would grow a delicate green mantle to harmonize more with the pines, but the leaves would turn golden in autumn.

As they stood in the right recess gazing at the flowing water and renewing the night's reverie of timeless peace, she explained, 'This is the fourth bridge. The first two were of stone, the latter being built by Telford, but floods carried them away. The community could not afford a third stone structure, so a wooden one was erected. The present very strong, four arch one was opened by Queen Victoria in 1885, and she called it the Royal Bridge.'

A tall woman in her thirties stopped and Iona said with a smile, 'This is Ishbel Wilkie, my Roman Catholic friend. Gavin Fraser and I only met on Friday. He is a Gordon Highlander on furlough.'

Ishbel, who had trimmed black hair, sharp features and penetrating brown eyes, gazed critically at the stranger, which made him feel as if he was a piece of seaweed from Aberdeen Bay. Before her austere, inclusive 'Hello' could be followed by further conversation, his heart sank as they turned to see Morag and a male friend bearing down on them.

'This is Colin Spence,' she said in a lukewarm manner, before exclaiming, 'Ishbel! I saw you walk beneath a ladder in Bridge Street. You shouldn't tempt fate so.'

'Nonsense, Morag. It is an old Catholic custom to walk under a ladder, because one would have leaned against the Lord's Cross, the symbol of our salvation. Also the ladder and the vertical complete a triangle, representing the Holy Trinity and the mystery of God. Later anti-Catholic Puritans turned walking under a ladder from an act of religious devotion into one of bad luck. Both Catholics and Protestants, however, believe in Providence and free will, not in fate.'

As Morag still frowned in disapproval, Iona tactfully changed the subject: 'Miss Clark used to compare the Dee to the different stages of life.'

Morag added with much exaggeration of the teacher's voice and gestures, 'Yes, she compared the river to the drama of birth, the rigours of infancy, the meandering paradise of youth, the stately flow of maturity and ending in the eternal sea!'

She concluded by excitedly jabbing her left forefinger downriver, but then, turning her stupefied smile in that direction, she met the dark looks of the Rev. Farquharson and his wife, who thought that they were being mocked.

'Sorry, Rev. Farquharson. Come, Colin, I am making a fool of myself.'

The trio were relieved to be left in peace, and the women were like sisters as they animatedly exchanged details about the morning's texts and sermons. There was a special intimacy about this aspect of Iona's world, including tones of speech and delicate smiles, into which Gavin could not enter, only quietly observe. He was charmed when the talking burst into mirth, for it was like the laughter of angels. Yet listening to Ishbel he remembered associating Roman Catholicism with statues and incense burning, but he was vague about its doctrines.

As she was about to go striding ahead, he asked her, 'Do you not sometimes wish to attend a service of the Church of Scotland, the dominant institution?'

Looking at him as if he was poor seaweed indeed, she replied, 'I attend a carol service at Glenmuick Parish Church each year, because then I am on common ground. Only the Catholic Church, however, knows with certainty the conditions for gaining eternal life. As God revealed to Peter that Jesus was Christ, the Son of God, Jesus made Peter the rock of his Church. Moreover, he gave him the keys of the Kingdom of Heaven, so that he would have authority to govern the Church, absolve sins and make doctrinal judgements and disciplinary decisions. To Peter, the other Apostles and their successors Jesus entrusted the teaching of his religion to all nations until the end of the world. The Holy Spirit was to guide them in the right direction and the Church was to be united. It is wrong to regard the Bible as the only authority, because it can be interpreted in various ways. Not surprisingly Protestantism is fractured in many sects and sub-sects.

On the night of the Last Supper Jesus united himself with his current and later disciples, offering the broken bread as his body and the cup of wine as his blood for the remission of sins. We Catholics at Masses, which are not just held on Sundays, put last things first, and in receiving the bread and wine of Heaven believe that beneath the physical appearance they conceal Christ himself. We experience a cumulative peace and joy as we proceed to the coming of the Kingdom.'

After exchanging a smile with Iona, she walked on and Gavin remarked, 'Her Christian name sounds appropriate.'

'Yes, it is a Scottish form of Isobel, which in turn is a form of Elizabeth, the name of John the Baptist's mother and which comes ultimately from the Hebrew meaning oath of God. She cares for her elderly parents, Ruth and Gregor.'

As they crossed to the bridge's left recess, he asked, 'Has she tried to persuade you to become a Catholic?'

'No, we discuss religious matters, but never argue, so we find that there is far more which unites than divides us. You got a forceful reply, because you put your question critically. As she attends a carol service each year in my church, I reciprocate by attending a Mass each Easter in her St Nathalan's Church. It is much smaller than mine, only being built in 1905, yet its intimacy encourages devotion. The use of Latin appeals to me, particularly as it emphasizes the long tradition of the Catholic Church and its global reach. Only Catholics can receive the bread and wine, but I cross my arms to show that I am a non-Catholic and the priest blesses me. It is not possible for me to consider becoming a Catholic. My father is a staunch Protestant and he loves me being in the church choir. My mother was a chorister in Ireland. When he sees me singing he almost feels that we three are together again.

Recently Ishbel and Miss Clark, a Protestant, discussed transubstantiation in the shop. As Ishbel could draw on her Church's long teaching, I was not surprised that she could answer Miss Clark's objections. My father was astonished that she could argue so forcefully, while Morag was very amused.'

They looked down at three parallel little islands covered in vegetation, which were previous bridge foundations, and then at the river flowing open wide, before it bent south and was hidden by trees, which made him smile wryly and say, 'It is better that we do not know what the future holds. Our lives are in God's hands.'

Continuing they turned right at the junction and strolled along the road, the only traffic being a horse and carriage, a car and two cyclists. On the riverbanks were coniferous and deciduous trees, plus ubiquitous ferns. Some trees bent down to the river, as if in obeisance to the water of life. Children played and laughed on the other side, one of them wearing a red jumper. They were so far away that Iona thought as if she was looking not only across the river of time to a parallel event, but also back to her own childhood, when she played carefree on the banks and was captivated by the magic of bright colours. Now she had an inner heaven, not just the bliss which a child felt around him in Nature, where the exterior was master and he was the simple, trusting servant. The growing devotion of Iona and Gavin was part of Nature, and their future with its trials and triumphs would draw inspiration from her changeless change. She would teach them more about the spirit, yet their mystic union would transcend her. Love's star belonged to no earthly place, but to the joyful peace of eternity. Iona recalled the unalloyed optimism which she had as a child. Now she knew that the bliss of new love had a chastened glory. He was a soldier, so there would be tension between the mortal and immortal aspects. Also, as life developed there would be gain and loss, but their loving spirits would keep them always young.

As they continued to walk near the Dee's wide bend, she observed, 'The finest views are higher up in the Balmoral area, where it becomes truly Royal Deeside.'

'This part is beautiful enough for me,' he replied, which made her look modestly aside.

Soon after crossing the bridge over the Brackley Burn, they turned north-west and stood on the Bridge of Muick where she said, 'The year 1878 is inscribed on facing larger stones on the parapets, and gaps between the stones generally on the tops give a pleasing rough, semi-battlemented appearance. The bridge replaced an awkward humpback one built about 1745. Let us continue and see where the Muick joins the right side of the Dee as it sweeps round.'

When they stopped to observe the union she commented, 'My father once said that the Dee was shaped like a shepherd's crook in this area, and it was fitting that it should be marked by Glenmuick Parish Church. Psalm 23, of course, begins with the words, "The Lord is my shepherd." My father was reminded of the legend that St Columba sent St Machar from Iona to travel east on the mainland, until he came to a place where a river, as it approached the sea, "lyk was then as it a bishopis staf had been." The River Don bent in that shape before it entered the sea. Around there St Machar built a church. Now St Machar's Cathedral overlooks the river's bend. It is particularly fitting that a bell from it is in our church.

In the past a belief in magic meant that where waters met there were special influences. Water from under a bridge where the living and the dead passed over was especially powerful. A burial ground is further on to the left of the road. In the last century a young sister and brother died in separate accidents involving horses in the area of the bridge. Yet, as Ishbel has said, we must reject fatalism.'

He nodded and said, 'In the peaceful joining of the rivers and our ineffable union, I see that harmony and love will always conquer in the end.'

'That is a strange remark for a soldier to make.'

'If I fight it will be to defend my love for you and Scotland, which is stronger than hate.'

'Did you have a hero like Robert the Bruce or William Wallace when you were younger?'

'They were the idols of some of my peers, but I preferred Hannibal of the third century BC. His desire for freedom from Rome inspired him to form a united army of different nationalities and various skills and take it, with elephants as a terror weapon, over the Alps. He evoked loyalty on the journey by leadership and identifying himself with the common soldiers, sharing their lot, even though nearly half were lost through the elements and starvation. Against the foe he was the master of the unexpected, achieving three crushing victories in Italy. Ironically, although the enemy regarded him as a barbarian, he showed magnanimity in not attacking Rome. Yet this failure to understand the imperious Roman spirit eventually led to his downfall and the obliteration of his native Carthage. He lacked the ruthlessness of some leaders. Your father and the Rev. Farquharson fear that Germany will seek to expand by conquest.'

As they gazed at the peaceful Dee, he remembered that he was on holiday, so relaxing he continued, 'When I spoke of my love for you just now, I showed my esteem and more. Some men regard women simply as women. I do not. I distinguish between the angels, the decent and the fallen. I would charitably put Morag broadly in the second category. She seems reasonably happy.'

'She may smile at a passing pleasure or to express her hopes and dreams, but basically she is sad at heart. The recently acquired friend Colin is not her ideal man. If he was, she would not have tried to draw your group's attention on Friday. When you visit the shop, please be restrained. I do not want her to become too envious of me.'

After walking some distance along the South Deeside Road they took a sequestered side road which curved up north-west, until she stopped and pointing east beyond a field commented, 'That ruined tower is Knock Castle, the first word meaning a knoll. As a Gordon Highlander you will be interested to know that Alexander Gordon is believed to have rebuilt it around 1600. Just as there were elements of Romeo and Juliet about William Cameron and Elasaid Gordon, there were such qualities in one version of a story here. Alexander Gordon's family had a feud with Arthur Forbes of Strathgirnoc, a western neighbour. The third Gordon son, Francis, and Forbes's only daughter were in love. Francis went to ask to marry her, but the bad-tempered old Forbes lashed out at him with his sheathed sword. The scabbard flew off and the suitor was decapitated. The feud was resumed with reprisals on both sides. Then one day a group led by Forbes killed Gordon's other seven sons when they were casting peats. Their heads were tied to the cross tops of the spades, which were then stuck in the ground. The father was at the top of the spiral stone stairs in the castle when a servant brought the news. The distraught old man fell to his death. Forbes was hanged and his property passed into Gordon hands. Knock Castle is a tragic memorial. Much of the shell is well preserved, but it is as if the ruined, tapered tops are raised in anguish to Heaven. After this bloodthirsty detour let us resume the Seven Bridges Circular Walk.'

After they had returned a short distance on the South Deeside Road, she pointed at a monolith in a field to the right and explained, 'That is the Scurriestone. It is partly covered in Nature's green embrace. Several explanations have been given for the name. One is that it means peaked or rugged, another refers to its use as a scratching post by animals, and another relates to a ford. Fords of the Dee and Muick were not far away, and the stone would have shown the way to drovers across the Muick and on to Glen Clova.'

Soon they took a gently rising, curving, north-west track, with the Dee and golf course beyond to the right. From a field to the left Highland cattle with long horns gazed at them impassively through thick hair. In Dalhefour Wood long, straight vistas of tall pine trunks casting shadows over the sunlit track gave noble dignity and peace. There was a wide range of vegetation, with attractive slopes on the left. The audible river was out of sight, but beyond was a fine view of Craigendarroch and other hills.

They walked in silent bliss for a while, before she enthused, 'One could take this walk countless times with delight.'

Near the end of the wood the track descended and curved round south-west, until just outside he said, 'That young rowan has fallen but still thrives.'

A black, shaggy pony dashed to them from the other side of a field to the north. She flung her arms round his head, as if they were old friends, and Mike vigorously wagged his tail in approval. When they walked on the pony followed a little way, reluctant to part.

As they turned north-west she said, 'We will cross the Dee by the white suspension Polhollick Bridge. It is graceful with trelliswork. Poll Chollaig may have meant the pool of the hazel place. It is also said to refer to little Coll, a saint who baptized just above the bridge. The structure is sturdy, but no more than four people should cross at once. Here and there one causes an amusing slight movement beneath, as if one is on a vessel.'

They lingered in the middle to admire the calm, dimpled Dee, and she said, 'Would that life's river was so serene, but we must be challenged to mature. The Dee has its placid and turbulent stretches.'

On the far side she pointed at a metal plaque on the left vertical and commented, 'As a Gordon Highlander you will like to read about the bridge being provided to the public by Alexander Gordon, Southwood, Hildenborough, Kent, in 1892. A famous Deeside engineer, brewer and philanthropist, he is reputed when young in 1824 to have seen an accident further up the river at Abergeldie. Two newly-weds were crossing in a wooden cradle, when the mechanism failed and, falling from the cradle, were drowned. Gordon promised that he would replace the ferry here with a bridge.'

Following a track to the Braemar-Ballater road, they admired to the west a shimmering, long, partly forested low hill. They walked east along the road, until they paused on the impressive single arch of the Bridge of Gairn. The tree-lined river, a tributary of the Dee, flowed quietly above the bridge, but raucously over rocks below it.

She explained, 'Gairn may appropriately mean crying one, and it supplies Ballater's water.'

Soon they took a path leading south and down. There was a large area of pasture on their right, which was more charming when seen from an oak wood. Then the majestic Dee swept round. Whereas in Dalhefour Wood it was out of sight, now its breadth and clamour dominated the view, although it was far below. They crossed in single file a small yet picturesque flat bridge which was wooden fenced at the sides. Beneath a token burn plunged down to the river. As they continued the peaceful path was between the river, birdsong from treetops and the sound of a car ascending the east road.

As the descending way drew nearer the river, ironically it became quieter and Iona said, 'This path is known as the Old Line. Queen Victoria did not wish the railway to continue to Braemar, as she valued her privacy at Balmoral. The section which had been engineered to the Bridge of Gairn became superfluous. It is fitting that Nature should sometimes triumph over the machine mentality.'

Gavin added gently, 'The path makes a fine lovers' walk.'

When they entered the outskirts of Ballater, on her suggestion they climbed Craigendarroch, and as they wended up to the right side of the hill she commented, 'The lowest one third on the south side is covered with the largest old oak wood in the valley. The oak is the best tree for attracting insects, and it has adapted by often growing a second set of leaves in summer to replace those eaten in spring. The recent severe frost will thus only be a temporary setback. Oak leaves represent courage. On the hill above are self-sown birches and pines. The round hill is made of granite, with crags, screes and an ice smoothed top. Here the oak leaves on both sides lie so deep, if it were not for the peaceful glint of Sabbath sunlight and young scattered ferns the ground would be like a crypt. The feeling of late autumn in summer makes death and rebirth seem strangely mingled. Next month, however, there should be more greenery.'

He light-heartedly replied, 'When the trees are in leaf they will harmonize with young yet strong love.'

As they ascended children's laughter and shouts welling up from the base of the hill caused her to say, 'It is as if the boughs are pointing down to my old school, and my childhood calls urgently, asking me to realize that my new joy is not separate from the past, but part of the wider wonder.'

To the left of the broad path were tree topped crags, with birches on high ledges. Enamoured moss clung to rocks, trees and little trodden parts of the path. Amid a medley of birdsong a great spotted woodpecker's sharp 'chack' and other notes came from a nearby oak's highest branch. They climbed up a more sharply ascending stretch, but soon when among pines and birches, with fewer bird notes, pine needles were underfoot. A steeper, twisting, narrower path had embedded stones and occasional downward sloping rocks which would need extra care when descending.

As they were more enclosed the alternation between feminine deciduous and masculine coniferous trees emphasized the balance and completeness. Profuse bright green blaeberry beside light dots on heather increased the enchantment. In the calm air and climbing steeply he felt the warmth, but she continued to tread lightly. The way became easier near the top, but more than once the approach was longer than he expected, because the view was hidden mainly by pines. Then on the right a fallen pine trunk lay in a large pool, and a small, grey camouflaged moth darted from heather, before trees gave way to the summit.

At its edge she paused beside a pool in a rock and said, 'It is like a huge baptismal font. Morag regards it as a bird bath.'

She secured Mike, but Gavin scarcely felt the cooling breeze when they halted at the top. His heart had risen near it, and now he longed to hold her, not with wild ecstasy, but gently by the waist. She did not turn to look at him. It was as if she knew instinctively how he felt, and thus, just as his hope of reaching the summit had been deferred more than once, so he must be patient before he could hold her freely in his arms.

'There is a fine view of Lochnagar,' she said, pointing south-west. 'The remnants of snow, winter in summer, make the mystic mountain look as timeless as the stars. Yet its loyalties are not divided, for it intercedes between the heavens and earth.' Descending a short way to the cairn she added, 'Ballater, on the other hand, looks like a toy village and life in miniature. It is cradled in hills, and they are sheltered in turn by higher hills and mountains. The moorland beyond Craig Coillich is more prominent from here. Now look further left at the Dee flowing peacefully on its way to the sea, and large areas of broom near it.' Walking round the cairn to the north-west she said, 'There the river turns south. The trunk of that fallen yet firmly rooted pine a few yards away is weathered, but the red boughs are protected by the evergreen canopy. The cones are like candles.'

They sat by the cairn's east side which shielded them from the breeze, and she continued, 'Among the large rocky slabs we see a little heather, a small birch sapling, living and dead moss, with fallen pine cones and needles in grooves. Death is not finality in Nature. It helps to perpetuate the recurring life cycle. This summit at 1,319 feet is only a little higher than that of Craig Coillich, but it is cooler because it is more open to the breeze. Also, as we view Ballater from this side of the Dee, we should feel closer kinship with it. Yet the burgh looks even further away than this summit does when seen from Ballater.'

Thinking that she was not showing her normal good sense, he innocently teased her by stretching his right arm, and, repeatedly rotating his index finger towards the burgh, said, 'A single, three-dimensional location of varied beauty would seem larger than an expansive, comparatively two-dimensional, regulated and homogeneous entity.'

She playfully pushed her right hand against his shoulder for such verbosity, before changing the topic. 'When Morag and I were children, we sometimes came up here. She has always been fanciful. She needs a great joy, or God forbid a deep sorrow, before she sees life whole. Our temperaments have diverged for years. I hope that the time will come when we are closer again. She is not even happy with her forename. At school Miss Clark told her that it was originally a pet form of the Gaelic name Mór, meaning large. Soon afterwards, when the teacher said that the asphodel was an immortal flower in Elysium, Morag tried to get us to use it as her name, but of course we did not try.

Miss Clark also taught us about superstitions. When Morag saw me once admiring the wonders of Nature, she playfully said, "Don't dally with the fairies, or they will kidnap you." Ironically it was she who accepted some superstitions literally. She made a fool of herself by entering a neighbour's house and telling the mother that a mirror would have to be covered lest fairies took the baby's image. Even now she insists that when she marries it will have to be on a Friday or Venus' day and there must be six small ornamental silver horseshoes and white heather on the wedding cake.'

Iona freed Mike for the descent, and they rejoined a track which went round the hill's north side, until they were opposite the crags which Gavin had scaled on Friday, and she explained, 'The pass runs along a fault line in the rock, making it easier for the glacier filling Deeside in the Ice Age to push its way through. The ice melted before it could widen the gap, so the pass was narrow. From here climbers are so small on the opposite heights, one is only aware of them on hearing their calls or metallic equipment. The sounds echo so strongly that the men seem closer than they are. They have to move before one sees them easily.'

As they walked carefully on the narrow path along a steep slope, she added, 'Like Lochnagar this side faces north, so it does not get much sunlight. It stays cool and damp most of the time, which is ideal for moisture loving trees and mosses. Yet as the pines are close and tall the branches are high up, and now the sun shines on the track. See that red squirrel racing up the pine to the right.'

Shortly she pointed left and said, 'That is a huge ants' nest made of pine needles. It contains a queen, some winged males and thousands of workers which travel daily to collect food for the colony. Look at ants walking past your feet from the nest. The workers are remarkably strong and can carry food a good five times their own weight.'

On the other side the crags had given way to a light green expanse and hillocks, while on the south side birches were less close than pines, so they had more branches, but she commented, 'See that hoof fungus on the old birch to the left. Most of the fungus consists of fine threads which are inside and rotting the tree. Soon the path will broaden and we will come to sturdy oaks as we approach the end of walking round the hill.'

Returning to the burgh they paused to look down at the railway station, and she remarked, 'When Queen Victoria saw this bridge, she must have been glad that at least she had turned it into a white elephant, because of her opposition to the line's extension to Braemar.'

They went to the living quarters above the shop. Mr Gordon greeted them warmly, being pleased to tell from their happy faces that the relationship was strong. As they began to eat trout cooked in oatmeal with peas and potatoes, he enquired about Gavin's family.

On hearing that his surname was Fraser, he said, 'Traditionally the Frasers are associated with the Inverness area. They are renowned for their steadfast courage in battle, which accords with the Gordon

Highlanders' motto. I belonged to the 2nd Gordons, my best comrade being Robert Maclean. The surname means son of a devotee of St John. I admire the Macleans' maxim that they must never turn their backs to a foe. We arrived at Durban in early October 1899, on the eve of the Second Boer War. There was a strong force of Boers at Elandslaagte, seventeen miles north of Ladysmith. I was in one of several Gordons' companies in advance. We nimbly avoided exploding shells and the ridge was taken in a series of rushes. To the accompaniment of bugles and pipes the Gordons' final charge surged over the crest, with the Boers fleeing before bayonets. Yet, as the general situation had deteriorated, we retired behind the fourteen mile perimeter defence of Ladysmith and protected the south-west. There was enemy fire for 122 days. We also had to contend with the heat, flies, dust, rainstorms, flooding and disease. Rationing was followed by starvation. Cavalry horses had to be slaughtered for food. In February the sound of approaching friendly guns was heard. Until the 23rd Boer guns fired more or less normally, but thereafter was the first evidence of withdrawal. General Sir Redvers Buller and his army were played into the town on 3 March by our pipers. On 24 July, however, in the first action of Rooi Kopjes or Red Hills my right leg was wounded by cannon fire. My career was over, but I had married Marie whom I met on holiday in Coleraine in 1894. She bore Iona there in 1896 and was enraptured by her. Yet she was weak for a while afterwards and got pneumonia. She knew that she was sinking, but the Irish cross on the mantelpiece was near and strong faith turned death into victory.'

After they had eaten scones, bread and honey with tea, Iona left the room and returned with a christening robe which she showed to Gavin, saying, 'My mother embroidered it before I was born. There are lilies of the valley. The plant was once known as Our Lady's tears, because it was said to have grown from Mary's tears at the Cross. It was also known as Ladder to Heaven, since the tiny flower bells looked like steps up each stem meaning return to happiness. The robe has only been used once.'

When she reappeared after replacing it, her father said, 'Please play and sing some Irish songs. She has her mother's graceful and nimble hands. We and our Irish relatives spend summer holidays alternately in each other's home. We are due to go there in August. Iona has such romantic notions about the island, I have been half afraid until your arrival that she might refuse to return permanently.'

Sitting down at the piano she said that, as Gavin and she had seen the union of the Dee and Muick earlier, an appropriate song was 'The Meeting of the Waters' written by Thomas Moore who died in 1852. He was inspired by a visit with friends to the valley of Avoca in County Wicklow, where 'the bright waters,' the Avonmor and Avonbeg, met and flowed to the Irish Sea. Yet the lyrics expressed the conviction that it was not the very fine scenery which mattered most, but beloved friends. They have felt how Nature's best charms increase, 'When we see them reflected from looks that we love.' The writer could rest in the valley's shady bosom with friends, 'Where the storms that we feel in this cold world should cease / And our hearts, like thy waters, be mingled in peace.'

After performing other songs she commented to Gavin on the final item, '"The Londonderry Air" is anonymous, but it is believed to be a genuine Irish folk tune. It was made available last century by the folk song collector Miss Jane Ross, who with her sister recorded folk tunes from peasants who visited Limavady on market day. The place was between Coleraine to the north-east and Londonderry to the south-west, and they were within easy travelling distance of each other. The lyrics titled "Danny Boy" were written by F.E. Weatherly in 1910 and set to the tune last year.'

Her playing and singing were most expressive. The pipes are calling and summer is gone, but Danny will be welcome if he returns in summer or winter. If the singer is dead, she wishes him to say an 'Ave' by her grave, and if he tells her that he loves her, 'I'll simply sleep in peace until you come to me.' To judge from Mr Gordon's reaction it was his favourite piece, the words having personal significance. The room filled with waves of sublime passion, as love's eternal joy triumphed over its mortal sadness and light banished darkness. Now and again, when the paraffin lamp lit Iona's face at a particular angle, it was briefly transformed into that of an entrancing angelic child. He felt as if he had known her all his life, and he recalled how childlike virtues lay at the heart of Christianity. The qualities had matured in her, so that she was both the dutiful daughter and the spiritual woman who performed for the men and practised for Irish relatives, but also had her mother in mind, so that in death the three were not divided. In the first and final poignant pieces in particular Gavin heard her crystal muse.

After tea and biscuits she went into the kitchen. When Gavin joined her she thanked him with powerful, beaming eyes. She washed items from the table and he dried them. As they did the chore little was said, but she quietly smiled. He recalled her saying on Craig Coillich that love was a song without words.

When they returned to the living room Mr Gordon warned them, 'As Highland weather is changeable, make sure that you are properly clad tomorrow. A Scotch mist can easily occur in the hills and even develop into heavier rain, irrespective of the weather elsewhere.'

She replied, 'We will visit Pannanich Wells and later climb Lochnagar.'

The couple walked to his holiday address. At the front door she laid her hands gently on his chest, and advancing her shining eyes lightly kissed his left cheek, whispering, 'Good evening. Please return at 9 a.m.' As there were other people about, she did not wait for a return kiss, but slipped away. Both of them knew that the love was real and kisses were only tokens.

4: Pannanich Wells–Lochnagar

Rising next morning he saw that it was cloudier than the day before. He recalled Mr Gordon's recent prophecy of war, but his new love shone above the clouds both literal and figurative. After a cheerful breakfast he entered Bridge Street. Iona wore a light blue frock with Mike beside her, while she spoke to her father in the shop's doorway. She smiled gratefully at Gavin's haversack, for he had thoughtfully foreseen that she would be bringing back water for her father, to whom she handed her own bag. The men greeted each other and Gavin took four bottles from her.

After crossing the bridge the walkers turned left at the junction. There was very little traffic, for the road was quieter than the main north one to Aberdeen. The gentle rise was to become steeper. On the right slope birdsong came from birches which inclined towards the road, as if it was a river. A flock of sheep mainly grazed to the left, a few lying as still as white stones, just their ears quickly twitching because of flies, and from beyond came the sound of the Dee. The walkers chatted as Mike gazed intently at some sheep standing near the fence. Whereas the pony on Sunday had rushed to them, the sheep nervously scampered away.

Iona commented, 'Jesus said in John 10.3-5 that the shepherd called his sheep by name, and they followed him, for they knew his voice, but fled from a stranger, because they did not know the voice of strangers.

My life has been based beside rivers, earliest memories being of walking beside the River Bann as it left Coleraine on its way to join the Atlantic Ocean. The town's history goes back to the time of St Patrick. He described an area near the river as the ferry corner, and it was from the Irish for that description that the name Coleraine came. The present St Patrick's Church is on the original site chosen by the saint to build his own church. My parents were married there. I love its warm and welcoming appearance. It has a square tower and pinnacles, with clear spaces high up like windows of the soul. Arched doorways and windows raise the heart to Heaven. As one passes trees and gravestones outside, one is reminded that the living and the dead are one in Christ. Inside is an air of timeless tranquillity.

I remember being taken in summer to the fishing village of Portrush, with the ruined medieval Dunluce Castle looking down on the east strand and framed by white cliffs. One evening I was struck by the mystic glory of gathered clouds and intervening breaks suffused with golden light. It was almost like an apparition. Portstewart was nearer, where we also walked beside zestful, crashing waves.'

Returning to the present scene she explained, 'That is the Dalmochie Burn, the first word meaning haugh of pig field. The burn comes from high on the moor to the south, before passing beneath the road and flowing gently to the Dee.'

Later she looked through binoculars at the river, before handing them to him as she pointed at a figure. Gavin saw a retired man with white hair wearing a cloth cap, dark green waterproof jacket and waders, standing some distance out from the far bank. Facing downriver he swung the rod with both hands, flinging the line towards the middle, before drawing in sections of the line with his right hand. Shortly, ahead on the Dee's north side, they could see part of a picturesque huge island. Birches lay on either side of the road for a while, but she pointed to the Craigs of Pannanich amid pines higher up to the right.

About ten minutes later they crossed over to the Pannanich Wells Hotel. It was a plain two-storey building above the road behind a high stone wall. The hotel was popular, having a small nine hole golf course. They went to one of the wells at the back, halting before a fashioned structure with large stones below and above thinner stones which formed an artistic pyramid.

Bending down he sampled the water pouring from a small pipe into a drain, and he remarked, 'It is very pure.'

As he filled a bottle she replied, 'I have an understanding with the lessee. Queen Victoria recorded in her journal that on 3 October 1870 she tasted the water here, where she had been many years before, and that when John Brown had stayed as a servant for a year there were many horses and goats.'

After Gavin had placed the final bottle in his bag, she suggested walking a short way along the road before turning back. They were drawn by a rill's animated sound to the right, as it poured white down rocks, at one place being divided, and set in summer greenery. Then she led him to a water trough on that side. It projected at right angles from a rocky mass, and an inscription on the front commemorated Queen Victoria's Diamond Jubilee in 1897.

Iona explained, 'The letters "R I" are an abbreviation of the Latin "Regina et Imperatrix," meaning Queen and Empress. If she had seen the tribute, I think she would have been amused by such a humble object being so dignified. Equally she would have appreciated her long reign being associated with the water of life.'

On the way back they were nearing Ballater, when her face lit up on seeing blue sky in the direction of Lochnagar, as if it was inviting them, and she said, 'We will eat, relax and later cycle up Glen Muick to climb the mountain.'

When they entered her living room she lifted the Irish cross and commented, 'Kells in County Meath is particularly associated with the book of the Gospels, but it also has four medieval, sculptured high crosses. When my mother's father, Sean O'Donovan, learned that she was to marry a Scot, he appropriately carved a small wooden replica of the Cross of Saints Patrick and Columba. It is a Celtic halo cross like this one round my neck. Ishbel has told me that the word halo comes from the Greek "halos" meaning the disc of or round the sun or moon. There are figures carved on its four faces. On the east one, at the crossing near the top, is Christ with sceptre and cross in the Last Judgement. He is surrounded by the symbols of the Evangelists. Above is St Matthew holding a medallion with the Lamb of God (Christ the suffering servant and symbol of redemption), to the left is St Mark's lion (Christ's resurrection), to the right is St Luke's winged ox (Christ's sacrifice) and below is St John's eagle (Christ's divinity). The upper panel in the shaft below depicts the Crucifixion. At the base are two horsemen followed by a dog and a chariot with two men. One of them holds what may be a Druid's rod. Chariots were used in Ireland during that period.

You can browse through those books about the island while I prepare lamb, cabbage and potatoes with apple pie and custard.'

At lunch Mr Gordon beamed with delight at her radiance, as she spoke excitedly about climbing her favourite mountain with Gavin. 'Some people like to climb it at night and see the dawn, but we will go earlier and linger until the stars appear.'

'Don't practise your dancing near a cliff edge,' her father joked.

Gavin asked her, 'Do you prefer Irish or Scottish dancing?'

'There is a formal precision in the Irish dances which I have seen, with the arms held down at the sides when not in use, and the heads do not turn independently. I prefer the comparative informality of Scottish dances, and there is not the same emphasis on the dynamism of legs.

A cool breeze will likely blow on Lochnagar's summit, particularly when the sun goes down, so I will wear extra clothing. Do you need something else?'

He smilingly shook his head as he stroked Mike's coat. Her father finished his cup of tea and wishing them a happy trip returned to work. They relaxed for a while, looking at an album of Irish photographs, before having an early tea. Then she packed some food for their supper.

When they set out there was a sunny freshness in the air, and they smiled at the Linn of Muick. Over a higher stretch of the river, where the view gave way to moorland, a glow lay like a benediction. They left their machines in the pine plantation to the north-east of Loch Muick. Many trees had been slightly bent to the right by past strong winds. Instead of heading to the loch they took a north-west track. The peat bogs on either side were homes to many specialized plants and insects, besides being used for nests and feeding by migratory birds. About one third of the way along the track a wooden bridge crossed the infant River Muick. There were more stones in the stretch of water after the bridge than before it, producing a slightly raucous sound, a hint of the later thunder. After leaving the track they soon took a gently rising, rocky path to the left of a stable which was a little distance from Allt-na-giubhsaich Lodge. They walked through pines which cast a mosaic of shapes, the main burn being audible some way off. Then they emerged in the open on a broad, rising path which meandered west through heather for a while. To the right lay a solitary foxglove. The original seed had apparently either been dropped by a bird or blown high up in a gale and deposited far from the plant's normal habitat. The burn rang loudly on the rocky bed to the right, until they came to a dip in the track where the water cut across at a ford. Laughing she tripped lightly over stones, gracefully holding up the right side of her long skirt.

When they were both across she suggested, 'Let us drink from the burn and leave our bottles full. The water is normal today, but after heavy rain it has a slightly brown, peaty look.'

Soon on the left were the mini cascades of a burn which was strengthened by the Allt na Giubhsaich which came with its mini cascades a little to the south-west. Occasionally water trickled across the track from the right. To the left were light and dark green steep banks.

She pointed south-west and explained, 'There is Little Pap. North-west of it is the large flat mass of Cuidhe Crom or crooked wreath, which is named after a snowfield lying late into summer on the steep grassy face north of the top. To its north is the big cone of Meikle Pap.' Soon she added, 'On the left is Clais Rathadan or rat gully, although the usual local form means hollow of the mastiff.'

Earlier they glimpsed the cliffs of dark Lochnagar, but now tantalizingly they were hidden. The way turned north, yet before long they took a path to the left which dipped, a plank aiding them across the boggy centre. Then the meandering stony path headed up to the graceful gap between Cuidhe Crom and Meikle Pap. After much toil they paused at a natural mass of large stones.

She said, 'This is the beautiful spring of Fox Cairn Well. An old fox that had caused havoc among sheep was killed in its den here in 1840.'

As sometimes happened in the Highlands the general plain aspect preceded sublimity. Near the top of the gap, with each step more of the crescent of crags of Lochnagar's east corrie appeared, until the mystic grandeur was complete. They gazed down at the lochan, followed by a series of five pools, the effect being of a large sapphire with smaller attendant ones. The Lochnagar Burn fed the Gelder Burn which contributed to the distant Dee. The towering dark cliffs with screes at their base cast a slight shadow on most of the tarn, but the narrower part was more like the azure sky.

She commented, 'Lochnagar means the tarn of the noisy sound, which probably refers to the wind rushing among the crags. Sheltered from the sun patches of snow linger long into summer. Over time frost splits up the rock and disintegrates the surface by freezing water between the particles. In a storm the corrie will be a great amphitheatre of the elements. It is ancient and so unique, with weather conditions at this height varying so much, that each time one comes in a sense it is like finding a new creation.'

He replied, 'Our relationship is new, although it is moulded by countless previous generations.'

As he admired her, she asked with a serene smile, 'Why do you love me?'

'Because you are beauty's spirit and spirit's beauty.'

'How much do you love me?'

'Ask me not now.'

'When?'

'At the end of time. True love is inspired by sublime passion. Nature's wonders reflect our purest feelings.'

'Yes, some people find Lochnagar dour and forbidding. I never have. To me it is a temple to the heavens, awesome, noble and enduring. Let us climb to the summit and wait for the stars to appear.'

'Day is love's night and night is love's day. We will stay until it is night and day.'

There were many boulders by the corrie's edge, so they retreated as she explained, 'We will climb a zigzag, rocky staircase called the Ladder to the plateau. Normally on the upper part at this time are large areas tinged with pink, creeping azalea.'

After ascending about half of the Ladder they paused, and looking back saw a mountain hare moving quickly far below. Gaining the plateau they took a stony track which was set back from the cliff. When they drew parallel with the Red Spout, its edge marked by the hue, they crossed over to look at the top of the wide gully which contained granite gravel.

She commented, 'The rock's feldspar is this colour. The granite is similar to that of the Cairngorms, and also the Pass of Ballater where it is better preserved because of less weathering.'

Shortly, when they were proceeding on the track, she exchanged a wave with a man walking briskly with a stick near the cliff, and she said, 'He is Angus Bremner, a retired gamekeeper. He is what I call a Lochnagarian, someone who can climb the mountain without having any problems with the rocky terrain.'

They took the path which swung initially round rising ground to the north. Climbing gradually to the higher plateau, they saw ahead a stag with three younger ones, plus another further off, stop to gaze at them before leisurely retreating.

She observed, 'They have climbed to eat tender new growth left by the receding snow and avoid flies lower down.'

There were mossy rocks on the plateau. Diverging to the right they walked along the cliff top. Here and there the plateau projected and gave impressive views of the cliffs. They looked across to the Black Spout, the largest gully in the corrie and filled with scree. Turning west a little they passed to the left of a small tor surmounted by a subsidiary cairn. The ground was level for a short distance, before dipping and rising again. A wide path led up the steep slope to the summit, which protruded like a natural fortification as a great mass of granite weathered into huge rocks.

They crossed broad slabs and then climbed north-east over rocks between facing massive boulders, before turning north-west into the viewing chamber with boulders which offered shelter from the elements. They gazed at each other and the panorama with ineffable bliss.

She pointed south-west and said, 'There is a perfect view of Coire Lochan nan Eun or corrie of lochs of the birds. Its remoteness attracts a summer colony of common gulls. Green and peaceful, it may be seen as a female complement to the awesome east corrie with its charged atmosphere. Left of this loch is The Stuic or projecting hill. Hidden beyond it are two tiny lochans, the larger called Lochan na Feadaige or tarn of the golden plover and the smaller Lochan Tàrmachan or tarn of ptarmigan. To their north is the Sandy Loch. South-east of The Stuic across the plateau is the green Coire Boidheach or beautiful corrie, which is favoured by hinds and their young calves in late summer.'

Handing him a small telescope she pointed initially to the distant south-west and said, 'There is Ben Lomond and west is Ben Nevis, north-west are the Cairngorms, including Braeriach, the source of the Dee, and Ben Macdui, there are the northern Caithness hills and much nearer is green Morven overlooking Ballater, which is buried in peace. Why do you smile?'

'Because we have climbed the mountain ostensibly to admire the views, but I am struck more seeing you transformed from a nymph into a sylph, a spirit of the air.'

She demurely looked aside and replied, 'We climb mountains to increase our fear and love of God. We come as pilgrims, so that ironically after all the exertion we feel disembodied and our spirits are set free to feel closer to God and find our purer selves on the journey to eternity. It is far better when two united spirits share the experience.'

'Yes, finding a soulmate is like climbing a mountain. It is inevitable that for many people they believe several times that the summit is near, only to be disappointed. We only see life whole when we meet the ordained spirit. That relationship eclipses any carnal love. It is a glimpse of Heaven.'

After they had eaten sandwiches and drank water, they enjoyed the hallowed time when day and night embraced and passed with a spreading glow. A golden red sunset spread over the Cairngorms.

She smiled and said, 'It will be a little while before the stars appear in full. You can take a nap if you like. It is milder than I have expected.'

'No thanks.'

'Then I will have one. Wake me when it is time.'

She laid her head on his larger bag and gratefully said, 'Thank you,' when he took off his coat and laid it over her. Although the light summer breeze belied patches of snow in the corries, the temperature would fall.

As she closed her eyes he saw a stray lock across her brow which did not mar but perfected her beauty, as a sign of humanity. He gently moved it back into place. Then he stood and saw the earth cast in twilight reflection and peace, as the sunset gradually turned to pink. Yet he struggled with the tumult of contrasting forces in his spirit. Before the visit to Ballater his vision had been a light beyond the mountains of his youth, and he had been self-reliant. Now his vision was the rare, unearthly beauty below him, much closer and yet more mysterious. He gazed at her for some time, while forming a résumé of his musing.

'Happy is the man who sees the quintessence of woman, not a fleeting beauty which enchants then dies in the heart, but a spirit which awakes his finest being. Oh sublime enigma! You have bid me sleep, but you will not let me rest. I must wrestle with my spirit for love's sake. Before I met you I saw too often the cold sea of life. Now a heavenly guest, the Paraclete, shines on your face. Upon this earthly bed his gifts are finely arrayed. Love the pattern of all the virtues is attended by perfect peace. On Craig Coillich I referred to you as a dove, a symbol of the Holy Spirit, the giver of life and the power of tranquillity. Now the rest of innocence is equated with eternal peace.

A product of two countries you draw strength from your early years which nourish your goodness. You are rich in the childlike virtues of humility, faith, charity, cheerfulness, innocence, spontaneity, contentment and gratitude. You are full of simple joys, while your pure mind transcends the physical innocence of childhood.

The life of your body and the life of your spirit are blended in Nature. The sense of freedom in Nature corresponds to your spiritual freedom. God's glory in Creation links it to Heaven. Deeply versed in Nature's lore you see continuity in change, corresponding to the constant heart in which joys and sorrows are reconciled, for spiritual not physical death is to be feared. Mature beyond your years you would become stronger in adversity.

Uncorrupted by the world you give so greatly, for you have bountiful grace. Classless and outward looking, blending the private and public sides, you have a stabilizing influence on others in these unpredictable times. An agent of redemption, you see good qualities in people which put their faults in perspective.

Composed and chaste you lie, and sealed are the eyes which reflect a myriad of thoughts and feelings. Yet your entrancing face interprets for me the changing wonders of the heavens. Let the fiery ardour which inspires your soul shine in my dark, wild night. You are patient and faithful, and my trust will have a positive return. To be equal before Heaven a master must show a servant's love. I will give gentle strength and you will be strong in gentleness. Through love and manly deeds my disciplined heart and spirit will be filled with favour.'

As he gazed aloft to find that twilight had bowed out before transcendent night, he murmured, 'Too soon the heavens have filled with glory! Too soon the stars have kissed Loch nan Eun! I would muse till dawn on the loving beauty which never sleeps, but you must greet your shining paramours.'

As he slid his right fingers between those of her upper hand, he thought, 'Angelic beauty beggars earthly gems. Your eyes and face in mystic locks alone are set, as stars adorn the night.'

Waking she smiled, and, her eyes shining into his, she asked, 'Why did you not wake me with a kiss?'

'You would have dreamed on with but one kiss.'

'You could have kissed me until I woke.'

'Kisses alone are a finite feast. Loving spirits meet with radiant bliss and tender kisses follow. Never has Aurora risen in all her glory like this blissful dawn of night.'

He helped her to rise and she saw the moonlit Coire Lochan nan Eun, before their joyful spirits flew together through the heavenly grandeur, at one with the cosmic pulse.

Looking north-west through the telescope she said, 'Mercury is setting and it will be followed by Venus which is not far from it. Venus is the brightest object in the sky after the sun and moon.'

He remarked, 'As befits the Roman goddess of love.'

'In contrast Mars is too far away now for useful observation.'

He wistfully replied, 'Would that prospects for war were equally distant and only love prevailed.'

She continued, 'Other interesting features are low down. West is Leo or the Lion. South-west is Virgo or the Virgin, said to represent a maiden or goddess associated with the harvest, and made conspicuous by bright Spica, literally referring to an ear of wheat in her hand. South is Scorpio or the Scorpion, and to its right is Libra or the Scales. Above Scorpio is Serpens and over the Serpent is a little coronet called Corona Borealis or the Northern Crown. To its right is Boötes or the Herdsman, with its bright giant sun Arcturus or the Bear Guard, because of its position in line with the tail of Ursa Major or the Great Bear. Left of the Northern Crown is Hercules. East is Cygnus or the Swan. It is also known as the Northern Cross, because it resembles the Cross of Crucifixion when it slides down towards the west horizon. Below Cygnus and to the right is Delphinus or the Dolphin. Near it is Aquila or the Eagle. Take the telescope. Why look at me?'

'Here is my fixed star.'

They gazed into each other's soul and kissed at the unhewn altar of love.

He embraced her for a while, but when they parted a cool breeze blew, and she said, 'It is getting late. We must descend the mountain carefully, although we will pause at the dip between Cuidhe Crom and Meikle Pap to see the stars shining on the east tarn.'

He was glad of her familiarity with the zigzag route between the lower plateau and the dip. Then they admired the lochan and lower pools, with a perfect union of heavenly light and water. He placed his right arm round her shoulder, as they smiled at each other, the heights and depths of their love united.

'I take it that being with me is your first joy,' she said. 'What is the second?'

'Thinking about you.'

'Perhaps you think too much about me. You remember Byron's words, "Man's love is of man's life a thing apart. 'Tis woman's whole existence."'

'His passions were sometimes most irregular.'

'Implying that ours will be most regular.'

'I suspect that our love which has been nurtured on the wild heights of harmony will be like yon rugged cliffs, sublimely irregular. They who scale love's heights must also feel its sorrows. Yet there is a divinity which joins them, so we will live and love supremely.'

As they descended the rest of the mountain moonlight picked out the stony path more distinctly than the heather and other vegetation which lay as an amorphous dream. Then they rejoined the main track and walked side by side. They said little but looked about, as if sharing one pair of eyes. When they saw the shining Allt na Giubhsaich they felt thirsty and drank the remnants of their bottles. At the ford they refilled them, the water flowing in as a mystic draught. The track led down to pines, where they walked through an inner night of scented calm. He thought of their joyful love contrasting with the humour arising from Morag's petty remarks. Soon they were in the open, with a peat bog on either side, but as they crossed the young River Muick he was reminded of how new their love was. Away from the spiritual strength of the mountain, he felt a sense of foreboding. He recalled Mr Gordon's fear of impending war. Would the innocent love shine amid events beyond their control, arising from the Fall of Man through Adam and Eve's disobedience?

He did not mention the matter to her, but seeing his pensive expression she said cheerfully, 'I suggest that we spend the last few days of our holiday visiting Upper Deeside and the Cairngorms. I have read about the mountains and been given accounts by walkers, but I have never been there, so it is a fine opportunity.'

'What a good idea,' he replied, shedding his brief sadness.

When they took the east road he would have cycled beside her, but she foresaw that unsuspecting small animals would face less risk if she followed him. Lower down a brown hare bolted out of the way. The largely descending return was relaxing.

As they quietly pushed their machines to the back of the shop after 1 a.m., she told him, 'Have a good sleep. At 10 a.m. we will leisurely cycle up the valley and stay with my aunt and uncle in Braemar. They are expecting us.'

5: To Braemar and the Cairngorms–Valediction

He slept lightly in spite of his exertions, for he longed to be with her again and make the most of their remaining holiday. On entering the shop a little early he was told by Mr Gordon that she was exercising Mike down by the Dee. He saw her on the north-west bank throwing a stick further up for the dog to recover, while she conserved her energy. Gavin took over the stick routine to Mike's delight, for the object flew higher and further, enabling the dog to show greater prowess. Finally the stick was flung into the river and Mike bounded off in pursuit, as it bobbed and twisted in the water. After it had been triumphantly recovered they returned up Bridge Street.

Soon the pair left Ballater and cycled up the sharply rising Braemar Road lined by varied trees. He had taken that way with his comrades on their rock climbing expedition. Now the situation was transformed, for he was parallel with not receding from her, and he recalled her remarks about stasis in motion. As some branches projected far across the road, at one point nearly meeting, he saw the Highland nymph's joyful face. She was looking forward to showing him Upper Deeside and sharing the excitement of visiting the Cairngorms for the first time.

She said, 'I am often busy in the shop and there are many human contacts. Shut away from great Nature and surrounded by thousands of items, however, it is a restricted existence. Now our united spirits are free again.'

Leaving the Pass of Ballater on the right, the road soon swung south-west, and as it descended the grand partly moorland, partly wooded hill called Geallaig or white one came fully into sight. They were reminded of their Sunday afternoon walk as they passed over the Bridge of Gairn and enjoyed a view of rounded, tree clad hills. Soon the sun lit the trunks of nearby silver birches and conifers, cattle and sheep grazed, while now and again the river ran near the road before moving away.

She observed, 'The old coaching inn of Coilacreich is to the right.'

Later they stopped as she pointed to the south bank and commented, 'Abergeldie Castle probably dates from the mid sixteenth century, the most likely builder being Sir Alexander Gordon of Midmar, later Earl of Huntly. It has a tower house style, the front facing the south road. The rectangular main building has a round stair tower in the south-west angle. A clock and cupola were added much later. Just to the south-east is Creag nam Ban or rocky hill of the women, but it is better known as Witches Hill. There were witch-hunts in the late sixteenth century, victims being confined in the castle before being burned on the hilltop. In 1603 Kittie or Kitty Rankine was an example, but in accordance with Scottish custom she was probably strangled first. There are stories about the women in which fact and fiction are mixed up, with an element of black humour. After the "Glorious Revolution" the castle formed part of struggles between Jacobites, including John Farquharson the Black Colonel, and government forces which won.

When we were at Polhollick Bridge I said that young Alexander Gordon was reputed to have seen an accident here in 1824. Barbara Brown, the "Flower of Deeside," was newly married to Peter Frankie, but when they were crossing the river in a wooden cradle from the south bank the windlass apparently malfunctioned, the rope broke and the couple was thrown out and drowned. This and other accidents produced a long public campaign for a safer crossing, and in 1885 Queen Victoria, who leased the castle, provided this suspension footbridge.'

Shortly before reaching Crathie she said, 'Not far to the south is the Royal Lochnagar Distillery. Water from the mountain goes into the whisky. Ishbel's father used to work in the distillery and recently he showed us round. Malted barley was added to hot water, the liquid being mixed with yeast and left to ferment, before distilling occurred in huge copper stills. This process was repeated three times. The liquid was moved to a locked safe before maturing in oak casks. The whisky took little more than a week to make, but over twelve years to mature.'

Soon Crathie Church appeared, elevated up a slope to the right, and they turned into the drive to look at it. Dominated by a massive square tower, it was made of grey granite with a red roof and was cruciform in plan with a semicircular apse. There was an open porch in the west gable.

She said, 'The church was built between 1893 and 1895. Queen Victoria had long worshipped at the previous church on the site. The present royal entrance, the Queen's Porch, gives access to the south transept. The quality of the choir and music has long been famous.'

Shortly they stopped again, as she gazed critically to the left and commented, 'That is Balmoral Bridge. The castle was finished in 1856 in the nineteenth century Scottish baronial style, and there was need for greater privacy. The South Deeside Road went through the estate to the Old Invercauld Bridge near Braemar. Prince Albert built the bridge here, so that the road was diverted to join this one. He erected a new bridge at Invercauld, a short distance west of the other, which then became private. The Balmoral Bridge was designed by Isambard Brunel and built between 1856 and 1857. The new material of wrought iron was used and it was to be his only Scottish bridge. Queen Victoria doubtless disapproved of the redundant railway bridge at Ballater, and it was said that she never spoke of this one, because she despised it. Plain and functional, albeit with latticework, the broad tops to the sides with so many bosses must have appalled her. The design is fitting for an urban road or railway bridge, but not here. She may have been reminded of man's naked power and ambition, which taken to excess in other ways had caused so much trouble in the world. The iron is painted in deep forest green, but it is just camouflage, a poor sop to Nature. To harmonize with the castle, although some distance away, a granite bridge with decorative battlements was needed. Whereas gaps on real parapets were used for firing guns, here they would have given variety, light and peace. In 1857, however, she was happy to open the Linn of Dee Bridge, which was made of granite and had a Gothic design.'

After they had covered a stretch on the rising road, she observed, 'I love this sublime view of tall conifers acting as guardians of the peace beside a bend in the Dee. Bare stones beside the banks show the summer drop in the water level, but the areas are less pronounced than by Ballater, enhancing the scene.'

He turned to admire her radiant smile. She looked not just with the eyes of young, bright beauty. Her gentleness, springing from inner strength and serenity, was at one with the vista.

She said, 'For much of the remaining journey to Braemar the Dee is close to the road. One may reach greater spiritual heights on a mountain, but the scenery now begins to impart such regal joy, I feel that this is the heart of north-east Scotland.'

Continuing on their way, soon she nodded and said, 'There is Balmoral Castle's clock tower topped by a round turret with a flagstaff peering over the trees. When the King is in residence the royal flag is a stirring and unifying sight. Balmoral's privacy has been increased by careful tree planting and time has naturalized the additions. High above Crathie the whole castle can be seen.'

Shortly she added, 'On 13 October 1856 Queen Victoria recorded in her journal that every year her heart became "more fixed in this dear Paradise," much more so then, when all had become Albert's creation, as at Osborne. There, however, is Prince Albert's Cairn, a thirty-five foot high pyramid of fashioned granite stones on Creag an Lurachain, one of the tops of Craig Gowan which rises south of the castle. The site was chosen so that the monument would be seen down the valley. The inscription recorded that the memorial was "raised by his broken-hearted widow" in 1862 and carried lines from the Wisdom of Solomon beginning, "He being made perfect in a short time fulfilled a long time." The large structure almost makes it look as if both the hill and the pyramid are to Albert's memory. He was a pharaoh or king in his widow's eyes. Also that year a marble statue of him was placed at the foot of the staircase in the castle. On 15 October 1867, the twenty-eighth anniversary of their engagement, she attended the unveiling of the second colossal version in bronze which stood on huge rocks in the estate. He was depicted wearing Highland dress and the Garter, with his retriever and gun. The day was rainy and the covering caught for a little while, before she admired her beloved from beneath an umbrella!'

Later Lochnagar to the south looked very mystical in vast luminous mist. At Inver was another old coaching inn, and beyond the valley narrowed with wooded slopes. The next picturesque feature was the romantic Old Invercauld Bridge on the left, built in 1752 by Major William Caulfield as part of a military road. Its graceful, long, gentle camber with six arches increasing in size to the centre, plus triangular shaped buttresses, set against the Ballochbuie pines, impressed them with a unique peaceful grandeur.

When they crossed the imposing granite bridge which Prince Albert built as a public replacement, she said excitedly, 'How much better this bridge is than Brunel's one. Also, there is airy rapture, for instead of valley sides we see the Dee descending from north to south beneath us in little rapids.'

As they advanced Highland cattle grazed on a haugh with scattered pines north of the Dee, and she observed, 'That is Invercauld House on a grassy rise. Most people regard it as a house, but some think it is a castle. From its central keep wings project on three sides. It includes parts of the Farquharson stronghold dating from the sixteenth century, although later it has been much altered.'

While the river flowed serenely to the right, the descending road hugged on the left the verge of steep wooded slopes, and she explained, 'That cliff is the Lion's Face, although the leonine contour has been hidden by trees. It is on the east side of Creag Choinnich or Kenneth's Rock, a hill overlooking Braemar. King Kenneth II in the tenth century had a hunting seat at Braemar, and according to tradition he watched the chase from the rock.'

Just before the road swung south to enter the village, they turned right to Braemar Castle on a little knoll, and when they were outside she commented, 'The tall turreted building is of the L-plan, with a large round stair tower, being built by the seventh Earl of Mar in 1628. One dawn in 1689 the Black Colonel and many of his men rushed down Creag Choinnich and fired guns on the sleeping garrison of dragoons at the castle. Some soldiers rode away, but many horses had galloped off in panic. Dead soldiers were thrown in the Dee, although a large number of prisoners were freed to tell of the attack. The castle was burned down. After the 1745 Rebellion it was leased to the British War Office as a barracks for troops to keep watch on the Highlands. Around the rebuilt castle was raised a rectangular wall, and a salient pointed from each face to form an eight pointed star, the flanks of which were pierced for muskets. Later changes were made to the building. Let us leave it dreaming of the past, but looking peaceful in the present. I expected you to be more enthusiastic about the military details.'

'If I was here just with my comrades, Sergeant Mackay dramatizing the castle's past, I would be suitably attentive. With you, however, I live for the joyful present and the way you interpret the past.'

On the outskirts of the village they paused by the Invercauld Arms Hotel, as she explained, 'Last century a historic rock was largely blasted away to allow an extension of the hotel to be built. On the rock on 6 September 1715 the Earl of Mar raised the standard of James VIII, the Old Pretender. As the standard was raised, however, the gilt finial topping the flagstaff fell to the ground, which many were to regard as an ill omen.'

Soon she led him on a little detour to the south and stopped at The Cottage in Castleton, the east part of the village, and said, 'Robert Louis Stevenson wrote the first part of *Treasure Island* here in August and September 1881. As he had tuberculosis he finished the work later that year in the clear mountain air of Davos, Switzerland. Around 1850 the village was rebuilt with fine stone houses.'

Shortly they stood on a bridge and gazed south up a rocky gorge, as she commented, 'The Clunie is named after the plain or meadowland through which it flows. In front is a calm stretch, but further up the water is forced to our left side in a white frenzy. Part of the hill Morrone is visible in the distance. The ruins of the royal castle of Kindrochit or bridge end on the east bank recall the greatest strongholds of the fourteenth century. It is most likely that Malcolm III (1057-1093), surnamed Canmore meaning big head or, more flatteringly, great head or chief, erected a bridge and place of strength here to secure communications with more settled districts to the south. It would also have been a base for deer hunting. In 1057 his army defeated Macbeth's at the Battle of Lumphanan, Macbeth being slain. There is a legend that he held a great gathering by Braemar with many sporting competitions to select the strongest, swiftest and most skilful warriors, and that this was the origin of the Highland Games.

According to a bizarre legend he had a monster called Tad-Losgann, variously identified as a toad-frog, a wild boar or even a crocodile. He lived beside the Clunie and grew larger and larger, lots being drawn to feed him on cattle owned by local people. A poor widow called McLeod had her one cow selected. Her son Sandy, about fifteen years old, shot the monster with an arrow. He was caught and sentenced to death, but his mother appealed to the King. Malcolm ordered her to stand on the rocky ledge across the Clunie from which the arrow had been fired. Sandy was to stand on the drawbridge, and, if he could pierce a peat on her head, he could go free. The feat was achieved.'

Gavin replied, 'He was a worthy forerunner of the Swiss William Tell, another legendary symbol of freedom.'

She continued, 'More appealing was a story about Malcolm's saintly wife Queen Margaret by her biographer, likely Turgot, a monk and her chaplain for some time. He recounted how her favourite volume was a Gospel-book covered in jewels and gold, with the capital letters in gold. A man was crossing a ford when he carelessly dropped the volume in the river. It was found later lying open at the bottom, its pages swept back and forth by the water. Miraculously the only damage was slight moisture on the end leaves. Then Margaret loved the book even more. A poem added to the beginning of the volume also described the events. Neither source identified the river or a nearby place. Here, however, the story is associated with the Dee and Braemar.'

The Clunie flowed north to the Dee, but they passed on and turned south to explore its further attractions. After cottage gardens and the crescendo of the gorge, they cycled beside deciduous trees and more peaceful flowing water, until they stopped by a colony of ducks partly on the bank and partly in the river. Those near rushed fearlessly to the visitors, which indicated that they were used to being fed. She produced from her bag a loaf which was slightly too stale for shop use. She gave him half and they threw bits widely to ensure a fair distribution. Continuing they soon saw foaming water coursing round a broad bend. The urgent splashing on small rocks was refreshing and harmonious, while rapid birdsong plus the wild calls of gulls blended with it.

She said, 'In March I saw two heather stretches on Meall an t-Sluichd to the south-east being burned.'

Returning to the village they went west into the other half, Auchendryne, and dismounted by a modest cottage as she said, 'I like its quiet charm.' (He thought that the description fitted her, quite apart from deeper qualities.) 'Malcolm Gordon is my father's elder brother. A joiner, he is on holiday this week. Aunt Barbara has two daughters who work in Aberdeen. We are here!' she called out informally on opening the unlocked door.

Her jovial uncle appeared, being taller and thinner than her father. He welcomed and guided them as they pushed their bicycles through and stored them in a shed. The plump aunt followed and, exchanging greetings, was immediately at ease with Gavin's polite, friendly manner.

While the hosts got lunch ready, the arrivals went into the living room, where he smiled at a picture over the mantelpiece, saying, 'We are looking south-east up the Himalayan type Glen Nevis Gorge. I have climbed the mountain and visited the gorge to its south.'

She replied, 'My aunt and uncle went there during their honeymoon.'

'An excellent choice. It is one of the finest scenes in Scotland. Deciduous and coniferous trees line the sides as the water hurries down towards you with rocky thunder. Beyond the gorge is a glimpse of meadow, and then there is the very grand 350 foot Steall Waterfall which widens and is partly divided by massive rocks. In the distance is the sublime long, left declining outline of a Munro of the Mamores Ridge, An Gearanach. It has been differently translated as the short ridge and the complainer or the sad place. To the right are a few snowfields and a cloud has been painted to the left, partly for symmetry and partly to emphasize that even in summer haze the mountain is involved in Nature's animation.'

As they ate beef, roast potatoes and Brussels sprouts, which showed the high regard in which Iona was held, Malcolm said to Gavin, 'Iona's father and I were raised in Ballater, but I met Barbara at a ceilidh in Braemar. We have settled here, so that she can be near her relatives. Our elder daughter, Eilidh, is a lawyer's secretary in Aberdeen, where Elspeth teaches music.'

Barbara added, 'We have mixed feelings about them being there. It is better for their work and marriage prospects. Elspeth has formed a serious relationship, and it is likely that she will marry before her elder sister. It is surprising, because Eilidh is better looking, although Elspeth is more sociable. We hope that Eilidh will be encouraged to go out more. On the other hand we are concerned about contagious diseases there. Last December a girl in Elspeth's lodgings caught scarlet fever, but fortunately she made a good recovery.'

With a mischievous glint in his eyes, Malcolm said, 'To use an old English expression a little loosely, Iona has scarlet fever of the jocular type, a tendency to fall in love with soldiers.'

'Only one.'

'I thought that a previous suitor became a soldier.'

'He did, but I was not in love with him and he had only a fleeting interest in me.'

Continuing to tease her, he asked, 'Have you nipped up Morrone to scan the Cairngorms for any residual snowfields?'

'No, we have just leisurely cycled from Ballater, although yesterday we climbed Lochnagar. We are conserving our energies for tackling the Cairngorms.'

Malcolm explained to Gavin, 'Morrone means big point or big nose and is 2,819 feet. It is south of the site offered by the Duke of Fife and accepted in 1905 as a permanent arena for the annual Braemar Gathering. I have taken Iona up the hill several times, and the top offers a panorama of the Cairngorms. At first they look like a mass of static waves. With her binoculars she soon learned with my help to differentiate them. Last year I could tell that she longed to go there, but time was lacking. I am glad that now she can. Normally I climb Morrone by myself. Recently the doctor advised Barbara to slim, however, so on Sunday afternoon we went together. Through my binoculars I saw some lingering snowfields on Cairn Toul and Braeriach, with streaky stretches on Ben Macdui's broad dome to the east. Ben Macdui is nearer, although it is a little higher. In the Cairngorms you should avoid a steep path if there is a sizeable bank of snow higher up, because of the risk of an avalanche. Keep clear as well of snow near a sharp drop, lest you slide through an overhang and fall to your death. Angus Bremner, the retired gamekeeper, has also informed Iona about the Cairngorms. Is he keeping well?'

'Yes, together with his nephew and niece, Hamish and Fiona Macpherson.'

'Good. When I lived in Ballater I liked Hamish's grandfather, John, a former blacksmith. He was a real character. On his eightieth birthday he joked, "I am too old to die." Yet the poor man died suddenly just two months later. In the midst of life we are in death.'

He politely inquired about Gavin's upbringing and current occupation, but he conversed mainly with Iona. Not only were they related, but also Gavin learned that he played a fiddle at ceilidhs and had broad musical interests. He asked about the church's music and various old acquaintances in Ballater. Gavin was charmed to hear Iona pour out information which showed her deep interest in people. Whereas he suspected that prim Miss Clark tended to be struck by a person's faults rather than his virtues, with Iona it was the reverse. While she concentrated on the recent past, her uncle filled in historical details and the talk flowed on until after teatime.

Then Malcolm produced his fiddle and said, 'If our guests were more light-hearted, Robert Burns's "A Red, Red Rose" would be suitable, particularly as it is June. Lifelong fidelity is promised, but some of the language is extravagant. Instead, Iona, please sing "By cool Siloam's shady rill" (Belmont), and I will play. You said last time that you were going to explore the background of this popular baptismal hymn.'

'Yes, it was written by Reginald Heber who died in 1826. He was the Church of England's Bishop of Calcutta which then included all of India, Ceylon and Australia. He worked tirelessly to spread Christianity through the East. He is now remembered mainly as a hymnographer. Siloam was the name of a spring and pool near Jerusalem. When Jesus, after declaring, "I am the light of the world," anointed with clay made from his own spittle the eyes of a man who was blind from birth, he told him to wash in the pool of Siloam, "(which is by interpretation, Sent.)" Thereby he gained sight. (John 9.5-7.) In the hymn's first stanza are also included the fair lily and "Sharon's dewy rose!" Yet the flowers are contrasted with the first line, for they refer to the Song of Solomon 2.1: "I am the rose of Shâr'-on, and the lily of the valleys." Sharon is a fertile coastal plain between the Mediterranean Sea and the hills of Samaria. The rose of Sharon, however, has been variously described as a tulip, crocus, etc. By inference in the hymn the child Jesus' heart was drawn not to earthly charms, but to God. The lily and rose will fade, and soon man's "wintry hour" will shake his "soul with sorrow's power" and "passion's rage." Jesus was early in his "Father's shrine" and his whole life was divine. The last stanza begins by referring to the Holy Spirit, "Dependent on Thy bounteous breath," as we seek Jesus' grace throughout life and in death, "To keep us still Thine own."'

After her very moving singing Malcolm played and sang 'Lachin y Gair,' a musical setting of the poem by George Gordon, Lord Byron, whose mother Catherine was a former Gordon of Gight, Aberdeenshire. England's rose gardens and other tame beauties are rejected for rocks where snow lies, but which 'are sacred to freedom and love.' He longs in particular for the valley of Lochnagar which he has known as a child. His heroic soul exults in the storm clouds which 'encircle the forms of my fathers,' while winter presides. He longs for the wild, majestic crags, 'The steep frowning glories of dark Loch na Garr.' After the song ended Gavin told Iona that while Byron gained inspiration from the Alpine like mountain, Hannibal regarded the Alps as Rome's ramparts, a defence to be overcome.

After Malcolm played and sang some other pieces supper was served quickly, so that the guests could have a good sleep before making an early start. Iona went to a spare bedroom, while Gavin occupied the settee in the living room. They were full of energy when they cycled south-west in the morning, but they paused on the outskirts to gaze at the peaceful arena which one day each year was a romantic swirl of music, colour and action with the piping, dancing and athletics of the Braemar Gathering.

Then they took a rising, winding road which was accompanied by birches. The nearby Dee meandered in dreamy rapture, passing over gravel beds and past occasional sandbanks. The scenery for the next six miles was rich and varied. They were met by a fresh, pure mountain breeze which with the view instilled deep peace and joy. To the north some conifers relieved the broad, bare, stony Carn Dearg. Avian chirps emanated from trees up a mound away to the south.

As they passed a loud rill which split lower down to the left, she said, 'A number of burns pass below the road on their way to the Dee. Eilidh and Elspeth are familiar with them all. Each has its own tune, although an occasional one may dry up in summer.'

They stopped at a burn which parted between fantastic, very closely set slender trees, and she enthused, 'This is our favourite, the sweet sound emulating that of some birds. On either side the water trips higher up over little, natural, stony steps, the edges glistening in the sun, before widening and making larger falls. The primary flow is on the left, dividing several times before mainly uniting near the base. Here and there are frisky spurts. When Elspeth was little she thought that they were caused by dancing fairies who only revealed their delicate hues to the moon.'

Nodding he replied, 'Sometimes there is sense in nonsense.'

Later they crossed to the other side of the road and paused as she said,

'There is the impressive winding delta of Quoich Water on its way to the Dee. Its leisurely course contrasts with the strong mountain flow above which pours over schists and forms deep potholes. According to tradition in 1715 at the Earl of Mar's Punch Bowl the Jacobite leader treated his supporters to toasts in punch which had been poured into a huge pothole. The picturesque Linn of Quoich is further down.'

They continued as Creag Bhalg dominated the view ahead. Conifers at its south-east side and up the steep north part were very attractive. Grey hills peered from further north. Soon from in front to the left they heard a muffled roar. Then they drew abreast of little cascades high up between conifers, the flow narrowing further down. Between broom bushes on the other side of the road they were charmed to see the water continue as a long burn descending between heathery banks and then meander before joining the Dee. In the background to the north was Carn na Criche with a long snowfield beneath the top.

She pointed west and said, 'There is a beautiful distant view of red roofed, neo-Tudor Mar Lodge north of the river. It is backed by trees and the long, upward, east sloping Creag Bhalg.'

They halted next on the far side of a flat bridge to admire the Corriemulzie Burn. A tall spruce bent its graceful branches from the right, as if enamoured of the burn. She gave an enchanting smile as the gently sounding water far below stirred her heart. She led him down to the Linn of Corriemulzie, an impressive fall of fifty feet in two parallel sheets. The silvery hue harmonized with the bark of birches. The bridge's high arch enhanced the background view of trees further up.

As they withdrew she explained, 'The name Corriemulzie suggests the corrie's burn being used to provide power for a mill. For many years the burn has supplied heating and lighting at Mar Lodge. It will be wonderful if Ballater can have electricity in time for Christmas.'

Soon they freewheeled down a long, steep, winding, tree-lined stage. At the bottom, in a parallel stretch with the Dee, they stopped near the three span Victoria Bridge leading to Mar Lodge. The South Lodge on the left side of the road opposite the crossing was built for a servant who operated the bridge's gates. The visitors were amused by the humble dwelling being dignified by a porch with four columns and a pediment to hint at the nobility owning Mar Lodge itself. The horseshoe arch over the bridge was inscribed '1848 Victoria 1848' on the front and '1905 Edward VII 1905' at the back to commemorate the building of the first and second bridges.

She commented, 'The sixth Earl of Fife was created the first Duke of Fife when he married Princess Louise, the eldest daughter of Edward VII. This lattice girder bridge is far more artistically designed than the Brunel one. There is a flower on each gate and the lattice effect is varied by a railing on each side with a regular light, decorative theme in the middle. Whereas an urban bridge is associated with bustle, this symbol of peace is subordinated to the river and pines.'

Yet scarcely had they continued than she pointed left to an old relic up the bank, stating that it was the 'Gallows Tree.' They focused on the view ahead, and beneath lower branches the serene Dee shone like a mystic heart. There was a louder tone, however, when the water poured round a large, grassy island.

They passed cottages of Meikle Inverey to the right, and then as they stopped on a humped bridge she said, 'Beneath the noisy Ey Water heads to the Dee. Little Inverey lies to the west, while south-west across the tributary is Creag a' Chait, a large rock formation which juts out above the woodlands. There was the Colonel's Cave from which he watched government troops burn his castle to the ground. The ruins lie north of the road. A mile and a quarter up Glen Ey a footpath descends to a recess in the gorge of the Ey. This was the Colonel's Bed where he hid from his pursuers. Food was brought to him by faithful Annie Ban–Fair Annie. He died in 1698, having wished to be buried beside her at Inverey. The wish was ignored, possibly because they had not been married, and his body was buried in Braemar. Legend had it that on three successive days the coffin was placed in its grave, only to reappear on the surface next morning. The night before the third occurrence the relatives were visited by his angry ghost. The coffin was towed upriver and buried beside the remains of Annie Ban.'

Nearing the Dee again, shortly they heard a rocky ford, before to the north was the stirring sight of Lui Water meeting the river. The area after the union was narrow and resonant, but then the flow widened. Soon tall conifers lined both sides of the road. When the road dipped they were captivated by the royal river's shining surface and dark interior attaining a perfect blend of opposites.

Curving round they halted on the Linn of Dee Bridge with its graceful sharp arch and ornamental battlements. A wooded hill lay away to the west and a more austere hill beyond. They went down on that side where just ahead the broad river entered a narrow gorge of schistose rocks in a wild rapture of light green and white foam. A plaque on the bridge stated that it was erected by James, fifth Earl of Fife, and opened by Queen Victoria on 8 September 1857. Gavin was told that the monarch noted in her journal that the royal party was dressed in a Highland manner, Prince Albert in a Royal Stuart plaid and she and the girls in skirts of the same design. The toast in whisky was 'prosperity to the bridge.' Now the pair gazed down on the other side where the narrow gorge continued and the water twisted on its tortuous way, before opening out in serene pools. They sat below the bridge's east side and heard a rhythmic roar echoing from the depths.

She commented, 'A river's heart is in its broad sweep, but its spirit is in a waterfall. Here the flow has worn so deep that the linn only just qualifies as a waterfall. When I was a child I used to come here with Uncle Malcolm's family. My older cousins and I were warned of the danger, so, instead of associating the foam with fairies, we saw it as a fearsome wonder and played by the calm water below. Now my awe is mystical, as I find beauty and harmony amid chaos.

The roaring surge would have captivated young Byron. His lame foot got caught in heather and he fell, but in rolling down he was fortunately caught by the attendant. When I read his poem, *Childe Harold's Pilgrimage*, in Canto II I was struck by the line, "Alone o'er steeps and foaming falls to lean." It was as well that he was not here by himself that day! The rush and fall of the water would have stunned him, before he drowned in the deep pool.

Look at those salmon! They are doing the opposite, gradually leaping up the fall! My grandfather in Coleraine once told me that in Irish Celtic mythology the salmon was a symbol of wisdom and knowledge. For me a leaping salmon is like a soul in search of God. When Jesus walked by the Sea of Galilee he saw Simon called Peter and Andrew his brother casting a net into the sea. He said to them, "Follow me, and I will make you fishers of men" (Matthew 4.19). Fish and bread were used to feed the 5,000, representing the material and spiritual food offered by Christ. In early times of persecution in the Church the image of the fish was used to signify Christ. The word ichthus, from the Greek "ikhthus" meaning fish, gives the initial letters of the acrostic, "Iesous Christos, Theou Uios, Soter— Jesus Christ, Son of God, Saviour." Less seriously I was born on 1 March 1896 under the sign of Pisces or the Fishes.'

Gavin replied, 'I was born on 30 December 1894 under Capricorn,' adding excitedly, 'The fishes' performance has given me an idea. I reckon I could jump across the narrow channel.'

'It is not difficult to jump over to a lower ledge, but returning is harder.

Several unfortunates are known to have perished in the attempt, so it would be foolhardy to try. You should conserve your energy for the journey. Come, we have a long way to go.'

He smiled at her Irish-Scottish wisdom as they remounted their machines. Curving round they cycled east on the north Deeside road, until they paused on the Lui Bridge. Small and set on a quiet road, it did not attract tourists like the Linn of Dee. Yet Nature did not need to be grand to impress her votaries. Even a burn could refresh the spirit. On the north side the flow, after sweeping round in a brief east stretch, was divided by huge shelves of rock, while on the south side it passed to the right of a long shelf and was guarded by trees until joining the Dee, which they had seen earlier.

They cycled back a short way, and, as they walked with their machines north-west up a narrow and sometimes rough road, she gazed right over the broad, shining, stony Lui Water and said, 'My cousins and I used to play on the other side. Unlike the dangerous Linn of Dee it is safe. Yet the wild aspect enhanced by rugged old pines and birches rouses people of different ages. I love the large idyllic island with pines and heather. That tree's lower branches abnormally point down, but they are part of Nature's often sublime abandonment. What has been our Treasure Island appeals to me differently now.'

Soon they left the road, ascended a slope and hid their bicycles in thick conifers above the Lui. Continuing they were rewarded by enchanting waterfalls and pools. The irony struck them that while the Linn of Dee attracted many tourists, relatively few people came to this much more extensive sequence. The first falls were mainly gentle, tripping over long schistose slabs which gave the water a beautiful blue-green colour. The rocky sides became massive and narrow with an often tortuous flow. The walkers' wonder suddenly mounted on seeing ahead a long, much sharper drop of white roaring splendour. Occasionally the view was hidden, but higher up were instances of cascading at bizarre angles. Twisting made the course of falls and pools seem even longer, and it was impossible fully to understand in a short time all the varied, intricate details which had taken thousands of years to form. Above the clamour was an attendant host of peaceful trees. It was a unique, unforgettable experience. Then the bed broadened in a placid, meandering flow.

They rejoined the road, and, when they paused on the Black Bridge over the Lui, she observed, 'The route is new now for both of us, but I have been informed and read about it. Further up to the right of the Lui on the green you can see two symmetrical knolls named Dà Shìthean or two fairy hillocks. Particularly in light mist and/or moonlight they will have a supernatural aspect. Scottish fairies are reputedly capricious and can be mischievous if resentful. They live inside green hills, chiefly conical in shape, on which they dance by moonlight, making marks of circles on the surface, within which it is dangerous to sleep or be found at night!'

Smiling he replied, 'I prefer the nymph who is beyond my imagination. You had a nap on Lochnagar. We can rest occasionally, if you prefer.'

She said resolutely, 'That was at twilight. This is morning.'

The bridge marked a gradual transition from the lower glen, with its plentiful conifers characteristic of Deeside, to the steadily plainer upper part. He was glad that the scenery was becoming more elemental and sublime, as it accorded with their spiritual union.

She explained, 'This road is part of the major Cairngorm pass, the Lairig an Laoigh, which means the pass of Lui or calf-one, referring to Lui Water. The pass connects Abernethy to the north with Braemar. To the west is the Lairig Ghru, the pass of Dhru or Druie, which probably means oozing, referring to the stream draining the north side. Connecting Aviemore with Braemar the rougher route is said to have been used for older cattle. There were townships or groups of agricultural smallholdings in Glen Lui with summer grazing, which explains green stretches. In 1726 people were removed while timber was felled for four or five years, while in 1776 the settlements were cleared, the glen being used mainly for money obtained from recreational shooting of deer. Thus there is a dearth of trees.'

As the road crossed a stream pouring down from the north-east, she said, 'This is the Allt a` Mhadaidh or burn of the wolf,' and then, after a total of four miles, she looked right and observed, 'That is Derry Lodge with its warm red and grey granite in the quiet charm of an east-west, narrow pine plantation. The front of the building, including a porch, faces south. Mr Bremner used to be based there. He said that the tranquil setting was appreciated after the occupants had spent a day arranged in shooting parties. Derry comes from the Gaelic meaning grove.'

As they crossed a footbridge she explained, 'This Derry Burn comes from the north to join just south the Luibeg Burn from the west and form Lui Water. Luibeg means little calf-one and refers to the stream.'

Turning to the idyllic Glen Luibeg, with its dreaming, fragrant pines, they passed through a broad pasture before joining a rising path. On the left were two knolls and a dead silvery trunk bending over to the ground in a semicircle.

As the track bent round a slope to the right, they gazed left at a group of stags and he said, 'They are growing new antlers. A royal stag is one with a head of twelve or more points. It is rare, for only one per cent have so many. It was a memorable day when I saw one.'

Soon there were clusters of pines around a stretch of the burn and the path which drew near it. An extraordinary trunk bent down then up, and yet the branches at the top were perfectly level. She photographed him with the pines and burn as background. Then he snapped her in the same position, so that when the duplicates were developed they could each put a pair of the prints together.

Shortly she remarked, 'I like the charming little cascades above the path to the right and a trickling flow below it, for their immediate gentle, feminine sounds balance the burn's rocky call. Why do you gaze at me so?'

'You and your remarks are the prime subject, wherever we are. Yet you look even more beautiful here than in the shop, mainly because you are in your element in the wild, and partly because you can give me more of your attention.'

Soon she pointed north and said, 'That old solitary pine is in Carn Crom's Coire Craobh an Oir or curved hill's corrie with the tree of the gold. According to a legend a crock of stolen gold was buried there by Mackenzie, laird of Dalmore in Mar, at a spot struck by the sun's first rays at midsummer, but he later moved it to near the top of Cairn Geldie, under a big stone with the figure of a horseshoe carved on it.'

The burn meandered separately in the winding glen. Attractive white rocks lay on and beside the path, which was adorned with occasional bouquets of heather sheltered by large stones. On either side were light and dark green grasses. They came to the ford across the rocky Luibeg Burn pouring down from the north. Just to the north-west was the east side of Carn a' Mhaim with two large exposed stretches and a saddle above. The walkers paused on sand above the ford and gazed at the red and whitish, often moss stained rocks below. After topping up their bottles they crossed the swift yet shallow flow, avoiding slippery surfaces.

There was a rugged, steep ascent and the sun beat down. Now and again they walked on or beside huge rocky slabs. When the way became easier they appreciated the austere scenery with the Allt Preas nam Meirleach, or burn of copse of the robbers, flowing below to the Luibeg Burn. As they gradually curved round Carn a' Mhaim they saw broad Glen Geusachan, with its meandering burn flowing to the Dee, on the other side of the Lairig Ghru. They realized that the stretch they were leaving was a transition between the gentle beauty of Glen Luibeg and the sublime glory of the main pass.

She explained, 'Glen Geusachan means glen of the little pine wood, although now there is just a grassy floor. The wild rocky sides are partly relieved by greenery. Carn a' Mhaim means hill of the pass.'

Turning north they saw ahead to the left The Devil's Point, dark and forbidding with a huge glistening slab on its east side, and pointing beyond it in due course she said, 'That is Corrour Bothy. It is named after Coire Odhar or dun corrie behind. Mr Bremner once told me that gamekeepers stayed in such huts at times, so they could keep track of the deer and prevent walkers from disturbing them and getting in range of the guns. Let us cross the Dee and take the path up the corrie behind the bothy. Although it is June a small snowfield lingers at the top, but it looks manageable and there will be a fine view from there.'

After crossing the river they laughed on finding that the route to the bothy was part path and part boggy hollows. Experienced walkers would have known a precise way, but they proceeded cautiously, looking for occasional stepping stones. Frustration was replaced by exhilaration when, passing the bothy, they climbed up beside the steep, winding, cascading burn. Its young and purposeful qualities found kinship with them. At one place a foaming fall steadied on a ledge, before it plunged so deeply that, if they had tried to see the full extent, they would have toppled over. Nearer the summit was an air of fantasy about the burn dividing into three down a broad rocky face. Around the top tiny currents flowing down through grass backed by snow added to the main flow. It was when they turned, however, and saw a long cloud clear to show the awesome cliff cirque of Ben Macdui to the north-east, that the Cairngorms cast their abiding spell. To have gone north on the heights would have been rocky with snowfields, so they returned to walking up the pass.

Before long she pointed right and said, 'There is Clach nan Taillear or stone of the tailors, but it is a group of ribbed stones. According to tradition one New Year's Eve in the late eighteenth century three men perished there in the snow. They had wagered that they would dance at Abernethy, Rothiemurchus and Dalmore within twenty-four hours, and they were walking south to the last place. To the west above a steep green slope is Coire an t-Saighdeir or corrie of the soldier. Its burn flows down to the Dee.'

Although they walked briskly on the rough path, the towering mountains and corries made progress seem slow, so they could leisurely admire the magnificent views. Equally they had more time to observe each other. She had never been with such a happy man. There was depth too, for his shining eyes would suddenly change and fix thoughtfully on part of the view which particularly moved him, before he relaxed with a deceptive boyish smile. She was impressed by his devotion to her and his commitment to life in general.

After a while she looked left and said, 'That is Cairn Toul or hill of the barn, for it looks square shaped when seen from the west. Here it is far more attractive, with its conical peak, long, graceful south-east and north-east ridges, the steep green side and lofty east Coire an t-Sabhail or corrie of the barn, from which a burn foams down to the Dee.'

He added, 'High up to the right of the burn are rocky outcrops, the main ones forming what look like vestiges of a huge, natural sheep pen, although it is too steep for grazing.'

Then to the east the largely green sided ridge of Carn a' Mhaim dipped down to a col, before exposed huge screes dominated over green areas on the side of Ben Macdui, and she said, 'In the dip pours down the Allt Clach nan Taillear or burn of stone of the tailors on its way to the Dee. The stream's name is by extension very appropriate, for Scottish dance music sometimes reminds me of lively, flowing water. The strathspey is named after the valley of the Spey. Now living water dances past the monument to where the men died on their way to a final dance.'

They gazed at the vast upper cliff cirque of Ben Macdui. Only a small misty cloud at the west end impaired a perfect view. They eagerly pressed forward, for they were entering the heart of the Cairngorms. Toiling in such grandeur had long helped form the proud, independent spirit of the Highlander, who strove to be both the master and servant of his environment.

She commented, 'Braeriach lies ahead to the west. The name means brindled upland. When seen from Strathspey clouds scudding across the mountain give the heather grasses a speckled look. Now an interlude in which passing light clouds has ended, huge, high, gaunt Coire Bhrochain is fully revealed. The name might literally mean corrie of the porridge. According to a story cattle followed the grazing to the high plateau, but in poor weather they fell over the edge. The smashed remains resembled porridge. Alternatively Bhrochain may refer to the little pieces of the exceptional huge screes on the floor.'

He replied, 'The corrie looks like a timeless, scarred battleground of the elements.'

After a further advance she observed, 'The corrie overlooks the vast An Garbh Choire or the rough corrie to the west, the finest in the Cairngorms. On the south side of An Garbh Choire is Cairn Toul's lofty Coire an Lochain Uaine or corrie of the green tarn. You can see the falling water which joins the Allt a' Gharbh-choire. To the west of Coire an Lochain Uaine is Sgòr an Lochain Uaine or peak of the green tarn. It is also called The Angel's Peak to contrast with The Devil's Point. At the end of the main corrie a broad nose separates Garbh Choire Mór or big rough corrie, which has Scotland's longest lasting snowfield, and to the north Garbh Choire Dhàidh or rough corrie of Dee. Beneath a snow bridge you can see the upper part of the Falls of Dee cascading south-east. Let us go further up the Lairig Ghru and visit the Pools of Dee. The huge, long Sròn na Lairige or nose of the pass is to their west.'

The pass narrowed as they ascended, until the floor was covered with boulders. Carefully they made their way over the west edge, and suddenly they felt peaceful tumult on seeing a very large pool stretching across the pass.

As they had lunch beside it she said, 'The boulders have tumbled down the steep sides. A short distance ahead is the March Burn. It is a few yards within the march or boundary with Inverness-shire, and it plunges from the east, disappearing among boulders and emerging on the Dee side of the summit as one large and three smaller pools. This is the big one. Their old name was Lochan Dubh na Làirige or black tarns of the pass. Today the rugged sides with green stretches cast a dark green reflection on the water. All around is debris left by the Ice Age 10,000 years ago. Although it is summer there is a chill in the air. It is like a meeting of the ages and the seasons. Over there a ptarmigan in summer grey plumage flies south. Near us are lichens and blaeberry. In a normal year sturdy marigolds are here. The first part of the flower's name is from Mary, probably the Virgin, and in the language of flowers the marigold represents grief, because, after following the sun's course each summer's day, it mourns its setting which forces the petals to close.'

'It is strange that gilded grief will be at the furthest point of our walk.'

'Yes, but the flowers will be beside the pure water of life, which is associated with the Holy Spirit.'

After eating they rose to gaze into the pool's mossy, rocky bottom and she exclaimed, 'Look! Trout are swimming.'

A breeze blew ripples towards them and a refreshing light shower began. Curiosity led them to walk a short way to the next pool which had an irregular shape. When the shower stopped they photographed each other against the main pool and the rough upper pass, which in the distance turned west out of sight. As they looked north for the last time before returning, they smiled at each other on sharing the thought that the challenging prospect, the peaceful pool and the chastened glory of the later flowers symbolized their spiritual journey.

Back in Braemar was a well spread evening meal. They resolved to spend the last day climbing Ben Macdui. She told him that the name's origin was obscure, but in translation the most likely derivations were hill of the black pig, in allusion to its shape, and hill of Macduff, as the Macduffs or Earls of Fife had long owned the Aberdeenshire part of Ben Macdui.

A westerly light wind blew early next morning when they set out. It was a little cooler, but walking was easier after they left their bicycles in the same area as before. They turned west soon after passing Derry Lodge, but, instead of crossing the ford again over the Luibeg Burn, they ascended north to its right and between Carn Crom and Carn a' Mhaim's east side. Soon the rocky burn lay far below.

Gazing ahead she said, 'There is the dome of Ben Macdui, but cut on its east side by the cliff lined cirque of Coire Sputan Dearg or corrie with red little spouts, referring to the red screes in the main gullies. The cliff ridge sweeps up to the majestic pyramid shaped peak before descending.'

They felt that they were on a great adventure approaching the second highest mountain in the country after Ben Nevis. Dark stretches of the Luibeg Burn alternated with foaming ones. They came to a busy ford where water pouring down from the Coire Sputan Dearg swept across to join the Allt Carn a' Mhaim from the west and form the Luibeg Burn. They saw that there would be a series of ascents to the summit, so they drank well with bottles in reserve.

They had enjoyed being hemmed in by heather, before grass increased and they climbed the long ridge, the Sròn Riach or brindled nose. To the east from high up came a distant dog's barking, with two burns cascading down deep furrows between heather and grass. The first aim of the climb was to reach a gap between large rocks. Beyond them weathered smoothing imparted a huddled look to groups of rocks. Relief came when the way was less steep. A light wind sang through wild grass and a fissured boulder. A short but steep slope was followed by another easier stretch where lay a gouged rock. Then they ascended round a dark tor before reaching a less steep area with several huge weathered rocks which lay like fossilized beasts. A larger climb included clambering over a long stretch of boulders higher up. They headed for a cairn and to the west admired Cairn Toul's high east corrie looking closer than the day before. Wandering over rocky terrain to another cairn, they advanced to a further one by the east cliff edge.

When he dubbed the cairns the 'Three Wise Men,' her reply was more serious. 'Nearby to the north-east is Coire Clach nan Taillear. The three men were not wise to go down the Lairig Ghru.'

They gazed from the cliff top far below at Lochan Uaine or green tarn, but which now mirrored the blue area of sky. Like Lochnagar's two tarns its lower section was narrower than the main part, and it contrasted with patches of snow. A path near it showed how many walkers had been drawn to the vast corrie.

As they turned away and continued, she observed, 'See that mountain hare ahead raise his ears among boulders. Now he bolts to hide among rocks near the cliff edge. He is wise to be cautious. A golden eagle generally makes a surprise low-level attack to catch a hare or ptarmigan.'

The walkers envied the hare's alacrity when they faced the stern challenge of climbing boulders to the pyramid shaped peak. The higher they climbed the wildness increased, but the interplay of sun and mist created sublime, peaceful shades of green. From the peak was a very fine view of the meandering, silvery Luibeg Burn and further away a wave of hills. Turning south-west they were glad to reach the gentler incline of the very broad dome of Ben Macdui and the roof of Scotland. Avoiding small snowfields they found the gravelly path which was occasionally interrupted by huge rocky slabs, but they looked ahead to see the continuation.

As they passed a ruined dwelling, she explained, 'That was the Sappers' Bothy erected by the Ordnance Survey,' and soon, when they reached the very wide summit cairn, she added, 'The Ordnance Survey set up a trigonometrical station in 1847, which was marked by a hole six inches deep and sunk in a huge stone upon which a cairn was built.'

They had lunch on the flat, waist-high cairn as she commented, 'I have long thought from pictures of Ben Macdui's majestic height and Braeriach with its nascent, nurturing river, that they are the King and Queen of the Cairngorms. The inspired union of masculine and feminine qualities in Nature corresponds to the love of a man and woman, which they feel is externalized and strengthened. The sublime purifies the spirit and fills it with awe. They who worship beauty for beauty's sake mistake the form for the spiritual essence. Ironically here one does not feel the elation experienced on Lochnagar's summit, where there are commanding views both near and far. This broad dome only allows us to see the tops of nearby mountains, although further views are extensive. Basically, however, we survey more cloudscape than landscape, particularly as clouds now hide the sun and so the mountains are less distinct. The humble conviction is learned that it is not a particular place we should seek, but a feeling of sublime solitude in which we may gain mystical communion with God. I recall words in Luke 21.27 about Judgement Day, of "the Son of man coming in a cloud with power and great glory." The passage warns by extension that we should be prepared. It is symbolically appropriate that we are waiting for the sun to peer through the clouds, for it reminds me of man waiting for Jesus' Second Coming.'

Recalling Gavin's reference to the Three Wise Men, she added, 'The Magi followed a star to the Epiphany, the manifestation of Christ. Yet they had expected to see a future earthly king, and so they brought royal gifts. They must have felt doubly humbled to find Christ in a manger. The shepherds represented Jesus' own people, while the visiting astronomers represented Gentiles, all the rest of the world. We will see Jesus in Heaven, but on earth we may experience epiphanic moments when we appreciate more than usually God's love and glory. Filled with the Holy Spirit, the giver of life, we must give in return.'

They were united as they communed with the clouds, nearby mountains and distant landscapes, awestruck by God's power and favour. On Lochnagar they had shared the ecstasy of seeing the cosmos by night. Yesterday they had seen the Falls of Dee pouring down like grace. Now the spiritual heights were experienced more broadly in the sober light of day.

He commented, 'By the Pools of Dee you said that the marigold represented grief. Life is sometimes a vale of tears, but inspired by God love is stronger than grief, stronger than life itself.'

She nodded but replied, 'I have heard tales that when mist covers the dome, the stillness can have a haunting quality which induces an eerie, other-worldly feeling. Mysticism is replaced by plain mystery and foreboding, which are increased by the fatigue caused by climbing the mountain. The way becomes indistinct; there is the fear of losing direction. Sounds are creepy and subdued. One becomes disorientated with a false perception of distance. Some people have spoken of hearing following footsteps, while others have actually seen a giant spectre called Am Fear Liath Mór or the big grey man. He has a large hat! Mr Bremner has climbed the mountain a number of times, but he has not heard of anyone who has seen the spectre in clear daylight. He believes, therefore, that it is a mirage, ironically an enlarged shadow of the observer projected onto mist by the sun. He vows that if he sees the apparition, he will not run away like others, but operate his arms as if using semaphore. If the spectre duplicates his movements, he will be certain that it is just a trick of the light and mist! I think that stories of the apparition and related sounds are the Devil's parables of men losing their spiritual way through lack of faith. More positively Queen Victoria had lunch here on 7 October 1859 and recorded superlative praise. On the night of her Golden Jubilee in 1887 a party climbed the mountain and set off fireworks. Many bonfires were seen on peaks, chiefly north and east.'

A glimpse of the sun brought out the camera. Another couple was there, and the man photographed Iona and Gavin smiling on the stony throne. There was only a light breeze and they were relaxed. As the sun shone through more breaks in the clouds, they descended west on the dome to get a better view. To the north was a distant partial green view of Speyside. Then came Sròn na Lairige and Braeriach.

He said, 'From here the other side looks softened, like a vast elephant's hide. The addition of snow reminds me of Hannibal's elephants crossing the Alps!'

She observed, 'There the Allt a' Gharbh-choire glistens through the haze as it flows east. The stream joins the Allt na Lairig Ghru to form the River Dee. Two descending ridges of Cairn Toul look grand from this commanding view, and The Devil's Point is even more compact against the long, gradually rising Beinn Bhrotain or hill of Brodan, which was Fingal's dog.'

As they wandered some distance along the sloping summit, marvelling at the vast granite formations resulting from molten rock and how glaciers had shaped the pass and the corries opposite, she commented, 'The jumbled stones which crunch beneath us have been formed by freezing, thawing and weathering. They look dour without their white coat. In this arctic setting evolution is far more evident than in the varied consistency of sand beside Loch Muick.'

Although they had seen Nature and time in much better perspective, ironically when they returned to the cairn they could not see the precise direction in which the path lay. Then they remembered that it passed near the Sappers' Bothy, so they crossed over rocks to it and descended from the dome. Misty wreaths wafted around elevations and gullies of Coire Sputan Dearg. Taking a north-east gravelly path they passed on the left a large pool fed by a higher source. From the pool flowed a number of rills which made a rough passage. They walked carefully, because the path briefly divided occasionally and water flowed here and there, so it was like treading through a small burn.

Laughing she said, 'I feel at home, because the conditions remind me of the prose of life. Above on each side is a wild, rocky scene, and there is some snow in hollows. The way lies below the swelling spur of Sròn an Daimh or promontory of the stag.'

Suddenly her eyes lit with passion at the scene ahead, far below to the left, as she exclaimed, 'Pure Loch Etchachan and Little Loch Etchachan! Like aspiring souls they mirror the heavens!'

After a while the path went down steeply, and, when they reached the ford over the outlet from the smaller loch, she observed, 'As water leaves here the main loch is renewed, so there is stasis in motion. Wild grass and thrift on the margins are a striking combination. The arctic purity is perfected by the soaring, austere cliff of Carn Etchachan on the north-west side. This is the largest stretch of water at such a height in Britain. It tends to have some ice for more than half the year. Let us refill our bottles. The fresh, bountiful water hidden so high up, like grace abounding, waits to refresh wayfarers. Etchachan likely means expansive place, which relates to the huge bowl of the corrie below and that wide loch at the head. East of Carn Etchachan is a col leading to Glen Avon and Cairn Gorm rises north of it. Let us make a diversion to the glen.'

Crossing the ford they walked through a wide basin which became very rocky, as they traversed fords between pools and streams feeding what she identified as the Allt nan Stacan Dubha or stream of the black precipices to the right. They made a very steep descent of 600 feet to near Loch Avon's head. As when descending Craig Coillich and Craigendarroch, he went first because it would not have mattered so much if she had bumped into him. Even so the risk was that if they slid they might have overbalanced and fallen heavily. Thus they unceremoniously crouched and used their feet and hands to lever forward. They were rewarded by the breathtaking sight of more and more of the loch coming into view.

On reaching the floor of the glen she said, 'It is regarded as the finest loch in the Highlands for solitude and wild grandeur. Queen Victoria was here on 28 September 1861 and recorded highest praise. In the distant past huge pieces of rock have fallen from the crags of Carn Etchachan.'

He replied, 'We saw past ages on Ben Macdui, and now it is like walking in prehistoric times among these rocks. Yet their falling has been nothing compared to what will happen on the last day.'

As they advanced she said, 'The great, dark, square topped Shelter Stone Crag is to the left, and this nearest and largest of the many big boulders beneath it is Clach Dhion or stone of the shelter. It fell on smaller blocks. A chamber is left in which we can creep. Although we have to stoop the roof slopes upward over the heather strewn floor, so we can almost stand erect at the back. Old descriptions of the stone referred to it as a retreat for armed freebooters. It was fitting that in more peaceful times the Cairngorm Club, the first climbing one in Scotland, originated at the Shelter Stone and that it was associated with the camaraderie of climbers. It was founded here on the morning after the night of Queen Victoria's Golden Jubilee, on 24 June 1887.'

Even in the dim light he loved to hear her fresh, clear voice full of peaceful joy. The gentle tone was intensified in the quiet chamber. They rested briefly in silence, before curiosity about the glen drove them out. She emerged first, and he thought what an empty shell the chamber was without her, like the shop in Ballater he had entered after rock climbing, only to be told that she was elsewhere.

When he saw her luminous, blissful eyes gazing at the loch, he realized that, while their spirits had united on the summits of Lochnagar and Ben Macdui, their hearts were one at the dance and in the rocky retreat, while their forms were ghostly in the faint light. When they had been at the Falls of the Glasallt she was not sure of her commitment, and her eyes and lips expressed restraint. Now her face's rare transcendent beauty showed love's rich simplicity which was beyond words.

Advancing across the glen's head they saw to the left a lofty, long, horizontal snowfield beneath the edge of the upper corrie, and a shorter one a little below. The great cliffs and immense screes had a very wild aspect. She identified the Féith Buidhe or yellow bog-stream which foamed in splendour, being joined lower down from the south by the two combined streams of the Garbh Uisge or rough water from Ben Macdui. Then from the north-west the Allt Coire Domhain connected, and the whole poured into the loch through a fertile area of turf on the north side called Meur na Banaraich or finger stream of the dairymaid. They crossed a ford to that green place, which normally had summer flowers. Then they advanced over white sand to golden sand by the loch, the edge of which was tinged with green. Cataracts descended from the sides.

He said, 'This is the strangest place I have ever visited. There is a curious combination of great beauty and awesome desolation.'

She replied, 'Where man seeks sublime beauty he makes a path to

God. The steep sided loch is a little mysterious. The loch is about one and a half miles long and a quarter of a mile across. The glen is so secluded that no boat or bothy has been here. Last century older people at Tomintoul told a story about how once a fine horse roamed on the shores of this loch. Many a man tried to capture it, but it dashed into the water and the man was drowned. Then a man took a silver bridle and slipped it over the horse's head. The kelpie was powerless and it was led back to Tomintoul. A tale of triumph over death would have appealed to older people.'

Pointing high up to the right she said, 'Those great tors on the top are the Barns of Beinn Mheadhoin or middle hill, as it is between the loch and Glen Derry. Unimaginative people call them warts.'

They gazed down the virginal glen, their young, innocent love in greater union with Nature, until at his suggestion they criss-crossed their hands on each other's wrists and spun, as they did in the Circassian Circle Dance. So they laughingly formed an eternal circle on the golden sand, where there was no tide to flow and ebb.

Then she said, 'It would be very beautiful and peaceful to walk beside the loch and a stretch of the River Avon, before returning south. I think it would be even better, as well as save time, if we retrace part of the way and descend Coire Etchachan.'

They were surprised that climbing out of the glen was easier and quicker than they expected. When negotiating the rocky stretch beyond, however, she slipped when mounting a boulder, but fell back into his strong arms.

The south-east path down Coire Etchachan was surrounded by boulders, yet steep and easy, causing her to enthuse, 'It is like descending a ladder from Heaven. I love the long, roaring cascades on the left. Masculine power and feminine grace combine, because from the rocks luxuriant green tresses stream like a woman's locks and they are followed by long white plumes. Dwarf juniper is a noticeable feature in the corrie.'

After greeting an ascending male walker they gazed at Stob (point of) Coire Etchachan to the left, and later as they looked back she said, 'The Creagan a' Choire Etchachan or crags of Coire Etchachan are on the south and west sides. The huge, dark and bare ones on the west wall are especially a worthy awesome sight on the approach to Ben Macdui.'

Lower down the way became less steep and the burn meandered. They crossed to the other side, noticing many small moraines at the corrie's foot. Then they turned south down the Lairig an Laoigh. At one point to the right they saw the Coire Etchachan Burn still flow in some little cascades. When he helped her across a rocky ford he loved the firm, warm grasp of her hand, before she observed that this Glas Allt Mór or big green burn pouring from the north-east joined the other flow to form the Derry Burn. As they pressed on down a long, austere stretch of the steep sided pass, to the west were the slopes of Derry Cairngorm, including a stream falling over the cliffs of lofty Coire an Lochain Uaine, although the tarn was hidden from them.

Occasionally the path was wet, and at one point he fell heavily after his right foot caught in a hollow concealed by rough grass, but she said sympathetically, 'As we have both slipped, it is unlikely we will lose our balance again. One of the finest pieces of ancient pine forest in Scotland lies ahead, although Mr Bremner has warned me that some roots in it travel across and even above the paths.'

When pines began to increase she pointed to the right, explaining, 'Those are the remains of the artificial dam built about 1820 by Sandy Davidson across the breach in the prehistoric Derry Dam. The water was suddenly released by a sluice to float logs down the burn. Yet he became financially ruined, because he badly miscalculated the cost of conveying the heavy timber of Glen Derry to Aberdeen. Let us continue a short way and see the stretch of the beautiful Derry Falls and shelving rocks. Then we will return and cross by that footbridge to the forest.'

Later they mounted the steep slope on the other side, before passing through the first trees she laughed and said, 'We are doing the opposite of what Mr Bremner has advised me. He says that ideally one should walk through the forest for the first time at dawn, when strong light waves surge through a wild wonderland of soaring old pines and fresh, vibrant, undulating heather, as the main path and broad, bright, clamorous burn occasionally converge, but otherwise take their own winding ways. An evening walk here may induce general thoughts of the morning and resurrection, but I can imagine that the drama of dawn is special. Birds sing cheerfully as trees gleam with enchanted tones in quickening light. Soon the whole sky brightens and the earth is clear to the horizon. Nature moulds the present with the past to produce the fresh face of creation.'

At the top of the heathery mound they paused, held by the sheltering peaceful beauty. They photographed each other, with tall pines around and the gaunt upper pass behind. The undulating ground continued to force the path to meander, but occasionally, when it drew near the burn, the main surging current and quiet pools beside the bank were matched by joyful hearts and serene spirits. At one point the water was divided by a sizeable island.

They noticed oddities in which beauty and harmony emerged amid chaos. To the east was a great pine which had only a token small dead branch on the north side, but normal branches on the other side. Even complete death seemed positive, for the colours grew lighter, partly enhanced by Nature's green livery. Several dead, pale grey pines still stood defiantly. Very long bleached trunks lay on the ground, as did smaller trees and branches, partly destroyed and twisted in fantastic shapes, imparting a mute but dramatic ghostly eloquence. The walkers were charmed by a living tree which bent over the path from the right and rested its branches on the ground to the left, forming a natural arch.

She pointed right and said, 'Two close rowan saplings are by that mound. Wire mesh has been wrapped round to protect them from grazing deer. The seeds may well have come from an older one some distance back on the left. The leaves will flame russet in autumn sunlight, setting the trees apart from evergreens.'

They crossed the burn and soon passed Derry Lodge. Regaining their bicycles they glanced west when crossing the Linn of Dee, but the hills which were clearly visible earlier now only showed their outlines through mist. Yet it was balance and completeness, while their spirits were high after the successful mission. Apart from the steep climb beyond Victoria Bridge the ride was easy back to Braemar. After a final meal they refilled the bottles, thanked their hosts and turned back in twilight to Ballater. Their hearts leaped at the renewed airy sensation of passing over Invercauld Bridge. The cooling darkness also gave the impression that they travelled faster than they did.

A stop was made to drink by the stretch of the Dee north of the Balmoral Estate which had enchanted her on the outward journey. The stars were largely hidden and only muted moonlight lay on the river, but now they felt greater joy because they were closer. Mountains and rivers were manifestations of God, and Royal Deeside was an eminent example, yet the crown was two united hearts and spirits.

He commented, 'Love is not love which does not flow in royal blood. It is as if we have been on a platonic honeymoon before a wedding.'

She replied, 'Yet strangely honey plus moon originally referred to waning affection. To me true love is a constant bright star which shines above the vagaries of time.'

Shortly after they advanced she said, 'Let us be charitable to Brunel and use his bridge to cross the river. We will reach Ballater sooner, and I do not want to keep my father up too late.'

As they cycled across the bridge he smiled and said, 'Nature's bosses are more artistic.'

The front of Abergeldie Castle was tranquil in the pale moonlight, and they particularly enjoyed the familiar final stretch, crossing bridges over the Muick and Dee, arriving in Ballater before midnight. Even so, when Mr Gordon opened the door, he was a little concerned that they had returned so late, but he understood their wish to make the most of the last full day. She suddenly looked tired and Gavin was worried that she might have overexerted herself. Yet when they had locked their machines in the shed at the back, she gave him a smiling embrace and said that she would see him off next morning.

Back in the square he felt weary climbing upstairs, and, all the exertions of the past week over, he slept deeply. In the morning Donald had to wake him. After breakfast he packed his bag upstairs, and as he looked across to the church he saw Iona strolling with Mike in sunshine on the green. The railway's mechanical time and army discipline waited, but sublime passion would transform mundane externals. He thanked Donald's aunt and bid her goodbye, telling his friend that he would see him at the station. Some people were streaming there as he headed to Iona. Mike veered sharply towards him, so he took the lead. She laughed because she had a packet of sandwiches, and she exchanged it for the lead, while he put the food in his bag. As they walked on she asked what he would be doing in the near future, and he told her to look forward to their next meeting. They were about to leave the green and cross the road, when they saw her father waving at them from the south end. He was clearly in some discomfort trying to rush with his bad leg, so they hastened to him.

Unsheathing a dirk he said, 'I hope that war will not break out, but if it does this friend could be useful. I know that there is prejudice in the Army against using a knife, but in close combat a backhanded jab in the face is the most effective way of getting in first at one man and then others nearby. The victims are so astonished they are incapacitated. There is a word for it.'

'Flabbergasted,' Gavin replied.

'That's it, flabb-er-gasted!'

As her father stabbed the air with the knife, Iona warned him, 'You are disturbing Mrs Leslie who is passing.'

Turning to the nearby frowning mother of Callum and Helen, he thoughtlessly pointed the weapon at her and called, 'Sorry, Mary,' but she responded with a flabbergasted look.

Sheathing the knife he continued, 'I am not impressed by dirks which are currently on the market, but this one is efficient. Best wishes!'

'Thank you, Mr Gordon, and the same to you.'

As the couple continued she smiled wryly and said, 'What a perfect end to our holiday.'

At the station's entrance Donald waved at them to hurry, and soon, as they walked beside the train, she explained, 'The long, curving platform has been built to accommodate the royal train, and foreign royals have also arrived here, including Tsar Nicholas II in 1896.'

As they stood by an open carriage door, he stretched himself and declared, 'I prefer your angelic grace to any special train and pomp. This has been the most wonderful and most arduous holiday of my life. You have been a very fine guide to Upper Deeside and the Cairngorms, giving vivid details capped with philosophical and religious remarks. Scotland's peaceful beauty is a fine example to less fortunate parts of the world. Keep me informed about you, your father and little Switzerland. I will write. Do you want anything else?'

With eyes of strong devotion she shook her head and gently replied, 'Love is the perfect gift. Would you like me to send a lock of my hair with the photographs?'

'No, let your beauty shine in perfection.'

'You must have some reservations about me.'

'Truth has no caveats. When I return I will chase you round a pine, the king of trees,' he joked to ease the pang of parting, as he kissed her left cheek.

'No, I will kiss you by a birch, the queen of trees,' she responded with a kiss, only a slight tremor of her hands showing reluctance to see him go.

He was the last passenger to board the train. Mike was both unwilling to part and excited by the noise and bustle, so seconds later, when the whistle blew and the train began to move, he strained at the lead to keep pace. Laughing Iona willingly complied, and they advanced until they stood near the end of the platform. Gavin waved from an open window and she waved back, until he was hidden by dark smoke. They were to see that machine with its sombre clouds bearing him away from their idyllic holiday as a portent of hell. He was to recall that whistle, when in the trenches he heard another whistle sound for him and his comrades to go over the top.

6: The Early Storms

He described in a letter to her the very different environment of the 1st Battalion of the Gordon Highlanders at Crownhill Hutments, Plymouth. The quarters were indifferent, but the Royal Scots were also there, while the Royal Irish and Middlesex regiments and the Navy were at Devonport. His pitch was enthusiastic, for he felt a new man, giving thanks for her love and hospitality. 'Your angelic presence still abides, with the joyful tones and smiles which are the music of light.' They and her letters would sustain him until their next meeting, hopefully as soon as Christmas. The strong spiritual bond meant there was no brooding, yet, to ease a certain emotional numbness after their parting, he expressed the whimsical thought that the present was but a fleeting interface between the past and the future, and they were united in the unfolding future.

In his next letter he stated that on 22 June he had gone to Willsworthy, Dartmoor, for rifle and battalion training. She was not told that for a long time senior officers had believed war would come. Infinite care was taken in rifle training, because of the tactical significance. She was informed instead about Dartmoor, which had been a royal forest in Saxon times. The small, hardy ponies roaming free together made him sympathize with the solitary one she had embraced outside Ballater.

Shortly before he moved to Willsworthy he was delighted to receive her first letter with a set of photographs carefully annotated on the back. She wrote of daily summer coaches travelling from Aberdeen to Balmoral and Braemar, and excursion trains from Aberdeen to Ballater every Wednesday and Saturday afternoon, with a link by road to Balmoral. Each Saturday that month there was a Deeside and Donside circular tour by rail and motor, and daily from July to September there were the 'Three Rivers Tours' by the Dee, Don and Spey, using a combination of rail, motor and coach. She had heard affluent customers in the shop talk of hiring landaulets and open cars in the burgh, as well as planning to go on holiday in Belgium or Paris.

She hoped that he had enjoyed some English strawberries. They were arriving in Aberdeen each morning fresh from the growers. He was reminded that frost had ruined the Deeside crop in many places. There were new summer vegetables and French cherries.

She deplored the sacrilege committed in Edward the Confessor's Chapel in Westminster Abbey on the evening of 11 June, when they were still on holiday. Slight damage was caused by a bomb to the Stone of Scone, or the Stone of Destiny, lying beneath the Coronation Chair. A woman's feather boa or throat wrap and other items were found on a nearby chair. Presumably the explosion was caused by militant suffragettes who were aware of the debate on the Home Office's action regarding their body. At the time a deputation of Irish suffragettes was visiting the House of Commons where the blast was heard. Iona reminded him that the mystic stone, made of pinkish sandstone and surrounded by legends, was stolen from Scotland by Edward I in 1296. Scots associated it with the struggle for independence, recalling the victories of Andrew Murray and William Wallace at Stirling Bridge in 1297 and of Robert I at Bannockburn in 1314. The Prime Minister, Mr Asquith, however, rejected a proposal by the MP for East Aberdeen that the stone should be moved for safer keeping back to Scotland!

Before closing with her love she gently criticized him for suggesting that they were together in the unfolding future. When he heard the Rev. Farquharson's sermon based on part of Christ's Sermon on the Mount, they were exhorted to seek God's Kingdom by living each day to the full. 'Sufficient unto the day is the evil thereof.' Sergeant Mackay also quoted the words in the shop, when her father spoke of his apprehension of war.

Later she informed him that in the early morning of 16 June she and other residents were woken by the church bell ringing an alarm. Her father cycled along and learned of a serious blaze at wooden stables in Braemar Road. He and many others hurried there, but the fire hose's water supply was inadequate and the stables were destroyed. Four horses were saved, although six terrified ones defied rescue efforts and sadly perished. For the helpers it was distressing to hear the screams of such noble, powerful creatures made impotent by fear.

Gavin was told of a severe thunderstorm in the north of Scotland on 18 June. The rain was welcome to farmers. Finally there was a development in the proposed Ballater electric lighting scheme. The Deeside District Committee had met at Aboyne on 27 June and discussed twenty-five poles being erected from a point west of Ballater Bridge to Glenmuick Manse. As the South Deeside Road was very narrow in several places and the poles were unsightly, it was suggested that they be kept on the north side of the river up to the golf course and then cross over at the manse. The matter was ongoing.

On Sunday, 28 June, however, four days after the 600th anniversary of Bannockburn, a cataclysm was caused by the inglorious assassination of Archduke Franz Ferdinand of Austria and his wife, who was pregnant with their fourth child, in Sarajevo. Iona was warned by her father about the grave international danger, yet she wrote positively to Gavin about the romantic attachment of the late couple. Unlike most of the aristocracy of the Austro-Hungarian Empire they did not marry for wealth or power but for love. She was of low birth status relative to him, having been Countess Sophie Chotek, a lady-in-waiting to Princess Stephanie, a member of an old Bohemian family of noble descent. Sophie could not become Empress of Austria and Queen of Hungary, and nor could her son become Emperor and King. The Archduke had his faults and was spurned by Viennese society, although about a year before he and his wife were very popular royal guests at Windsor.

The Black Hand secret society's aim was to recover Bosnia from the Austro-Hungarian Empire and recreate the greater Serbia. Ironically 28 June was the most sacred day in the Serbian Orthodox calendar, commemorating the crushing of greater Serbia seven centuries before. The Archduke's visit was thus a great provocation. He planned to initiate reforms when his uncle died, but they would have pacified Bosnian Serbs, and the Black Hand wanted armed revolution.

Iona thought what a tragic, pitiful figure was the nineteen year old assassin, Gavrilo Princip, compared to Gavin. His tortured life had been the opposite of the freedom and good health enjoyed by the young in the Scottish Highlands. He had been part of an oppressed Serbian peasant family. His parents had to pay imperial taxes and could not afford to feed him, so at the age of thirteen he was sent to Sarajevo to live with a brother. His animosity increased when martial law was imposed to control Bosnian Serbs, and terminal tuberculosis intensified his determination to be a martyr. Now he stood outside a patisserie, fortified by a sandwich which was a travesty of the sacred bread which the royal couple received earlier at a special Mass to mark their fourteenth wedding anniversary. As a symbolic prelude to the inexorable machinery of war, the Archduke's chauffeur took the wrong turning, stopped near Princip and tried to reverse, but the gears jammed and the assassin took revenge for himself and suffering families.

He wished the couple to share his premature death. The tragic end of their romance, a victim of international politics, was the first of millions. When it was established that Serbia had provided the conspirators' arms, it was the pretext rather than the cause for war. The Austro-Hungarian Empire got the support of its ally Germany against Serbia, and it in turn had a pact with Russia which was allied with France and Britain. Thus instead of inciting rebellion in Bosnia alone, the opportunistic assassin precipitated the Great War. Yet the spirit of Bannockburn would help bring aid to oppressed peoples.

Iona understood the irony of Gavin's request to be kept informed about her area, for cheerful and light-hearted news was now even more important to him. He learned of a heatwave at the end of June which concluded in a thunderstorm on 2 July, but the rain helped the crops and the contrasting weather enabled the scenery, so much prized by tourists, to recover quickly from the frost. Quite a number of larger houses in Ballater were let for three or four months, and most of the big houses were wired already for electricity.

She was glad that early on 8 July an attempt by two suffragettes to set fire to and blow up the Burns Cottage near Ayr was foiled by the nightwatchman! In contrast on the evening of 13 July Morag attended a hoeing match in a field near Ballater, a male cousin being an entrant. Competition for prizes was keen, but to add to the tone of rustic innocence and humour there was a prize for the best looking hoer and one for the hoer with the largest family. Morag's cousin did not win anything.

On Friday, 17 July, Aberdeen and a number of other Scottish cities broke up for the summer holiday. In Gordons' shop several strangers discussed St Swithin's Day, 15 July. She explained there was some evidence that Swithin's remains were moved inside Winchester Cathedral on or around 15 July 971, but a legend had grown that rain on 15 July and for forty subsequent days, a sign of God's displeasure, persuaded monks to leave the body where it was. This situation produced the maxim that if rain fell on 15 July it would prevail more or less for forty days. Two tourists in the shop agreed that it had been dry on 15 July, and so the breakdown of weather afterwards disproved the adage. A third holidaymaker, however, observed that rain had fallen in Aberdeen shortly before midnight on 15 July. Morag disliked pedantry and gave a comical nonplussed look at the ceiling, before stating it was the general case that showery weather could be expected at that time of year.

At the beginning of August the general outlook for the Twelfth was indeed glorious, with no disease among the birds. Yet with Britain's commitment to protect Belgian integrity the international news was about Armageddon. On 2 and 3 August Royal Naval Reservists from Fraserburgh, Peterhead and Aberdeen left Aberdeen Joint Station for Portsmouth, Britain declaring war on the 4th. The day before Iona received a short letter from Gavin, which indicated that he was busy. On 29 July he had returned from Willsworthy to Crownhill. She was warned that when his battalion was abroad for security he could only send limited information. If there was a delay in the arrival of any of his letters, it might not be due to bad news, but because he was on the move or engaged in action. The suffragettes' militant behaviour would soon seem like childish pinpricks compared to coming events. Instead of bemoaning his lot, he was thankful that they had enjoyed a blissful holiday, and he asked her to convey his thanks to her father for his foresight in enabling it to happen. 'The darker the prospect the brighter shines your spirit. If I fall in battle, I have seen my vision.'

His battalion received the mobilization order by telephone at 5.20 p.m. on 4 August at Crownhill. Next day the mobilization equipment and small arms ammunition were drawn. About half of the battalion's strength consisted of reservists, and the first batch arrived from the depot at Aberdeen on 6 August. He thought how ironic it was that in a sermon in June the Rev. Farquharson spoke of 6 August as the day they would celebrate Christ's Transfiguration which anticipated his death on Calvary and the resurrection of the dead on the last day. Gavin was reminded that he had to take up his own cross. The next day another batch of reservists arrived.

In her next letter Iona quoted Psalm 91.2, 'I will say of the Lord, He is my refuge and my fortress: my God; in him will I trust.' She also recommended him to read from St Paul's Epistle to the Romans the latter part of chapter 8, especially verse 35, 'Who shall separate us from the love of Christ? shall tribulation, or distress, or persecution, or famine, or nakedness, or peril, or sword?'

In contrast she commented that on 6 August a lot of local people were diverted from the day's religious significance by making such a run on sugar that her father had to ration it. Many people used it at every meal. Food prices had risen, but the initial rush to lay in a stock of provisions had abated, because reassurance had been given about the extent of food supplies in the country. While the shop would be visited by fewer tourists, it did not matter. Hotels faced a more serious situation. Later she remarked that it was ideal weather for the Twelfth, but activity was much reduced. Keepers were out on the Balmoral moors, and a large box of grouse was sent by rail from Ballater to the King, arriving next day.

Also on 13 August the 1st Gordon Highlanders began to move to France. At Southampton the men lined up and the King's telegram was read. They were to fight for the safety and honour of his Empire. Duty was their watchword. He would follow their every movement with greatest interest. He prayed that God would bless and guard them, and bring them back victorious. Gavin was to inform Iona that when he raised his glengarry in three rousing cheers for His Majesty, he was proud to be a Gordon. The black cap had a band of diced red and white. Where the horizontal red stripe kept crossing vertical red stripes was a black square. The badge on the left side had been described by Mr Gordon when Gavin first entered the shop. The dark tartan was that of the Black Watch, consisting of black and blue with green, but with the variant of a yellow line.

Each man carried in his active service pay book a little printed paper by Lord Kitchener. Courage, energy and patience were needed. The British Army's honour depended on individual conduct. Equally, very friendly relations were to be maintained with those they helped. Looting was to be regarded as disgraceful. To maintain health temptations of wine and women were to be resisted. God was to be feared and the King honoured.

Most of the 1st Gordon Highlanders, including Gavin, left Southampton at 2.45 p.m. on the hired ship *Abinsi*, the rest aboard *SS Mombassa*, which were under sealed orders with a naval escort. The gentle, playful swell at the start of the voyage gave way to the symphony of the sea. His initial feelings of the unpredictable and precarious were assuaged by the deeper harmony of the mystic infinity of wave patterns and the endless roar. He hummed a medley of tunes, including his regimental march 'Highland Laddie' and battle march 'Cock o' the North.' The racing music accorded with the joyful spirit of freedom which moved in wind and sea. He felt calm as he recalled how Iona's still spirit was at one with the peaceful tumult of waterfalls. War was life in little. Whatever tragedies befell individuals the blast of conflict would be lost in the awesome, silent heavens, and man's noble destiny would be reasserted.

Packed like sheep on the vessel most of the other occupants were not so philosophical. Older men tended to be grim and said little, some wondering if the national euphoria might be misplaced and many of them could be slaughtered. Young ones were filled with a sense of adventure, particularly as they were going abroad for the first time, and tended to give brave smiles.

They arrived at 4.15 a.m. next day at Boulogne and disembarked, camping at St Martin on the outskirts. The Entente Cordiale had been formed between Britain and France in 1904, and King George V had recently visited Paris to cement the relationship. On the 16th the battalion went by train from Boulogne to Aulnoye in the zone of concentration. Then the troops marched, halting only at dark and moving on at dawn. The sun's burning heat in this early period took a lot out of them, turning them very brown and even black. Yet he liked the honest marching sound as opposed to the pretentious goose-step used formally in the German Army. He contrasted the train journey to Ballater and peaceful walks, however, with the continental train journey and marches to war. He was behind the sergeant who smoked his pipe, which became irritating, but he knew that it was nothing compared to the smoke of battle.

On 21 August they passed through Maubeuge to Goegnies-Chaussée on the Belgian frontier. The day was hot and sultry, and marching on a cobbled road was tiring, but he was better prepared after long Highland stony walks. Also, he knew the importance of soaping socks and putting them on precisely to prevent blisters. In compensation the soldiers' fine physique and brown, cheerful faces, distinctive glengarries and swinging kilts made a positive impression in Maubeuge, and women offered wine and food. Sergeant Mackay graciously accepted the gifts, but turned down kisses, explaining loudly that he was married. With magnanimous sweeps of a hand holding a long French loaf, he indicated that they should embrace comrades around him.

As Gavin diverted some of them to Donald and others who were happy to participate, he saw the brief encounters and contrasting them with his relationship thought, 'They but share a mortal kiss, while we enjoy immortal bliss.'

Then young girls, stirred by so many Scottish soldiers, daintily skipped with outstretched arms to keep up with the marchers for hundreds of yards. The girls' long white dresses stood out from the subdued khaki, and their light spirits further marked them as individuals. Reminded of Iona's light movements and her remarks about the dance of life, his spirit rose, although he walked in a long line of ranks of four amid a forest of rifles.

The next night's halt was at the village of Hyon, less than a mile south of Mons. The aim was to defend the latter place. He was struck by the irony of its Latin name meaning hill. Mons was the centre of a coal mining district, and he realized the further irony of how the pointed slag heaps contrasted with the glories of dark Lochnagar. It was like Purgatory after Heaven.

While he marched, however, the food situation in Gordons' shop continued to ease. There were large supplies of butter, eggs and even sugar in the country. The outbreak of war stopped shipments from Denmark, but, as the Royal Navy ensured that the North Sea was relatively safe, accumulated Danish butter was flooding in, so prices had fallen considerably. Moreover, British sea power removed enemy commerce from the oceans.

Yet the news from Belgium about the general German advance was desperate. When Iona learned of Mons, she anxiously read about the little red-brick town in a book. It was originally a Roman camp in the third century, but it grew around an abbey formed about 650 by St Waudru, daughter of the Count of Hainaut. It was attacked and occupied by various European countries, including the English, in the sixteenth to eighteenth centuries. An educational centre, it had the fine buildings of the Church of St Waudru and town hall.

News of approaching large German forces turned a great advance by the British Expeditionary Force into a defensive operation. The 1st Gordon Highlanders got its initial sight of the Germans on the night of 22 August, and about 7 p.m. saw an enemy aeroplane brought down. Sunday the 23rd came in with mist and scattered showers. Whereas Princip's bullets had broken one Sabbath calm, now another was to be shattered by war. The Gordons stood to arms at 4.30 a.m. and moved off about 7, taking up a position behind Mons and by the road to Beaumont, facing east-north-east. With the 2nd Royal Scots on the right they cleared the foreground of anything which gave head cover, such as willow, beans or wheat, to produce a clear rifle range apart from buildings. Then they dug small trenches. In green woods behind were many guns.

In the wider scene all bridges over the canal which had not been blown up were commanded by machine guns and barricaded by interlocking huge cable drums. The canal, bordered by railway sidings and industrial rear yards, was black with slime and stank of chemical refuse. It contrasted with the pure, serene Dee. The citizens of Mons went to Mass in black Sunday clothes. The bells might as well have tolled for the coming slaughter.

Some of the Gordons, including Gavin's company, had finished entrenching and had lunch, while others had nearly completed work and were about to eat, when word came that the enemy was approaching.

They were told to fall in and take their places in the line. Two minutes later they saw the Germans in grey field uniforms crowding over the top of the hills in front in very dense formation. A terrible artillery duel began. About noon German troops began advancing by rushes obliquely across the front of the Gordons and the 2nd Royal Scots in the direction of Hill 93. They went forward in companies of 150 men in files five deep. The defenders steadied their rifles on the edges of the trenches and were still until officers gave the word, when devastating fire was made with two machine guns for each battalion and fifteen aimed bullets per rifle per minute, almost in enfilade. The Germans thought that the rifle fire itself came from machine guns. The enemy made easy targets, many bullets passing through one man and lodging in the next one, or finding two billets as the succinct expression put it. Machine gun fire caused them to go over in heaps like sheep. The first company was blasted away. Other companies kept advancing very slowly, using dead comrades as cover, but they had no chance. The victims tended to stagger before they fell, travestying the dance of life. The riflemen fired with cool precision, although their weapons became hot. If any of the Huns used rifles, they only fired from the hip. Extra help was given by a battery firing shrapnel over the Gordons from the high ridge of Bois la Haut. So dense were the enemy ranks that gaps made by exploding shells were plainly visible. The enemy was stopped. Shortly before 4 p.m., when the leading company of a German battalion advanced on Bois la Haut, the left-centre of the Gordons lay low until the company was within 500 yards, and then rapid fire pinned survivors to the ground.

The German artillery was much more formidable. During the day Gordons heard shells whining through the air and bursting all around them with huge bangs and great flashes. They ducked to avoid showers of shrapnel consisting of lumps of iron and rusty nails. Sometimes three or four shells landed at the same time. Adding to the uncertainty were instances when they ducked on hearing an approaching shell, but as there was no explosion they cautiously raised their heads, wondering if there might be a belated blast or whether the shell was a dud. Casualties were light under the circumstances. What angered the Gordons was the treatment of a nearby nunnery which had been converted into a hospital. The Germans must have seen the Red Cross flag flying, but they shelled the hospital from a relatively short range and killed everyone inside.

North and west of Mons the German pressure had been heavier, and the town was abandoned. In late afternoon a Gordons' platoon, including Sergeant Mackay, Gavin, Donald and Hector, escorted the 23rd Battery

Royal Field Artillery which was in a dangerous position on the top of Bois la Haut. The column tried to reach the north-south road through Hyon by a sunken lane. One section passed through, but then fire came from a party of Germans barricaded at right angles to the end of the lane. The horses of the first gun were shot. When Gavin and others struggled to bring the remaining horses under control, as they screamed and repeatedly reared and plunged in terror, he recalled the incident in Ballater when frightened horses died in a stable fire. At least that had been an accident, but the sufferings of dumb, defenceless animals in war were particularly cruel. Hector's exceptional strength and Mackay's rallying voice helped, besides the spur of the dangerous situation, in the very arduous task of dragging the carcasses to the banks. A small attack was repulsed and five prisoners were captured. They repositioned the gun and surviving horses and the battery withdrew.

At 9 p.m. the 1st Gordon Highlanders and 2nd Royal Scots were ordered back to Nouvelles. The younger Gordons were proud to have stayed cool and assisted in keeping the flower of the German Army at bay. They were told, however, that they were to keep on retiring until the Germans opposed to them were drawn away from the Germans fighting Russia, to let the French in between and thus cut them off.

At 5.30 a.m. on 24 August the 8th Brigade was ordered to withdraw, but the Gordons did not move until several hours later. They were lucky to disengage unscathed after some German shelling. Following a long march and no sleep the previous night, they were very tired when they reached Amfroipret, on the Forêt de Mormal's north fringe, at 2 a.m. on the 25th. The great forest was a wedge forcing General Sir Douglas Hague's I Corps to turn east. The 1st Gordon Highlanders was part of General Sir Horace Smith-Dorrien's II Corps, which later on the 25th moved towards Le Cateau.

The troops were glad to have left the black country around Mons for the rich, rolling fields of France. Fruit was plentiful, even growing on the wayside. Yet they were in no mood to sing. Apart from fatigue, which meant that their packs and nine pound rifles seemed to weigh more, the weather varied between scorching heat—the sweat poured off—and sudden downpours, the foe was close behind and the night sky was lit by villages in flames. At one point Sergeant Mackay tried to encourage those around him by joking to Donald that he was out of step. Gavin thought that the increasing part of humanity caught up in the war had forgotten the spiritual dance of life, particularly as there were large numbers of pensive refugees who had conscripted a sad motley of transport. He gazed enviously, however, at those on bicycles, as he recalled cycling with Iona in Glen Muick and along Deeside. There was a tragic atmosphere about the *via dolorosa*, but her bright spirit shone above the cross he had to bear. Each step took him further away from her, but so also was the enemy. If the British Expeditionary Force and Royal Navy did their duty well, the Germans would be prevented from invading Britain. The idea of Scotland especially being subjected to wanton damage and atrocities was abominable.

Later Iona learned of confused reports about the Angels of Mons. It was uncertain if the apparition was authentic or the result of hallucinations due to tiredness and great nervous strain. She asked Gavin if he or any of his comrades had seen the vision, but he replied in the negative, reminding her that he had his own angel already. When she discussed the matter with Ishbel in the shop, her friend was sceptical about an apparition, because divine ministry through angels closed with the New Testament. She maintained that God did not work through such direct revelations to the multitude, because then he might be taken for granted. We had to seek him spiritually. St Paul wrote in Romans 8.25, 'if we hope for that we see not, then do we with patience wait for it.' Moreover, the Holy Spirit within intercedes 'for us with groanings which cannot be uttered' (v. 26).

Light was later shed when Ishbel lent Iona her copy of Arthur Machen's *The Angels of Mons: The Bowmen and Other Legends of the War* (London, 1915). He stated that 'The Bowmen' had first appeared in the *Evening News* on 29 September 1914. The story had no factual foundation. A soldier saw beyond the trench a long line of shining shapes. They were bowmen brought by St George from Agincourt to help the English. The bowmen had been misinterpreted as angels, reports of which were thus mere hearsay. Ishbel also lent Iona her copy of Harold Begbie's *On the Side of the Angels* (London, 1915), which rejected Machen's case, but the evidence of sightings which he gave was unverifiable. Ishbel learned that when the Society for Psychical Research investigated the matter in 1915, it received no first-hand testimony. Later she said that while there were some stories about angels before Machen's piece appeared, and there were reports from French soldiers about apparitions, she believed that the story developed through rumours and mass hysteria. Tales of battlefield visions occurred in medieval and ancient warfare. Much later in 1930 she drew Iona's attention to a *Daily News* report that according to a staff member of the War Office official archives contained no record to support any statement that an apparition was seen at Mons by British troops. Ishbel remarked that it appeared the angels were a fiction arising from a misunderstanding of another fiction.

In retreating from Mons the II Corps was exhausted, and so on 26 August the commander decided to stand and fight, outnumbered and outgunned, at and around Le Cateau. Hopefully the corps would then be able to retreat in less danger. The position allotted to the 1st Gordon Highlanders was about 1,000 yards long and just north-west of the village of Audencourt, which was six miles west of Le Cateau. About 5 a.m. the Gordons went to prepared trenches, but they gave finishing touches. It was a good position with a large field of fire. Heavy enemy artillery opened at 8 a.m. They were not hard-pressed initially, because the Germans saw a better opportunity to the west at Caudry. A number of times Gordons' fire had a marked effect, but elsewhere the foe advanced, some machine guns even being used from the spire of Le Cateau church, and a further general retreat was essential. At 4.30 p.m. Gavin's company was ordered by the brigade major to retire, although one of the four platoons could not be contacted. At dusk the rest had to crawl quite some distance on their stomachs in the open, with bullets spitting all around them, before they reached cover.

He was later to understand that the brigade major had been shot dead when riding on to order the rest of the battalion to withdraw from the trenches. When Gavin and others had got safely away and the roll was called, there were only about 170. Next morning another group joined them, bringing the total to about 210. They marched all day fighting a rearguard action, and they lay in trenches at night until all the cavalry brigade had arrived.

Then they saw a lone horseman coming over the brow of a hill, and, as he rode towards them, Sergeant Mackay exclaimed, 'It's Captain Sandy Phemister!'

The arrival's haggard expression and downcast eyes foretold terrible news, before he said, 'There has been a disaster, boys. We got the order to withdraw very late, and only moved off at 12.30 a.m. We reached Montigny, a little over two miles south of Audencourt, where a family said that British troops had moved through Bertry to the south-east. A man guided us to the Bertry road. At 2 a.m., however, the head of the column was fired on south-west of Bertry. Fire was returned, but, because of the darkness and the unknown strength of the enemy, we were ordered to fall back along the Montigny road. Yet we were very tired and kept on south-west to Clary. Suddenly a field gun faced us down the road. It was seized before it could be fired, although the rear of the column was fired on from the south. Fire was returned while the head tried to break through Clary. An hour long firefight ensued, but we were outnumbered and the Germans were mainly firing from cover from all sides. We surrendered after suffering heavy casualties. I was taken prisoner, but managed to escape. Possibly others did so.'

Mackay commented, 'The Gordons' continued resistance helped other troops whose withdrawal from Audencourt had started. Yet the disaster is all the more saddening because we have got off comparatively lightly at Mons. So many men of a high standard have been removed, particularly the officers. The Highlanders' reputation is so great that the German generals have probably picked them out for special attention, in the hope of weakening the British Army's strongest links.'

As Gavin and his comrades continued to march that night, he gazed aloft and recalled the myth that everything which was wasted on earth, such as unfulfilled dreams, was treasured on the moon. He smiled at the legend of Endymion, a shepherd son, to whom Zeus gave eternal life and youth by allowing him to sleep perpetually on Mount Latmos, and Selene the moon goddess came down nightly to embrace him and bear fifty daughters. The classical images vanished from his mind as the stuff of dreams, while he gazed at the moon which had no protective atmospheric shield, and countless bodies had struck and cratered it, producing the semblance of a vast battleground.

Yet then clouds intervened and emphasized its peaceful silvery light. He remembered how the angel Gabriel used the image of a cloud when he appeared before the Virgin Mary and said, 'The Holy Ghost shall come upon thee, and the power of the Highest shall overshadow thee: therefore also that holy thing which shall be born of thee shall be called the Son of God' (Luke 1.35). Gavin understood why the moon appeared so often in paintings of the Virgin Mary. Her face, moreover, was a constant sphere ruling love's forever flowing tide. He thought of Our Lady of Dolours with her seven sorrows, which were more than matched by her seven joys, and of Our Lady of Mercy gently spreading out her mantle and gathering sinners beneath it.

He remembered Iona say that when she was younger she associated the goddess Diana with the moon and chastity, so he took out a photograph of her and mused, 'The moon shines on your face in France and the eyes a purer light return. Your name is a chain of stars which maps the shining compass of my ardour. Without your name my love would wander lost through the heavens.'

The Gordons reached the Somme at Ham at 9 a.m. on 28 August. After a rest they marched another twelve miles or so to bivouac for the night beside the village of Genvry, north of Noyon. Moving away from snoring Hector Gavin fell asleep, but his subconscious woke and sublime images filled his dream. Through the grandeur of the night his spirit winged to the Dee. Light, water and earth expressed the Holy Spirit's omnipresence. The moon reclaimed its haunts and the scenery around Ballater was bathed in glory. While the stars cast their spell he roamed by the river where he saw his joy, his vision of everness.

'Walk forth in the moonlight and scorn the shades, for they are envious of your beauty and would claim you for their own. Like the tranquil moon bide by me. To lovers' souls the moon is more potent than the sun. Let us walk on the banks of time while the beam follows us over the water. Sublime is your form, but in the eyes I see you whole, for they reflect love's infinity. Their mystic hues speak as if you were to whisper in my ear till dawn.'

The retreating Gordons reached the south bank of the Aisne at Courtieux. Then they entered a beautiful country of forests and rivers, but hoofs, feet and wheels threw up clouds of dust and shady trees created a stagnant atmosphere. The men swayed for lack of sleep towards the end of each march, yet their spirits remained resolute.

In early September she was greatly relieved to receive a letter from him. On Sunday, 30 August there had been a special edition of the *Times* which gave the impression that the British Expeditionary Force had been practically annihilated. The Press Bureau promptly issued an account of the great heroism and skill shown by British soldiers round Mons, Maubeuge and Cambrai. Soon the *Times* story was attributed to coming indirectly from prisoners with an inaccurate view, and ironically it was a strong spur to national recruitment, but it had caused much anxiety.

In his letter Gavin recounted details of his reverie and dream, and he expressed gratitude for their Highland walks in a practical sense, because they had helped train him for long marches on the Continent. He added the nostalgic remark, 'You led me on peaceful paths and wherever we roamed was fairer than the gardens of kings.'

Commenting on recent events he stated that it had been a miracle he was not hit by bullets when withdrawing from near Audencourt. Echoing Sergeant Mackay he commented that what was particularly tragic about the German ambush of the bulk of his battalion was that so many fine officers were missing. Their main concern had always been for the safety of the men whom they exhorted where possible to take cover, while they exposed themselves with extraordinary courage to enemy fire. A danger for all the men was that the kilt exposed knees as a clear target for bullets. Prejudice was strong among the Highland regiments in favour of the traditional picturesque kilt which linked them to military glory won in past conflicts. The men had recently found, however, in battles and severe forced marches, especially in the rain, it was a considerable hindrance. In attack the heavy soaked kilt impeded the soldier's movements, and it chafed his limbs on a long march or hot pursuit. While it put fear into some Germans, it caused amusement to others. The men would prefer trousers.

Naturally he could not disclose his present whereabouts, but they had kept on retiring. The rumour was that they were going back to be reinforced and fully equipped. Much of their equipment had been left in the scramble for life. It was pitiful to see whole families tramping to refuge from death and destruction. Many places had been laid waste by the enemy.

In her reply Iona thanked him for inventing the neologism of everness about her, but she advised him not to mention it to his comrades, because they might misunderstand and could conclude that he was suffering from shell shock!

While he thought it was miraculous to be unscathed, she had read of a wounded French officer who said that British soldiers themselves had performed miracles. They went into fighting as if it was a football match, and the more they had of it the more they seemed to like it. The cause was strengthened by the fact that while the Germans were proud of their culture, they were philistines towards the cultures of countries they invaded. Louvain, the St Andrews or Oxford of Belgium, so rich in literary and artistic treasures, plus beautiful historic buildings, had been set on fire. Germans were creating hell on earth, instead of spreading the Holy Spirit's loving flames.

She was glad to tell him that on Friday evening, 4 September, there was an enthusiastic recruitment meeting in Ballater's Victoria Hall. Beforehand sixty National Reservists mustered in the barrack square, and led by pipers marched through the burgh, then filed into the hall. Watching children were excited by the romantic glamour, but they were ignorant of the reality, the pain and suffering, the totality of war. Her father sat at the back inside, learning that 2,000 recruits were needed to bring the Aberdeenshire contribution up to war strength. The British Army was small and needed large reinforcements to deal with this unprecedented threat to the British Empire. Reassurances were given that employers would look after families dependent on men who joined up. After the meeting eighteen young men enrolled, three reservists rejoined and late on Saturday morning there was a solemn atmosphere in the shop as word came that large numbers of young men were enrolling.

Never had people been in greater need of God. It was common to hear and read of churches attracting large congregations. While Germans thought that God was on their side, many Britons likened the Kaiser to the Devil. True greatness was based on humility, not on worship of Mammon. It was a fight not only for national existence, but also for righteousness. Many sons had joined the services and many daughters had become nurses. She thought that her place continued to be in the shop, because her father's war wound sometimes forced him to rest, but she knitted comforts for soldiers abroad in her spare time.

On 5 September the 1st Gordon Highlanders received reinforcements in the wooded area south of Tournan. The British Expeditionary Force turned about on the 6th, the German Army having wheeled aside. More reinforcements arrived and on the 8th the troops marched with the advanced guard to the Petit Morin, where the enemy made a stand, but in the afternoon it began to withdraw because of pressure further west, and the Gordons crossed despite heavy fire. They reached Oulchy-la-Ville on the 11th and next day became Army Troops. Too weak to act as a battalion in battle, they provided guards for German prisoners being sent down to the base, the largest number being 783, who were escorted to St-Nazaire on the Atlantic coast.

In a letter Gavin stated that many French people had fled. Those they did see tended to show their hatred for Germans by hooting at prisoners, but cheered the guards. He and his comrades were not allowed to fraternize with prisoners, and had no wish to do so. One day, however, he was standing over a group sitting on the ground, when a German with a disarming smile held up a photograph of his sweetheart to him. She was a pretty but serious blonde. Gavin showed him a photograph of Iona in return, as love interests were a neutral subject. The German gazed at Iona's angelic features and appreciatively nodded his head, before looking curiously up at him, as if he was very lucky.

During the month the battalion's strength grew. On the 26th it was reorganized on the basis of headquarters, a machine gun section and three companies. It was well on the return to normal. On the 30th it rejoined the 8th Brigade. By this time the British Expeditionary Force was about to begin its move towards the coast.

Iona wrote that his reverie and dream beneath the moon contrasted with an incident in Aberdeen on the night of 10 September. A large crowd gathered at Schoolhill, because it was believed that an airship had been sighted. A sentry at the railway tunnel was alerted and he fired a shot. When the clouds cleared, however, it was just the moon! The citizens were more nervous than youngest soldiers at the front.

Later that month she recorded that the merciless German bombardment of Reims had even included the Cathedral, and only its four charred walls and towers remained. Such sacrilege was regarded as worse than the sacking of Louvain. In a further letter she commented that in these times when truth was stranger than fiction, it was not surprising that the press carried Thomas Hardy's letter protesting against the attack on the Cathedral as a loss to the world of a very fine specimen of medieval architecture. When he was young French architecture of the best period was much studied, and some traceries and mouldings as those at Reims were copied by architects' pupils, including him. If the destruction was a premeditated example of the German ruling class's wilful power, it indicated a disastrous effect of the writings of the megalomaniac Nietzsche and his followers who had for the time being supplanted true philosophers such as Kant and Schopenhauer. For Iona it was not so much the building itself, but the assault on spiritual and religious values which mattered. Years later Ishbel said she believed that Hardy had misunderstood Nietzsche, because he was strongly opposed to nationalism and power politics. His sister Elisabeth married a leading chauvinist and anti-Semite, Bernhard Förster, and, after his suicide in 1889, driven by greed she worked to remould Nietzsche in Förster's image by misusing her brother's literary estate. For a long time she misled a host of readers, including commentators.

Iona lamented with Gavin at how innocents suffered in war. Ironically much hardship was caused to German women and children. Prices had risen very sharply, and in Hamburg for example fresh meat was unavailable because the cattle had been requisitioned, the tiny supply of milk and butter had been reserved for hospitals, and there were not milk and prepared food for babies.

The 1st Gordon Highlanders took part in the British Expeditionary Force's move north, entraining at Pont Saint-Maxence, near Senlis, to the Abbeville area, and then moved by road, on foot or in buses provided by the French, in the direction of Béthune. On 12 October Gavin thought fondly of the peaceful Royal Bridge at Ballater, when his battalion was ordered to seize the bridge over the Lawe at Fosse. The enemy held the bridge and houses in Fosse on the far side and a nearby wood. It took the Gordons and two other battalions to expel him. Then Gavin saw a dead German officer and he was struck by the helmet's badge. It featured a spread eagle with crown, one claw holding the sceptre and the other the ball and cross, the whole being beautifully gilded. He contrasted it with the eagle of mythology which represented spiritual power opposing the physical and material dark powers. The eagle always won, but not in this misused case. Iona was later told that while some of his comrades took trophies, he found the practice repugnant.

The advance was resumed next day over flat country intersected by dykes. Movement was checked within two miles and the left of the Gordons was counter-attacked. The dykes had often to be bridged with boards, and smoke shells or bombs to hide such work were unavailable.

Gavin learned that on 14 October a company advancing from Béthune was exposed in an open field. The captain saw a rise in the ground ahead and ordered the men to follow him. Twenty-one who heard him, for they were in extended formation, ran after him to cover. He was shot dead when observing the foe. The rest lay for a while, but then risked fire rather than face probable capture, and fled back over two fields to their old trenches. Eighteen of twenty-one got back, but only seven escaped being hit. Gavin remembered Mr Gordon's admiration for the Macleans' maxim that they never turned their backs to a foe. If Mr Gordon had been in that situation, doubtless he would have treated it as a worthy exception to the rule.

On 15 October the battalion reached the main La Bassée-Estaires road. On the 22nd the French cavalry appeared unable to hold Fromelles, and the II Corps retired under darkness to this line. The Germans attacked on the morning of the 24th, but the British artillery was mainly responsible for holding them off. As they were easy daylight targets in this plain, the Germans made a series of night attacks. One involved the 1st Gordon Highlanders. It was on the left of the 8th Brigade's front, with a gap dividing it from the 15th Sikhs of the Jullundur Brigade. Promised barbed wire, which was so scarce that it was taken from field fencing, did not arrive. A German attack broke through the Gordons' right company, and because of pressure all the Gordons withdrew to the main Neuve Chapelle-Armentières road. About midnight the 4th Middlesex supported by the Gordons regained lost trenches. The Scots learned by hard experience to operate effectively.

Gavin informed Iona that the Germans had shelled their positions at a terrible rate, although the danger on the other side was evenly shared. The men who carried rations to them had to keep well under cover, as they were always shot at. While they got plenty to eat, the rain fell heavily and there was no shelter. In contrast, as writing paper was scarce in the trenches, he was amused to see a comrade write a letter to his girlfriend round the margins of part of an old newspaper which had blown over from an enemy trench. A pencil was used and the strips from the edges were torn, forming an unbroken ribbon to signify his unwavering love. More formally Gavin was proud of his comrades. They were heroic in action and the wounded were just as brave in suffering.

In a lull in his exertions it was sweet to receive a letter from Iona. The very handwriting on the envelope was an agent of the Holy Spirit breathing peace through him. She knew how important it was for him to see life as a whole, and appreciate the background care being shown to him and his comrades. She was glad to convey news of members of his battalion who were prisoners of war in Germany. One of them was not allowed to disclose where he was interned, but another was at Leo-Konvikt, Paderborn, and he could send a postcard once a fortnight. Ishbel had told her that Konvikt meant seminary! Paderborn was in Central Germany, taking its name from the numerous springs immediately to the north of the Cathedral. It was the birthplace of the Holy Roman Empire when Charlemagne or Charles the Great met Pope Leo III there in 799 to discuss the founding of a German nation. As the first Holy Roman Emperor Charlemagne promoted the arts and education. Particularly in view of Gavin's remark that he and his fellows would prefer to wear trousers, for his amusement she stated that in a prisoner of war camp at Doeberitz near Berlin Highlanders were offered German Army trousers to protect them from the cold, but the otter was indignantly refused!

For Highlanders at the front Lady Tullibardine was collecting 15,000 hose-tops to protect against catching chills by exposing knees to wintry weather. They were to be knitted in khaki or other dull shades of wool and sent out on 14 November. In view of the short time she suggested that donations be sent to her to enable the wool to be knitted by the many fisher girls who had been made redundant by war. Parcels were to be sent to her at Kettering, Northamptonshire.

It was a great shock to the inhabitants of peaceful Ballater that on 15 October *HMS Hawke*, a light cruiser, was sunk by a German submarine off the Aberdeenshire coast. Seventy were saved, but 500 were missing. It was learned on 20 October that two German submarines had followed three rafts bearing survivors in hope of sinking any British warships which might approach to rescue them. Ironically the submarines were sunk at

Scapa Flow by British warships. After twenty-four hours of exposure at sea, however, about 150 men spread across three rafts were tragically reduced to a total of only twenty.

The disaster helped to bring closer ties of humanity with Allies and make distances seem to shrink. Iona reported the tragedy of Antwerp being bombarded night and day. The editor of the *Journal de Mons* was in Aberdeen. He was part of a convoy of wounded and sick Belgians driven from the hospitals of Antwerp and Ostend by the German invasion. In a letter which appeared in the local press he praised the beauty of Aberdeen which he was told compared with Louvain as an intellectual centre.

Iona liked to mention comic ironies to relieve the tragic side. She observed that occasionally soldiers reassured those back home that they were in the pink of condition, ignoring the mortal dangers. The expression had been adopted in an Aberdeen store's advertisement which warned of October's chilly nights and recommended woollen Scottish bath blankets which had been carefully finished during the summer and were thus in the pink of condition. The city's Lord Provost had recently requested blanket donations, old and new, for Kitchener's Army to be sent to the local Red Cross Depot. It was clearly irrelevant whether or not they were carefully finished! Some manufacturers and stores gave the impression in advertisements that customers patronizing them would also be patriotic by keeping the economy going. Iona's father respected the judgement of his customers on the right balance between patriotism and prudence.

Although Gavin somewhat unusually did not smoke, he would not be surprised that there was much talk in the burgh about sending smoking materials to servicemen. Recently, however, when a wife said in the shop that she had included tobacco in a parcel for her husband, Morag tactlessly spoke in her hearing of a wish to attend a dance in Aberdeen. When the customer had left Mr Gordon turned on her, saying that she was empty-headed and frivolous. Morag protested that Aberdonians went to see films and plays, but he replied that such activities did at least engage the mind, and she should spend her spare time knitting comforts for troops like Iona.

Whereas children in Ballater were educated in accordance with church teaching and domestic principles, G.K. Chesterton revealed how the official educational system in Germany consumed childhood. The early hours, huge schools, long lessons and ponderous discipline contradicted the position of children in German homes, for no other country valued them as much.

Iona recalled walking with Gavin among the oaks of Craigendarroch, when she read that pressure on food supplies in Germany was so great that ground acorns were recommended for adding to coffee, while it was affirmed that chestnuts strengthened flour. In her own country during times of famine people used to collect acorns and ground them into flour to make bread, although acorn flour was very bitter.

She knew he would smile on learning that the Acting Secretary of the Cairngorm Club had replied to fears expressed by a neurotic person writing to the press. As regards the apprehension that Zeppelins might land on or in the neighbourhood of our remote mountains, there would be no purpose in observation, dropping bombs or landing soldiers there. Scepticism was expressed about the appearance of lights and discharge of rockets at night from some of the highest mountains. Who and where were the people to receive the signals?

7: The Ypres Salient and Ballater, November-December 1914

The 1st Gordon Highlanders was detached to the 7th Brigade, which was to move north and replace exhausted troops on the Ypres front. The little city's proximity to the Channel ports made it vitally important. In the region of Hooge to the east the 7th Brigade relieved the 20th on 5 November. The battle had begun in good weather, but from about the 5th there were constant rain, sleet and snow creating an enemy for both sides. During the heavy fighting of the 7th and 8th the 1st Gordons remained in support in Shrewsbury Forest. On the 9th it was in the firing line, and on the 11th a German bombardment increased until between 8 and 9 a.m. it was the heaviest ever experienced by the British. Most of the men crouched in inadequate and soon battered trenches. At 9 a.m. German infantry attacked on a broad front. The 4th Division, a highly rated Pomeranian and West Prussian formation, was repulsed by the Gordons. The standard of rifle fire may have fallen off because of losses by the British Expeditionary Force, but it was still good. Attack waves were also broken by shrapnel. The general rebuff of the enemy decided the First Battle of Ypres, although the British did not know it. On the 12th a heavy bombardment caused more casualties among the Gordons than the day before, and on the 13th Germans broke in on the left, but Gavin's company with another drove them out.

The Gordons had gained fresh laurels which were excellent for morale. Heavy shelling continued, but they showed great endurance. A 'Jack Johnson,' a great shell named after a black boxer and fired by a German big gun, could kill, wound or bury them. Repeatedly men had to be dug out from earth and debris which a shell blast heaped up. A hollow ten to twelve feet deep was sometimes made. The fighting was terribly severe. The Germans persistently tried to break through, coming in heaps, sometimes shouting and singing. By experience the Gordons waited until they were not more than fifty yards away, and then turned on their firepower, always putting the wind out of them. They lost heart and rushed back to their trenches. Sometimes the dead were piled up in front of the riflemen–an awesome sight. There were reports of Huns being driven to attack at the point of officers' revolvers.

During this engagement hot food for the Gordons was an exception to the rule, and in some instances they lived for days on rum and ration biscuits which resembled dog biscuits. Sergeant Mackay rallied his men by quipping that they were dogs of war. They did their best to sleep in the open. When necessary they drew on deepest reserves of strength to face attack. They were not relieved by French troops until 20 November. Gavin and the rest were to learn that on the broad front the Germans had not exploited gains, because they thought the British had more reserves than was the case. He knew that he was not allowed to convey such sensitive information in a letter to his parents or Iona. The Gordons marched south-west to Westoutre on the French frontier.

Explaining to Iona that military action had much delayed the writing of his letter, he thanked her for sending a pair of socks. He expressed the conviction that it was much colder there than in Ballater. As his mother was currently unwell, he asked if she could send warm items for his head and throat, preferably of course knitted by her. He added that success in the field maintained high morale, in spite of the elements. His comrades' spirits were further lifted by singing Scottish songs as well as the 'Marseillaise' and 'Tipperary,' but he was inspired more by memories of her singing. When he joined in the Irish song he saw himself as Paddy, her as Molly and thought of Ballater. The item was composed by Jack Judge whose grandparents came from Tipperary. He was performing at The Grand Theatre in Stalybridge, England, and sang it on 31 January 1912. It was popularized in the music hall circuit in Britain and adopted by the 2nd Battalion of the Connaught Rangers Regiment of the British Army. The regiment had connections with Tipperary Town. The Rangers went to France at the start of the war, and the song's rousing strains meant that it was becoming the Army's unofficial anthem. Finally, she would be glad to learn that British horses were better maintained than those of the French and Germans.

In a letter which accompanied the socks she deplored that on Sunday morning, All Saints' Day, 1 November, at the time of High Mass in the Cathedral of St Martin in Ypres, German shells began to fall. The enemy had apparently chosen that time, risking the lives of old men, women and children who were about to pray for their dead. Ishbel had told her that the Cathedral contained the tomb of Cornelius Jansen, Bishop of Ypres and father of Jansenism, a Roman Catholic movement of unorthodox tendencies. In view of the onslaught on the city, it was ironic that he and his followers exalted the initiation of grace made available by Christ the Redeemer and placed less emphasis on human responsibility. The shelling was a sign of desperation. The Kaiser was reported to be a shadow of his old self, suffering from insomnia. There were no confident imperial messages about Germany's God. He was worried by great losses and the death of many friends. Hubris led to a slow nemesis.

Iona was pleased to learn that British horses were well looked after, but she was sad to learn of a report from Norfolk, Virginia, of 800 horses bound for France being lost in a fire on the steamer *Rembrandt*. She was reminded of the stable fire in Ballater. Later that month she told him that Miss Clark had spoken in the shop of Our Dumb Friends' League starting in 1912 the Blue Cross Fund which aimed to care for wounded horses in wartime. The French Minister of War had authorized installing eight horse hospitals in France, and donations from the public were being sought. The hospitals would save much suffering, fatigue and starvation, the mortally wounded being humanely destroyed. The poor, innocent creatures did not understand the war and wondered at some men's cruelty. It was conservatively estimated that there were one million horses engaged in the conflict.

While life continued outwardly peaceful in her area, with municipal elections having been held in Ballater, people were increasingly affected by the war. There was talk of enlistment having caused a shortage of rural labour, with the fear that a prolonged conflict would worsen the situation. Farmers visiting the shop spoke of their dilemma. The military authorities urged them to send their sons and servants, for they were more acclimatized to the outdoor life than city dwellers, besides being used to hard manual work, whereas the Board of Agriculture urged more ploughing and raising more stock, which needed labour.

She informed Gavin that the Admiralty and War Office sent telegrams to post offices to relieve public anxiety on Sundays. There had been some discussion in the shop about the Sabbath rest being partly broken by the production of Sunday newspaper war editions. Miss Clark was opposed to them, but Mr Gordon said that as the war continued on the Sabbath, it was right for those at home to continue to take an interest in them. Members of the clergy were not unanimous about the matter. On 17 November the Deeside United Free Presbytery met at Aboyne and discussed a circular from the convener of the Assembly Committee on Life and Work and Public Morals protesting against the sale of Sunday newspapers. Because of the value of war news, however, the general view was that the matter should be left to people's own consciences. Iona commented that respecting Sabbath rest was more of a problem in large cities.

She observed that normally her father read about the war in newspapers in grim silence, which lightened when the Allies made progress. On 18 November, however, he laughed heartily about an item regarding two Gordon officers who were prisoners of war and were alleged by the Germans to have signed a statement that they had been supplied with dumdum bullets. Her father explained that they were soft-nosed bullets which expanded on impact and inflicted lacerations. What amused him was that in a War Office memorandum Sir Victor Horsley considered the modern pointed nickel-sheathed bullet to be 'probably the most humane projectile yet devised.' Mr Gordon joked that they would be producing a humane shell next! German statements that British troops were using projectiles prohibited by The Hague Convention were untrue, and seemed to have been made to justify the use by German troops of projectiles which did contravene it.

She was glad to inform Gavin that on the evening of 19 November there was a successful second Army recruitment meeting in Ballater. Her father again sat at the back. It was claimed that Germany had planned war for twenty-five years, and we had to fight or go under. Fifteen men were attested. Gavin already knew that Kitchener's Army Battalions of his regiment were the 8th, 9th and 10th. The nucleus of the 11th Service Battalion had been formed at Aldershot. She added that while she appreciated he would always do his duty, he should avoid being foolhardy. She had read of a lieutenant of the 2nd Gordon Highlanders who had ventured from the trenches near Ypres, during a brief lull in shelling, and amused the men by dancing the Highland fling. It was originally performed, however, to celebrate victory.

She was pleased to learn on 21 November that Lady Tullibardine's appeal for hose-tops to prevent the Highlander's cold knees had been successful. Three yards of gartering braid and two large safety pins were sent with each pair. The combination replaced string which Highlanders had used for gartering, but which in many cases had led to varicose veins. Iona warned Gavin that many of the hose-tops had been cast off too tightly, so if he received such a pair he should give it away and she would send a replacement.

After posting a letter to him, she received his request for more warm clothing. She did not have it, a batch having just been sent, but her father was reluctant to let her visit large stores in Aberdeen for the wider choice, because of a scarlet fever epidemic and an alarming number of diphtheria cases. She reassured him that she would only be there for a short time, and the risk was tiny compared to the dangers which Gavin faced. She visited two stores in the city and posted a Namur khaki knitted woollen helmet, with the part over the ears knitted fine to allow hearing, and a sleeping cap in khaki wool which could also be worn as a scarf. Notepaper and envelopes were included. In the middle of the month she was glad to learn that Army orders notified an increase per soldier to three shirts and three pairs of socks.

Later she told him that a café chantant was held on Friday evening, 27 November, in Ballater's Albert Memorial Hall. The sum of £60 was raised for the Belgian Relief Fund, the country being appropriately headed by King Albert. (Moreover, Ishbel said that St Albert was his patron. In 1192 the cleric was consecrated Bishop of Liège in Reims. While Emperor Heinrich VI opposed his appointment, there was no evidence implicating him in his murder outside Reims by three German knights. Now the Catholic countries of Belgium and France had been invaded by German defenders of Lutheranism, although secular power was again the basic aim.) The wife of the Belgian Consul in Aberdeen declared the function open. Miss Clark did not enter at first into the spirit of the occasion, making the pedantic objection that café meant coffee, but tea was being served. Morag, who beside Iona poured her tea, retorted in pique that soldiers at the front did not object to drinking large quantities of the brew. Furthermore, a café chantant on the Continent often made music and other entertainments available in the open air, but as it was a November night doubtless Miss Clark approved of them being held indoors. The varied programme included vocal and instrumental music, dramatic recitals, morris dances, etc. There were not only local artists, but also a lady from Australia, four performers from Aberdeen and an elocutionist from Glasgow. The highlight, however, was the passionate singing by four Belgian soldiers of their national anthem, 'La Brabançonne' or 'The Brabant Song,' which was cheered by the large audience. Miss Clark redeemed herself by first giving an explanation. Jenneval, a Frenchman whose real name was Alexandre Dechet, wrote the lyrics. At the time he was working at the Brussels theatre where, in 1830, the revolution started which led to independence from the Netherlands. He died in the war. The composition was literary and gained in fervour towards the end, but it was underlined by tragic pathos in the current situation of the martyred country, particularly in the affirmation that it would be 'always great and beautiful.' The song was mainly based on the 'Marseillaise,' but the Belgian version promoted constitutional monarchy, pledging loyalty at the end to 'The King, the Law, Liberty!'

Iona proudly informed Gavin that not only did Ballater's figure for supplying fighting men compare favourably with much larger towns, but also now it contributed in a new way to the war effort. It had a zealous branch of the Red Cross Society. Since the outbreak of war its members had become very efficient in all branches of the work, and several months before the Women's Voluntary Aid Detachment raised about £160 in the burgh and district for equipping a convalescent hospital as well as garments and other necessaries for wounded soldiers. As the Victoria Hall had been used for Army recruitment, it had appropriately been transformed in a week or two into a hospital with twenty-one beds.

On Monday, 30 November, the first group of patients arrived. As a mark of respect the shop closed for a short time and the staff joined a large number of people heading for the station to give them a warm welcome. Normally a crowd only gathered by the station if British or foreign royalty was arriving en route for Balmoral and other royal holiday homes. Now honour was given to brave ordinary men. When the fifteen patients had originally arrived in Aberdeen, they were well aware on seeing the crowd how their condition aroused deep wells of compassion. They were a little surprised to see so many people greeting them at Ballater, but they responded heartily as they proceeded to the Victoria Hall which was conveniently opposite. They came from a range of British regiments, one belonging to the Royal Flying Corps.

Iona was excited to learn that three of them came from Gavin's battalion, and after work she said to her father, 'Most of the patients' relatives live a long way off, and the soldiers would welcome a visit, even from strangers. Earlier I heard a patient say that the sixteen hour ambulance train journey from Southampton to Aberdeen was smooth and comfortable, but so long he thought that he was travelling to the North Pole! We could go together and enquire about the welfare of Gavin's fellow Gordons in particular, and see if any of them know him well.'

He replied, 'I would advise caution. Accompanying me would emphasize that you are a single woman. Also, you might well be a little anxious. While an ordinary woman under some stress looks weak, the addition of your strong spirit would make you appear even more beautiful and irresistible to lonely, unattached men. I will therefore go alone.'

'If we make it clear that Gavin is my boyfriend, I am sure they will understand. My presence could result in information about him being more forthcoming.'

'All right, then.'

'We could take a gift.'

'Like others we have already given items, but we will find out if anything else is needed.'

It was only a short walk to the Victoria Hall, but they appreciated the warmth inside. He smiled, for the last times he was there it rang with patriotic speeches to boost Army recruitment. Now there was a bright, spotless ward with a long, white covered table section in the middle between two lines of beds. A chair lay uniformly at the end of each bed. The effect of complete consistency was only marred by the bedsteads which were not all of the same design, hinting at speed in preparation. The underlying tone was mainly of female discipline. The work as a whole was done by half the detachment under the matron and sister, the other half being in the kitchen under the quartermaster. Some of the men were in bed, and there was no loose soldiers' talk. He recalled how Iona had spoken of a balance of male and female elements in Nature and society.

Approaching a nurse, a gentle crusader bearing a Geneva red cross on her uniform, he said, 'Good evening, Agnes. I believe that there are three 1st Gordon Highlanders here.'

Pointing Miss Gauld replied, 'One of them is asleep over there, but I will take you to the others.'

She led them into a large, cheerful smoking room where a group relaxed before a bright fire. Yet he was amused by the cigarette and pipe smoke, because it was at odds with Ballater's reputation for pure, dry and bracing mountain air. Iona was surprised by the courteous looks which the humble heroes gave them.

After the nurse introduced the patients as Jim Lorimer and David Wood and gave the visitors' names, Mr Gordon shook hands with them, saying, 'I served with the 2nd Gordon Highlanders during the Second Boer War.'

Jim replied, 'We are sorry we cannot rise quickly to greet you, but we are recovering from shrapnel wounds to the legs. We are very grateful at the prospect of being pampered here for three weeks, with a more varied diet than on the Continent and entertainments being arranged, before going home for Christmas.'

Mr Gordon responded, 'I commiserate with you. It was a leg wound which ended my military career.'

There had always been great camaraderie among members of the regiment, and conversation flowed freely, the patients laughing when he said, 'You will be pleased to be clean and fresh all the time now, although your spirits will shine whether you are filthy or clean.'

When Iona asked if they knew Gavin Fraser, David replied, 'Yes, I am from his company. He is steady, reliable and cheerful. His experience as a stalker is valuable, because he never loses his bearings and is expert at taking cover. He observes things which are invisible to comrades, for example when a sudden change of wind disturbs camouflage to reveal a German sniper's position.'

Mr Gordon nodded and remarked, 'The Lovat Scouts, a corps of mounted infantry raised by the sixteenth Baron Lovat and composed largely of shepherds, gillies, etc., proved of wider similar worth in the Second Boer War.'

David continued, 'He is also a generous and intelligent man who spends more time than average writing letters. There is clearly an uncommon bond between him and his young lady. He was in good health the last time I saw him, not mentioning rheumatic twinges which affected many men in all that muddy water. He believes that abstinence from smoking helps his health.'

After a further discussion about conditions at the front Mr Gordon said, 'Thank you for the information. I wish both of you well. Would you like a present?'

Jim replied, 'More interesting books would be appreciated.'

Iona informed Gavin that next day her father lent an assortment of non-fictional and fictional works for the rest of the war. He displayed a notice in the shop exhorting customers to do likewise. Towards the end of the letter she looked forward to Christmas, regretting that she was not allowed to send perishable goods. She would have liked to send him dates from Tunis, plums from Portugal and muscatels or raisins from Malaga. He would receive instead tins of oatcakes, shortbread and assorted biscuits which he could share with comrades. She asked him to give more details about trench life in further letters, so that she could understand the atmosphere even better.

By December he and other surviving original members of the British

Expeditionary Force felt that they were veterans of the war. Young men who had not been abroad before reflected on the initial naive belief that they were embarking on a short conflict which would be over by Christmas. Early losses had brought instead a sense of the brevity of life itself. Gavin occasionally read newspaper accounts of his battalion's actions as if they were history.

As Iona was mature for her years, he considered it wise not to diminish the dangers of war, lest she should be misled into thinking that he was safer than he was, and thus death or serious injury would have been a greater shock to her. Equally the world of men would have seemed strange, so he contrasted the Western Front with Deeside, and wrote as if he was speaking to her, to give a greater directness and immediacy.

In letters that month he described the routines which prevailed through the uncertainty, of how for example before moving up to the trenches he would have an evening meal, gaining spiritual strength from Christ's fortitude at the Last Supper, even though he knew that he faced death. After a roll-call which was reminiscent of schooldays, but technically to check for deserters not truants, he would set off just before darkness, loaded with trench stores. He envied the ants of Craigendarroch that could carry a good five times their weight. He was in a platoon of sixty to reduce the risk of heavy casualties from shellfire which could be expected on approach roads and communication trenches at that time. Mechanical and impersonal, such fire mocked the spectacle of the old open theatre of war. Yet in any age physical fear was controlled by moral courage. The ground shook and visibility was hampered by drifting smoke, contrasting with Deeside's gentle mist. Apart from the rising noise, shell flashes and smoke were the Very lights sent up at five minute intervals along the line. Even the name Very was ambiguous. The flare was named after the inventor, Edward W. Very, an American naval officer, but it was indeed so very bright that it was like daylight. Gavin saw it as a shooting star contrasting with the light years of the stars above. One of his comrades, a wag, seeing one coquettishly moving repeatedly from side to side shortly before it fell to the ground, likened it to a lady of the night, a euphemism for a prostitute. The light was both beautiful and eerie, and Gavin knew that the Very pistol was used not only for temporarily illuminating part of a battlefield, but also for signalling. Therefore any cessation or variation in its use by the enemy roused suspicion.

Despite the din, when the relieving soldiers approached the front trench, if the opposing trench was near there had to be no rattle of equipment, otherwise the enemy would know that soldiers were entering and leaving at the same time, and both would attract shellfire. Sentries were posted at once, one for every three men on the line. Normally a line was thought of as straight or curved, but here were traverses or quadruple right angles in the trench to prevent enfilading or sweeping fire from end to end by soldiers on foot or by an aircraft. These fire bays contrasted with the forest firebreaks of Deeside. Even the same trench line was rarely straight, but snaked along. Ironically while British and German trenches had a similar appearance, French ones had a leisurely zigzag pattern. When Gavin faced danger from shelling in a snaking trench, he thought fondly of the peaceful, more angular part of the path leading to the Falls of the Glasallt above Loch Muick.

The parados or rear shelter was the mound along the back of the trench to secure from reverse attack or fire. Both it and the parapet at the front were normally made of sandbags and earth. Early in the war wooden planks lined the trench's base. Two or three feet above the planks was the fire step. Yet there was so much rain that Gavin and his comrades had to make great efforts to keep the trenches drained. They stood in mud and water, shivering with cold. If a trench was made tolerable a thaw after frost was a test. While Highlanders prided themselves on being trim and clean, it was unrealistic in that situation, where the trenches were often more like ditches. The men had to be careful to walk on the planks, because if they left them it was possible in some places to sink to the waist. It was common to lose shoes and hose. They left the trenches looking like miners emerging from a pit.

At least the rifles were always kept clean with oil. Even they could get frostbitten, however, and sometimes were ruptured by sudden expansion on being fired. Water bottles could freeze too and had to be thawed out. The men did not leave anything about which an airman could easily see. Empty bully beef tins were not thrown out at the back of a trench, because if the sun appeared the flash was visible for miles and the trench could be heavily shelled.

Paradoxically the cold and damp affected them more than the firing. They got used to snipers' buzzing bullets and even became accustomed to shrapnel. Yet the climate induced dreams of eating steak pudding beside a large domestic fire. For Gavin the bullets were replaced by a memory of Iona laughing at midges.

What put their hardships in perspective were the wanton damage and persecution of civilians by the Germans. The Gordons had gone through

Ypres and passed close to the magnificent, huge Cloth Hall begun in the thirteenth century, but which he was to read in a newspaper the enemy shelled and burned to the ground. He looked around in the trenches and in some places could see a number of farms burned down. The most pitiful sights were not the Gordons' own casualties, for they were the valorous price of war, but Belgian refugees and ruined homes from which they had been driven.

Each soldier was trained in the use of a hand grenade or bomb, and the rifle-grenade which travelled further and was often used against machine gun positions. Snipers continued to be important. In 1884 the Maxim gun was designed, the first fully automatic water-cooled machine gun. It was named after Sir Hiram S. Maxim, the American-born British inventor. By the Great War the British Vickers machine gun was an improved and redesigned Maxim, while ironically the German machine gun was closely based on the original Maxim.

Bayonets were fixed in the front line, with a round in the chamber of each rifle. Half an hour before sunset and half an hour afterwards, as well as around dawn, there was stand-to on the fire step in case of an attack. A night sentry kept still with his head and shoulders above the parapet to reduce the risk of being shot in the head. He strained his eyes looking for any movement, including Huns pushing straw or other camouflage. On one occasion when Gavin performed the relatively passive night sentry duty, he thought that if he had to die in the war, it would be better if it happened at such a time, instantly by a sniper's bullet, so he would be translated to eternity when he was at peace with the stars and the love of his soul. At once, however, his Highland spirit scorned such a fate.

Training occurred at the rear of the battle area, with work in the morning and games in the afternoon. Gavin informed her that football was most popular, not just as a relaxation from discipline, but also, as even the Germans allowed, it taught something about war tactics and camaraderie. Some soldiers participated in boxing and running. He liked the last pursuit best, although he won no prizes. Emerging from the trenches was like a bird released from a cage, and running appealed to his free Highland nature. The men generally got a lot of running at night. It was good for the circulation in such cold weather and helped them to sleep.

On 2 December his battalion rejoined the 8th Brigade at Locre. The move was part of a reorganization under which all the Ypres Salient was handed to the French and the British took over a sector from the La Bassée Canal to a point west of the village of Wytschaete south of Ypres.

Early that month certain indications along the Western Front made Allied commanders believe that the Germans had withdrawn considerable forces. On Monday the 14th the 8th Brigade attacked with the 1st Gordon Highlanders on the right against the farmed Maedelstede Spur near Wytschaete, and the 2nd Royal Scots on the left against Petit Bois. Normally such a scene was associated with God's plenty and peace, but in war the situation was easily inverted. At dawn the artillery of three divisions made a preliminary bombardment, but for want of ammunition it lasted only three quarters of an hour. Gavin and his comrades occupied a position some 400 yards south of the German line. At 7.45 they charged over a level plain devoid of cover and swept by heavy machine gun and rifle fire. Initially it was terrible for Gavin, as they leaped from the trenches and met the full enemy fire. Then cool discipline and the red mist of battle blood made him impervious to fear. His recent running helped, and he knew that if he was to die it would be better that Iona should remember him as a man of action. Several men fell before they reached the first trench, but scarcely had Gavin and others entered it, where he dispatched a Hun with Mr Gordon's dirk, than they clambered over earthen breastworks towards further trenches. Men dropped increasingly, including brave Hector whose lifeless form still pointed his fixed bayonet at the enemy. The fewer who remained in the advance the more fervent became their resolve, until they lay for a few minutes in a dip in the ground, regaining their breath and smeared with mud. Then they charged through a hail of bullets. Only twelve to fifteen paces away lay the intact barbed wire and trenches with snipers' loopholes. As it was impossible to proceed further, there came the signal to retire. Regaining the dip they dug head cover with entrenching tools, before bandaging their wounded. They lay in mortal danger for the rest of the day. In the dark they warily stole back with their wounded to the front line, for snipers were active, aided by star lights.

It was one of the hottest fights the Gordons had ever taken part in. An officer compared it very favourably to the famous Dargai charge in India in 1897, when the 1st Gordon Highlanders drove tribesmen from Dargai on a rocky spur in the Chagru Valley. Generals French, Smith-Dorrien and Haldane observed the action from a neighbouring hill and gave high praise. The 2nd Royal Scots got in and took some prisoners, but the Gordons' objective had been more formidable. The attempt to take the German trenches did not succeed, but it was chiefly attributed to the heavy artillery bombardment not having been sufficiently effective. The general desired effect was achieved, the enemy's losses being very heavy.

For the rest of the winter the 1st Gordon Highlanders was confined to trenches on the Vierstraat-Wytschaete road, a little north of those from which it had attacked on 14 December, and its billets in La Clytte two and a half miles behind. As soon as Gavin reached a billet he resumed writing to Iona, describing the action in general terms as if it was work. After such heavy casualties some soldiers would attribute their survival to luck, but he was among those who ascribed it to God's grace or Providence. Only if a soldier wrote to a male friend would he mention the stark realities of war, that sometimes victims were buried in six pieces, but oftener in sacks, while some were blown to atoms, and rats grew fat eating human flesh. Gavin did inform Iona that occasionally he heard a comrade boast about having bagged a German, as if there was a parallel with shooting grouse on a moor.

He contrasted Pannanich Wells' very pure water and the Dee's plentiful pure flow with the situation on the Ypres front, where there was sometimes the double discomfort of standing in water up to the knees or even waist and frequent difficulty of getting drinkable water into the trenches. It was as in 'The Rime of the Ancient Mariner,' Pt II, with 'Water, water, every where, / Nor any drop to drink.' They had learned to use empty tins to catch a little rain, and occasionally fresh snow, a godsend, was used when it was unsafe for people to move about. 'Yet closer than snow is your surpassing arctic purity.'

Their shaggy winter jackets were warm, reminding him of a heavy rug before the fireplace at Iona's home. He wished her a happy festive season. He and his comrades were used to presents, for they were getting a generous supply of comforts, such as socks, shirts and mitts. An evening concert was planned before they returned to the trenches.

His Christmas Day passed quietly, but it was very cold. He thanked her for the extra card for his twentieth birthday on the 30th and the food parcel which included cocoa as a variant to tea. He and his comrades shared gifts of food. Each of them received a card from the King and Queen. On one side were portraits of them, the King in khaki field service dress, and on the other side was a greeting in facsimile of the King's handwriting, offering 'best wishes for Christmas' and the words, 'May God protect you and bring you home safe.' From HRH Princess Mary's Soldiers' and Sailors' Christmas Fund came a present. Gavin received a non-smoker's one, plus a photograph of the princess and a card conveying 'best wishes for a Happy Christmas, and a victorious New Year.'

Earlier that month Iona informed him that although the King thought it was his duty to stay in or near London during the war, it was in his name as donor that the head gamekeeper on the Balmoral Estate sent venison and rabbits to the Ballater Red Cross Hospital. Like her father a number of people seemed to have asked what was needed, because there was a great range of gifts, from basics such as oatmeal, milk, eggs, bacon, potatoes, fresh and tinned fruit and sticks, to cakes, toffee, macaroni and vermicelli, crumpets, shortbread, tea bread and honey. She emphasized that she was simply showing how well the men were being cared for, not teasing him! To complete the patients' comfort there were games, books, newspapers, notepaper, clocks, the fitting up of a bathroom and a telephone. A garage proprietor had driven all the patients in cars to Balmoral Castle, where they were entertained to tea by the housekeeper and presented with cigarettes by male servants.

Recalling how some pre-war actions by suffragettes had let down their sex and cause, she was glad that members of the Aberdeen Association for Woman's Suffrage (Law-abiding) had been busy with various patriotic efforts since the war started. Danger had induced sobriety and unity against the common foe. The Kaiser's slow nemesis continued. He spoke of 'humbly receiving fortune and misfortune from God's gracious hand.'

As Gavin had commented on 'Tipperary' in a letter, he would be amused to learn that the Germans, through prejudice, disinformation or ignorance, failed to recognize it as a stirring, romantic and by extension patriotic marching song. They did not understand the British soldier's fondness for a frivolous composition made in America (actually England!) about an Irishman's longing for his home (in fact sweetheart) in Tipperary. It was thought that when the first English troops arrived in France they had no war song, and one of them sang this one which he had heard in a London music hall. The French on the other hand had the 'Marseillaise,' and the Germans had 'Gloria, Victoria, with Hand and Heart for Fatherland' and 'Die Wacht am Rhein.'

In view of Gavin's fondness for horses, she informed him that the novelist John Galsworthy had appealed for the RSPCA Fund for Sick and Wounded Horses. By 16 October the Army Veterinary Corps had already dealt with some 27,000 horses, saving the lives of many. Over half of the horses which had passed through its hands had been made well. Among other items twenty-five horse-drawn ambulances were required to convey horses from railway stations to convalescent farms. Twenty-five lorries were badly needed for rapidly carrying fodder from base hospitals to con-valescent farms and fields. This was the greatest current need, for with winter coming on the horses could not graze. The dumb creatures did not, as the prayer for them claimed, 'offer their guileless lives for the well-being of their countries.' An RSPCA inspector commented, however, that the motto at the front was 'Horse first, man afterwards.' Apart from humanity there was the motive of economy in saving as many horses as possible.

Considering the immense efforts on the Western Front and the Royal Navy's zeal, she hoped Gavin would not be too offended or amused to learn that precautions were being taken in case of a hostile raid by the enemy in Aberdeenshire. There were a Central Committee and Emergency Committees for the county's various districts. The public had been reassured there was no need for panic or alarm!

She was glad that a heavy snowfall occurred in Upper Deeside the weekend before the Gordons' charge near Ypres. The people of Ballater's struggle with the elements helped them in retrospect to sympathize with the greater battle. The snow began to fall on Saturday evening and continued with little respite until noon. A gale also occurred and snow drifted in many parts into large banks, making traffic almost impossible between Ballater and Braemar. The average depth of snow was two feet. The skeletal beauty of silver birches on the lower slopes of Craig Coillich and the proud evergreen battalions above were masked in snow. Dark Lochnagar was transformed into a pristine white mountain and the Dee flowed past ermine banks. Sunshine filtering through clouds cast a gentle sheen on a valley which was half asleep. The vast frozen reservoir of snow contrasted with the frequent lack of drinking water in trenches on the Ypres Salient. Later on Sunday there were signs of a thaw, but on Monday Braemar was still cut off.

She told him that a pair of warm gloves was to be given for Christmas to each member of the 1st, 2nd and 6th Battalions of his regiment. Half the cost was to be met by the Town Council of Aberdeen, the other half being raised by the county. Such items doubtless soon wore out, so a fresh pair would be welcome. A similar arrangement applied for sending these soldiers a plum pudding for the New Year. Moreover, from the Scottish National Flag Day Fund were being sent packages, each containing a currant loaf and cake of shortbread, as New Year gifts to members of Scottish regiments at the front. With the approach of the festive season in particular she was very sympathetic to relatives who had been informed that a military husband or son was missing. All the uncertainty would seem like a living death. At least the International Red Cross Society, based in Geneva, could sometimes trace a missing soldier, say, to a prisoner of war camp.

She was pleased that the hard-pressed fisherwomen of east Scotland got good news before Christmas. They excelled as knitters and there was an urgent need for 40,000 pairs of socks for troops at the front. The order had been placed with the women of a number of fishing villages on the Scottish east coast, more particularly Aberdeenshire.

Gavin would recall meeting the young brother and sister, Callum and Helen Leslie, on Craig Coillich. They attended the United Free Church Sunday School and had received book prizes for success in memory work!

When he was in Ballater she told him it was hoped to install electric lighting by the end of the year. Despite the war it was achieved on 23 December. The original prime motive was to extend the tourist season by a fortnight or even a month. It was fitting that among early visitors to benefit would be patients in the Red Cross Hospital. Actually the first group left on 21 December, but the next one would arrive on Hogmanay. The inaugural ceremony occurred at the new power station near the railway station at 4 p.m. before the Town Council and others. The design and physical work had been done by outsiders, apart from a Ballater painter! The engines were started and the electric light was switched on, illuminating all the streets. The company adjourned to the more hospitable venue of the Invercauld Arms Hotel for a cake and wine banquet at which the main speeches were made and several toasts were proposed. It was pointed out that women would be able to use the power for cooking stoves and irons, etc. When used in daytime it helped to stop the current going to waste.

Shortly before the inaugural ceremony Mr Gordon and others visited the power station. They enthused over the two sixty-eight brake horsepower suction gas engines and suction gas generators, and how each engine was coupled to a dynamo of forty-two kilowatts, while there was a storage battery. He commented that it was good to see machines being used for peaceful purposes.

As he returned to the shop he smiled as Iona and others standing in the doorway were suddenly illuminated. She was charmed to see children who, already excited at the approach of Christmas, were given extra cheer. She thought how fortunate they were compared to those in Aberdeen, which being by the sea had to endure strict controls over lighting. Moreover, it was risky for pedestrians, particularly children, to cross the roads with far more traffic. Ballater was both literally and symbolically a haven of light, and Christmas celebrated the coming of the Light of the World. They entered the shop and Mr Gordon switched on their electric lighting, while she extinguished the paraffin lamps which would only be needed as an emergency backup in future. She thought of Gavin and other soldiers on the Western Front, where darkness was relieved only by Very lights, exploding shells and firing of bullets.

Her father gave best wishes to Miss Clark on her retirement and nodded when she said, 'It is disgraceful that the River Gairn, which supplies the burgh's water, has not also been used to generate electricity, because it has a good fall. Old-fashioned factors attach more importance to the trout, if you please. Yet when visitors, whose complaints about paraffin lamps have prompted change, arrive by rail to enjoy our pure air, what will they see but a nearby power station operated by coal! Have you ever heard of anything so absurd? Also some Stone Age locals are against the burgh being lit by electricity at all! It might cost extra, but it will be more than compensated for by a longer tourist season.'

After a busy day in the shop on Christmas Eve, Iona walked with her father through the crisp air, under a beautiful starry sky, as the church bell rang for a carol service. Hearts in the large congregation which were on the Continent felt comfort rather than joy, but Iona's heart and spirit, fortified by Ishbel's presence, were finely attuned, so she felt no divided loyalties.

Later she took Mike for a walk, turning right at the junction beyond the Royal Bridge. After a while she paused at the spot where she and Gavin had stood near the meeting of the waters and close to the Bridge of Muick, where the living and the dead passed over. She recalled how beneath the summer sky he spoke of Hannibal. Now like his hero he had to contend with snow. She also remembered that he said in the union of the rivers and of them he saw that harmony and love would always conquer in the end. Alone in the frosty night she realized his remark contained an implicit warning, that if he sacrificed his life it would be to save their love.

8: The Ypres Salient and Ballater, January-July 1915

He admitted to her that the trenches continued to be wretched, often half filled with liquid mud. A kilt's ten yards of cloth were a burden there. Some of his comrades suffered from the condition of trench foot which was caused by standing in water little above freezing point. The feet were apt to swell with sloughing of dead tissue. Eventually the malady was counteracted by rubbing feet with whale oil and sending dry socks nightly with rations, before gumboots were generally worn. Yet it was common to have a touch of rheumatism. Those who had been in the war from the outset experienced the extremes of continental climate, periods of oppressive heat and now often hard frosts at night. Near Ypres many men with frostbitten feet had to be evacuated. On the other hand midwinter nights were very dark, giving an opportunity to attend to wire defences. Equally special vigilance was necessary in case of a surprise German attack, especially when there was heavy rain.

Sometimes they were covered in clay from head to foot an inch thick. It impressed on them that they were mortal clay. Yet the worse the mud, rain and cold the more exposed were the men's elemental natures, and, as they fought for Heaven's cause, the cheerier they became and their spirits grew. There was practically no crime or drunkenness among the Highlanders. They were stiffened by resolve as well as by corporate discipline, which complemented each other. Amid the dreary war and weather, when they might be blown to oblivion any moment by a missile or a mine from below, in their nothingness they found their all. With death so near they feared not the foe but God, who was greater in the hell of war. What were the enmities of men contrasted with the power and glory of God's love which encompassed the living and the dead?

At church parade on Sunday there were a psalm or paraphrase, a prayer, a scripture reading and a short sermon. Familiar hymns, such as 'Rock of Ages,' 'Nearer, my God, to Thee,' 'Jesus, lover of my soul' and 'Lead, kindly Light,' sung in an unfamiliar environment helped them to feel that God was sheltering them and their loved ones. An interval was given for them to engage in silent prayer, when Iona's bright spirit filled Gavin's devotion.

In the New Year he received a parcel from her which contained at his request candles and more soft biscuits as opposed to hard Army ones. The accompanying letter included information about Ballater's new electric lighting and power. That shining haven of peace differed strikingly from hidden, elemental candlelight in a dugout. He recalled her saying the previous summer that the snowdrop, her favourite flower, meant hope and purity, the white blooms having symbolized Candlemas, a festival held on 2 February to commemorate the Virgin Mary's purification and Jesus' presentation in the Temple, when candles were blessed. He read Psalm 23 and was transported from the valley of the shadow of death to Iona's side by the Pools of Dee. His soul was restored. Then he remembered her remarking by the Linn of Muick that some Highland flowers were small, but there could be myriads of them like stars. He reflected that mortals reached their physical prime then faded, yet their spirits continued to grow in the Holy Spirit and shine like candles or stars.

He informed her that he and his comrades had much enjoyed the New Year gifts which she had mentioned, a plum pudding from Aberdeen plus a currant loaf and shortbread from the Scottish National Flag Day Fund. Generally there was ample food and it was well prepared, but variety was welcome. He liked bully beef, although some soldiers were so tired of it they vowed never to have it again when the war ended.

He told her that when he was behind the firing line on long, tedious evenings in particular, he would welcome a mouth organ to perform a solo or accompany singing by his comrades. The cheerful sound would be an antidote to the war, promoting inner and corporate harmony. He had attained some proficiency with a mouth organ as a schoolboy, but he had given it away when he turned to other pursuits. The instrument did not have the simple purity of pan pipes and certainly none of a church organ's glory, but it would be appropriate in the current setting.

When she sent him a mouth organ, she explained that her father had kept it as a memento of his childhood, because of its pretty design. He was glad that it was going to be properly used again. Ironically it was made in Germany! So many soldiers had requested them that hardly any London wholesalers had any left. America had not been able to match the demand, or to make them as efficiently as the Germans.

She told him that twenty wounded soldiers from various regiments arrived at Ballater on Hogmanay. The hospital continued to receive many gifts of food and other items. Game had been given on the King's behalf. Hares had been received and even fish which had trebled in price because of the limited area in which fishing was allowed and the risks involved. Items had come from beyond Deeside, including Edinburgh and London.

What a contrast the changing of sentries at the front was to the changing of staff at the hospital! Two nurses did night duty together for a week at a time, from 9.45 until 8.30, when the patients' breakfast was served and the day nurses came on. They worked in relays changing at 1 and 6 p.m. The kitchen staff changed to the ward and the ward staff to the kitchen at the end of each week. Morag thought that those in the kitchen away from all those fine men would feel it was like Purgatory after Heaven. The clergy took much interest in the patients. One of them was always there to take prayers at 9 a.m. and conduct a short service each Sunday evening.

At the King's suggestion on 3 January, the first Sabbath in the New Year, the churches observed a Day of Intercession to give thanks, to remember and to appeal. While not unmindful of its own shortcomings, the nation felt that it had God's approval in the war. The idea was adopted in France, Belgium and in Russia by the Orthodox Church. Iona gained strength from this international bond.

She had read of an informal Christmas truce along parts of the Western Front. There were instances where British and German soldiers met, literally and symbolically, halfway across no-man's-land, wishing each other a merry Christmas and shaking hands. As a result of meeting the enemy as individual human beings, it was even felt that, if it was left to the men, there would be no war. German leaders, however, were driven by imperial vainglory. Jesus thought not of nations or empires, but of redeeming individual souls for the Kingdom of Heaven.

In view of Gavin's remark that his kilt was unsuitable for flooded trenches, she wrote that the War Office had introduced so-called drab military kilts, which only had five yards of cloth! They were a temporary measure because of difficulty in obtaining a supply of tartan. Prompt action by the Kilt Society of Inverness, however, had ensured that the tartan would be used again as quickly as possible. When she read that he was sometimes covered in an inch of clay, she thought of the contrasting scene when irresolute, disillusioned Hamlet held Yorick's skull and said, 'get you to my lady's chamber, and tell her, let her paint an inch thick, to this favour she must come; make her laugh at that.'

Iona was glad that Gavin was well fed. Back home food prices had risen, but customers in their shop understood the reasons and appreciated that her father was not profiteering. So many British fishing vessels and ships had been requisitioned by the government for the war. There were heavy freight charges and increased rates of insurance. The price of wheat had risen because ordinary supplies from Russia had ceased and drought had caused a serious shortage in Australia. Whereas 'Bydand' was the Gordons' motto, economy was the watchword of the ordinary housewife. The shop no longer kept the same stocks of little luxuries. Yet the country was fortunate in food supplies relative to its Allies and enemies. In Germany white bread was reserved mainly for the wounded. When Miss Clark recently bought a loaf in the shop, she said she was pleased that the Kaiser was reported to be sharing with his people what was known as war bread, made largely from potatoes and not very palatable. Moreover, the Germans no longer had good news from the front.

Iona wished that the discipline and humble gratitude for gifts shown by British soldiers abroad would have a positive effect on all those back home. Sadly, some people who earned good wages through government contracts indulged in drink and drunkenness had increased in Scotland.

She assured him that she continued to be busy helping the war effort in her spare time. As a member of the Glenmuick Parish Church Work Party she made comforts. Between them they produced shirts, belts, socks, hose-tops, mufflers, helmets, mitts and wrist cuffs. She liked to work with another member in either of their homes, as the conversation lightened the labour. It was also encouraging to know that their efforts were part of a far greater activity involving girls as well as women.

Morag's boyfriend, Colin Spence, had wanted to help the war effort more directly than just being a butcher's assistant in the burgh. As he did not see himself as a soldier, in the New Year he began work in a ship repair yard in Aberdeen. When the Gordons' shop opened on the last Saturday of the month, however, Morag's mother, Maggie Brockie, entered in a shocked state.

'Morag will not be coming today. Last night she learned that Colin lost his footing on a platform in the yard and, falling awkwardly, was killed instantly. There was no question of drink being involved; it was just a freak accident. Yet Morag became hysterical, threatening to throw herself off

Craigendarroch. We gave her some drams to calm her. She should be back at work on Monday.'

In the evening Iona went round to comfort her, but as she approached Morag stood unsteadily in the doorway, which was three further on from that of Donald's aunt, and exclaimed to a female neighbour, 'I'll soon be awa to Tomintoul's tottering, tufted top!'

Her befuddled gaze swept round to see Iona discreetly turn round and slip away, but she apologized next day after church, saying, 'I drank too much. Colin was not my ideal, but he was a good man. I will miss him.'

In February Gavin told Iona his comrades were optimistic that when the bad weather was over the Allies would make a big advance. A few even thought that the Germans would be beaten in a matter of months. Privately he was not so confident. Having climbed mountains with her, he knew that a summit was hidden by intermediate stages. Like a true Christian in life's battle he made the most of each day and left the future in God's hands. Some less religious men referred to Father Time when danger loomed.

He expressed great thanks for the mouth organ. A number of them had now been given to the battalion. The music was much appreciated by his comrades when singing. Nature was full of elemental music, including that from birds, burns and even a breeze among trees. Man's music gave beauty to emotion and made him feel closer to Creation and loved ones, besides relieving the sad heart when the mind brooded over fallen comrades. During yelling but disciplined charges, among showers of bullets and shrapnel, there had been occasions when a pal by his side had suddenly fallen in the silence of death. Now the joy and hope of music turned winter into spring, helping him to stop looking backwards and to think of those friends as having gone forward, free of earthly cares.

He told her that the daily rum ration was a fine stimulant to men standing in icy water and exposed to chilly winds. He gained more benefit from the rum than men who had previously drunk heavily. As for his feet, if he felt numbness he loosened his shoes a little and moved the toes and other parts to help the circulation and keep frostbite at bay. He did not wear two pairs of socks, because they increased pressure in the shoes and round the ankles.

On 27 February the Territorial battalion, the 4th Gordon Highlanders, joined the 8th Brigade of the 3rd Division at La Clytte. The regulars advised the new men and warm friendships were made. Gavin found that one Territorial had originally come from Ballater, so he mentioned him to Iona, thinking that she would probably know him, particularly as his parents still lived in the burgh.

When Gavin referred to a big advance, she knew that it could not be achieved without much sacrifice. Just as he spared her the gruesome details of war, so she did not mention to him that the Gordons had suffered the dreadful toll of 1,600 casualties, being exceeded by only one regiment in the British Army, the Coldstream Guards, whose losses were over 2,000. She was glad, however, that she and other members of the Work Party had continued making comforts with the same energy, because Field Marshal Sir John French's wife had announced a material decline in the supply of such items at her depot, and wished it to be reversed, particularly as clothing wore out very quickly in such demanding conditions.

Iona told Gavin that Deeside had also had heavy rain. While some of his comrades were too optimistic about the war, there had been undue hope in the valley about the opening of the spring salmon fishing season on 11 February! With a recent spate in the Dee salmon had been early in the lower reaches. Yet on the 11th the river was in flood. Heavy rains had brought down melting snow which deterred fish from reaching pools in the upper reaches.

Recalling their summer holiday, she reminded him that when they gazed across at Birkhall in Glen Muick, she spoke of Florence Nightingale having been a guest there. A statue of her had now been unveiled in Waterloo Place, London, standing next to one of Sidney Herbert, who as War Minister granted her permission for the mission to Scutari. The 'Lady with the Lamp' was a fine example of how women could excel in war. It was the first public statue of a woman in London except those of royal ladies.

In March Gavin told her that the grim contrast between the Scottish Highlands and Flanders' plains made him and his comrades appreciate even more gifts from their territorial district in particular. They drew strength from the heartfelt unity shown by people at home, which was why soldiers sent warm, grateful letters to donors when they gave their names and addresses. A comrade had written to thank a young girl in Aberdeen for knitting a pair of socks, stating that he would remember the gift as long as he lived. Later he smiled wryly and said that it would be ironic if he was killed soon wearing the socks!

While members of the battalion were optimistic about the outcome of the war, Gavin did not tell her that they were realistic about their own chances of survival in this conflict of attrition. As it was common to have had many narrow escapes from death or serious injury, a lot of men had made their wills. Normally it was the elderly who had rheumatic aches and made wills, but war changed the situation.

He did warn her that danger was not reserved to the trenches and no-man's-land. The battalion had done an extra day's duty, because of thinning of the line caused by recent fighting. A company when relieved at night from the trenches came to a support farm instead of going further back to La Clytte. During the day on 17 March the Germans shelled the position very heavily with shrapnel. About 2 p.m. a shell from a gun behind a hill came through the door of one of the barns, killing five men and wounding another eleven. It was difficult to bandage the worst wounds. Yet those men lay patiently suffering behind the farm, until stretcher-bearers arrived at dusk to carry them back to the dressing station. One of them died before they reached there. Even so, officially the six men died on active service, which would be comforting for their relatives, but it was not how the men would have wished to go. Although shells had come whistling like a strong wind before exploding, birds sang in trees conscious only of the advent of spring.

He assured her that she did not need to send him books. They received a supply of books and magazines which were given by many people back home and sent out from a central depot to the front. After a good initial rest in a billet, it was relaxing and stimulating to read a variety of material, although the New Testament remained the favourite. His copy had been damaged by falling debris after a shell exploded, but he would replace it. He had learned that German soldiers at the front also read the New Testament! In addition, besides service manuals and guides to foreign languages, Goethe's *Faust* and Nietzsche's *Thus Spake Zarathustra* were popular. He had heard Miss Clark speak briefly of *Faust* in the shop in Ballater. Could Iona please ask her or Ishbel about the significance of these works and send him information?

In her first letter that month she thanked him for his greetings, conveyed in a folded sheet with a drawing of them on Lochnagar's summit, for her nineteenth birthday on the 1st. Continuing on a gentle note, she stated that Lady Smith-Dorrien was appealing for contributions to the Blue Cross Fund for our Allies. There were four horse hospitals already in France. It was hoped to establish a further base for Belgian horses, and even to extend the help to Russia and elsewhere. On a more sombre note she informed him that normally tragedies affecting ordinary people were a private matter, mainly involving relatives and close friends. In the war, just as decorations for valour were reported in the press, so there sometimes appeared tributes to fallen men, including letters of condolence from superiors to next of kin. Pride in success and sorrow was shared publicly.

Her father continued to visit soldiers at the hospital. She did not tell Gavin a patient had observed that when he saw a red cross on a nurse's uniform he thought he was lucky not to be buried with many of his comrades on the Continent beneath a wooden one. She did report another patient saying that the stay in Ballater was so interesting, particularly with entertainments being provided, it was like a holiday which passed all too quickly. They had been shown both much respect and great kindness. Soon they would leave for various parts of the country, most proceeding south, and probably never to meet each other again. Yet they would remember their stay in this haven of peace amid a world at war as one of the brightest periods of their lives. Morag, on the other hand, was amused to learn that the hospital had been given from Aberdeen twenty soldier's housewives, or cases for holding needles and thread, etc. She had fancied working with the patients, but she found that first aid and home nursing certificates were required.

In reply to his enquiry about *Faust* and *Thus Spake Zarathustra*, Ishbel had commented that Goethe's masterpiece was about a necromancer transformed into a personification of the struggle between the noble and ignoble sides of man. Faust's curse was the desire for the power of excitement offered by the life of sense, and he made a pact with Mephistopheles, the spirit of the Devil. Innocent Gretchen stirred his higher senses, but she was seduced. Yet Goethe's philosophy of hope ensured that Faust was saved. Out of his love for classical Helen was born a spirit which drew him back into the world of action. At the end of his pilgrimage Gretchen completed his redemption. German soldiers reading the work would think that they were the enemies of Mephistopheles, but the Allies would believe the reverse. Now also the Devil would finally lose, as the troubles he caused helped humanity to find wisdom and grace. Years later, when Nietzsche's works were more clearly understood, Ishbel showed how his masterpiece, *Thus Spake Zarathustra*, had been misinterpreted during the war by the foe. Nietzsche chose Zarathustra, the ancient Persian prophet, because he saw him as the first thinker to regard the battle of good and evil as basic to the linear view of time. Nietzsche's central concept was of eternal recurrence. The person who craved the infinite repetition of each moment of his life with its horrors would be superhuman. Nietzsche struggled with nihilism which debased the values associated with the ascetic ideal. Yet the work contained the dictum 'God is dead.' He replaced the Holy Spirit with the human spirit, besides rejecting Christianity's concepts of good and evil and faith in an afterlife. He believed that morality was a way of living with one's passions and different people needed different ways. The best people came from an environment which valued the individual over the masses.

On 17 March, the day that the tragedies occurred abroad in the barn, after a week of beautiful spring weather there was a snowstorm. The laden branches on Craig Coillich and Craigendarroch looked charming, although spring flowers were covered.

Her father had found an alternative to her knitting comforts. As importing rural home craft products, including wooden and stuffed toys, from Germany, Austria and Hungary was prevented, the Rural League in London had seen an opportunity. Her father had obtained advice and information, plus a supply of raw materials and tools. She warned him not to make stuffed dolls, because she feared that she would have to come to his rescue. Instead he was very good at making toy wooden soldiers, so she could concentrate on knitting comforts for real ones. Learning about the new activity, young Callum Leslie was now helping him, so as not to be outdone by his sister Helen who was producing comforts.

A Great North of Scotland Railway Company booklet was a reminder that the holiday season was approaching. There was a list of furnished lodgings in districts served by the railway, plus a descriptive sketch of some of the health resorts on it. Those were alphabetically arranged, so Ballater was well placed. It was likely that summer and autumn would be better than last year, because of the need for a holiday or change to aid health and give a little pleasure. With the Continent closed the homeland beckoned. Seasonal special excursions were to be resumed–the 'Three Rivers Tours' via the Dee, Don and Spey, half-day excursions from Aberdeen every Wednesday and Saturday from June to September and the motor omnibus services.

On 3 April Gavin described his National Bible Society of Scotland 'Active Service' New Testament. Opposite the title page was in facsimile a message from the veteran Field Marshal Lord Roberts in his own handwriting, dated 25 August 1914. 'I ask you to put your trust in God. He will watch over you and strengthen you. You will find in this little Book guidance when you are in health, comfort when you are in sickness, and strength when you are in adversity.' It was neatly and strongly bound, printed in clear type and yet weighed less than four ounces. It also contained the Psalms of David in metre which recalled for the reader the finest memories of his home and youth. When reading a psalm in the bedlam of war, Gavin was at peace and heard the still music of the soul. Together with Iona's love the much taxed soldier was helped to feel his natural age.

Also on 3 April he recorded that they had spent eighteen days in the trenches, so the four days in and four days out scheme was currently in abeyance. Yet the next day they would go back to rest, hopefully for six days. Casualties were caused by some men not keeping their heads down, so they were picked off by snipers. It was a senseless loss of life. On Easter Sunday he noted that recent cold weather had been replaced by dampness. Further down the line the Germans had tried to fraternize with their men, as they did at Christmas time, probably to try and learn information, but their approaches were firmly rebuffed. On 12 April he was glad of better weather, because they were going to the fire trenches on the night of the 13th. The 4th Territorial Battalion was linked to them, half of each being in the trenches while the other halves rested. The Territorials were very keen, but they were not of the same standard and so did not hold the line by themselves.

They were in picturesque country and birds sang enthusiastically in the mornings, children played and men worked in the fields to the sounds of rattling rifles and booming big guns. There was an occasional lull, but the bucolic scene was spoiled by ruined houses and some huge holes in the fields caused by shells from a large howitzer. He was thankful that Scotland was safe and there was no danger to its children from flying or unexploded shells.

When they took over a trench on the night of the 13th, they were not more than 100 yards away from the enemy, but bullets came from the left rear. They strengthened the trench and in the morning found that the German line swung round behind to their left!

His battalion was only affected to a limited degree by Second Ypres of 1915. The 3rd Division's right faced Wytschaete and its left was a little east of St Eloi, so its nearest troops were about seven and a half miles from the trenches from which chlorine gas was discharged at 5 p.m. on 22 April. The Germans defied The Hague Convention which outlawed chemical warfare. Yet some of the 1st Gordon Highlanders, including Gavin, who were holding a narrow front with a half battalion, suffered from sore eyes. Probably they were slightly affected by leakage from cylinders which had been dug in on this front. Cloth and extra tins of water were sent to the Gordons. The wet cloth was tied over the nose and mouth.

Iona informed him that the Secretary of the War Office had announced there was such a large stock of clothing and mufflers, etc., overseas and at home, no further supplies of warm clothing needed to be sent to the troops. If he required anything of which there was no local supply, he should of course let his mother or her know.

As some heavy shells were named after Jack Johnson, the black boxer, he would be interested to learn that it was reported from Havana he had been defeated in the twenty-sixth round of a forty-five round fight on 5 April by a knockout punch from a cowboy, Jesse Willard, who was now the world champion. The crowd's sympathy had been with the challenger. Very unsportingly it jeered at the black man during the whole fight.

After reading Gavin's remarks about birds in Flanders, she reported that spring proper had been delayed on Deeside by bad weather, although crows had been building nests. She and Mike had enjoyed some early morning walks. Twice she had seen a lark ascend to greet the rising sun. It was a joy to hear blackbirds' flute like warbling and thrushes' songs reaching crescendo as they welcomed spring. Yet thrushes sang loudest when rain was imminent! She had also seen bullfinches, chaffinches, goldfinches and linnets. If boys were about, however, she did not linger to listen to birds, in case they were tempted to steal eggs. Miss Clark said life in Germany was so regulated that some bullfinches were taught to whistle two or three tunes. It was far better to hear their natural ecstatic notes relieve the sylvan silence. Generally the lady preferred to keep quiet about her German nest box. There was a small entrance near the top, inclining down outside to keep out rain. She put a little food and water out for the thrushes that used the box. They had repaid her, however, by attacking yellow crocuses, reminiscent of the sun, to eat the anthers.

Iona stated that the Red Cross's heavy need for accommodation in the north-east had caused the King to reconsider a proposal to transfer Balmoral to the naval and military authorities for use as a hospital. He could not relinquish all the rooms, because those which had been occupied by Queen Victoria were in exactly the same state in which she left them, and he desired that they should not be disturbed. Iona's father thought that Aboyne Castle further down the valley would be a better site. The burgh was on the railway and the castle was only half a mile to the north, whereas Balmoral could be cut off if heavy snow blocked the roads connecting it with Ballater.

In early May Gavin reported that conditions were relatively quiet. They did not see a lot of German aeroplanes fly over their area, and those that did were very high. He believed that two had been downed on 29 April near Ypres, which was only about four miles away. On the negative side a shell landed in one of their trenches and wounded two men, one seriously. The effects of chlorine gas were now being taken much more seriously. Apparently it either killed at once or within seven days, or if you survived you got consumption or chronic bronchitis. The Germans would poison the water if they had to retire. On 10 May he recorded that they had been withdrawn to La Clytte, and formed part of a sort of flying column which might have to rush anywhere, producing an unsettling effect. There was a northerly wind, but it was too strong for gas at present!

They had learned of the sinking of the *Lusitania*, Cunard's flagship passenger liner. On 7 May she was torpedoed off Ireland and sank. Among the 1,201 who died were many women and children, including 128 neutral Americans. The German government had issued warnings against travelling in her and she carried a cargo of arms. Yet Gavin commented that while normally attention was focused on casualties among fighting men, now the fate of innocent civilians roused international outrage. A comrade knew someone who had his wife on board, so he would be anxiously waiting news.

Continuing on the 11th he stated that he had been interrupted the day before by a sudden practice turnout. The enemy was pushing north of Ypres and used gas freely. Yet simple respirators were proving fairly effective, and during the last attack covered by gas Germans advanced expecting to find a trench containing only dead and dying soldiers, but they suffered a heavy loss. Also the attacks seemed to be less disciplined, although a big effort continued to be made. The weather was glorious, but it still got very cold in the evenings and they had had to reduce their kits. Moreover, as they were ready to move quickly, he could not get away for running. An aeroplane duel occurred over their trenches the other day, the German being brought down.

On the evening of 12 May the 1st Gordon Highlanders took over a section of the front facing Hill 60, which was an artificial heap formed by material excavated from the railway cutting. It was used as an observation post, looking north-west towards Ypres. The Gordons had the grim task of burying the bodies of many men who had been killed by gas a week before. Yet they were glad to find hundreds of rifles, the British being in short supply. The Germans fired incendiary shells into Ypres, as if recreating Dante's Inferno. Over their left shoulders the Gordons saw dense columns of smoke and by night the glow of big fires in the city. Shelling was almost continuous night and day. Bombers of the 1st Gordon Highlanders twice attacked the enemy, in one case Gavin and others crawling up an abandoned communication trench to do so. The 8th Brigade was relieved on 20 May and retired next morning to La Clytte. Gavin informed Iona that he had been having a hot time, leaving her to imagine the details. He did reveal that British troops had been warned that a river near Ypres was believed to have been poisoned with arsenic by the Germans. The contrast with the pure Dee could not have been greater. Very early in the morning of Whit Monday, 24 May, the enemy released gas on a far bigger scale. The 8th Brigade was out of the line, but it was ordered to march. On 25 May the 1st and 4th Gordon Highlanders worked on a reserve trench east of Zillebeke. The Germans, however, had called off the offensive after the failure of the 24th. On 26 May the 8th Brigade marched through Ypres and took over the front from Hooge to the railway. As ground had been lost the line was new, the trench being only half dug.

Gavin thanked Iona for sending him a newspaper cutting which reproduced a picture at the headquarters of the Scottish Branch of the British Red Cross Society in Glasgow, depicting Florence Nightingale as she received the sick and wounded at the Barracks Hospital in Scutari after the Battle of Inkermann in 1854. As a symbol of grace and light she reminded him much of Iona, and he preserved the item inside his New Testament.

She told him that John Galsworthy, who had previously appealed for sick and wounded horses, now appealed for the starving Belgian people. We the richest country owed Belgium a great debt for standing firm. If each of us set aside one penny for every pound of income, which would yield nearly three million pounds, that people would be saved.

On the afternoon of Thursday, 6 May, there had been a severe thunderstorm on Deeside. At one stage some people sheltered in the shop until it abated. When bad weather struck she felt particularly proud of how Gavin and his comrades bravely and cheerfully faced the dangers and hardships. They needed drink only to fortify their bodies, for their own spirits shone against all adversity. The government was worried, however, about the effect of drink on the war effort at home. Normally she was placid, but inwardly she was angry that much of the domestic trouble from drink, especially in the northern yards, rose from raw, cheap, fiery spirits. She was annoyed at the government's mishandling of the situation and the confusion which arose. Prices on drink had been raised in Aberdeen on 3 May, due to the increased duty which was to be imposed. Yet elsewhere in the county spirits and beer were being sold at old prices. On 7 May the new liquor taxes were abandoned, apparently because they roused such animosity national unity was considered more important! Whisky under three years old, however, was prohibited. She had seen Morag, who showed signs of war weariness, secretively receiving a bag of clinking bottles from a female friend in the shop, claiming they were for her father. As Iona suspected that she was indulging in secret drinking, she warned Mr Gordon in private. He quietly mentioned the matter to Morag's mother when she next left the shop. She denied that her daughter had supplied Philip with drink, and said she would persuade her to reduce her intake.

Iona's animosity over excessive drinking was nothing compared to what she felt at the depths to which the German armed services had plumbed. There was the appalling disaster of the *Lusitania*, and enemy submarines engaged in cowardly piratical behaviour off the Aberdeenshire coast and elsewhere in the North Sea. Many fishing vessels had been destroyed. To her the poisonous gas which the Germans used at the front symbolized their corrupt spirits.

The Ballater Red Cross Hospital continued to receive generous support. In the King's name potatoes and oatmeal were given from Balmoral. Items from other places included fifteen pairs of slippers, baskets of fruit and flowers, a lord and knight gave salmon, while a commoner gave kippers. Drives would have been particularly appreciated by patients in the better spring weather. At the end of their stay they were probably almost as reluctant to leave Ballater as Queen Victoria was to leave Balmoral!

On 1 June German fire swelled up again, but the British artillery was very short of ammunition. Ypres finally perished on 2 June, some 500 shells being fired into it. The 1st Gordon Highlanders' trenches were badly damaged, the occupants having a hellish time and suffering many casualties. On 10 June Gavin recorded that they had just been relieved after spending thirteen days in a particularly poisonous part of the line. On 16 June other British forces made the First Attack on Bellewaarde between the Menin Road and the Ypres-Roulers Railway. There was partial success. The 1st Gordon Highlanders and a company of the 4th took over the captured trenches which were full of dead and wounded, chiefly British, resulting mainly from the German artillery bombardment which the British had neither guns nor ammunition enough to check. The enemy now switched to using gas shells on a big scale, but respirators continued to be reasonably effective, and, although some men were affected, no men in Gavin's battalion were overcome. The 8th Brigade was relieved on 19 June.

Nonetheless the 1st Gordon Highlanders suffered 126 casualties between 15 and 19 June, but they were more than made up by a draft of 144 on 24 June. Moreover, the men were of very high quality, half a dozen having been in the United States Army. Their American accents boosted morale, besides producing subconscious humour. They served in the kilt with pride.

On 20 June Gavin wrote to Iona, asking for a few tins of condensed food, oatcakes, acid drops and peppermints. Cigarette smoking had given Donald a cough, so as he had switched to confectionery which he shared, he thought he should reciprocate. Yet the most important hour for him was when the postal orderly arrived with an item from her. He valued it more than rations. A letter expressed her love and everything about a parcel showed her care. Occasionally there was a delay during a sudden movement of men or fighting, although the general service of the field post office was excellent. His watch had broken down, but, as there was a range of military ones in Aberdeen which were luminous in the dark, he had asked his father to send him one.

Iona warned him she had learned that in early May some stretcher-bearers were on duty with a battalion which was advancing on Hill 60, south-east of Ypres. Looking for wounded to the left, they passed a barn. On the door two men had been crucified with nails or spikes driven through the palms of their hands. One victim appeared to have had a fire lit beneath him, because his clothes were black and there were what seemed like embers beneath him.

She was proud that so far Britain's armed forces had been manned by volunteers. In Germany, on the other hand, even university members of staff as well as the students had been conscripted. There was a contrast too between the King's noble principles and the Kaiser's malevolence and deceitfulness.

While the situation for British horses at the front was excellent, with an Army Veterinary Service supplemented by civilian vets, The Animals Guardian Guild based in London was appealing for help, because the French Army's horses badly needed more veterinary staff at the front. To carry injured horses in trucks a long way to a base camp or base hospital increased the suffering.

She had resumed knitting comforts, as there would be renewed heavy demand for them later in the year. The Ballater Red Cross Hospital had received salmon from the King, while other gifts included twelve pyjamas, fish from Aberdeen, turkeys, ducks' eggs, an elastic kneecap and flowers, with car and carriage drives. The only drama in the burgh had been a slight outbreak of fire in a wash house and coal shed on Queen's Road on 15 June. About 4 a.m. a neighbour saw thick smoke and gave the alarm, the flames being soon extinguished. What a contrast the incident was to Ypres!

The only disharmony in the shop was when Miss Clark, for whom economy was the essence of patriotism, grumbled that while flour was much cheaper, bread had not been reduced in price, although she acknowledged that Mr Gordon had no control over the matter. She did speak positively about the rush for the new War Loan, praising the issue of 5 sh. vouchers, because they were a fine opportunity for small investors. The customer added that while everyone was equal under God and the law, the war was achieving a degree of equality in other directions, and some aspects disturbed her. On realizing that Morag's neurosis about her complexion showed war fatigue, Miss Clark reassured her, saying that she was far too young to need skin cream.

Writing on 23 June Iona referred to a fortnight's bright sunshine on Deeside. Farmers had not welcomed the dry season, for the hay crop would be lighter and turnips had suffered much. Yet the weather was very pleasant for walking, cycling, motoring or riding in a horse-drawn vehicle. There would be few American and Colonial tourists that season, however, particularly after the *Lusitania* disaster. Normally they visited Edinburgh before travelling to Aberdeen and Deeside, and then to Inverness and the Highlands beyond. Yet the Continent was practically closed to the British public and Deeside was well patronized.

Gavin reported near Poperinge on 7 July that his battalion had been rejuvenated by a good rest, the weather being pleasantly warm. Her reference to cycling on Deeside reminded him of their idyllic rides last summer. Donald and he had met some children and taught them a little English, in return learning a little Flemish, a version of Dutch. They were to return to the trenches on Sunday night, the 11th. The bombers and snipers had been organized in a separate unit.

On 19 July the battalion's machine-gunners, bombers and snipers supported the 4th Middlesex in attacking a little German salient at the western end of Hooge. A tunnelling company had driven a gallery 190 feet beneath the enemy's support line, and the exploding mine at 7 p.m., forming a huge crater, was the signal for attack. The bombers or grenadiers, those who threw grenades, were courageous and skilful, but not all the gains were held. The Gordons suffered from shellfire during and just after they relieved the Middlesex on 20 July. On the 24th the 8th Brigade took over a sector between Verbranden Molen and St Eloi.

Gavin stated that the trenches were like a prison. In dry weather the dust gathered and the atmosphere was stuffy. Showers were welcome because they partly cleared the air. Yet unless they had work, there was lack of exercise. Much of the time life was monotonous, relieved by occasional exciting events. Constant vigilance and readiness were essential, however, whether or not shrapnel and high explosive shells came. The conditions had a wearing effect, but the men's spirits were high. They were most alive when death was closest.

Last Christmas was a watershed. Afterwards the enemy was regarded as a treacherous brute. Since the spring the war itself had changed, with the general initiative passing into Allied hands. Endurance and sacrifice were their cross, but faith and courage were their star. In this war of attrition Britain and Russia had inexhaustible resources. By earnest prayer and brave deeds God's will would be done, and the enemy's infernal machines and gas would be defeated. For him and his comrades the Highlands were reality, not this passing nightmare of bedlam and mud or dust.

Iona told him that a number of children in Ballater, including the two he met, had heard about an appeal in Aberdeen for children to send stamps for letters written by sick and wounded soldiers in local hospitals. They had handed some stamps in to their own one. She hoped that he would not be reduced to the level of a Gordon Highlander who, as a prisoner of war in Germany, had written a message to his sweetheart in his own blood on a piece of ragged canvas which had previously been used as a handkerchief. It was sent by a comrade.

Gavin's remark that Britain and Russia had limitless resources was noted. Russia's sacrifice could not be overestimated, however, and on Saturday, 10 July, a Russian Flag Day was held in Aberdeen and other places in the north-east, including Ballater, for the Russian Red Cross Society. It was the holiday month with many people away from Aberdeen. Yet the total was estimated at nearly £1,000, Ballater raising over £30.

She was sad to learn that on 6 July, in a German bombardment of Arras, shells were fired on the Cathedral, the roof being destroyed. Her father was incensed, and, on reading an appeal for civilians to supply prism binoculars, which were compact, for the Army, he sent their good pair as a gift, even though a London firm was prepared to buy suitable ones.

Miss Clark was unusually jubilant in the shop when she spoke of the Chancellor of the Exchequer having announced on 13 July that the amount subscribed through the Bank of England and the Post Office to the new War Loan was £585,000,000. The total was larger than any amount ever subscribed in the history of the world!

Iona reported that while Gavin welcomed showers to improve the atmosphere, the rain on St Swithin's Day, 15 July, in the north-east of Scotland was appreciated by farmers and others. Rain on Monday the 19th, which was part of Aberdeen's midsummer holiday, aided indoor entertainments there, and many passengers travelled by rail up Deeside, the effect being noticed in the shop.

On 14 July Lord Lovat's bill to allow grouse shooting in Scotland to begin on 5 August instead of the 12th was passed by the Lords. Mr Bremner told her that it was on the whole well received in the Ballater area. This year the young birds were fairly well formed and the stock of old birds was so large that the 5th was not too early for a start. Moreover, overstocked moors tended to produce disease, one or two cases having been noticed already. Yet bad springs were the rule, and so generally the 12th was early enough. The measure could not affect the food supply much, because the prices usually charged made them a luxury. On 22 July the Prime Minister announced that it was not proposed to proceed with the bill. Radical MP's had killed it, because no private MP's bills were allowed that year, so one by a private peer could not be allowed to pass. Some people attributed the motive to spite, but others conceded that with the nation at war there was more important legislation. Iona referred to customers saying that the delayed start would deprive wounded soldiers of a welcome gift, and farmers' stooks would be vulnerable to large coveys. The disease problem on the moors would doubtless worsen.

As she was too busy working on 20 July, she was not in the Albert Memorial Hall in the afternoon to hear a paper read by a lady who, with her sister, the matron of a military hospital, had spent a fortnight in May visiting some French hospitals, where they were impressed by the fine work being done. Ishbel said that she dealt especially with the Scottish Red Cross Hospital at Rouen. The audience contributed to the funds of the local Red Cross.

On Wednesday afternoon, 21 July, Iona did attend the annual United Free Church sale of work in the same hall. An Aberdeen lady sang two songs and the church organist played pianoforte selections at intervals. Miss Clark's booming voice was heard across the hall, as she explained to a group of ladies at the tea stall that the word pianoforte was from the Italian 'piano e forte' meaning soft and loud. The sale realized over

£51, which was much more than had been expected, although of course tourists helped. Iona wandered among the stalls—coloured fancy-work, white fancy-work, bric-a-brac, plain work, woollens, sweets and cakes and the tea stall—before buying some flowers at the section tended by dark haired and petite Mrs Mary Leslie, the mother of Callum and Helen and who worked in a fruit and flower shop. Her husband was still serving in the 6th Gordon Highlanders. She was very gentle, and clearly taxed by the war found relief in discussing with Iona the conditions in which Kyle and Gavin were fighting and the huge sacrifices which were being made to protect such peaceful events at home.

Mary said, 'On 3 June Kyle was in one of two companies involved in an action against a strong point on the Givenchy Bluff held by the Germans to the east of Béthune and on the north bank of the La Bassée Canal. At 9.30 p.m. a big mine exploded at the top of the salient and the assault succeeded, although an enemy counter-attack in darkness next morning forced a retreat. There were heavy casualties. Fortunately it has been quiet since. Out of the line men have trained in the mornings and in the afternoons have bathed or basked in orchards. Sundays in billets have been rest days with a church parade. The sequel to a stay in billets has been a concert, when possible being held in the open air.'

Iona was particularly glad for the children that on the evenings of 26 to 28 July a conjuror, who was on a caravan tour of Scotland with a South African tenor, gave an open air bohemian variety concert in Station Square. The spectators were much entertained by conjuring tricks, ventriloquist sketches and some Irish and Scottish songs. On the first evening the collection of over £3 was, in accordance with the conjuror's custom in each place he visited, given to the local Red Cross. A new programme was presented on each occasion.

Gavin may have wondered why men from various British regiments had been sent to Ballater Red Cross Hospital. On 26 July the Under Secretary for War stated that every effort was made to send patients arriving from abroad to hospitals in the area of their homes, but, as men were sent in ambulance trains, each carrying 100 or more, it was not always possible. In many cases it was unwise for patients to be sent on a long rail journey. When Iona's father visited the local hospital, he saw men with serious injuries and even amputated limbs, and occasionally poisoned by gas breathing heavily. Yet they were bright and optimistic, bearing the pain and discomfort without complaint.

9: On Furlough in Aberdeen

On Thursday morning, 5 August, as Iona served in the shop she was briefly apprehensive hearing her father say on the telephone, 'Yes, Mr Fraser,' but when shortly he cheerfully replied, 'I will be happy to let her come,' she knew that it was good news.

Replacing the receiver he beamed at her and said, 'Gavin has written to tell his parents that he will arrive on furlough in Aberdeen on Saturday for a long weekend. You have been invited. He hopes to alight from a King's Cross train in mid-morning. You can take what you please as gifts from the shop.'

Later that morning she received a letter from Gavin in which he stated that his battalion had moved to a less hostile part of the front, and he announced his coming leave. He would not have time to visit Ballater, but he would like to see as much of her as was compatible with her duties in the shop. He exhorted her, 'Wear nothing new, for your love is more current than the latest fashion.' His parents would lay in ample food, so she need not bring any perishable items, unless they were for her. Some confectionery from Ballater would be welcome in memory of the previous summer. He modestly cautioned against building up a glamorous image of him as a military figure. 'Most of us are not heroes who come home to rest. Comrades who lie in foreign fields are immortals, the bravest and the best.' He concluded, 'Keep well until we meet with loving lips and hearts which weep with joy.'

During the past year she would have liked to meet his parents, but, as he faced mortal danger at the front and their relationship was informal, she thought it better for any information about her to be channelled through him to them. These coming brief but blissful days would enable her to meet them all. While a censor had read Gavin's letters, he had not met her, and Gavin could express his mature love without inhibition. Yet the long separation would soon be replaced by communing looks and words.

Arriving in Aberdeen he and Donald were very impressed by how the old, dingy Joint Station had been transformed with huge glass roofing, spacious platforms and other features, even though their parents had told them. On the platform was a lady collector wearing a white sash with a red border and 'Alexandra Day' in gold lettering in the centre. She was surrounded by passengers as she sold artificial but charming wild pink roses from a tray. The two soldiers were weary after their long journey and passed on. Beyond the platform barrier they were delighted to see their parents. Suddenly Iona's and Gavin's eyes met in wonder. His description had enabled his parents to recognize her. Wearing a navy blue coat she looked as fresh as the day they parted, and he was bronzed but a little drawn. His whole being was filled with her joyful smile and still, angelic beauty. He greeted his parents and kissed his mother, before Iona and he kissed and embraced.

'You are still a nymph.'

'I will always be Iona, never a Venus.'

As they drew apart he said, 'You are wearing a wild rose in connection with Alexandra Day.'

'Yes, it is to raise money for local causes, including the hospitals. The idea of the design comes from Queen Alexandra's badge. The roses have been made by the blind and crippled girls of the John Groom Crippleage in London.'

As they walked away she was proud of his uniform, with a rifle slung over a shoulder, and of the man, so by the station entrance, when she bought a rose from a lady with a basket and pinned it to his chest, evoking the comment, 'It is prettier than a medal,' they knew that it also represented their love.

Before he and Donald parted, his father informed them that a picnic for Gordon Highlanders and their families and friends was to occur that afternoon outside Seaton House. The privilege was due to a convalescent Gordon officer. The comrades agreed to meet there. A short time was spare before the next tram went in the direction of Gavin's home in Old Aberdeen to the north, so the quartet strolled along Union Street, the city's main thoroughfare. Iona had no interest in the summer sales.

Laughing he said, 'There is the Froghall Nannie. My mother has told me that a man living in Froghall Terrace regularly lends his goat as a mascot for charity collections.'

As they passed the animal that was suitably bedecked, with children placing pennies in the attached collecting boxes, Iona reminded him, 'You were born under Capricorn or the Goat.'

At a corner of a junction with a side street was a car filled with real roses for sale, but she commented, 'I said last summer that I preferred wild roses to cultivated ones, particularly as they were associated with the five wounds of Christ. Now the artificial roses seem more natural than real ones.'

He nodded and added, 'It is a dull day, but, with almost everyone participating, the atmosphere contrasts with the Western Front.'

They boarded a tram which at the east end of Union Street turned north up King Street. Dismounting they walked west along the south side of King's College and its playing fields, before turning north past the College's front, including the early sixteenth century Chapel and Crown Tower. The quaint High Street, which narrowed, intensified the difference between peaceful Old Aberdeen and the bustling city. They crossed St Machar Drive and went briefly up the west side of Don Street, which meandered like the river of that name, to which it made its northerly way.

Entering the living room of the terraced house Iona looked vital in a green dress, and the parents treated her almost deferentially, so she perceived that Gavin must have given them a high opinion of her. Jenny was fair and thin with a light, cheerful voice. Ivor had his son's features, and while he was broader and somewhat older than Iona had imagined, she knew that extra years could make a man more paternal.

Pointing at Gavin's bulging bag his mother said, 'You could let me have any clothes which need washing.'

As he produced some items he said, 'I will show you my back room, Iona.'

They went upstairs and seeing the rear garden of a large house she asked, 'Is a gardener employed there? Peaceful masses of beautiful flowers surround a perfectly trimmed lawn.'

'No, it's a labour of love for a retired professor and his wife. It's good to see beauty and order in this warring world.'

Turning she smiled at a picture of the Alps over his bed and remarked, 'Clearly it reminds you of Hannibal.'

As he unpacked his bag she saw him place a New Testament on a bedside table, and she recognized a protruding newspaper cutting which depicted Florence Nightingale. Alongside he laid the mouth organ which her father had given him. She saw on a bookcase some works on ancient history which covered Hannibal's period, with others on Scottish wildlife.

He laid a small Belgian flag on a lower shelf and explained, 'I mentioned in a letter that Donald and I taught children a little English, and in return they taught us some Flemish. Unusually they did not ask for a memento, but instead gave me the tricolour. We were told that the colours were based on the Duchy of Brabant's coat of arms, black symbolizing determination, yellow generosity and red valour. The gift reminds me of a happy time out there.'

As they enjoyed a hearty meal, the main course consisting of beef and vegetables from the back garden, Jenny asked Iona about her, her father and life in Ballater. Then Gavin said that his battalion had recently moved near to Givenchy. He also filled in some other military details which for security he could not divulge in letters.

Ivor informed Iona, who simply knew that the parents were involved in clothing, 'I work at Grandholm Mills on the far side of the River Don. We are very busy fulfilling a big government contract to make khaki for troops. The word is from Urdu meaning dust-coloured. The sight of so much material is both patriotic and sobering.'

Jenny said, 'I work for one of the clothiers making uniforms. Other textile manufacturers in Aberdeen make woollen materials for troops and preserving works produce rations for them.'

Ivor added, 'The granite trade prospers. Shipping is much reduced, for many seamen are in the Naval Reserve, and fishing is much curtailed, many fishing vessels and crews being in the naval service. Moreover the Continent, the chief market for cured herring, is cut off and fishing only occurs in a limited area. Yet shipbuilding yards make repairs and build steam trawlers to replace wastage. As Aberdeen plays a significant role in the economic war effort, however, it has not contributed in the same proportion as other parts to the Army. That is why I am particularly proud of Gavin.'

Jenny said, 'Living in peaceful Old Aberdeen we are less nervous than people in the city about the dangers of a naval bombardment or Zeppelin raid. Yet reports of enemy submarines operating in the North Sea, including off the Aberdeenshire coast, have caused some parents to reassure their children that Germans will not land in the dark and prowl along the streets.'

Afterwards, as the women did the washing-up, the men discussed recent military events in the back garden, before Ivor said, 'I am much impressed by Iona, but, in view of the uncertain future and the heightened emotional nature of this short furlough, it would be unwise to formalize your relationship at present. You should wait until you have more time together and there is a realistic expectation of you being able to live as man and wife.'

Gavin gazed at her in the kitchen and nodding replied, 'We are sure about our relationship, but the medium term horizon is beyond our control.'

When they returned inside Jenny, perceiving that the young couple would prefer to speak mainly to each other that afternoon, tactfully said to Gavin, 'I hope that Iona and you enjoy the Gordon Highlanders' social event. Ivor and I will go to the summer dog show at the Belmont Auction Mart in Kittybrewster, a city area to the south-west.'

After the young people walked a short way round west by St Machar Drive, they headed north up the long straight section of the Chanonry, where the canons of St Machar's Cathedral originally lived. She noticed the contrast between the humble yet homely dwellings abutting Don Street and these large, detached houses set back behind walls and impressive trees. At the end on the east side they reached the Cathedral with its gatehouses.

They stopped to gaze at the imposing building as he commented, 'You know the legend that St Columba sent St Machar from Iona on a mission to the mainland. He was to travel east until he came to a place where a river as it approached the sea bent in the shape of a bishop's staff. He may have built a church here, safe from flooding above the River Don. For 400 years the Celtic Church ruled, then until the Reformation the Roman Church prevailed, and in this period the current architecture was built. Unlike your parish church the Cathedral faces west. The two great towers at the front were originally erected as for a castle, but Bishop Dunbar, who shared my Christian name, added two spires. In 1690, after the Revolution, the Church of Scotland adopted the Presbyterian order.

There is an intriguing story about the wooden statue of Our Lady of Aberdeen and baby Jesus. Dunbar gave it to the new chapel at the north-east corner of the Bridge of Dee which was finished in 1527. Here travellers could pray for Mary's protection before setting off on a journey or give a prayer of thankfulness after completing it. The statue was saved from destruction during the Reformation and later shipped to safety in the Low Countries, being presented to Isabella, Infanta of Spain (1566-1633), who ruled in the Spanish Netherlands. She defeated the Dutch and the statue was venerated as having brought victory. It has since been known as Our Lady of Good Success in Belgium. For 100 years it has been kept and greatly honoured in the Church of Our Lady of Finisterre in Brussels. Since the restoration of the Scottish Roman Catholic hierarchy in 1878 devotion to Our Lady in the diocese and further afield has focused on copies of the statue. In February my mother told me that its restitution was probable. Hopes in such matters, however, have often been disappointed. We will worship there tomorrow.'

Just west of the Cathedral they passed through a gateway and gazed down on a haugh of the Don. The river curving ahead was heartening, but it lacked the Dee's broad, regal serenity. As they descended they saw a colourful concourse on Seaton House's spacious park which was bordered by beautiful trees. Strolling through the crowd they met Donald and spoke with him for a while about the previous summer holiday and wider matters, before he thoughtfully kept his distance. When there were over 200 people the entertainments began, catering for old and young. The brass bands of the 1st and 2nd Gordon Highlanders played and a pipe band also performed for the dancers. Games for young people included activities such as football, dart throwing and Aunt Sally, where players threw sticks at a pipe in the mouth of a wooden woman's head.

Gavin remarked to Iona, 'I am thankful that the children are spared the dangers and hardships faced by those in Belgium and France.'

When she took photographs of him he understood how much they would mean to her in his absence, and particularly if he did not return again. Enjoying the Gordons' proud camaraderie they had no wish to withdraw from the throng and rest against a tree on the margin.

To some children who asked to be photographed she smilingly replied, 'Yes, but I will take group not solo pictures. I will send them to the Gordon Highlanders' Memorial Institute in the city's Belmont Street, where an official will know how best to distribute them.' She quietly added to Gavin, 'I fear that some of the children have lost their fathers in the war, so this event is especially important to them.'

He was charmed that, although they had not seen her before, they were drawn instinctively to her. He did his part by joking with them. When the last picture was due to be taken, he asked her to pose with a few children, so that he could have a memento.

Then they sauntered back to his home, but this time passing through the very quiet part of the Chanonry which bordered the south side of the Cathedral before bending down into Don Street. They were glad that during the day there had been only one or two light showers, which were balanced by short intervals of sunshine. They were gladder still that the private and public expressions of their relationship were seamlessly interwoven. Love was a blessing to be shared, not a trophy to be guarded.

Returning home they found that his parents were still away. As he entered the front room to see old family possessions, she said that she would bring in some washing which his mother had hung on the line before going to the station, and then she would make coffee. After the washing had been neatly piled inside ready for ironing, she went to ask him if he would like anything to eat. She found him lying fast asleep on the sofa. After his long journey from abroad she was surprised that he had been so alert all day. Now she realized that the joyful reunion with his parents and her, plus the pride of attending his regimental event, had stimulated him, but alone he was suddenly exhausted.

She tiptoed across the room and sat in an armchair. She recalled that on Lochnagar's summit he had watched over her as she slept. Now the roles were reversed. His pleasant smile and cheerful demeanour were gone. It was as if he was snatching sleep in the trenches. His face was set with quiet courage and devotion to duty. While he saw her as the angelic consummation of many generations of women, in his stern features she beheld the valour which had been handed down through generations of Scots, and which could enable ordinary men to commit heroic deeds and sacrifices. Her gaze wandered over every detail of his uniform, and she smiled at tiny scorch marks on his kilt. She perceived that the candles she sent him had been used partly to get rid of lice. He had not mentioned the problem in letters. Her suspicion was confirmed that he had hidden much from her, because he wished to concentrate on what they had in common, so they could continue to achieve a better understanding of each other.

Hearing his parents return outside, she rushed to open the front door and whispered that Gavin was asleep in the front room. Ivor was very amused that she should behave as if his military son was a baby. The trio had a cup of coffee in the living room. Jenny quietly said that the number of entries at the dog show was lower because of the war, but the quality was above average. She spoke of various pedigrees, until a barking mongrel down the street roused Gavin and he joined them, apologizing for nodding off as if he was just a civilian. His mother exerted her authority and told him to go upstairs, change clothes and bring down his uniform for washing. When he returned Iona was charmed to see him wearing similar clothing to that he had on last summer, which increased her enjoyment of eating haddock and more fresh vegetables.

Jenny commented, 'It is appropriate for a soldier or naval man in particular to eat what fishermen have risked much to catch. A decrease in the supply of haddock is more marked in Aberdeen than any other Scottish port. Yet it is a pity you just have a long weekend.'

'I feel fortunate, actually. Earlier this year I heard of a soldier in the Argyle and Sutherland Highlanders who was only able to stay one day at Campbeltown in Kintyre. I know of instances where soldiers have taken an extra day's furlough and returned to face the consequences. I could not do that, because if a man who fills my place during that time were to be killed or injured, it would weigh on my conscience.'

As his mother served the dessert she said, 'I am adding Deeside strawberries to the sponge and custard. Grapes and peaches with shortbread will follow.'

He smiled at Iona, for they were from her valley, and he joked, 'This dish is preferable to what my comrades describe as trench pudding—jam spread over a boiled Army biscuit.'

His father commented, 'The meals we have this weekend are special for us all. To help the food supply in a small way, twice a week we have cheese instead of meat. Moreover, as barley, wheat and maize are used for making beer and spirits, I have stopped drinking both for the rest of the war. Also, I have given up the pipe. Jenny has stopped eating sweets.'

'Sweets?' asked Gavin, as he gave a knowing look at Iona, because he had asked her to bring some confectionery for him.

His mother replied, 'Sugar has high food value, especially for children, but sweets are the most expensive form of sugar.'

Ivor added, 'A good part of the money we save overall goes into War Loan. Yet such details are trivial compared to your duties. Have you any more thoughts about the Germans?'

'It is as well that God judges us by what we are and not by how we seem. Many of my comrades tend to stray from the King's English, and they are not as well read as most German soldiers, but they are closer to God, the supreme spiritual leader, than the Germans with their imperial ethos where the individual is subordinated. Education is supposed to nurture a person by drawing out goodness in his nature and counter the influence of original sin. German education has the opposite effect.

The enemy envies our mobility in battle, when on being driven from one point we often quickly occupy another firm position and counter-attack. To them it is sportsmanship in the purely physical sense. For us the word also means in battle generous valour, reminiscent of medieval chivalry involving devotion to defending the weaker party, particularly women and children.

In May I saw a gasping, badly wounded German officer being carried on a stretcher down a communication trench. As my fallen foe was my brother, I raised a water bottle to his parched lips.

Seeing the reality of life he feebly muttered, "Thank you. It is tragic when Christians fight Christians. After the sleep of death and my soul is refined, I hope to see the eyes of Christ at last."'

There was a sudden bang as a neighbour's back door was firmly shut. Gavin quickly turned his head, as if he was at the front, only to smile at being sensitive to such an insignificant matter. Iona noticed that while he did not take himself too seriously, he was deeply concerned about other people and just causes. She said little, being preoccupied with observing how his fine qualities had been strengthened in war. He was more of a complete man, although still young.

After the meal the women first washed items from the table and then his clothing, while the men went into the front room. Shortly after the washing had been hung outside, his Uncle Ross and Aunt Lizzie Fowlie arrived from the city. Jenny ushered them into the front room and they warmly greeted Gavin. Lizzie, rotund and self-opinionated, perfunctorily shook Iona's hand, but did not remove her tall, dark blue hat with a white ribbon. The thin uncle, a clerk, was unprepared for Iona's Highland grace and beauty, and he shyly smiled and quietly greeted her as they shook hands.

'I like your new hat, Lizzie,' said Jenny.

The aunt replied, 'There is too much drinking in the city. As a member of the World's Woman's Christian Temperance Union, I show my opposition by wearing the badge of a white ribbon prominently on my hat.'

Her younger brother laughed and said, 'There is no drinking here during the war.'

Iona indicated to Lizzie that she could sit in the armchair near the window which she had left, while she gestured to Gavin that he was to stay in his armchair, the rest occupying the sofa. While the aunt sat stiffly upright, Iona curled her knees on the carpet and leaned against a hand as informally as when she and Gavin picnicked by the Falls of the Glasallt.

Turning to her nephew Lizzie said, 'I hope that you and your young lady are going to hit the town during your furlough. I can recommend the variety performances at the Tivoli Theatre.'

'I leave on Tuesday morning after a long weekend, so I prefer to rest and take exercise.'

'But surely you can take a few extra days?'

'I am afraid not. There is a war on.'

'Yes, yes,' she grudgingly replied. 'The lighting restrictions in Aberdeen are ridiculous. People bump into each other and lamp posts, while they take their lives in their hands crossing a busy road.'

A Highland fire burned in Iona's eyes and her lower jaw was set in a way Gavin had not seen before. He intuitively realized that she thought charging across no-man's-land was far more dangerous than a civilian crossing a dark road.

Unaware of the offence she had caused Lizzie continued, 'We are so far north it seems most unlikely to me that we will suffer a naval bombardment or Zeppelin raid. All that the cowardly Germans do at this latitude is to hide in sneaky submarines and attack unarmed merchant shipping and trawlers. In May, for example, the Aberdeen trawler *Glencarse* was captured and taken to a German port. The Aberdeen trawler *Lucerne* was forced to stop by bullets from a submarine. The idiotic Germans insisted on paying 2 marks for fish for their own use, although the trawler and the rest of the catch were blown up with explosives! The eight man crew's small boat was damaged bumping against the submarine, but the men were put aboard the Danish sailing ship *Urda*. The situation has worsened. The weekend before last was very black for our port. On the Sunday news of the disaster to the trawler *Briton* was published, involving the captain's death, five missing presumed drowned and two injured. That night came news of the destruction of *SS Firth* with the loss of four lives. The following Wednesday it was reported that twenty-nine fishing vessels–trawlers and liners–belonging to Aberdeen had been lost through German submarines during the war. Ridiculous German propaganda claims that British fishing vessels are all armed and crewed with the best naval fighting men. It is asserted that because of the vessels' large numbers and manoeuvrability they are a great danger to German submarines, and the greater the number which are sunk the more is reduced the secure ring round the British Isles.'

Addressing Iona she said, 'I dare say that coming from your Highland retreat the wild sea must be a forbidding sight.'

Iona shook her head and replied, 'A river is many streams and a sea is many rivers.'

Lizzie raised her right index finger, as if she was about to clinch the argument, and said, 'But the sea is salty, whereas a river is not.'

Iona obstinately answered, 'Actually, rainwater dissolves minerals containing sodium and chlorine in rocks and soil and rivers carry these minerals to the sea where the salt accumulates.'

Lizzie furiously stirred her tea before saying to Gavin, 'It is a pity that you will not be here for the Glorious Twelfth. There was very little shooting last year. Thus the current stock of grouse is exceptionally large. You would have had fine sport, but it is more important that you should bag some Germans.'

She laughed at her own joke, until, perceiving that the others did not think that the firing line was a comic matter, tried to qualify what she had said, adding, 'Anyway, grouse is not for an ordinary man's table.'

Iona corrected her, 'A retired gamekeeper who is a friend of mine believes that several Aberdeenshire lairds will not forget sick and wounded soldiers in hospitals. In peacetime many dead birds were not used. It is a pity that it has taken a war to teach the need for economy. Nothing is wasted in Nature.'

Trying to silence the tiresome young woman, Lizzie addressed Gavin again, 'The National Register forms are due to start being distributed on Monday morning. If you leave before yours arrives, I am sure that your parents will forward it.'

Iona quietly corrected her again, 'The armed services are exempt.'

Lizzie affected social maturity by complaining, 'It pains me to see the war breaking down the old, respected order of the classes and women taking over men's jobs. I shudder to think where it will all end.'

The old order included younger generations being subservient to older ones, but Iona spoke up, 'As officers lead their men into battle, they face a higher risk of being killed. The levelling brought about by war in the classes and between men and women may ultimately produce greater equality and freedom.'

Thunderstruck Lizzie was determined to have the last word, and, affecting knowledge of agricultural matters, commented, 'My cousin Tam Brown's well managed farm in Buchan is helping the general war effort. The potato crop is expected to be very fine, the only unsatisfactory crop being hay, because of damage caused by drought followed by rain.'

Fearing that Iona might counter-attack, she suddenly announced, 'We must visit our daughter Maisie and her family in King Street. Take care at the front, Gavin,' and, in a dry aside to Iona, she said, 'I wish you a safe **return** to Ballater.'

When they were gone Jenny and Ivor went to the living room, and Iona, resting her head on Gavin's lap on the sofa, said softly, 'I did not like to cross your aunt, but she appeared to treat your service abroad lightly, rather than tactfully trying to sound a note of normality.'

'We should show her compassion. Unlike Uncle Ross she was blind to your physical and spiritual grace. At least the exchanges between you meant that she did not even mention astrology. She likes to talk about it at length. Her birthday is on 15 March which makes her a Pisces like you. Yet while you show the strong qualities associated with the sign–friendly, imaginative, intelligent and sensitive–she exhibits weak aspects, being driven by emotions rather than reason and she dithers. As a Capricorn I have to take life seriously, overcome hardships and enjoy the challenge of difficult problems. I am to be a loyal friend. If I am stubborn at times, however, I hope that my opinions are right. Leaving astrology aside, the trials of these times should not only chasten our bodies, but also purify our spirits. In war I have learned that the words peace, joy and love have deeper meanings.'

'What is peace?'

'Harmony between God and man.'

'What is joy?'

'Love's radiant delight.'

'What is love?'

'A shared foretaste of Heaven. Not of this world alone are we who are in love. The enemy is focused on this world. When one of his large shells explodes, after the initial flame there is smoke which robs the sight of life's wider colours, leaving only black and grey, the hues of death. Such materialistic power is spiritual nemesis which will lead to downfall, with the Allies becoming more determined. Reports of a food shortage in Germany betray spiritual starvation, a failure to provide for non-military essentials, because of preoccupation with the war.

Some of my comrades are so zealous they insist on staying in the firing line for hours after they are supposed to have gone to a reserve trench. As I think that the conflict could drag on much longer, courage should be tempered with patience. The longer I serve the risk of death or serious injury increases not diminishes. Yet my faith and your love sustain me. When I am on sentry duty at night and gaze at the moon wounded by meteorites, I realize that the solar system, although divinely ordered, is dynamic not gentle. It is because we are separated by time and space that we see the hand of God evolving peace and harmony from chaos. His influence also works in the affairs of men.'

She looked into his eyes, as if she understood him completely, even better than he did himself. The light of her strong spirit illuminated the inner darkness, and his whole being was filled with bliss.

He stroked her hair which like her frame was a perfect embodiment of her heart and spirit, and said, 'You wisely know that you must never bind your locks, even in a ribbon, still less in braided chains. Sublime beauty is elemental and free of circumstances. My mother and Aunt Lizzie think that the furlough is too short, but you do not complain. Some couples would lament having to make the most of so little time, but our love is timeless.'

She replied, 'Last summer we experienced great joy in the Highlands. Later tribulations have merely made our reunion sweeter. Events have troubled our hearts, but our spirits have stayed calm above the storm, braver and more united. Love is God's Kingdom on earth.'

A wireless or gramophone was not needed. The ensuing silence was more potent than music. The spiritual heights and emotional depths were one in the music of transcendent love. Its mystic chords flowed between and within them. What did his life matter, when she had regenerated his soul? June had incurred heavy casualties for his battalion, an inversion of Nature's most benign season. Yet now away from the stale, sometimes fetid air in the trenches and martial sounds, he found spiritual freshness. He fell into a reverie and they flew ardent and free above the valley of the shadow.

After a while she pressed his right hand and whispered, 'Are you asleep?'

He murmured, 'Sleep, sleep, night's sweet potion. How often abroad it has come in snatches, when I desired it most. Shortly I must reluctantly succumb to it fully. Let us have supper, so I can be ready for tomorrow.'

She went into the living room and returned with a tray. While they ate his mother pointedly entered with bedclothes and said Iona had agreed that, as there was no extra room upstairs, she would sleep on the sofa. He did not wish to spoil a perfect evening, apart from his aunt's visit, by arguing. It would have been two against one, and, accepting that discretion was the better part of valour, when he was ready he wished and kissed Iona goodnight.

He rose quickly on finding that he had overslept and it was nearly 9 a.m. The others had already breakfasted, and he was amused that two women tended him while he ate and chatted to his father. Then he expressed a wish to go early to the Cathedral, so that he could show Iona some points of interest in the interior. She suspected that by being discreet he also modestly wished to minimize the attention which would be given to a soldier on furlough.

Walking up Don Street they turned into the Chanonry and entered the Cathedral from the south. Only the visiting preacher, the Rev. Hugh Irvine, and an elderly couple speaking with him near the sanctuary had preceded them. They gazed at the seven lights above the west doorway. They depicted a series of figures of Jesus and his disciples, and beneath were emblematic representations of their deaths.

Gavin pointed at the foot of the central panel and explained, 'There is the Gordon coat of arms and those on the sides are of related families. The glass dates from 1867.'

Then he led her further up the building and commented, 'Bishop Dunbar had installed a flat ceiling of panelled oak about 1520. It contains forty-eight shields arranged in three lines. It has long been a joke in this Protestant Cathedral that the arms of Pope Leo X, albeit a great patron of arts and letters during the Renaissance, should occupy the prestigious first position in the middle rank at the east end. Behind him are the bishops of Scotland. On the north side Emperor Charles V is backed by the kings and dukes of Christendom, the King of England following those of France and Spain. On the south side King James V is first, then a minor and later the father of Mary, Queen of Scots. I draw your attention with particular pride to the following arms of St Margaret, Queen of Malcolm Canmore, preceding those of Scottish earls. Through all the ecclesiastical changes in Scotland her memory remains fresh as a tender and wise wife and mother, as well as a saint. At the west end of the series of shields from north to south are the arms of Old Aberdeen (including lilies because of the Virgin Mary's patronage), the University and King's College of Old Aberdeen founded in 1495 and the city of Aberdeen.'

The minister approached them and Gavin explained that Iona was from Ballater, modestly only adding that he was local, to try and prevent him asking anxious questions about his role in the war. Having seen the lilies she was reminded of the statue of Our Lady of Aberdeen in Brussels, and she asked the minister if he knew of any progress about its return.

With a resigned smile he replied, 'No, but Our Lady is needed even more in Brussels just now than here.'

To Gavin's relief he blessed them and turned to greet other worshippers. The couple sat at the back to the left. She gazed at the east window with its clear glass and ornamental stone tracery, the natural world aptly leading into the supernatural one. The building's great strength impressed her, particularly the two lines of huge pillars with linked arches east to west. She thought of the contrasting more modern sets of pillars in her church.

They were joined by his parents, and a few other worshippers who wished him well were introduced to Iona. The deep chords of the very fine organ announced the first hymn, 'All people that on earth do dwell,' which was based on Psalm 100. Iona's pure, cheerful voice accorded with the direction of the words and filled him with the joy of which they had spoken the previous evening. The hymn referred to people being God's sheep, to his enduring mercy and truth, and affirmed that earth and Heaven adored him.

The first reading was Ezekiel 34.11-22, in which the Lord stated that he would seek his flock, feed it and would judge between the members. The second reading was Matthew 25.31-40, in which Jesus told his disciples that he would come escorted by the angels and sit on his throne of glory, separating men from one another like sheep from goats. Those who had been charitable to the least of his brothers did so to him and would go to Heaven. In his sermon the minister said that in this worst of wars thoughts turned more to eschatology and the Day of Judgement in particular. The Lamb of God was also the Divine Shepherd who would lead them to rest and eternal peace. The prophet Isaiah wrote of 'The Prince of Peace' (9.6). St Paul in Ephesians showed how Christ by the Cross reconciled men with God and made his Church the sacrament of the unity of humanity and of its union with God. Jesus 'is our peace' (2.14). In the Sermon on the Mount Jesus said, 'Blessed are the peacemakers: for they shall be called the children of God' (Matthew 5.9). Our armed forces strove for peace in a spirit of justice, not out of murderous hatred. Civilians supported the war effort directly and by charity. He pointed to St Margaret's shield on the ceiling. She was born in Hungary which was associated with another royal saint, Elizabeth. Both of them were concerned for the poor. The light of faith would guide those who mourned the fallen, until they were seen again in the celestial radiance of God the Father and his Son. The blessing of Providence was sought for the present armed men, so that peace, justice and equality could be restored and there was charity between the nations.

After the service ended with a stirring rendering of 'Love divine, all loves excelling' and the benediction, Gavin, his parents and Iona chatted briefly with some worshippers before walking back between rows of gravestones of people long since dead. Gavin thought of the rough graves being dug daily along the Western Front with wooden crosses, but he was humbly grateful for God's care and the promise of eternal life. He was also thankful for parental support and the sustaining loving peace between Iona and him as they retraced the quiet way back home.

Over a fine lunch they compared religious services in Old Aberdeen, Ballater and abroad, but Iona noticed the parents dart occasional anxious looks at him, and she gently said, 'Last summer Sergeant Mackay, the Rev. Farquharson and I reminded Gavin of Jesus' words in Matthew 6.34, "Sufficient unto the day is the evil thereof."'

Gavin smiled and replied, 'As Iona cannot take me on a stiff Highland walk this afternoon, I will take her on a leisurely stroll.'

They walked east down St Machar Drive and turned north-east up King Street, until they halted on the long, handsome Bridge of Don. Looking down the estuary they saw the river flow to the wild North Sea. They crossed to the other side and walked further west well above the river.

He pointed and said, 'There are two seals basking on that island. Ahead is the Gothic Brig o' Balgownie with strong buttresses and a pointed arch. Legend suggests the bridge having been started by Bishop Henry Cheyne in the late thirteenth or early fourteenth century and completed by King Robert the Bruce. The current bridge definitely resulted from rebuilding in the early seventeenth century. It is so well endowed that ironically money from its fund has paid for its much larger neighbour. I am reminded somewhat of the Linn of Dee Bridge, but whereas it is surrounded by conifers and we have seen salmon leaping up the narrow channel, here are deciduous trees and the Don flows sedately from a gentle gorge beneath the bridge, with a deep salmon pool below known as the Black Neuk. According to an old tradition it was of unknown depth and haunted by a spirit who, before a storm or when a disaster was impending, made strange noises in the pool.'

When they stood on the cobbled bridge, they had an old-world feeling as he continued, 'Just as Byron nearly slipped to his death at the Linn of Dee, he was apprehensive of this bridge. He regularly crossed on his pony, and he was afraid that he was referred to in Thomas the Rhymer's prophecy that the bridge would collapse if an only son crossed it on a mare's only foal. It was a strange fear. Particularly in winter, when Nature has retreated, the strong bridge appears to reign in timeless grace.'

Turning back they rested on the bank near it, and she laid her hands gracefully on the grass. Even away from the Highlands he was deeply charmed by her hair curtaining part of the high neck, while the locks were swept back behind the ears to show an open face. The Sabbath and summer peace encouraged relaxation, so he was surprised by the powerful gaze of her blue-green eyes as they turned alternately to him and the river. She had a stronger spirit than many older, taller women to face the challenges of life's sea. With a thoughtful expression she delicately rubbed the end of her long nose, before gazing down with a critical frown to check that her dark blue dress was well arranged.

Trying to make her relax he said, 'When we met on Craig Coillich you said that you were not a sprite. Yet there is a puckish element in the way you have rubbed your nose, as if you might be a mischievous fairy.'

She gave a modest, girlish smile. Other women were apt to fidget, but her changing strong and tender expressions, with the movements, showed a unique combination of thoughts and feelings. Stroking her hair alternately with each hand, she then chewed on her lower lip as she looked down and lowered her eyelids as a veil.

She replied quietly, 'At the Falls of the Glasallt I said that if war came you would go abroad and see many attractive women.'

'A fickle heart may fall in love many times, but the spirit only once. My nourished heart was not fickle.'

Her radiant eyes were matched by drawn cheeks creased in a blissful smile. While Morag raised her eyebrows in affected surprise, Iona raised hers in love's delight. The genteel upper front teeth projected over the lower lip. She blinked hard to control herself and not dissolve in giggles. She demurely looked slightly away and her eyes shone with purest joy. It was not social but natural modesty born of innocence, adding to her incomparable beauty and mystery. Then her left hand touched the back of her hair, and protruding lips formed a little circle to indicate compressed thought, before she gazed at the sky with a pearly lustre in her eyes. He had not seen another woman who had such riches and who was so unmindful of them. His attention was repaid a hundredfold. She sought love for its sake alone. The war had strengthened their relationship.

They took the long Don Street to his home, where the cake baked by his mother made the evening meal special. He tried to divert attention from him by inquiring about his relatives in west Scotland and Iona's aunt and uncle in Braemar. Yet inevitably the conversation turned to the war. He spoke of its dual pitiless and noble aspects. Life generally was two-edged, darkness and light, suffering and joy, mortal and immortal. It was part of God's sometimes inscrutable design that unlikely comrades could become heroes when there was greatest need. It was broadly true that those on his side were spiritually and corporately united, whereas the Germans tended to be spiritually misguided and even dead. Yet sometimes when prisoners were taken, he thought that a few of them looked genial. Iona had informed him in a letter that some Germans and Britons left trenches on Christmas Day to achieve a brief, limited armistice. He believed that the Germans had been allowed to drink alcohol freely, but unlike their leaders some of them were messengers of the Holy Spirit. Recently he learned that the 2nd and 6th Gordon Highlanders participated in a truce, in the latter case it was claimed between Christmas and 3 January! Germans started it. The dead on both sides could be buried on no-man's-land. There was bartering of food, drink and smoking materials. Some of the Scots were even shaved by Germans who were barbers before the war.

God gave us liberty so that we could receive his free love and freely return it. One followed him in humility and hope. The future lay in his hands. Jesus gave his love first and his life as ransom for the world. In his joys and sorrows, loftier and deeper than ours, he was the peripatetic soldier of peace. In Matthew 10.28 he said to his disciples, 'fear not them which kill the body, but are not able to kill the soul.'

He did not see an early end to the war, but it was like a long Lent. One saw a spiritual mirror which was the opposite of narcissism, for it revealed imperfections. Yet, to change the image, one was reborn. There were both the military conflict and the inner, upward struggle. One remained resolutely cheerful, so that Christ was within one and one was within him.

'The slings and arrows of outrageous fortune' would be controlled. There was something spiritually hollow about the shells which were fired at the front. In fact one in three did not explode! Basically it was a fight for principles not power, for true peace not victory. In stillness and tumult the Holy Spirit moved and inspired. Faith and inner calm helped one to bear the chaos. Ironically if there was no noise from the enemy the silence was potentially dangerous, in case a ground assault was imminent!

When Iona and he were alone in the front room, she understood that, as they had only gone for a short walk that afternoon, he wished to rest. She therefore took the initiative, and as it was Sunday she produced her Bible.

'As you will not see the Highlands this time, I will read some references to mountains. They are important for personal encounters with God. When Moses was leading the Israelites from slavery in Egypt towards the Promised Land, on Mount Sinai he received from God the Ten Commandments, recorded in Exodus 20.2-17. Isaiah 52.7 prophesied Jesus' birth: "How beautiful upon the mountains are the feet of him that bringeth good tidings, that publisheth peace; that bringeth good tidings of good, that publisheth salvation; that saith unto Zion, Thy God reigneth!" Zion used to refer to the holy hill of Jerusalem on which the city of David was built, or more widely to the Hebrew theocracy. Now it also means the New Jerusalem or the Kingdom of Heaven. When I was a child and read Jesus' words in John 14.2, "In my Father's house are many mansions," I took them literally. What is meant is that Heaven is not for a select few, but for the souls of all the faithful.

Matthew 4 recorded how when Jesus was in the wilderness the Devil took him up a very high mountain, and, showing all the kingdoms of the earth, offered them if he would worship him. Yet Jesus, thinking of the Kingdom of Heaven, replied, "it is written, Thou shalt worship the Lord thy God, and him only shalt thou serve" (v. 10).

In Matthew 5 Jesus began the Sermon on the Mount. The eight Beatitudes or blessings are precepts not commandments. I find encouragement in the words, "Blessed are the poor in spirit: for theirs is the kingdom of heaven" (v. 3). All our goodness comes from God, and it is a cause for thanksgiving and praise. Yet love involves sacrifice. Jesus said, "Blessed are they which are persecuted for righteousness' sake: for theirs is the kingdom of heaven" (v. 10). He knew that his disciples would suffer for him, except one. Judas hanged himself from a tree because of his sin, whereas Jesus was crucified on a tree for the sins of mankind.

In Matthew 17 Jesus was transfigured before Peter, James and John on a high mountain, traditionally regarded as Mount Tabor, to reassure them who he was. His face shone "as the sun, and his raiment was white as the light" (v. 2). Moses and Elijah spoke to him, signifying that he had come to fulfil the law and the prophets. A voice from a bright cloud said, "This is my beloved Son, in whom I am well pleased; hear ye him" (v. 5). Hence, strengthened in faith like the three disciples we are prepared for the cruel ascent to the small hill of Calvary. In Genesis 22 it was on a mountain that Abraham's faith was proved, when he was prepared to sacrifice his only son Isaac, but the angel of the Lord stopped him just in time.

In the Revelation made to St John on the island of Patmos an angel "carried me away in the spirit to a great and high mountain, and shewed me that great city, the holy Jerusalem, descending out of heaven from God" (21.10). After a detailed description he added, "I saw no temple therein: for the Lord God Almighty and the Lamb are the temple of it. And the city had no need of the sun, neither of the moon, to shine in it: for the glory of God did lighten it, and the Lamb is the light thereof" (vv. 22-23).'

Gavin thanked her for the quotations and comments, but added, 'It is a pity that we have not been given a physical description of Jesus, although now he is transformed in Heaven.'

She replied, 'It was not customary then to give such details. In any case Jesus wishes us to concentrate on his living words, not on his appearance. God looks not at us but within us. The body is clay which is to be moulded by spiritual beauty and power. Adam and Eve were guilty of pride, the first of the seven deadly sins. Jesus the second Adam showed humility in assuming human flesh.

In Luke 1 Mary, after learning that she was to bear the Son of God, showed humility in the Magnificat. This second Eve has been given various poetical titles, but I think of her as the Mother of Jesus, of the Church and of humanity in its joys and sorrows. I see a degree of affinity between her and Jesus in some of his words in Matthew 11.28-30, and in which I feel closest to him. As both the Divine Shepherd and the Lamb of God he said, "Come unto me, all ye that labour and are heavy laden, and I will give you rest. Take my yoke upon you, and learn of me; for I am meek and lowly in heart: and ye shall find rest unto your souls. For my yoke is easy, and my burden is light." Later when Mary saw him slowly die, he was raised above the ground and interceding between Heaven and earth said, "Father, forgive them; for they know not what they do" (Luke 23.34). It took divine humility to show such selfless love. I believe that the second Eve, the most saintly of women, gazed compassionately also at the two thieves who were crucified on either side of him, and that one of them responded to her intercession and Jesus' example by saying, "Lord, remember me when thou comest into thy kingdom. And Jesus said unto him, Verily I say unto thee, Today shalt thou be with me in paradise" (Luke 23.42-43). The exchange prefigured Judgement Day when the saved would be separated from the lost. Later Mary was taken physically to Heaven, so that she would not suffer corruption. We approach her now mainly through prayer. Since the Fall of Man we are banished children. Baptism clears most of original sin, but there is still an element which falls into temptation. We seek her protection and guidance, and value her as a friend of the sick, in the journey to our heavenly home. It is fitting that she has long been the patron of Old Aberdeen.'

Gavin replied, 'Thank you. I would love to discuss St Paul with you, but we will do that tomorrow evening. Let us have an early supper again, so that we can make the most of our last full day.'

Even so he overslept and descending found that his parents had left for work. They knew that the young ones would prefer their own company. Iona served him porridge followed by bacon and eggs. Afterwards he suggested a longer walk than the day before. They crossed St Machar Drive and went down the High Street, stopping outside the Chapel and Crown Tower of King's College. The visitors saw a tall, elderly man accompanied by a small group. He appeared to be a retired scholar of the University, for he commented on the buildings with an air of authority. Iona and Gavin stood behind the group, as he explained that a Latin inscription on the north side of the Chapel's west entrance acknowledged James IV's support, although he was killed at the Battle of Flodden in 1513. Whereas the west towers of the Cathedral had spires, this tower was surmounted by four arched ribs topped by a lantern and crown. It was a closed imperial crown, because James IV saw himself as an emperor in his own kingdom. More generally the guide said it may have surprised them to learn that much of the rest of the College dated from the nineteenth century, but he would focus on earlier parts.

Leading the way into the quadrangle, he pointed at the slender hexagonal spire which almost divided the line of the Chapel roof into two. The spire had always raised the gaze of College members to Heaven, whereas if it was at the west end it would have been obscured for the inmates by the Crown Tower. The sundial at the top of the second Chapel buttress from the west at about thirty feet had been claimed to be the earliest single face sundial known in Scotland. An early two-storey structure on that side had included the Library's second position in the sixteenth century. In the eighteenth century the dilapidated construction, including the Library above, was rebuilt and enlarged because of Dr James Fraser's generosity, but it was dismantled in 1773 because as a false economy the College had not employed an external architect! The books were kept in the west end of the Chapel before being moved in 1870 to the building on the east side. The Chapel's south side, now faced in granite with buttresses, and the east face of the Crown Tower, had armorial bearings of worthies connected with the University from the sixteenth to the eighteenth centuries, such as the Lovat family, several members of the clan having been early members.

Iona whispered to Gavin, 'My father has sometimes spoken of Lovat Scouts serving in the Second Boer War.'

Entering the Chapel they admired the richly carved rood screen and choir stalls. The guide said that they were the finest surviving example of medieval Scottish ecclesiastical woodwork. The visitors' eyes were carried along each row of stalls to a broad band of carved oak leaves and acorns, vines and grapes, while the canopies above had fine pinnacles.

Gavin recalled Iona's remark on Craigendarroch that oak leaves represented courage, and she murmured Jesus' words, 'I am the vine, ye are the branches: He that abideth in me, and I in him, the same bringeth forth much fruit: for without me ye can do nothing' (John 15.5).

Centrally placed before the steps of the sanctuary was the tomb of the founder, Bishop William Elphinstone. Near to the south was a brass plate marking the grave of Hector Boece, who became the first Principal. Iona looked about and noted the pleasing combination of oak and plaster.

Back in the quadrangle they passed the so-called Cromwell Tower house in the north-east corner. They were told that it owed more to Cromwell's General Monk who came to Aberdeen in 1651. Then they were led through a passageway at the south-east corner. After advancing a short way they were asked to turn round, and Iona was surprised to see the stark, defensive Round Tower, its gunloop and small windows blocked up, but with larger modern windows. The guide stated there was reason to believe that the early Scorpio chamber, which housed the college armoury and was the Library's first position, was in the tower. (Iona and Gavin smiled on recalling how the previous innocent summer they had seen Scorpio from Lochnagar's summit.) The astrological meanings of Scorpio included northern, cold and watery, the night mansion of Mars. There was the possible threat of an attack from sea or inland. In the summers of 1496 and 1497 Aberdeen had been placed in a state of preparation for war because of the risk of an English invasion from the sea. The tower could well have helped the students ward off a mob of reformers who came from the Mearns in 1560 to try and destroy the College.

The couple then went north-east up King Street, before turning east along the first stretch of the Esplanade to the right of the Don estuary. They were vivified by the sea air, and, when they were about to go south down the two mile main Esplanade, their spirits were animated by the wild beauty and freedom of the sea, heightened by the long shoreline stretching from the distant north down to Aberdeen harbour. As they continued he thought that submarines might be lurking not far off, and he looked south-east in the direction of Flanders. Then he gazed sternly west across the Links at how a peaceful golf course had been utilized as a military training ground, before he followed Iona's eyes to the regulated, tumultuous waves.

She remarked, 'As each wave approaches the shore it forms for a moment the circle of eternity, before surrendering in white purity on the sand.'

Shortly she recognized a woman who walked in front with a man, and she called, 'Elspeth!'

The plump woman, who wore a pink dress with round white dots, turned to smile brightly, and Iona explained, 'This is my younger cousin whose parents live in Braemar. You will have heard of Gavin. He is a Gordon Highlander on furlough.'

Elspeth looked at him with deep compassion, as if he was a lamb temporarily removed from the slaughter, and she said, 'Hello, Gavin. This is Stuart Hardie. We both teach music.'

Iona asked her, 'Is your sister Eilidh well?'

'Yes, you know that she is a secretary at a legal firm. She is not so homesick now that she is going out with a lawyer.'

Stuart, who was a little taller than Gavin, with grey hair and a sallow complexion, said to him, 'You have been doing heroic deeds in Flanders.'

Gavin unassumingly replied, 'Its flatness contrasts with our Highland holiday last year.'

Stuart nodded and said, 'We spend one weekend each month with Elspeth's parents in Braemar. We have not got further than the Linn of Dee, however, as we are not the exploring type.'

Elspeth had been told of Gavin's candid manner, but she gazed at him curiously, wondering if war had changed him, possibly for the worse. She was reassured, for there was no brave posturing or tense puffing of cigarette smoke. Suddenly she felt self-conscious in case he regarded her dress as frivolous at that time compared to Iona's dark blue one, although he was out of uniform.

She was relieved and charmed when he said, 'Iona is an accomplished soprano. I have no natural abilities in art or music, except for a modest skill in playing the mouth organ. I admire aesthetes who lead us to sublime and even divine beauty. Do you both have a favourite instrument?'

Stuart replied, 'I specialize in the piano and Elspeth loves her clarinet. We have some ability, but much painstaking practice is needed. Our pupils have varied talents and levels of interest, but we instil discipline to produce satisfactory results. It is particularly therapeutic for them and us in these times to appreciate the deeper harmony of music. Yet sometimes when I fuss about the details of a score to bring out the emotional colouring, I think that I should be one of the shining spirits fighting in the dull monochrome of war.'

As they neared the end of the Esplanade Elspeth asked anxiously, 'When do you return, Gavin?'

'Tomorrow.'

'Oh dear, it is lovely to meet you, but you will want to share these precious hours together. We hope to see you both again. Goodbye.'

As Elspeth and Stuart crossed the road and returned to the city, Gavin pointed beyond the harbour entrance and said, 'Girdle Ness Lighthouse was built in 1833. It was designed by Robert Stevenson, the grandfather of Robert Louis whose holiday home in Braemar we saw last summer.

Let us go down to the beach and return beside the breaking billows.'

They walked on sand embedded with pebbles. By the shifting margin of the elements they had more privacy than when passing other promenaders on the Esplanade, and he put an arm round her. After walking some distance they sat and ate sandwiches which they had brought.

She commented, 'Last summer we heard rivers, burns and waterfalls praise the Creator. Now we hear the united voices of the sea. Originally the dark, primordial, chaotic waters of the deep were associated with spiritual darkness. Yet early in Genesis are the words, "the Spirit of God moved upon the face of the waters" (1.2). Baptism means plunging. When Jesus had been baptized in the Jordan by John, "he saw the Spirit of God descending like a dove, and lighting upon him" (Matthew 3.16). Baptismal water cleanses the person of sin, and he is given the new life of the Holy Spirit. Romans 6.4 asserts that when we are baptized in Jesus we are also baptized in his death, for as he has been raised from the dead, "we also should walk in newness of life."'

Picking up a freshly washed shell she continued, 'Ishbel has told me that the shell is a symbol of pilgrimage, being used in ancient times for eating and drinking. As it could be used for pouring water in baptism, it is also an emblem of baptism and of the Virgin Mary. St Augustine had a vision in which a child told him he would sooner be able to empty the oceans with a shell than for the human mind to understand the mystery of the Holy Trinity. Repentance is required of an adult who is baptized. When the disciples asked Jesus, "Who is the greatest in the kingdom of heaven?" he called a small child to him and, setting him in their midst, said, "Except ye be converted, and become as little children, ye shall not enter into the kingdom of heaven" (Matthew 18.1-3). Life may buffet us, but we will always be guided by God's divine breath. When we walked beside Loch Muick I spoke of finding my place in Creation. Now amid such physical and religious power we also learn humility and discover our real significance.'

Gavin replied, 'I will keep the shell as a memento. I had my baptism of fire at the Battle of Mons, in which I had a burning zeal for the glory of God which the overweening enemy sought to usurp.'

As they sat in silence for a while by the roaring sea and the tranquil sky bent over, they heard the rising chords of an inner tide. Only God and they knew the bliss of their perfect love.

When they were strolling back to Don Street, he suddenly understood that the trauma of the war coming so soon after their idyllic holiday had made her turn more to Ishbel for religious guidance to bolster her faith. She had hidden her anguish and restrained her religiosity in letters. Looking back he felt he should have understood that the tone of normality in her writing was somewhat unnatural. He was very grateful to Ishbel for helping to broaden and deepen her religious knowledge. He was confident that she had become so strong spiritually nothing could break her. There would be no tears, only joy at parting on the morrow.

She had fully integrated with the family, and during the evening meal Mrs Fraser asked about her Irish connections. Had it not been for the war, she explained, it would have been her Irish relatives' turn to visit them that summer. The matter of home rule for Ireland had been temporarily eclipsed by the island's duty to the Empire. Iona realized that Mrs Fraser had focused on her, so that Gavin could concentrate on eating and build up his strength for the long return journey. She thus expatiated on her Irish memories.

When she and Gavin were alone in the front room, they needed a higher strength, and he said, 'The word faith sounds a little impersonal, even minimal, implying basic belief. Real faith is fervent and personal, arising from joyful trust. St Paul's burning faith has always appealed to me. That is why I have suggested we discuss him now.'

She replied, 'Yes, he affirmed, "I can do all things through Christ which strengtheneth me" (Philippians 4.13). One of Jesus' greatest miracles was the conversion of Saul who had seen Christianity as a threat to Pharisaical Judaism which promoted purity and fidelity to the Law of Moses. When Stephen, one of the converts among Hellenists, or Greek speaking Jews, in Jerusalem, was stoned to death, the killers placed their clothes at the feet of the young man Saul (Acts 7.58). Three times in Acts it is related how, when he went to persecute Christians in Damascus, he saw a vision of Jesus in glory. Paul, to use his Roman name, himself stated that God revealed "his Son in me, that I might preach him among the heathen" (Galatians 1.16). He turned from external forms of purity to the pure heart, from hate to love, and from the Old Testament covenant between God and the Israelites to extending the covenant of Christianity to become a world religion.

Like many Jews he believed that the Day of Judgement was imminent, and so he saw himself as an apostle or missionary to prepare the people of every nation. When I spoke about baptism on the beach, I referred to this context in Romans 6.4, "we are buried with him [Jesus] by baptism into death: that like as Christ was raised up from the dead by the glory of the Father, even so we also should walk in newness of life." The chapter concludes with the words, "For the wages of sin is death; but the gift of God is eternal life through Jesus Christ our Lord" (v. 23). In 1 Corinthians 15.31 Paul wrote, "I protest by your rejoicing which I have in Christ Jesus our Lord, I die daily."

Jesus said to his disciples, "He that findeth his life shall lose it: and he that loseth his life for my sake shall find it" (Matthew 10.39). Jesus was born in a cave in Bethlehem in wretchedness and initial obscurity. Later he wept going to raise Lazarus of Bethany to life again from a cave, particularly as his sisters Martha and Mary were grieving (John 11). He foresaw the sorrow which Mary his mother would suffer at his death, after which his body would be laid in a rocky tomb, but from which he would be raised from the dead.'

Gavin commented, 'I have been in great danger many times at the front, but I have been reborn with spiritual power and felt fearless. During our holiday last summer I envied your grace. Now I have found grace through war. When I read John 2.14-16 in a dugout, I was moved by Jesus' righteous anger at seeing officials at the Temple in Jerusalem exchange ordinary money for temple currency to buy animals for sacrifice. Jesus "made a scourge of small cords" and drove the officials and animals out of the Temple for turning it into a house of commerce. It was not the brief disorder, but the restoration of sacred peace which impressed me. His divinity was lost on Roman soldiers who were to mock him as the King of the Jews. When he himself was scourged, as on the Cross he may have addressed his Father and even quoted from the scriptures. If so the scorn of the soldier who punished him would have increased, because Jesus' Father was not a Roman god, so for the soldier Jesus would have continued to blaspheme and rebel. There was no limit to the number of lashes, and sometimes the victim died while being scourged. Jesus was going to be crucified anyway, so it did not matter how barbaric was the punishment. Not surprisingly he was so weak walking to Calvary, but his divine grace was a pattern for Paul and others to follow in their sufferings.'

Iona added, 'Paul sometimes used athletic and military images, but for spiritual not physical prowess. He observed that of those who ran in a race only one received the prize. "So run, that ye may obtain." Those who strive for it are "temperate in all things. Now they do it to obtain a corruptible crown; but we an incorruptible. I therefore so run, not as uncertainly; so fight I, not as one that beateth the air" (1 Corinthians 9.24-26). Although it is believed that letters to Timothy have been written later in Paul's name to promote fidelity to his teaching, 1 Timothy 4.8 contains the curious remark, "bodily exercise profiteth little: but godliness is profitable unto all things, having promise of the life that now is, and of that which is to come."

In 2 Corinthians 10.10 Paul expressed others' views of him: "his letters, say they, are weighty and powerful; but his bodily presence is weak, and his speech contemptible." Yet he must have been filled with the Holy Spirit to accomplish what he did. Jesus knew how to keep out of physical danger until he faced his destiny in Jerusalem. Paul on the other hand suffered greatly as a missionary, 2 Corinthians 11.23-25 referring to beatings, imprisonments, a stoning and three shipwrecks. He had been through the valley of darkness. Yet in the same chapter there was something almost comical in the way he avoided arrest in Damascus, when through a window he was let down in a basket by the wall (vv. 32-33).

As for grace, while scholarly opinion is divided about whether Ephesians is genuine, Paul's teaching is expressed succinctly in 2.8-9: "For by grace are ye saved through faith; and that not of yourselves: it is the gift of God: Not of works, lest any man should boast." Jesus dealt with the matter in a characteristically practical way when he visited Martha's house. She was distracted by all the details of serving a meal, and, seeing her sister Mary sitting at his feet to hear him speak, asked him to tell her to help. He gently told her she worried too much, and that Mary had made the better choice (Luke 10.38-42). Faith took precedence and then came good works.

Paul followed his master when in Galatians 5.14 he wrote, "all the law is fulfilled in one word, even in this; Thou shalt love thy neighbour as thyself." In 1 Corinthians 13 he regarded it as the greatest gift of the Holy Spirit. Charity or love "Beareth all things, believeth all things, hopeth all things, endureth all things" (v. 7). For "now abideth faith, hope, charity, these three; but the greatest of these is charity" (v. 13).'

Gavin replied, 'Thank you again for the quotations and comments. Before I met you a narrow view of the spiritual life dominated me. You have taught me the ways of the heart, but I still envy your natural grace. As Jesus said in Matthew 5.8, "Blessed are the pure in heart: for they shall see God." Jesus was emotional. He did not wish to die, but he bowed to his Father's will. May my heart and spirit become more finely attuned, as ours are together.'

Resting her head on his lap, she smiled up at him before closing her eyes. Gazing down at length on her in silent peace, he recalled looking at her asleep on Lochnagar, and now even more she emanated the Holy

Spirit. After a while she stirred, and he said that they should have an early supper again, so they could make the most of their remaining hours together next day.

He descended early in uniform, but the women were already preparing breakfast and his sandwiches. Soon Ivor appeared and they all ate, before going into the back garden to take photographs. Gavin stood with a proud smile by himself, and then Iona photographed him with his parents, before the young couple posed. It was a happy event, but Gavin knew that if he did not return the photographs would be particularly treasured.

He had a short earnest conversation with his father in the front room, before seeing him off on his bicycle to work. Soon he left with the women and they took a tram down King Street, alighting in Union Street. They stood by a store window out of the way of passers-by, as his mother said to him, 'God bless you' with a kiss, and, giving a smiling 'Goodbye' to Iona, walked briefly away, before mother and son instinctively turned round for a last smile and wave.

He and Iona were buoyed by surrounding humanity. As they went down Bridge Street they saw other soldiers heading their way. She thought that they looked grim but more spirited than subdued men going mainly in the opposite direction to civilian jobs. They turned left into Guild Street and crossed the steel bridge by the station. Unusually the main girders separated the road from the footpaths which at the outer edges had cast iron parapets. She had a chilly feeling as she contrasted the safe bridge and a tram peacefully rattling by with the metal missiles which would soon threaten him, an expendable common soldier.

To her surprise, instead of focusing on the impending dangers, he gazed at her with great compassion and said, 'You need a proper holiday. I once visited Aviemore. It is the front entrance to the Cairngorms, because you see a whole mountain range with forests and lochs in the foreground. You and Ishbel could take a tent. In particular try and visit the Wells of Dee on Braeriach. If you send me the more vivid details with a few photographs, it would almost be like us being there together.'

As they crossed the road before entering the Joint Station she replied, 'I will ask my father and Ishbel about the matter.'

The north facing veranda of the new station cast a shadow as they gazed across the concourse and saw transport in transition, with a horse-drawn Royal Mail van and carts looking old-fashioned beside the cabs. Then the couple merged with the activity inside. The train was waiting and some passengers had already boarded. Donald stood by an open door bidding farewell to his parents. He nodded at Gavin and then nodded sideways to indicate that he and Iona should pass on, as he was comforting his distressed mother.

Standing by the next open door Gavin held Iona by her arms and said, 'I have not seen the Highlands this time, but you have brought your Highland spirit which is more important. I can never repay your loving care. I am not expecting to be involved in a major action soon, but, if there is a delay in the arrival of any of my letters, it may not necessarily be because of bad news.'

Resting her hands on his chest she kissed him and replied, 'Remember St Paul's words in 1 Corinthians 10.31, "whatsoever ye do, do all to the glory of God."'

'I will remember his valiant fight. The heart is not enough. When hearts and spirits are strong and united, we understand and serve God best. All will be well in the end,' he concluded with a kiss.

He found a seat by a near window and laid his bag and rifle on it, while she stepped out of the way. Standing by the window he met her gentle gaze. Amid the bustle there was a silent dialogue of souls. The whistle blew and the train drew away. She quickened her accompanying steps with a joyful face, as if she and Mike were running in the Highlands. Then she stopped to exchange a bright, brave smile, and the last he saw of her was an adorable rising, angelic hand. Soon the train passed over the sparkling Royal Dee, and he thought of her strong spirit returning to Ballater's pure air and blessed peace.

10: Iona and Ishbel in the Cairngorms

As Iona journeyed west she realized that Gavin had delayed suggesting a return to the Cairngorms, partly to ease the numbness after parting, but mainly to encourage her to gain a more complete appreciation of the mountains, as they had been a literal and figurative high point of their relationship which in a way would continue there. Particularly in wartime they were an exceptional spiritual retreat relating to their discussion of biblical references, and if he did not return she would associate them with him.

She resumed working that day, but in the evening with her father's approval she visited Ishbel whose father cordially agreed that the pair could start their holiday on Wednesday, returning on Saturday. He suggested that they took his old golf trolley to carry a bag containing the tent and other items. They appreciated the mobility, but to reach Aviemore by rail they had to travel to Aberdeen and then go through a wide westerly arc. Leisurely tourists would have passed through Elgin and stayed briefly in Inverness, before travelling south to Aviemore. This pair, however, wished to make the most of their visit to the Cairngorms, and they went via Keith lying south-east of Elgin. In due course their hearts leaped when they saw the broad River Spey, which was like a sister of the Dee.

As they stood on the south platform bridge at Aviemore admiring the panorama of the mountains' mystic lights and shades, Iona commented, 'They look grand beyond the ancient pine forest of Rothiemurchus, which probably means fort of Muircus, and Glen More or big valley. Corries of Braeriach and Cairn Gorm are visible. Ironically the most dramatic feature is the Lairig Ghru, the pass linking Aviemore to Braemar, with its huge V-shape. The north entrance is between Castle Hill and Carn Eilrig. Let us begin, however, by visiting the birch woodland before nearby Craigellachie, or rock of the stony place, west of here. The cliff used to be the venue of the Clan Grant, its slogan being "Stand fast, Craigellachie!"'

They walked beside little Loch Puladdern which bore charming white water lilies. Then rippling rings spread on the surface as a trout rose to snatch insects. The visitors felt somewhat greasy leaves of alders around the shore. North-west beyond the loch they passed silver birches. They were familiar with those on lower Craig Coillich, but in this setting the constant sway of the loosely hung leaves had a special cheerful peace.

Iona remarked, 'It is strange that the tree, a lover of light, is sometimes called the pendulous or weeping birch, although rain draws out its fragrance.'

From damp hollows came the sweet scent of dark green leaved bog myrtle, while on seeing the yellow flowers of bog asphodel Ishbel noted, 'The asphodel belongs to the lily family.'

Iona giggled and said, 'Poetically the asphodel was an immortal flower in Elysium. When Morag and I were at school, she tried unsuccessfully to get the rest of us to use it as her forename.'

The path went uphill and they met an old woman walking with her dog. She said that she kept him on a lead, because there were roe deer on the higher slopes. She added that the nearby little reservoir was created in 1880 to provide water for a hotel in Aviemore. There were some ducks on the reservoir. To the north-east red moss lay in a boggy hollow. Large quantities of sphagnum, of which the red type was a species, were collected for use as wound dressings during the war. They looked towards the steeper slopes. On rocky screes were scattered several kinds of trees, but the aspens with their long stalks causing the large leaves to flutter drew Iona's attention. She thought of the vibrant green lives on the Western Front, and wondered how many would be lost before the leaves above her fell. A hunting buzzard circled overhead, giving a long, low, plaintive whistle. Yet Iona knew that it was a characteristic cry, and she was not a prey to idle pathetic fallacies. Seeing the Cairngorms from the reservoir's west side, they resolved to go at once towards them. They moved quietly to avoid startling any roe deer which might be near. After the long rail journey, however, they were much refreshed by visiting this retreat of thickets and glades.

Crossing the Spey by a girder bridge they went south-east through Inverdruie, until they reached Coylum Bridge, where they gazed down the south side. From Iona's map they learned that from the right came the Am Beanaidh from Gleann Einich to the south. It included the Allt Druidh from the Lairig Ghru to the south-east. The Am Beanaidh swept round to meet the River Luineag from Loch Morlich and form the River Druie which they had seen coursing to the Spey. The reduced summer flow was mainly on their left side. From the right bank a tall birch with wildly dancing tresses bent over the shimmering water. The women crossed to the other side, where the banks were also lined with varied trees. Some way ahead a thick dead trunk lay over the river as a natural bridge.

Then they walked south-east on a forest track some distance to the west of the Am Beanaidh. There were pines, birches and juniper bushes which had a gentle green appearance but were prickly. A welcome southerly breeze came from the Cairngorms. Soon they were enclosed in pines which cast cool shades, with an occasional larger shadow as a cloud crossed the sun. Blaeberry, cowberry and mossy stones lay on the floor. Stretches of pine needles on the track had an autumnal brown hue which seemed to mix up the seasons, although sounds like kissing came from lofty crossbills, joyful songsters of the light. Next day the women would be spiritually uplifted among the mountains, but now they were glad to leave the fevered world for Nature's serene peace which soothed their hearts. (Many pines in Rothiemurchus were felled during the war, however, mostly for ammunition boxes.) At one point there was a glimpse of the Am Beanaidh roaring north, with a dead trunk across it reminding them of the one near Coylum Bridge. At length a wide heathery clearing gave a view of conical Carn Eilrig to the south-east and round Creag Dhubh to the south-west.

Iona said, 'The Cairngorm Club Footbridge is a short way on the left, and we will camp south of it overnight. Having made good progress, let us take that track to the right and visit Loch an Eilein.'

As they walked surrounded by heather, Ishbel left the bag and trolley out of sight over the bank to the right, an occasional tree acting as a marker. Before long charming Lochan Deò lay to the left, surrounded by pines on three sides. On reaching the intersection with the track leading to Gleann Einich to the south, they turned left to Lochan Deò's open side which had juniper bushes, heather and grass. Sitting on a rock they had lunch and admired the scene's composition. Tall trees cast long shadows over the water, but a large segment in front reflected the sky. The very tranquil surface was stirred only by a faint breeze. In the medium distance the bank on either side curved in somewhat, making the further stretch of water with its shining centre look even more sheltered. The tarn had much shrunk during the summer, and after eating the women found many deer tracks in the soft ground by the edge. Ishbel photographed Iona, as Gavin would appreciate seeing her against the peaceful lochan.

After they resumed walking west, Iona observed, 'I am reminded indirectly of Gavin. When he first visited the shop and said that he was originally from Lochaber, Morag teasingly remarked that cattle thieves used to come from there. This is part of the old Rathad nam Meirleach or road of the thieves which was used by Lochaber reivers when they raided Moray and the north-east.'

After a while suddenly through an extensive expanse of trees burst a scene of surpassing beauty, and Iona's eyes glistened as she exclaimed, 'The famed Loch an Eilein or loch of the island! The loch is less than a mile long, but it is large compared to its main attraction, an island with a ruined medieval castle lying nearer the west shore. Let us walk round the loch's narrowing north end and get a reasonably close view of the castle, particularly as I know that the west wall is better preserved.'

The loch was sheltered among high wooded slopes, and the track was some distance from the water. Curiosity led the women to descend through pines for a clearer east view of the island. Sunshine between two clouds laid a long path across the rippling water. Yet a heavy presence of trees on the island allowed only parts of the castle to be seen. Through Ishbel's binoculars the mysterious aspect was heightened by the trees and ruin casting green and grey hues on the water. They resumed walking on the track where red squirrels had dropped pine scales and cones. Here and there were blaeberry, juniper bushes and occasional birches. Then they admired larches on the shore with graceful branches and long, slender, light green needles. Cones on the ground prompted them to gaze aloft and see a crossbill removing seed from a cone with his twisted beak. Crossing the Milton Burn at the loch's exit, they walked down about one third on the far side until they were opposite the castle. An artist was painting the scene. Before the sun disappeared behind a cloud the women light-heartedly photographed each other against the ruin.

Then Iona commented, 'The island is thought to be at least partly artificial. In 1688 the wife of the laird of Rothiemurchus successfully defended the castle from an attack after the Battle of Cromdale by a party of supporters of James II under General Buchan. According to past locals there was a submerged zigzag causeway from the castle's door to the shore, the secret being always known to just three people. Until 1899 ospreys nested at the castle in spite of much human persecution. Now it shelters only a variety of trees and jackdaws. If the trees outside were less obtrusive they would help keep fresh the castle's appearance. As it is the sight of them towering above and besieging the ruin, including the green mantle on the walls, is bizarre. Yet the humbled but still strong monument of defence in times of trouble will resist the elements for centuries to come.

I am reminded of Miss Clark teaching us about the military significance of the twin lochs, Kinord and Davan, five miles north-east of Ballater. In 1648 by Act of Parliament the Castle of Kinord was ordered to be slighted. Some months after we learned about the islands my father took me to Loch Kinord. Amid the perfect peace it was difficult to believe that men had once fought there. Nature had reclaimed hers.'

She continued to make observations as the loch curved by the finely wooded Ord Bàn or fair round hill behind them. In old times signal fires were lit on it. They passed some very large pines which were probably seedlings during the Jacobite Rebellion of 1715. From above came the high trilling calls of crested tits, while sphagnum mosses were in hollows. Pine scales and cones on the way again showed that red squirrels had been busy. They saw a roe buck suddenly disappear. At the loch's west end white water lilies in a bay contrasted harmoniously with the heathery bank. Then they gazed up at the rocky buttresses of Kennapole Hill overlooking to the south-west.

Iona said, 'There is a cairn at the top with an inscription by the Duke of Bedford to the Duchess in 1834. She was a daughter of Jane, Duchess of Gordon, who retired to Kinrara on the other side of the Spey. The mother's influence was clear when in a few weeks a regiment could be raised on the Gordon estates.'

As the track bent away from the loch she suggested going south to the connected Loch Gamhna or loch of stirks. Leaving the serene order and spaciousness of Loch an Eilein with its broad track, they were enclosed in a narrow footpath. Loch Gamhna was itself more confined and even more peaceful, particularly as they saw no one else. They walked through secluded, wild abandonment. Water lilies added to the beauty, but there was not the same distinction between land and water, for the shallow loch had extensive reed beds. There were many plant species and the scene teemed with life, a natural diverse garden. Sheltering crags lay beyond, but to the south-east on steep hill slopes they saw through binoculars groups of hinds and stags against the heather.

At the north end a shining channel led to Loch an Eilein. On the east side of the larger loch they heard a female capercaillie's 'kock-kock' sound. In contrast an unseen wren filled the air with its warbling song which ended with a trill, and then a goldcrest darted above treetops. In a bay were more lilies and some ducks.

As they returned to the point at which they had originally approached the loch, Iona commented, 'Pine seeds have been blown and seedlings are evident some distance away. I am reminded of the Holy Spirit which animates all Creation. On another level recently my minister took for his sermon Matthew 13.37-38: "He that soweth the good seed is the Son of man; The field is the world; the good seed are the children of the kingdom; but the tares are the children of the wicked one." During his furlough Gavin said in effect that some ordinary German soldiers had redeeming qualities. Yet when he was previously at the front I informed him of how G.K. Chesterton deplored the repressive educational system in Germany which consumed childhood.'

Ishbel had said little during the trip, because she knew that Iona was gathering details for Gavin, but now she replied, 'Jean-Jacques Rousseau believed that lack of education caused people to misbehave. Germans receive too much factual education based on books and too little moral education. Man both as a race and individual, however, is tainted by original sin. Cardinal Newman used the words "aboriginal calamity." We all have a dark side, but potentially we are all capable of forgiveness. Jesus gained expiation for sins for all nations by his Atonement. He is the bridge between God and us. Adam and Eve were full of gladness at the beginning. By forgiveness from God and forgiving others, we can recapture our early innocent joy.'

Proceeding east they saw through trees the broad, resounding Am Beanaidh and the Cairngorm Club Footbridge. The bank was lower than the far one, so they climbed steps before walking on the iron bridge. Looking south-east the surging roar of dark blue water between outstretched pine branches stirred them, as did rocks beneath the surface in front shining golden in the evening sun. Downstream water seethed more over rocks, and a plaque on that side of the bridge stated that it was built in 1912 on the Lairig Ghru route by the Cairngorm Club, Aberdeen, through its committee and the help of 'many Mountain-Loving Friends.' A plaque on the other side gave times and distances for places along the route, ranging from Aviemore—one and a half hours, four miles—to Braemar—ten hours, twenty-four and a half miles.

Ishbel remarked, 'People will also use this bridge when walking to or from Loch Morlich to the north-east.'

Some tourists stepped carefree on the rocky west bank, but a young man in dark clothes stood still gazing thoughtfully at the fleeting water. As the two women left the bridge on that side, he suddenly turned and began to walk resolutely north-east. Ishbel was about to say, 'Good evening,' when she noticed his withdrawn look and said nothing.

Iona whispered, 'I think he has likely decided to join the Army.'

'Yes, you are probably right.'

Following the little used south-east track, for a short time they were surrounded by pines, ferns and heather, until they camped on soft grass to the left. It was sufficiently far from the Am Beanaidh to lessen its roar, and they were hidden from walkers on the other side. Then they walked briefly ahead until the track dipped down to the Am Beanaidh curving from the south-west, and which nearby to the east was joined by the Allt Druidh, before flowing on towards the bridge. The central swift current sent ripples to the margin where the women washed their hands and faces, before refilling the bottles.

Iona observed, 'The gentle harebells, the true bluebells of Scotland, and other flowers on the bank look exquisite in this wild setting.'

They rushed into the tent and quickly closed the flaps to minimize the midges which could enter. From outside the tent was modest in size, but inside the top looked high. After they had eaten Iona began to record observations in a notebook, Ishbel offering some contributions. Then they rested, brushing aside midges which settled on their faces. Iona thought that the pests were trifling compared to the bullets and far larger projectiles on the Western Front. Shortly after darkness fell the women giggled on hearing a stag's wheezy call.

Emerging early next morning they saw no low clouds, and so Iona said, 'Let us climb Braeriach and visit the Wells of Dee. Gavin asked me to go there in particular. It will be easier if we turn left past Lochan Deò and go up Gleann Einich or glen of marsh.'

Entering it they admired the spacious pine woodland which allowed an abundance of blooming heather. The grand view was enhanced by long, straight stretches of track. Then the way narrowed and rose between austere, conical Carn Eilrig to the left and Cadha Mór to the right. The track went high above the glen's floor on the left, and they were charmed as, surrounded by tall ferns and heather, they gazed down on the idyllic scene of the Am Beanaidh roaring over rocks and round boulders contrasting with the still peace of evergreen pines and rich green of summer. Then they descended, trees gradually petered out and the prospect revealed massive Braeriach rising like a whale to the south-east, with intermediate long knolls. They crossed a broad tributary of the Am Beanaidh, and, when they crossed the reduced summer flow of the river itself, there was a lovely clump of harebells on a tiny stony islet near the other side. The river now lay to the right, and they were to cross other tributaries which emphasized the still large volume of water passing through the glen.

Pointing up to the left Ishbel said, 'Look at that quaint line of boulders abandoned on the hilltop by the receding Ice Age.'

The steep sides of the glen's head were visible for a while, before they were excited by a mystic gleam on part of Loch Einich. The track bent down to the loch, and at its edge they watched powerful long ripples surge beneath awesome cliffs to the west. The latter were partly green, particularly lower down, and bare sections shone in ancient splendour.

Iona said, 'I am reminded somewhat of the even wilder head of Glen Avon. This loch is one and a quarter miles long with an average width of 600 yards. To the south waterfalls augment Coire Odhar's jagged main stream before it plunges into the loch. A boulder of about sixty tons, which in prehistoric times fell from Braeriach, turned over more than twenty years ago and moved some distance nearer to the loch's head. An avalanche was the likely cause.'

They refilled the bottles and returning a short distance along the track took the narrow stalkers' path which rose south-east through very picturesque scenery. They walked between carpets of heather which occasionally brushed their skirts. Iona picked up a ptarmigan's small feather and kept it as a memento. They forded the long white torrent of the Allt Coire Bogha-cloiche pouring over rocks covered in grass and moss. The burn descended to join the serpentine marshy section of the Am Beanaidh. As they forded other burns they saw how here and there the lesser flow enabled many rocks to be covered in lustrous thick mosses of different hues. These burns went down to the loch itself.

At a high level the women turned and Iona, pointing back some distance to the left up the glen, said, 'That is Loch Mhic Ghille-choil or tarn of the thin young man's son. It was hidden from us when we passed. He was said to be a brave pursuer of a party of Lochaber reivers who slew him on a Sunday.'

The walkers felt strangely at home in the gaunt Coire Dhondail, Iona explaining that the second word meant stirks' dell. Yet they were apprehensive about tackling for the first time the steep, zigzag higher section. In an exposed part they leaned against the side and clutched tufts of grass to help keep their balance. Then they scrambled up through a rocky groove and negotiated a massive rocky face down which poured two streams, the first concentrated and vigorous, the other more diffused.

They merged further down to form the Allt Coire Dhondail. Before fording the first stream the women drank from their bottles and topped them up. The path curved round up beside the other flow and ended on a terrace. Striding up long, steep slopes of turf and gravel, they paused to gaze back at the upper west cliffs overlooking Loch Einich. They took it in turns to look through binoculars in particular at a large, very smooth corrie with a burn pouring from it. Then they climbed to the plateau which consisted of stony, gravelly tundra.

As they strolled carefree north-east in the soothing pure air at 4,000 feet, Iona smiled and said, 'It is heavenly to walk on the roof of Scotland and I feel closer to Gavin. Last summer we were on Ben Macdui's summit to the east.'

Their hearts leaped on seeing the infant shining Dee meander ahead. They found the source which was marked on a bank by a little cairn of white quartz stones. Lower down grass and much moss were marred by muddy parts caused by walkers who had stooped to drink the water.

Iona commented, 'Normally the well is powerful, but now it is gentle. I have expected to drink from it, but we will watch from here and not add to the erosion. The spiritual effect is more important.'

Ishbel replied, 'Yes, I recall words from Isaiah 12.3, "with joy shall ye draw water out of the wells of salvation."'

The water swung round moss towards them on the left, quietly flowing over a rocky step. Iona was deeply stirred by the scene. The year of war with its chains of human sin had weighed on her. The long repetitive hours in her spare time spent knitting comforts had contributed to an inner weariness, with a suspicion of being self-righteous. Gavin's short furlough had been a great tonic, but it would be another year before she saw him again, if she was fortunate. On this holiday she envied the birds' songs which were full of thrilling creation. She remembered that Jesus said God knew if a single sparrow fell to the ground, yet each of his disciples was 'of more value than many sparrows' (Matthew 10.29,31). The long, magnificent walk up Gleann Einich, progressing from sensuous to more elemental beauty, and the stiff but uplifting ascent of the mountain, had prepared her. Now she felt a renewed sense of wonder and humility. Her spirit imbibed the peaceful water which released a purer fount of grace and joy. She was filled with life and the promise of eternal life. Henry Williams Baker's hymn, 'The King of love my shepherd is,' based on Psalm 23, rang in her ears, particularly the lines, 'Where streams of living water flow / my ransomed soul he leadeth.' While her heart and spirit had stayed united, now they shone together more broadly. She and Ishbel photographed each other by the well, and they continued as other wells increased the flow past mosses of different colours.

Soon Iona said, 'The water passes down east to the 500 foot falls. Gavin and I saw their upper part from the Lairig Ghru last summer. The Dee is the fastest flowing Scottish river.'

Near the head of the falls wild grass danced frantically, the seeds ready to be blown widely. Some distance ahead the cliffs gave way to an impressive bouldery slope. Climbing north-east through light mist up a steep mound, they were glad of each other's company, for it was the wildest and most remote part of the crescent shaped mountain. They reached the edge of Coire Bhrochain and walked along the top of its cliffs, with gullies and broken pinnacles, until they reached the summit where the mist gradually cleared, and they photographed each other beside the large rough cairn.

'The view is one of the finest in Scotland,' Iona enthused, as she took a further picture. 'Across the main corrie is Sgòr an Lochain Uaine or peak of the green tarn, also known as The Angel's Peak. Just to the south-east is Cairn Toul. On its steep north slopes is Coire an Lochain Uaine. The high, peaceful tarn is hidden to walkers below. Its stream plunges down wild rocky outcrops and screes. The Sgòr's North East Ridge leads from the tarn's shore. To the east the shining Dee meanders in the Lairig Ghru. On the other side of the pass are the unclouded, soaring dome of Ben Macdui and its arm of Sròn Riach.'

After lunch they progressed until they paused near the end of the north-west slanting Sròn na Lairige. Looking down the pass they saw the gleaming east flank of The Devil's Point and the Dee with hills in the background. From the map they identified just to the north-west of Ben Macdui's summit the foaming Allt a' Choire Mhóir which gracefully plunged to the pass. Walking up Sròn na Lairige they admired the upper, weathered opposite side of the Lairig Ghru. Then a very wide view appeared over Aviemore, Speyside and far beyond. There was a steep descent over boulders before Ishbel photographed Iona near an east crag of Sròn na Lairige, with Lurcher's Crag on the other side of the pass.

As the path bent down north-east they paused as Iona said, 'Creag an Leth-choin is often called Lurcher's Crag. According to tradition a deer chase which began at Ryvoan ended there, when a dog went over the cliff in the heat of the hunt, so hence the name. The crag is very exposed to high winds and its face is deeply lined even by Highland standards. The screes below tell their tale.'

Down beside the Allt Druidh they refilled the bottles before making a descending return. For a while they were hemmed in, but then the prospect opened to gentler scenery, although the path was rough. The way through the pines of Rothiemurchus was easier. When they saw the Am Beanaidh sweep round to meet the Allt Druidh they knew that the long journey was nearly over. Soon they gratefully crossed the Cairngorm Club Footbridge to return to their tent.

On Friday morning they decided to pitch it beside Loch Morlich, so that at the end of the day's walk they would have less distance to travel. They had enjoyed the first camping site, but, while the tent was on grass, midges had gathered from nearby heather. The swarm would have been denser and more vicious if they had camped on light heather. As Ishbel was taller and stronger, she carried the heavy bag across the Cairngorm Club Footbridge and Iona followed with the trolley. Then Ishbel insisted on pushing it, saying it was light labour. She did not want Iona to overexert herself, as she knew that she wished to send a full account to Gavin. They walked south-east within sight of the Allt Druidh, before the track turned north-east. Soon they glanced affectionately at the path branching off to the Lairig Ghru. Now the way gradually ascended through similar scenery of pines, heather and rich greenery. Then they made a long descent, until they were excited by a glimpse of Loch Morlich through pines. They took the peaceful path south of the loch rather than the road to the north.

Iona said, 'Loch Morlich may mean lake of a great slope. It is a mile long and much of it is over half a mile wide. Around it lies Glen More.'

Beyond the forest on the loch's north side were soothing hills. When they began to turn round the east end of the loch there were pines and deciduous trees. Framed between tall dark pines was a beautiful view to the west. They descended a trail of exposed tree roots which acted as steps down to the loch's edge. Beyond the wide water lay trees and the distant, partly sunlit hills of Am Monadh Liath. A stiff breeze drove ripples rapidly towards them. Continuing they saw preening ducks near the shore, one first dipping its beak in water. Then the prospect brightened with shining summer green and the pines yielded a more mellow hue. Filtered through branches the sun's rays were split as if it was a diamond. Slender deciduous trees bent gracefully over the broad, brown bedded Abhainn Ruigh-eunachan flowing gently to the loch.

'Even the myriads of animated leaves reflect the ferment of creation,' Ishbel remarked.

Iona replied, 'While water flows west to the loch, loud ripples on it sweep east before melting in silence on the shore.'

Walking on golden sand they saw near the water a dog's paw marks, the owner's footprints being further away. Soon they crossed a rill flowing over sand. They decided to pitch the tent near some outer pines which were some distance from the loch, but still surrounded by sand. Hopefully they would not be troubled by midges. Then walking north to the road which bent round south towards Cairn Gorm, they heard shouts and laughter from two youths in a rowing boat.

'I hope that the war ends before they are eligible to serve in it,' said Ishbel.

Turning right along the road they soon passed Glen More Lodge on a rise to the left. Its distinctive homely, long white frontage caught the eye. The winding uphill road with heather and flowers on the banks and Glen More forest raised their spirits.

Iona commented, however, 'People walking through the forest sometimes have a slightly desolate feeling. It was believed to be haunted by a spirit called Bodach na Laimhe Deirge or the old man of the red hand. He lived on the loch's east side and protected the deer and other animals. He challenged belated travellers to a fight. Doubtless he would not challenge women!' she lightly concluded.

They passed over the Abhainn Ruigh-eunachan which had been crossed lower down. Shortly they admired a quaint steep knoll covered in pines to the right. It looked quintessentially Scottish. Later Iona identified from the map a picturesque rocky stream pouring down towards them on the right as the Allt Mór. It passed beneath the road.

After advancing further they looked back and smiled at Loch Morlich spread out beneath them, but the tent lay in a hidden bay. Glen More Lodge was a landmark. Ahead lay lofty, round, green Cairn Gorm. Two long thin clouds hung over the mountain, but scarcely obscured any of it. They refilled their bottles in the stream of Coire Cas or steep corrie, the way being south-east. They passed a pair of middle-aged women, before being overtaken by a retired man and his dog.

Iona observed, 'There are small pines resulting from seeds blown from Glen More forest. Winds force them to grow along the ground.'

Higher up Ishbel remarked, 'There are examples of an ancient little plant, the fir clubmoss, which developed before flowering plants.'

They toiled south up the domed summit and photographed each other by the cairn. The retired man with a dog said on leaving that they were going to Ben Macdui. During lunch the women contrasted the gentle beauty of Glen More and Strathspey with the wild Cairngorms. Then a cool wind encouraged them to walk further across the summit.

Gazing south Iona's eyes lit up as she exclaimed, 'There is shining Loch Etchachan which Gavin and I visited last summer! A pool is in front and then the Allt nan Stacan Dubha plunges down into Loch Avon which is hidden deep below. We took a slanting course, but even so from here the side looks steeper. South-west of Loch Etchachan is the dome of Ben Macdui. Turning now much nearer to the south-east I see through the binoculars some people walking on top of an extended rocky mass, as if it is a natural fortress.'

They went a short way north-east and she said, 'In the hollow a stream furrow running east into the Garbh Allt is called Ciste Mhearad or Margaret's coffin. According to tradition about 300 years ago the woman pleaded in vain before Mackintosh to lift a death sentence on her lover. She went mad and about a fortnight later her body was found in the small corrie. Morag threatened to throw herself off Craigendarroch on learning of Colin's death, but the madness was transient for the passion was shallow. Just beyond to the north-east here is Cnap Coire na Spreidhe or knob of corrie of the cattle.'

Returning to the cairn they walked south-west near the high north edge. The way continued to be strewn with boulders. Past Coire Cas were two promontories, Fiacaill a' Choire Chais or ridge of the steep corrie and Fiacaill Coire an t-Sneachda or ridge of the corrie of snowing. The ridges were narrow and uneven, rather like a row of teeth.

Standing to the west of Fiacaill Coire an t-Sneachda on the subsidiary summit of Cairn Lochan, Iona commented, 'The second headland is reported to be one of the most wintry places in Scotland, particularly as it is away from the sun. I feel that we are here out of season, as if snow and ice are more natural. Below us are dramatic cliff faces. Ahead is Coire an Lochain or corrie of the tarn. The bare rocky stretch on that slope indicates where a regular avalanche prevents growth. The part green, part bare corries have a fitting chastening effect in this period, but they lack the romantic resonance of those of Lochnagar.'

Smiling Ishbel replied, 'I know that you are very fond of Lochnagar's corries.'

When they returned to the cairn for the last time, Iona gazed wistfully at the far south-west upper side of Glen Avon. At the head of its loch she and Gavin had criss-crossed their hands on each other's wrists and circled in harmony with the Lord of the Dance the previous innocent summer. She hoped that in the completed account she could convey her renewed strength, not that she feared he could be mentally or nervously corrupted by the hell of war and spiritually expelled from their wild Garden of Eden.

While descending the mountain they decided to finish by visiting a tourist attraction to the north-east of Loch Morlich. From near Glen More Lodge the meandering, rising way was lined with pines, and the peaceful atmosphere increased when the view narrowed in the steep sided Ryvoan Pass. The entrance to the path was surrounded by heather, and they were hemmed in by enchanting scenery of more heather, graceful birches and other deciduous trees, ferns, juniper bushes and flowers. Also, they were surprised by fantastic contorted shapes of old pines, moss relieving the hoary crusts. A long, mossy fallen trunk had its own sheen. There was added charm as they carefully made a steep, winding descent.

At the bottom Ishbel pointed and said, 'That is common wintergreen. It keeps its glossy leaves through winter, although its spikes of creamy flowers only appear in summer.'

In the centre of the pass they suddenly saw its gem, as Iona commented, 'That is An Lochan Uaine or the green tarn. The translucent, dark green water looks strange. A south-westerly breeze drives lively little ripples which further stir the senses and imagination. The mysterious appeal is heightened by the absence of an inlet or outlet above ground. Rocks give the colour, but there is a story about the fairy folk in the wood washing their clothes here, especially their king.'

As other tourists approached the pair walked by the tarn's left side. Reaching the far end they briefly looked north-east at the wider heathery view with some pines. Then they sat beside the tarn, with ripples flowing towards them and gently lapping at the edge. A skeletal light grey trunk lay in water to the right. The left slope was away from the sun for much of the day, but its large scree was relieved by a fair number of pines. The opposite slope was more richly clad, and on three sides the tarn was more sheltered by trees, some with exposed lengths of roots at the water's edge.

'Let us rest for a while,' said Ishbel, 'but not dreaming of little folk.'

'No, as children of the light we will enjoy the sublime harmony and peace.'

When they rose they photographed each other with the green water behind. Iona in particular looked the lady of the lochan. Climbing back up the steep path was ironically easier than the descent. It did not seem long before Loch Morlich was seen through pines. They ate heartily in the tent.

Before Iona fell asleep she listened to the loch's surging rhythm and recalled that she had always lived near flowing water. It was close to the union of the Dee and Muick Gavin said that if he had to fight it would be to defend his love for her and Scotland. At the Pools of Dee he remarked it was strange that the marigold's gilded grief would be at the furthest point of their walk. She had replied that it was fitting for it to be beside the pure water of life which was associated with the Holy Spirit. When they parted at Aberdeen Joint Station he said that all would be well in the end. She knew that he referred to God's general plan, not his own circumstances. He meant that it would be weakness for either of them to worry, and that if he gave his life it would be a test and affirmation, not a rejection of their love.

Next morning the women walked back to Aviemore by the upper side of Loch Morlich, looking fondly up at Cairn Gorm and the mountain range. They paused briefly to watch water flowing round grassy islands from the loch to form the River Luineag, with ducks floating at the side of a current.

Ishbel commented, 'The scene is picturesque, yet, while we are here for exercise and spiritual renewal, Nature is preoccupied with survival and growth within the order of Creation. Man is above the beasts, but the Allies are bravely fighting the Huns who have made God in their own image, inverted Creation and practise barbaric cruelty in pursuit of materialistic power.'

Iona understood that Ishbel spoke soberly to ease the transition for her to the grim reality of wartime. Yet they returned to Ballater tired but happy. Iona was glad to draw on the notebook when writing to Gavin. So much effort had been put into walking and there were so many images, that some of the sharper details and reflections would otherwise have been forgotten. She promised him a few photographs when they were developed.

11: The Prelude–Second Attack on Bellewaarde–Glenmuick Parish Church

The following Tuesday she received a cheerful letter in which he affirmed returning refreshed and with renewed zeal. The battalion was currently in the same less hostile location, and it was fervently hoped that it would be left there for the winter. They were busy building strong dugouts, which meant digging deep and providing good drainage, with a very strong roof consisting of beams and layers of corrugated iron above to support five or six rows of sandbags, a layer of broken bricks and two feet of earth on top. He concentrated on making dugouts for bombers and bomb stores, and others were provided behind machine gun emplacements.

Before his furlough he had become too used to harsh sounds at the front. Now amid the reduced cacophony of war he heard more of her euphonic voice which helped induce inner peace. Ironically he was on sentry duty the first night on returning to the trenches, when a shell bursting short of the trench showered him with debris. A comrade observed that they were like rats in an alley. While the incident was a reminder that they lived in death's shadow, the conditions also symbolized the passing hates and often shallow lives of this world. We had to feel something of Christ's wounds if we were to share in his glorification. In John 12.32 the Lord, foreseeing the manner of his own death, said, 'I, if I be lifted up from the earth, will draw all men unto me.' He referred here also to his Ascension into Heaven, the Cross beginning it. The body was just an outer garment, and, when it was beset by danger plus moral darkness, the spirit was fiery. In John 12.46 Jesus said, 'I am come a light into the world, that whosoever believeth on me should not abide in darkness.' Gavin reasserted that he found increased spiritual fulfilment in war. When he had seen Iona sleep on Lochnagar, he had to wrestle with his spirit to understand her ineffable peace and grace. Now he was refashioned, more completely a man. In the war there were four crosses—Legion of Honour, Victoria, Military and wooden ones. The last type was much commoner and plainer, but far more significant. The war would be won by the great, often complete sacrifices of many, not by the conspicuous gallantry of a few, inspiring though they were. The German Iron Cross travestied the true one.

Before he went to the trenches he heard Sergeant Mackay say to a new member of the platoon, 'Young Alec! We met in Ballater, when you were disturbed by artificial blood. What is your surname?'

'Reid, Sergeant.'

'Are you one of these under age boy soldiers? You are not replying. The bristling dog beside you looks more aggressive than his master. What's his name?'

'Thomas.'

'After your hero Aquinas I presume. He **will** be useful. Terriers are good at catching rats in the trenches.'

'That was what the dealer said.'

'It's a pity you haven't brought a ferret as well. They would have made a perfect hunting pair. In the firing line make sure you both keep below the parapet, or you could be shot by a trigger-happy sniper.'

'Yes, Sergeant.'

Two nights later Alec read a book by Aquinas in a dugout by candlelight, with a Bible to follow up references, and Gavin asked, 'What were Aquinas' views about war?'

'He wrote about the just war in the *Summa Theologiae*. His literal interpretation of the Old Testament image of Yahweh as a God of Battles influenced his support for Christian warfare. He observed that John the Baptist did not tell some soldiers to give up their occupation. Instead he said, "Do violence to no man, neither accuse any falsely; and be content with your wages" (Luke 3.14). By the words "Do violence to no man," apparently he meant that they were not to make an unauthorized attack. For Aquinas a just war required firstly the sovereign's authority, secondly a just cause and thirdly the intention of advancing good or avoiding evil. In the Sermon on the Mount Jesus said, "resist not evil" and "Love your enemies" (Matthew 5.39,44). It has generally been believed, however, that these are references only to personal foes. Aquinas and Augustine agreed that the Gospel precepts of non-resistance should be obeyed except when they contradicted the common good.'

Gavin remarked, 'So Gavrilo Princip's assassination of Archduke Franz

Ferdinand and his wife leading to the much wider war was a classic rejection of Aquinas' teaching.'

'Absolutely, particularly as the shootings occurred on a Sunday.'

'Yet Aquinas would not have disapproved of the Battle of Mons being fought on a Sunday?'

'Oh no. While the Old Testament prescribed rest on the Sabbath, Aquinas thought that the Maccabees' decision to fight on a Sabbath (Maccabees 2.41) showed such warfare had been blessed, although on this occasion a wish for survival probably came first. Aquinas noted that Jesus healed a man on the Sabbath (John 7.23), and to some questioning Jews the Lord said, "Judge not according to the appearance, but judge righteous judgment" (v. 24). Aquinas believed that to safeguard the common good by fighting was even more justified.'

Thomas the dog was lying at his master's feet, when he saw a plump rat emerge from behind a spade in a corner and creep towards some breadcrumbs beside the table. The dog sprang forward and chased the rat round the dugout and across it a few times, before Gavin moved a foot to slow the rat and it was quickly killed.

Alec commented, 'Would that our main enemy could be defeated so easily. To continue, Jesus said to his disciples, "Think not that I am come to send peace on earth: I come not to send peace, but a sword" (Matthew 10.34). Aquinas distinguished between good peace and bad peace. The good peace was that achieved by Jesus in his Atonement which won for man the possibility of reconciliation with God. Bad peace came from closest natural ties. Jesus came to remove this bad peace. The sword was the word of God in spiritual warfare to divide the closest unions which went against the love of God. When Peter drew his sword to defend Christ, he was told by him, "Put up again thy sword into his place: for all they that take the sword shall perish with the sword" (Matthew 26.52). Aquinas believed that instead of clerics fighting, they should be willing to shed their own blood for Christ's sake. More widely he argued that to "take the sword" meant only to take it unlawfully, and that the words "perish with the sword" did not necessarily mean death by a literal sword, but spiritual death.'

Gavin informed Iona that Alec and he agreed that Jesus did not teach about physical warfare, because his mission was to reconcile man and God. He said to Pilate, 'My kingdom is not of this world' (John 18.36). Moreover, if he had made such remarks they could have led to his premature arrest and death. Instead in the Sermon on the Mount he said, 'Blessed are the peacemakers: for they shall be called the children of God' (Matthew 5.9).

On a lighter level Gavin told her that he was looking forward to sharing a gift of oatmeal each breakfast when he was out of the trenches. He much appreciated porridge on furlough. In Scotland it was taken for granted, but out there it was a treat.

Later that month she informed him that the Alexandra Day in Aberdeen and district, in which he had participated, raised £667. In contrast to his remarks about crosses and great sacrifices, there was a sad dispute about war service badges in Aberdeen. The government had consented to some firms issuing them to their workers. There was a wish that employees at the Gas Works should get them!

Last December she had told him about an appeal for the RSPCA Fund for Sick and Wounded Horses. The fund had been launched with the Army Council's authority and it greatly helped the Army Veterinary Department. A report from the British Headquarters in France stated that the fund had, besides providing motor and horse-drawn horse ambulances, lorries and fodder petrol driven chaff-cutters and corn-crushers, plus many other accessories, erected three hospitals with places for 2,500 patients. Another hospital was to be built to house 1,250 horses. Requirements for treating the British Army's sick and wounded horses were increasing, so another appeal was made.

As for Deeside only the conditions last year justified the epithet in the Glorious Twelfth. This time even the weather was mixed, and figuratively the event was more overshadowed by the war. There were plenty of birds and the young ones were healthy, but there was a danger of the moors becoming overstocked with old ones. At Balmoral the King's keepers on Geallaig moors ignored showers and occasional thunderclaps, the usual box being sent to His Majesty. In the Ballater area only one moor was shot over on the opening day.

On Friday evening, 13 August, she and her father attended a concert in The Bungalow, adjoining the Loirston Hotel, in aid of the local branch of the Red Cross Society. The items were of a high standard and the presence of four uniformed nurses helped to produce the generous sum of 10 guineas. Such a social event was unusual and thus it was particularly enjoyed. She realized why concerts on the Western Front aroused such enthusiasm, as a relief to the war and bringing reminders of home. Early next morning there was a fire in the Gordon Institute in Ballater. Fortunately smoke was spotted and a band of workers with buckets of water soon had the flames under control. The cause may have been a lighted match or cigarette end thrown in one of the wooden spittoons in the billiard room! She helped at the annual Glenmuick Parish Church sale of work in the Albert Memorial Hall on the following Wednesday afternoon. There were many visitors as well as residents, and the very creditable sum of £75 was raised.

In a letter she received on 19 August he thanked her for the vivid and reflective account of her visit to the Cairngorms. The incident of a massive boulder having moved some distance nearer to Loch Einich's head and the water of life reminded him on a gargantuan scale of the stone, representing the sins of mankind, which in contrast was rolled away on Christ's resurrection. There were mortal and venial sins, but many venial ones could harm our love for God and neighbour. Yet as St Paul wrote in Romans 5.20, through Jesus, 'where sin abounded, grace did much more abound.' Young Alec had grown in maturity and grace since last summer, when he was easily struck by Morag's superficial charms. He gave an appreciative smile on seeing Gavin reading Iona's letter. It was clear that he recognized her inner worth. Life had taught him much, as well as books.

Gavin had just heard an illuminating sermon on Holy Communion. The original ecclesiastical Greek word for Eucharist meant thanksgiving. In the Eucharist we were united by the Holy Spirit with the risen Christ. Nourished by his body and blood we became one body and spirit in him. The blood and water which flowed from his side symbolized the Eucharist and baptism. The Eucharist represented not only Christ's sacrifice and ours, but also his abiding presence. Filled with the Spirit he shared in the Eucharist and in us. Outwardly the sacrament was simple, but it was a heavenly banquet. Gavin recalled Iona say on Craig Coillich that grace was not earned, but freely given by God to his humble and grateful children. In the midst of war and the works of the Devil one could still be thankful for gifts from the Father, material and spiritual. In Holy Communion we were cleansed from sin, preserved from future mortal sins and received hope, joy and peace. Jesus' resurrection and his main appearances to the Apostles before the Ascension occurred on the first day of the week, so Sunday had become the Sabbath. In the conflict it was still greatly treasured. On it in particular men of clay felt they had to die inwardly and be resurrected in common with Jesus. One day the war would end and mankind would grow together in Christ.

Meanwhile he recalled again the ants on Craigendarroch when he was a member of one of many bodies of men walking slowly with packs on their backs, going to or from the trenches. He was amused by Aunt Lizzie's complaint about lighting restrictions in Aberdeen, because they were much more stringent at the front, apart from Very lights. In the trenches there was extra risk of an attack around dawn and sunset, but the stars shed peace. Moreover, although living in the shadow, he recalled Loch Avon shining in a glen of light. Finally, he and his comrades were very satisfied with the hard work they had done in their present location, but they were not to reap the benefit, because they were returning to the hotter place they had been in before.

Iona understood at once that he referred to the area around Hooge. She felt uneasy, because she knew that it was the most dangerous location in the Ypres Salient, which itself was the worst area in the line. Struck by the religious tone of his last two letters, and in particular by the theme of sacrifice, she understood that he was warning her. Everyone knew that sometimes, shortly after a soldier returned to the war after a furlough, he was cruelly killed or badly injured. In her next letter she quoted from Joshua 1.9, 'Be strong and of a good courage; be not afraid, neither be thou dismayed: for the Lord thy God is with thee whithersoever thou goest.' She also quoted Psalm 91.2, as she had at the beginning of the war, 'I will say of the Lord, He is my refuge and my fortress: my God; in him will I trust.' She assured Gavin that he was constantly in her thoughts and prayers.

He was helped by news about Ballater, so in a later letter she stated that an accident could not occur at its railway terminus like that near Gretna Green on 22 May. It was the worst disaster in the history of British railways. A train carrying about 500 of the 7th Royal Scots (Territorials) to the south crashed into a stationary local train. A Euston express then collided with the wrecked trains. At least it was an accident caused by a signalman forgetting about the local train, not the kind of soulless carnage mechanically produced by the Germans. On Saturday evening, 28 August, at Ballater station an engine engaged in shunting operations was derailed. An accident train arrived from Kittybrewster—the area where his parents had attended the dog show!—on Sunday morning, and the engine was rerailed with the help of strong hydraulic jacks assisted by two engines. The engine was much damaged, but it could travel under its own steam to Aberdeen.

Gavin's next letter was short because he had a bad cold, but he expressed great thanks for recent photographs, particularly that of her by the source of the Dee. It was a powerful symbol of their sacred love. On 3 September he wrote about conditions. It had rained for the past twenty-four hours and the whole area was boggy, just as it was all winter. The occasional soft stretches they had encountered in the Highlands were nothing in comparison. Wintry weather was starting again, but while he and his comrades were currently resting the authorities had not provided huts or tents. The men were bivouacked in open fields with only waterproof sheets and blankets. Yet the traitors at home were worse than the enemy and the elements. The soldiers would like the strikers to be shot. Many thousands had died for their country and huge numbers faced great peril, yet the nation was disunited when it was fighting for its life.

Iona sought to balance his rigours somewhat with information about the Red Cross. On Friday afternoon, 10 September, a Ballater fishmonger was driving a lorry with passengers from Braemar, when one of them fell out at the back as the vehicle turned a sharp corner before heading south to Ballater. The doctor was called and the patient with a suspected fracture of the base of the skull was taken by the Red Cross ambulance to his home in the burgh. Normally the Red Cross was associated with the Geneva Convention. While there was no need for the latter in this haven of peace, the use of the ambulance for a civilian emergency, as well as for the convalescent hospital, helped to underline the burgh's link with the international organization.

Ishbel was in Aberdeen on Monday, 13 September, to buy warm clothing for her elderly parents, and she visited a new ambulance train which was exhibited that day and the next at the Joint Station on behalf of the Aberdeen Red Cross Transport Fund. The khaki train could carry around 450 patients and had been built by the Caledonian Railway Company. It was one of four built for service in France and several more were to be made. The site was a huge attraction. An archway admitting to the platform for guests was hung with the patriotic Royal Stuart tartan. Iona noted that the previous time she had mentioned that tartan to him was in reference to Queen Victoria and her family when she opened the Linn of Dee Bridge. Ishbel proudly showed her an autograph which a Victoria Cross soldier sold for the fund. The exhibition drew almost £1,000 at the Aberdeen stage of the itinerary.

Gavin's next letter was short because he stated that they were very busy. On 17 September he again stressed how occupied they were, but he was more informative. The artillery was firing heavy and light shells daily at least to damage the enemy's works and try to kill a few Huns. The bombardment was bad for the enemy's nerves and gave him a lot of labour. Yet they needed five times the supply of munitions to have a chance of beginning to finish the war. They were very short of materials for making dugouts, machine gun emplacements and trenches. Moreover, it was surprisingly difficult to know where one was in a maze of trenches. It was far harder here where the Germans had been in and out several times, and many trenches had been blown in and not used any more, with new ones having been dug. God's land in this area had been hideously deformed by shells which daily went each way in hundreds and often in thousands.

He balanced the dour news with more positive remarks. Soldiers loved to sing both hymns and native secular songs, and occasional other ones such as 'When Irish Eyes Are Smiling.' It made him recall Iona's Irish connections. The song was written by Chauncey Olcott and George Graff Jr, and set to music by Ernest Ball, for Olcott's production of 'The Isle O' Dreams.' It was first published in 1912, so it still sounded fairly fresh. He did not mention that recently a comrade enthusiastically sang the plaintive refrain, 'On the bonnie, bonnie banks o' Loch Lomond,' only to be killed next day by a sniper. Singing was not just to pass the time. Its main purpose was to express and deepen camaraderie, which was already strong because the men were there of their free will. German soldiers were conscripted and so were the French, but the latter's patriotism was soundly based.

In the camaraderie were Christian love and grace. He referred to points made in a recent sermon. Achieving a right relationship with the Holy Trinity also helped one to achieve communion with one's fellow men. It was through the Holy Spirit that the Virgin Mary conceived and gave birth to the Son of God. Through her the Holy Spirit brought men into communion with Christ. Grace was a personal relationship with the Holy Trinity. To attain it, just as Jesus was the Son of God, we had to become sons of God. As St Paul wrote in Galatians 4.6, 'because ye are sons, God hath sent forth the Spirit of his Son into your hearts, crying, Abba, Father.' The Holy Spirit completed the work of creation and salvation.

Gavin contrasted the murky, watery shell holes with the Pools of Dee as symbols of pure water. Just as the gestation of our physical birth occurred in water, so the water of baptism represented our being born into the divine life as given in the Holy Spirit. When a spear pierced Christ's side, blood and water issued. The Holy Spirit was this living water which would well up in us to eternal life. Gavin contrasted also the fires which the Germans started in Ypres and elsewhere, and their use of the flammenwerfer, with the inner fire signifying the transforming energy of the Holy Spirit. Also contrasted were the acrid, even poisonous clouds and false lights of war with the use of clouds and light as manifestations of the Holy Spirit, as on the mountain of Transfiguration and Christ's Ascension, as well as the foretelling of his Second Coming.

Gavin was neither allowed nor inclined to inform Iona that he was preparing for military action. On Saturday, 25 September, as subsidiary to the Battle of Loos, the 1st and 4th Gordon Highlanders were involved in the Second Attack on Bellewaarde. There had been more fighting in this area since the First Attack by other British forces on 16 June, and the 1st Gordons with a company of the 4th had taken over captured trenches. At the end of July the British had lost Hooge and were driven back 500 yards. The Germans had used the flammenwerfer. On 9 August the 6th Division regained the lost ground from the stables of Hooge Château westward.

On 25 September, just before the Gordons advanced to the assault at 4.10 a.m., Alec's tethered dog started barking and Sergeant Mackay furiously called out, 'Can't you keep him quiet?'

'He doesn't want to be left behind.'

'Hold him by the lead close beside you.'

As Alec's left hand was thus occupied, the right one held a little crucifix against his rifle, as he explained to Gavin, 'When Jesus said to Aquinas from a crucifix, "Well hast thou written of me, Thomas, what reward wouldst thou have?" he answered, "None, Lord, but Thee."'

Scarcely had Gavin nodded than the attack started, but the defensive wire was undamaged and some of it was so thick it defeated wire-cutters. In some parts, however, Royal Engineers of the 3rd Division had cut gaps with Bangalore torpedoes after explosions. The 4th Gordons reached the enemy's third line and caused heavy loss. As the 1st Gordons charged to the wire, Gavin's heart sank as he saw Donald felled silently by a bullet in the chest. Many others fell searching for gaps in the dark. The right company, including Gavin, found a gap and gained a footing in the front trench. About 4.30 the Germans started to bombard their lost trenches. Communication trenches were blocked, so that bombs, shovels and sandbags could not be delivered. Between 11 and noon the enemy attacked across the open and along the trenches. In fierce fighting the 4th Gordons and such of the 1st as had got in were driven out. Gavin had just scaled the trench, when he looked back and momentarily froze on seeing a comrade below shooting a Hun further along the trench, only to be killed by a bomb himself.

Mackay shouted from further down the top of the trench, 'Another bomb!'

Gavin began to sprint away, but there was an explosion and darkness fell.

It rained heavily that day in his city of Aberdeen, although collectors sold pretty little Union Jacks and badges with what was described in a newspaper as 'a coloured representation of a famous, grim Prussian dungeon-hold,' the Drachenfels or Dragon's Rock, built on the crag of that name. The money raised was to relieve prisoners of war from the north-east with parcels of food, clothing and other items. Iona reminded Ishbel that the scene roused the Gothic fantasy of many poets, including Byron, who wrote in *Childe Harold's Pilgrimage*, Canto III, 'The castled crag of Drachenfels / Frowns o'er the wide and winding Rhine,' which to him flowed through enchanted land. She added that she had quoted elsewhere from the poem when she and Gavin were at the Linn of Dee. Ishbel replied that her father had said the Drachenfels was south-east of Bonn, and in the seventeenth century the castle was pulled down apart from the donjon or high tower. The combination 'dungeon-hold' was ambiguous. Our patriots would tend to think that the tower had a strong underground cell for prisoners, so the badges would represent the plight of prisoners of war. The word dungeon, however, could refer to the tower itself, the word hold meaning stronghold. He was not aware of the tower being currently used for confining prisoners of war, so he believed that the illustration on the badges served as symbolic propaganda to contrast with the freedom associated with the Union Jacks.

Ishbel had read a version of a legend about Siegfried, the hero of the thirteenth century *Nibelungenlied* or *The Song of the Nibelungs*. He wished to possess a very beautiful Christian maiden who had been taken prisoner. Yet the heathen priestess decided that the girl would cause lasting animosity, and so she should be given to the dragon that dwelt in a cave on the Drachenfels. When she was led forth, however, she advanced resolutely as if fearless, and, as the dragon rushed towards her it suddenly fell to the ground, being slain by Siegfried with his sword. On learning that the sight of a cross had caused the dragon to fall, he was converted, married the maiden and built the Castle of Drachenfels.

In view of the bad weather few people in Aberdeen left for Deeside ahead of the local autumn holiday on the Monday, even compared with the war average. Yet the holiday season generally in the Highlands had been better than expected. Ordinary tourists mainly from the middle class, and who had the usual railway tickets, arrived in large numbers to rejuvenate themselves. There were safety and peace away from the danger zone at home and the war-torn Continent, where previously many people had paid an annual visit. Also, the summer heat being gone, visitors could exercise more easily.

Iona and other women in Ballater had looked ahead to winter and were spending more of their spare time knitting comforts for soldiers. Like everyone else they had been chastened by the war. Yet, as Iona worked in the shop on Monday, she felt sorry for the poorer people in Aberdeen bearing an increased cost of living and not being offered special excursion trains or reduced fares. She was pleased to learn, however, that the Suburban Company ran special buses to Banchory and Balmoral.

That day there was a sale of antique furniture in Ballater. In the evening Iona opened the shop door and was surprised to see her father and a cart driver carry inside a grandfather clock in a mahogany case with a brass and silver dial. Mr Gordon thought that the clock would be useful for themselves and customers, as well as adding tone to the shop. He had not told her earlier, so it would be a pleasant surprise.

When Morag saw the new addition next morning, she displeased the Gordons by quipping, 'Old Father Time!' partly because of lack of respect for an antique, but mainly because Father Time was associated with grievous loss of life in the war.

Later that morning Iona was restocking a shelf, when her father answered the telephone and said, 'Yes, Mr Fraser,' in a subdued tone, which made her look intently at him and freeze.

Mr Gordon listened for a while before replying, 'Yes, I'll do that. Give Mrs Fraser our sympathy. Goodbye.'

Turning gravely he strode to Iona and said gently, 'Gavin took part in an attack on Bellewaarde last Saturday. He was badly injured by a hand bomb. He is in a base hospital, but in a coma and has lost a lot of blood. The signs are not good. His father was half choked with grief. You can take time off to rest, if you like.'

Her downcast eyes were full of pain and sorrow, but suddenly they rose defiantly and she replied, 'I will get on with my work. It is Gavin who needs to rest.'

She hid her grief so well customers only noticed her enhanced noble beauty. That evening, after she and her father had eaten, she gazed at Gavin's photograph on the mantelpiece, the one taken of him in uniform in Old Aberdeen. Whereas some soldiers' photographs contained resigned expressions of duty until death, he gave a brave smile, signifying that was how he wished to be remembered if he did not return.

Her father quietly approached and said, 'You are very calm.'

'Like Job we sometimes wonder about things which happen to others and us. Yet we must accept the situation as God's will. Our minds are not big enough to understand him fully. As St Paul wrote in Romans 11.34, "For who hath known the mind of the Lord? or who hath been his counseller?" God knows the whole plan, whereas we know only part of it, so we rely on faith. Once when Jesus slept on a boat, a gale rose and his disciples were afraid that the vessel might be swamped. They woke Jesus who calmed the wind and sea, and he asked the disciples why they had no faith. God can control Nature and he can control our lives. Gavin himself has said that faith should not be just basic belief, but joyful trust. We must learn patience as exemplified by Job and as a fruit of the Holy Spirit. Gavin informed me in his first letter after returning to the front that he felt inner peace. Like the Psalmist we must praise God at all times, for his love, greater than the universe and gentler than a breeze, endures for ever.'

'It was ironic, though, that Gavin's last words to you were, "All will be well in the end."'

'He referred to God's general plan and the promise of eternal life. If the worst happens, it is not death to die, it is but au revoir.'

'It is not death to die!' her father retorted. 'You might as well say it is not life to live.'

'After the sleep of death we are purified and pass to another, fuller life in which we see God as he really is and we see each other as we really are, for we come into the perfection of the image in which he has created us.'

Still thinking that a young woman should focus on this life rather than the next, Mr Gordon replied, 'What I mean to say is, naturally I hope that Gavin recovers, but if not time heals. You have yet to experience different kinds of love. There are many stars in the heavens.'

'Only two, his and mine,' she said firmly. 'Your devotion to my mother's memory should tell you that people know when love is Heaven-sent.'

She found it difficult to sleep that night, so next day she worked harder in the shop and took Mike for more exercise than usual. The second night she had a brief dream. Amid sacred music she saw Mary, the Mother of God and Queen of the Angels, bathing her feet in the water of eternal life. Her eyes of blissful purity and peace were heightened by exquisite tapered features and fingers, with gentle, light, trailing locks. Her Son was to wash his disciples' feet, and later, apart from Judas, they understood the action as a lesson to follow him in humility, if need be all the way through martyrdom to glory.

A week later Iona was serving a customer, when her father received a more composed call from Mr Fraser, and afterwards he whispered to her, 'There has been little change, but he is holding his own.'

The following Friday she was artistically preparing a window display, when Mr Fraser rang again, and from the brighter response she was ready for better news, before her father replaced the receiver and called, 'Gavin has regained consciousness, but he is expected to remain in the hospital for a while. He is not well enough at present to write letters, but a chaplain or nurse can write at his dictation. His father has given me the address, so that you can send letters.'

Next Monday, 11 October, she received from Mrs Fraser a kind letter in which she expressed their great relief at his improvement. She enclosed the chaplain's last letter which gave details about the surroundings. The patient was in a great camp of three base hospitals with related sites. The tents were arranged in streets named after London ones. Winter was approaching, so huts were being built. As Gavin was a very serious case, he was already in one of them. They were beautiful, long buildings with a lot of light and were very comfortable.

When Gavin regained consciousness he asked him to write to his parents and get them to send his love to Iona. It was common for soldiers to bear great suffering with stoic silence, but, considering the immense trauma through which he had passed, he was remarkably serene and cheerful. He was much more concerned about worse cases around him. In view of the grave condition of a number of patients, a religious service could not be held there, but he had lent him a hymnal, so that he could read some of the soldiers' favourites, such as 'Eternal Father, strong to save' and 'Jesus, lover of my soul.' All that chafed him was enforced inactivity.

When Mr Gordon read the last remark, he advised Iona, 'You will have to exhort him to show some of Job's patience!'

Mrs Fraser had been too good mannered to ask for the return of the chaplain's letter, but it was copied and returned with thanks. Only two days later Iona was very pleased to get a letter from Gavin which had been dictated to the chaplain. He revealed that soon after regaining consciousness he had received a surprise visit from Sergeant Mackay, who was himself a patient but staying in a nearby hut.

Mackay beamed over him and said, 'I am glad to hear that you have come round.'

'Sergeant! I saw Donald fall silently and suspected that the wound was fatal, but it was how he would have wished to go, suddenly in a gallant charge.'

Mackay nodded and replied, 'I have followed up a lieutenant's letter to his parents with my condolences. Some superiors when writing to the next of kin of a fallen man are apt to state that he will be much missed by his comrades. I prefer to be positive and say that he will be remembered with **pride**.'

Gavin promised, 'I will write to his aunt in Ballater when I am better. She was very kind to us last summer. I was told that my life was saved because I was brought back immediately from beside the German trench. Did stretcher-bearers fetch me?'

Roaring with laughter Mackay replied, 'Stretcher-bearers among all those bombs and bullets?' On hearing a feminine 'Hush!' some yards away, he realized that there were grave cases around him, and he turned to apologize, 'Sorry, Sister.'

He fetched a chair by the end of the bed, and slowly sitting with a wince and lowering his voice said, 'You will soon regain your wits. I carried you back, although you looked barely alive when I lifted you. We were nearing our front line, when a German shell exploded some distance away, but I still got a sizeable piece of shrapnel in my side. Comrades quickly got you to safety, but Alec continued to expose himself in rescuing me, and he was hit by shrapnel. When we were lying in the trench I thanked him, but he murmured, "You should thank my hero, Sergeant. Has Thomas returned?" When I replied, "I'm afraid not," he said, "We have both found peace." A comrade felt for a pulse in his neck, but sadly shook his head. "Greater love hath no man than this, that a man lay down his life for his friends."'

'Yes, Jesus foresaw his own supreme sacrifice when he spoke those words to his disciples.'

Mackay continued, 'We were driven out of the enemy line because of heavier and more effective artillery. We attacked at a narrow salient where we faced artillery fire from three sides and could not deploy our guns properly. There were many better positions where we could have attacked with a greater chance of success, and which would have served as a diversion. Yet we and others engaged in the attack were splendid. We killed more of the enemy than they did of us, and I heard of 160 prisoners being taken, although we won no ground.

As for the main battle, oh the 2nd Gordons' piper of Loos! What spirit! A cloud of British gas had blown back, but he played through it to encourage the men. Yet the reserves were not brought up in time to exploit the initial success, the bombardment was inadequate and the wind was too light to carry the gas. Loos turned into a bitter defeat, costing far too many lives. Rudyard Kipling's son is among the missing. A captured German officer has said, "Your men are magnificent, but your staff work and generalship awful!"'

Gavin replied, 'God will give us victory when we deserve it.'

There was a thoughtful pause before Mackay said, 'There is a convalescent camp here, but it has been decided to send me to a convalescent hospital somewhere back home, followed by a furlough. We Gordons are men and do not welcome a wound which removes us from the action for a while. That said it will be pleasant to be pampered in a Scottish hospital. If when I disembark at Southampton an attempt is made for expediency to send me to an English hospital, I could be difficult.'

'Quite right, Sergeant.'

'It may take a while for your case to be assessed, but I hope we meet again. Give my regards to the Gordons in Ballater and best wishes to you.'

'And to you, with very grateful thanks for saving my life.'

Mackay nodded before smiling at the sister as he tiptoed out of the hut.

As the letter including a résumé of this meeting was dictated to the chaplain, Iona understood when Gavin concluded briefly with his love and looking forward to her next letter. Her father had not previously read letters from Gavin to her. As they were personal she had simply told him about items which would interest him. As this letter was written through an intermediary and Gavin had narrowly escaped death, he read it that evening. He was concerned that Gavin's love for her was not expressed more expansively.

'I hope that his feelings for you are undiminished, but sometimes when soldiers suffer a great trauma their personalities change. He may not be the same when you see him again. You should be cautious how you express your love for him in letters for the time being.'

Smiling she replied, 'I have never been effusive. He may have thought that if he had expanded on his love for me the chaplain might have misunderstood.'

She looked intently at his photograph on the mantelpiece. Had his proud martial spirit survived intact, but his great love for her been brought low? Had public duty eclipsed his private loyalties? She remembered how the year before they had stood near the union of the Dee and Muick as he said, 'If I fight it will be to defend my love for you and Scotland, which is stronger than hate.' She found it hard to believe that such a fine man could change.

In her letter of reply she hoped that his recovery would continue. Leaving her love implicit until the end, she told him that in the week after his military action sunshine and showers produced a number of rainbows on Deeside, and there was a lunar rainbow one night. His father or mother may have informed him that on Saturday, 2 October, there was an unprecedented parade of troops in Aberdeen, with a call for more recruits. On the next Saturday there was an Aberdeen flag day for Russian Jews. One of the cruellest aspects of the war was that Jews, finding themselves on opposite sides, were forced to kill each other. More broadly, however, the war had brought good people closer to God and each other. While in Britain some male civilians, both employers and employees, had used the conflict to extort financial gain, women had won respect for putting the nation first and serving in diverse ways. There was a greater equality among the sexes which would endure. She urged him to inform her of anything he needed.

She was delighted that he wrote his next letter himself, although it was short, indicating that he was still very tired. The tone was quiet and reflective, for while he was now in the convalescent section he was waiting for an assessment of his longer term level of fitness. Yet the old warmth was there. It was hard that he could not fully control his injured body, but he was slowly progressing and the void of uncertainty was filled with memories of her light, laughter and speech. 'Your remarks are wings of love, not flights of fancy where words are flies which dance in antic frenzy.' He agreed with her remark when they parted at Ballater, that love was the perfect gift. Understanding that his recent grave condition may have made her wonder if his mind was unimpaired, he reassured her. 'How could I forget the heart and vision of my life?' God's peace blessed the beginning and end of each day, and the drab trenches were replaced by much pure whiteness in the ward. He was also grateful for her prayers. He would appreciate some confectionery, both for its own sake and in memory of old times.

In a letter accompanying toffee and other items she informed him that the Marquess of Huntly had offered to lend Aboyne Castle to the Red Cross to be used as a hospital for wounded soldiers. She reminded him that as Aboyne was on the railway and the castle was only half a mile to the north, it would be more suitable in winter than Balmoral Castle which could be cut off by heavy snow. The climate was very favourable and there were large rooms and beautiful grounds.

As it was a year since Red Cross work was begun under the Joint Committee of the British Red Cross Society and the Order of St John throughout the Empire, the occasion was being marked by a special appeal to the country for extra funds. The King led with a cheque for £5,000 as a further gift. In the national and local press a Crimean illustration of the 'Lady with the Lamp' had been reproduced. On Saturday, 23 October, there was a flag day in Aberdeen. The design was a Red Cross on one side and on the other a crest of one of the twelve Scottish regiments. The proceeds of the flag day in Scotland were mainly for needs of Scottish regiments in the Dardanelles.

In the King's name more venison had been given from Balmoral to the Ballater Red Cross Hospital. Other gifts included a box of smokies from Station Square, fourteen dozen and four eggs from the National Egg Collection and the pupils of Ballater Primary School, gramophone records, golf clubs and balls. During his holiday based in Ballater they had been too busy exploring the Highlands for him to play golf!

The war was producing its own heroines. Mrs Pankhurst was helping women engaged in war work to be paid reasonably. Some employees had not been paid enough to keep them in good health. Far more poignant were Edith Cavell's last words to her chaplain before being executed. She willingly gave her life for her country. Having seen death so often, she was not afraid. 'I realize that patriotism is not enough. I must have no hatred or bitterness towards anyone.' Unlike soldiers she knew in advance the time of her death, but her spirit was strong to the last.

As it was an elemental spiritual as well as physical war, a convalescent soldier told her father that many men focused on the basic truths of Christianity, rather than the forms and dogmas which had been added over the centuries. There was a deep desire by soldiers for those at home to pray for them, not to achieve an easy victory, but for God's inspiration so that they would be worthy of it. On Wednesday, 28 October, there was a united gathering for intercession or prayer at West United Free Church in Aberdeen. It was a heavily attended interdenominational meeting and the first in a series proposed to be held until the war ended. Most Christian denominations in the city supported the services, and it was a positive aspect of the war that it had brought about such unity.

Finally, when Mr Gordon recently saw Morag playing hopscotch in the street, he called out, 'Stop playing with the children and get on with your work.'

Petulantly she returned to restocking a shelf, saying out of his hearing, 'Och, let's be childish now and then, and kindle the light of life again.'

In following days she spoke repeatedly of wishing to help the war effort by making soldiers' uniforms in Aberdeen. The day on which Iona wrote the letter Morag informed Mr Gordon that she would resign at the end of the year and move to the city. In the past she had sometimes expressed a dislike for cities because of serious infections. Iona suspected that the dearth of young men in Ballater had turned it into a ghost burgh for her, and she wished to meet a partner in Aberdeen.

Iona hoped for a letter from Gavin by the end of the first week in November. When one had not arrived by Tuesday the 9th she became a little concerned. A relapse in his condition seemed unlikely, and it was too early for heavy pre-Christmas posting to have an effect. Perhaps he had delayed writing until his longer term prospects were established.

Next morning she was about to serve Miss Clark when the postman entered, saying, 'Here you are, Iona, a letter from your man. I'm sorry it has been delayed from abroad, but at least it has arrived.'

'Thank you,' she replied with a relieved smile, before greeting the customer, 'Yes, Miss Clark.'

'Och, there's no hurry. I'm sure you are longing to read it.'

Her bright eyes grew brighter as she quickly scanned the contents and exclaimed, 'He is returning to Scotland! He has regained reasonable mobility, but not enough for the Army, so he is being discharged. The decision has been a disappointment, yet he is grateful not to be maimed and accepts the situation as God's will.'

'Wonderful news!' her father enthused and hugged her, adding, 'You can relax for the rest of the day. We will manage. I am very proud of Gavin and you.'

She continued, 'He commiserates with the King who, inspecting troops at the front on 28 October, was badly bruised when his horse disturbed by the cheering reared up and fell. Gavin jokes that he should have ridden the mare on which the Black Colonel escaped from the Pass of Ballater!'

After lunch she said to her father, 'I will take Mike for a good walk over Craig Coillich. I am too excited to sit still and will return at dusk.'

'Yes, take care.'

In the street young Helen Leslie called her, and pointing to the nearly deserted Church Square asked in a plaintive tone, 'What tune is the piper playing?'

Putting an arm round her she gently replied, 'It's the "Flowers of the Forest," a favourite at the funerals of brave servicemen who have given their lives for our well-loved King and country. The piper lost his nephew in the war earlier this year.'

Helen gazed pensively in her eyes, before nodding twice and considerately enquiring, 'How is your boyfriend?'

'He is much better, but he cannot resume soldiering and so is returning

218

to Scotland.'

Helen's eyes shone as she replied, 'Good! In his condition and the war continuing, he may delay asking you to marry him. You could ask him.'

'I cannot do that.'

'I could ask him for you.'

'You wouldn't dare!' was the smiling rebuke.

She walked through birches on the lower part of the hill, amid subdued light and shadows. In late autumn she always welcomed Nature's repose. Now she earnestly felt a requiescat for fallen servicemen, besides being grateful for Gavin's impending return. She smiled on recalling that when they parted at Ballater station she promised that on his next visit she would kiss him by a birch. Now the branches were virtually bare, and in any case it was likely that the next time she saw him would be in Aberdeen.

When she reached the cairn she paused to read lines from the letter which ran within her. 'I will miss marching with my comrades. It is believed that men in Scottish regiments have a more regular step and keep in closer form than others. No more for me drab sandbags and ghostly, even poisonous clouds of war. No more shells which can turn a trench from a comparative refuge into an infernal trap. No more zipping, zugging bullets. No more rats, lice and flies. No more Very lights which turn night briefly into unnatural day. Fare ill to the Huns. All their honour is not worth an ounce of Scottish earth. Why should the young men of Europe be used as sacrificial lambs for the German leaders' folly? Comrades who had the greatest zest for life were bravest in the fray and most likely to die.

I have done my best. Providence has smiled on me. I long for the sublime harpist who plucks my strings and the Highlands. We are at one by the crystal Dee, we are at one on the mystic heights and we are at one with the windscaped sky.'

She went to her haven beneath the waving pines. Yet Gavin's ecstasy of love and freedom had moved her so deeply, she wished to go to a more fitting place. Just as he had faced the challenge of climbing the precipice of the hawk in the Pass of Ballater, she had to lose herself to find herself in a scene of wild abandonment. She walked south until trees were left behind, and she stood on the primeval, very uneven, rocky moorland, where the bushy heather had never been burned and wore a savage aspect. She advanced across the forbidding terrain to the real summit of Craig Coillich, the witch's rocky crag. The dark desolation harmonized with the wider view and fortified her spirit. She raised her face and stretched out her arms to greet a passing shower. Now she was more prepared for

219

meeting Gavin.

Turning back she passed through close trees, avoiding a green bog lurking beneath the first one. She and Mike had not come this far before, and his curiosity led him to wander off, which delayed her. As the light was starting to fade she called him to her, and attaching the lead said firmly, 'Home!' To encourage him further she kept up a brisk pace, only releasing him when they were on familiar ground.

When she reached the cairn Ballater's street lights were being switched on. Towards the bottom of the hill, amid silver birches, she recalled more words from Gavin's letter: 'Both victors and vanquished are we. I see your eyes reflect an inner heaven. Come my perfect love, my heart of songs, come with radiant grace and smiles of light, my angel of the night.'

Without warning Mike, who was a little in front, shot round the end of the path and began to speed down the track leading to the road. Thinking that he had seen another dog, she laughed and ran after him, calling, 'Mike! Mike!' The dog halted beside a familiar form. As Iona turned into the track she gave an ineffable smile. More words from the letter streamed through her mind: 'We have a sacred tryst to keep, when eyes to eyes and soul to soul will speak. Let us be gentle when we meet, for great love can ache, although it is too strong for tears.' She rushed forward and met Gavin with a kiss by a birch, the queen of trees.

He kissed and embraced her, saying, 'No worldly fame have we, but close to God are we.'

On Saturday morning, 18 December, a few climbers were on white Lochnagar, but along Deeside preparations for the second Christmas of the war were muted. Yet at 11 a.m. many people in Ballater celebrated a local event. A group had gathered outside Glenmuick Parish Church, and warm greetings were given when the bride and her father arrived informally on foot from Bridge Street.

An awestruck little girl wearing a large blue scarf exclaimed, 'Bonny Iona!'

Helen Leslie and her younger cousin Brenda, the bridesmaids, were waiting in the vestibule, and at the first stroke of the bell on the hour the quartet walked up the left aisle. The choir led the singing of John Henry Newman's hymn, 'Praise to the Holiest in the height.' Great faith in Providence was expressed in the words, 'most sure in all his ways.' Christ's triumphant glory shone in the lines, 'a second Adam to the fight, / and to the rescue came.'

The semi-retired Rev. Farquharson officiated, because Gavin had heard him preach there the year before. The groom turned and gazed at his bride, who as she advanced gave angelic smiles at him and the guests, including Ishbel. The nearer she approached him the more she radiated love's light, ardour and purity.

He mused, 'Come our joy today and all our bright tomorrows. The flame and the light are one; our hearts and spirits are one.'

As she joined him, still and serene, bearing a bouquet of red roses for love, white ones for peace and together for unity, he thought, 'What are the harmonies of sound compared to the silence of love profound?'

When the hymn ended Miss Clark heard the right rear door open. She turned and exchanged a quizzical look with Morag who entered. The bride had arrived on time, but she was late. All were attentive as Mr Gordon read a passage from Genesis 1, including the verses, 'God created man in his own image, in the image of God created he him; male and female created he them. And God blessed them, and God said unto them, Be fruitful, and multiply, and replenish the earth, and subdue it: and have dominion over the fish of the sea, and over the fowl of the air, and over every living thing that moveth upon the earth' (vv. 27-28). Those present reflected on how men were fighting over a common inheritance. Miss Clark read Psalm 128 which began, 'Blessed is every one that feareth the Lord; that walketh in his ways.' Moreover, 'Thy wife shall be as a fruitful vine by the sides of thine house: thy children like olive plants round about thy table' (v. 3), and 'thou shalt see thy children's children' (v. 6). The Rev. Farquharson read the marriage feast of Cana passage from John 2. When Mary told her Son that the wine had run out, Jesus replied, 'Woman, what have I to do with thee? mine hour is not yet come' (v. 4). Yet she said to the servants, 'Whatsoever he saith unto you, do it' (v. 5). Jesus instructed them to fill with water six large stone water jars which were meant for ritual washing among the Jews. When the ruler of the feast tasted the water which had been turned into wine, he called the bridegroom and said that whereas normally good wine was served first, followed by worse wine, he had kept the better type until now.

In his short sermon the minister said, 'In a world darkened by evil we celebrate the sacrament of marriage with its love and goodness. It is fitting that the light of hope should shine amid us during Advent, for next Saturday on Christmas Day we will celebrate the birth of the Church's bridegroom and the Light of the World.

Details were not recorded about the couple at the marriage in Cana, which was attended by Jesus' mother—a woman with a quiet heart— her Son and his disciples. Yet it represents every marriage of Christian baptized couples. At the entrance to his public life Jesus' presence at the wedding confirmed the goodness of marriage and that henceforth it was a sign of his presence. Here he performed his first miracle–at his mother's request–turning elemental water into wine. He foresaw the shedding of his own blood and the offer of the wine of eternal life through the forgiveness of sins. A line from Richard Crashaw's poem, "Aquae in Vinum Versae," reads in translation, "The shamefaced water saw its Lord, and blushed." If we repent we can receive the grace of Christ and the promise of eternal life.

In his teaching Jesus expressed the original meaning of the union of man and woman as the Creator willed it from the beginning. Echoing words from Genesis 2 he stated that a man shall "leave father and mother, and shall cleave to his wife: and they twain shall be one flesh." Moreover, "What therefore God hath joined together, let not man put asunder." (Matthew 19.5-6.)

The whole Christian life shows the relationship between Christ and his bride the Church. St Paul in Ephesians 5.25-26 wrote, "Husbands, love your wives, even as Christ also loved the church, and gave himself for it; That he might sanctify and cleanse it with the washing of water by the word." Baptism precedes the wedding feast of the Eucharist. God loves us completely, having given up his only Son to save us. Husband and wife give themselves to each other. They are one flesh, one heart, one soul. They also give themselves to their family and the family of the Church, which is one with the body and blood of Christ.

Love grows and is fruitful like the vine. We have already seen an uncommon bond and maturity between Iona and Gavin. She reminds me of Proverbs 31.10, "Who can find a virtuous woman? for her price is far above rubies." It is an open secret that the couple will explore Iona on their honeymoon. The Church of Scotland has restored the Abbey since her parents' visit. Gavin has fought well, but he cannot continue with his military career. On their return he will work with his wife. By the strength of the Cross and the guidance of the Holy Spirit may their union continue to grow in love, and may they live to see their children's children.'

During the marriage rite, when Gavin vowed to be faithful until death parted them, he thought that nothing could trouble them in future as much as the recent trials when death had nearly separated them. Then she vowed to be faithful to him in a clear voice which could be heard through the silent church, and he was filled with peaceful joy.

After he placed a ring on her finger as a sign of love's eternal circle, with a gentle smile she lightly placed a ring on his finger, and he thought, 'Not of gold or silver, but of pure crystal is made love's shining chalice.'

At the signings he realized that henceforth she would sign with her married name, but for him she would always be the finer half. The organist played the triumphant chords of the Toccata from Widor's Fifth Symphony. The couple smiled at each other, as they recalled how when visiting the Falls of the Glasallt she said that the liberating cry reminded her of the Toccata and for Morag the sight resembled a wedding dress. Now Iona's sublime grace transcended her attire.

After the blessing the radiant couple walked down the right aisle to Dorothy Francis Gurney's beautiful hymn, 'O perfect love, / all human thought transcending.' In it those present prayed that the couple's love would have no end, for they were forever joined in one. Charity, faith, hope, endurance and trust were sought for them, as well as joy and peace. After the day of life it was wished for them 'the glorious unknown morrow' which dawned on 'eternal love and life.'

As they smiled at each other and the guests Gavin mused, 'So now beloved trace with me the maze of destiny. On our earthly journey we walk in light, we walk in darkness, in the beauty and glory of love divine. There is light in darkness and darkness in light.'

Outside, after photographs had been taken, as the bridesmaids strewed rose petals and cut oak leaves from baskets, a perplexed bystander asked, 'What are the oak leaves for?'

'Courage, Morag,' replied Miss Clark firmly.

Then Gavin raised his blissful bride aloft to make her more visible to the excited group, and with the veil streaming behind her on the breeze he said, 'Only in love's vision do we glimpse Heaven's endless light.'

As the couple and guests were about to walk to the nearby Loirston Hotel for the reception, he asked the piper to change from 'Cock o' the North' to 'Flowers of the Forest,' as he thought of the risen Christ with his loving arms outstretched to the living and the dead.

Lightning Source UK Ltd.
Milton Keynes UK
UKOW03f1819291113

222083UK00007B/480/P